Praise for
The Secret Lives of Country Gentlemen

"As always, Charles combines masterful prose, thrilling romance, fantastic wit, and gripping stakes. Her characters feel as real and relatable as a bruise. She is, in my opinion, a titan of her genre."

—Talia Hibbert, *New York Times* and
USA Today Bestselling Author

"KJ Charles weaves romance, intrigue, and history into one deliciously compelling read."

—Megan Frampton, author of *Four Weeks of Scandal*

"Once again KJ Charles has produced an absolute masterpiece! Joss and Gareth's cross-class, emotional struggle will have you rooting for them on every page. Charles is one of the best writers in the game, and her books never disappoint!"

—Joanna Shupe, *USA Today* Bestselling Author

"Dangerous smuggler meets rule-abiding baronet in this gorgeously written novel brimming with romance, wit, emotion and mystery."

—Maya Rodale, *USA Today* Bestselling Author

"*The Secret Lives of Country Gentlemen* is equal parts a tender romance and a riveting story of smuggling and adventure. [A] joy to read from start to finish."

—Martha Waters, author of *To Have and to Hoax*

"With sparkling prose, evocative descriptions of its coastal locale, and unforgettable characters, *The Secret Lives of Country Gentlemen*

THE SECRET LIVES OF COUNTRY GENTLEMEN

KJ CHARLES

sourcebooks
casablanca

Copyright © 2023 by KJ Charles
Cover and internal design © 2023 by Sourcebooks
Cover design by Stephanie Gafron/Sourcebooks
Cover art © Jyotirmaryee Patra
Internal design by Laura Boren/Sourcebooks

Published by Sourcebooks Casablanca, an imprint of Sourcebooks
P.O. Box 4410, Naperville, Illinois 60567–4410
(630) 961-3900
sourcebooks.com

Cataloging-in-Publication Data is on file with the Library of Congress.

Printed and bound in United States of America.
WOZ 10 9 8 7 6 5 4 3 2 1

For Mum, my first and best reader

The smuggler; a person who, though no doubt highly blameable for violating the laws of his country, is frequently incapable of violating those of natural justice, and would have been, in every respect, an excellent citizen, had not the laws of his country made that a crime which nature never meant to be so.

—Adam Smith, *An Inquiry into the Nature and Causes of the Wealth of Nations*

One

February 1810

KENT WAS STILL THERE.

Gareth had tumbled into the Three Ducks with his lungs burning from walking too fast in the cold night air, his face instantly reddening as the warm fug of the taproom assailed him. He didn't even know why he'd hurried: he was over two hours late and he'd told himself the whole way that Kent would have left already. If the situation were reversed, Gareth would have decided his lover for the night wasn't coming and left cursing the man's name. He'd fully expected Kent to do the same or, even more likely, find another warm body to go upstairs with.

He'd come anyway because...well, *because*, that was all. Because it was rude to miss an appointment, because he had nowhere else he wanted to go, because he hoped against hope that just this one thing might not be taken from him today.

And there Kent was, unmissable, the only man in a room crowded with men. He was sitting with a mug of ale and his feet up on a stool, chatting to the landlord without a care in the world. Then he looked round at the door and smiled, and the sight of him took Gareth's remaining breath.

The landlord slouched away as Gareth came to the table. "I'm so sorry I'm late."

"Watcher, London." *What cheer,* Gareth had worked out that phrase meant: Kent's version of *good evening.* Gareth would have been furious in his place, but the smile in Kent's warm golden-brown eyes looked entirely real. "Thought you weren't coming."

"I didn't mean to keep you waiting so long." *Thank you for staying,* Gareth wanted to say.

Kent waved a hand before he could go on, dismissing his failure to appear as though it didn't matter at all. "You look fraped. Everything all right?"

Gareth didn't know what *fraped* meant, but he had no doubt he looked it. "Not really. No. It's been rather a bad day. Terrible, really."

"Here, sit down. I'll get you a drink and you can tell me about it." He rose from his seat.

"No, don't." Gareth regretted the words as he spoke them. He would have liked very much to have a drink with Kent, to pour out what had happened and the bewildering uncertainty that now surrounded him. Except that if he tried to explain anything he'd have to explain everything, and he didn't want to do that. To present himself as a pitiable object, an unwanted thing, to easily confident Kent who didn't look like he'd been rejected in his life, then to watch him be repelled by the stench of failure, as people always were—No.

Anyway, Gareth had better ideas of how to spend the evening than brooding about his dismal situation. He had the rest of his life for that. "It doesn't matter. Could we go upstairs?"

Kent's thick brows angled. "In a hurry?"

"It's late. And I was looking forward to seeing you."

Kent frowned, just a little. Gareth probably didn't seem a particularly desirable prospect, sweaty and flustered as he was. Fraped, even. He reached for Kent's mug of ale, watching those glowing brown eyes watching him, and took a long, deliberate swallow.

"Thirsty?"

"In need," Gareth agreed, and dragged the back of his hand over his mouth in a meaningful fashion.

Kent's lips curved. "Better?"

"Getting there."

"Suppose we might as well go up, en."

The Three Ducks made the back room and the dark covered courtyard available for illicit fumbling and spending. Gareth knew the spaces well, having come here many times over the years. He'd always assumed the upstairs room was private, but Kent, who he'd never seen in here prior to this week, apparently had the privilege of using it. Perhaps he was an old friend of the landlord. Or perhaps it was just that smile of his, that wide, irresistible grin that sluiced you in happy anticipation and confidence and sheer joy of living. Gareth had gone down poleaxed at the first flash of that smile. He wasn't surprised the Ducks' taciturn landlord couldn't resist it either.

They crashed into the upstairs room together, already kissing wildly. Kent was strong, with broad shoulders and taut muscle, several inches under Gareth's height but a lot more solid, and he moved with all the confidence of his smile. He planted a hand on Gareth's arse, pulling him close, and Gareth sank into the sensation with a flood of relief.

Fingers grasping, lips and tongues locking, the press of thigh against thigh—Gareth got both hands into Kent's long, loose curls, the strands so thick and strong by comparison to his own flyaway hair. He held on hard as Kent kissed him, and felt Kent's smile against his mouth.

"London," Kent murmured. "I want you bare."

Gareth let go with a touch of reluctance: he liked Kent's hair. But Kent liked him undressed, so he stood as Kent pulled first coat then waistcoat off his shoulders; raised his arms obediently as Kent tugged his shirt over his head.

He'd worn trousers and shoes partly because the Three Ducks was not a place to dress well, partly because Kent dressed like a working man, and mostly because they came off easily. He kicked off his shoes, inhaled as Kent unfastened the buttons at his waist, and bent to peel off his stockings.

And there he was, exposed to Kent's gaze in the golden lamplight.

It had felt very odd the first time he'd stood naked like this under Kent's scrutiny. He'd never been fully bare with a lover before Kent. Surreptitious fumblings in dark corners didn't come with the luxury of time, or of more undressing than necessary. And he had no idea why Kent liked to look at him so much. Gareth was nothing special: tall but thin, pale and uninteresting. He wouldn't have noticed himself in a crowd, whereas a man could look at Kent's firm, fit body and that outrageous smile for hours.

Yet there was no mistaking the heat in Kent's eyes when he stood back and examined Gareth, and the frank appreciation tingled like a touch on his skin.

"Hearts alive, you're a pretty one," Kent said, voice a little deeper than usual. "Ah, London."

Gareth breathed the feeling in: naked, exposed, offering every inch of himself up and waiting for Kent's touch. His prick was stiff at the thought. "Christ," he said. "I love it when you look at me."

"Makes two of us."

Kent moved forward, slid his hand over Gareth's chest. It was narrower and far less impressive than Kent's own broad muscles, but Kent didn't seem to mind. His fingertips were light. Gareth quivered under the feathery touch as it roamed his skin, and couldn't help a gasp as Kent's hand finally closed around his jutting prick.

"Eager," Kent murmured. "You ready for me, London?"

"Whenever you are." Kent was still fully clad. "If you're joining me, that is."

"Oh, I'll be doing that."

Kent was smiling. Gareth smiled back, and his heart was pounding every bit as hard as the blood in his groin.

He'd only come into the Ducks last week for a drink with like-minded company. Of course he'd have taken a bit of pleasure if any offer came his way, but he'd have been perfectly happy with a mug of ale and a chance to breathe out from another day. He'd looked around to see who he knew—and then he'd seen *him*.

A working man, by his dress, in a long dark leather coat. Tawny brown skin; thick, wavy black hair loose to his shoulders; a faint shadow of black beard; a generous mouth. He was talking to a pretty youth of very similar colouring, and as Gareth watched, he had thrown his head back and laughed.

Yes, Gareth had watched. Stared, even. Very well, he'd gaped like a hopeless fool, but one didn't see a man, a smile, like that every day. He'd still been looking when, unexpectedly, the man had glanced over, and their eyes met.

Gareth had looked away at once, embarrassed and annoyed at himself for the needy display. He'd carefully stared into the opposite corner of the room to mark his lack of interest, until a throat was cleared close to him, and he realised someone was standing by his chair. Not just someone. *Him*.

"Watcher," he'd said. Gareth's cheeks instantly flamed because he'd unquestionably been watching, but the man went on without a pause, "Wondered if you might be wanting company."

That was bewildering. Was he being mocked for gawping so obviously?

The man gave him a quizzical look. "Did I startle you? You look like a sighted hare."

Gareth had no idea what that meant and it sounded oddly bucolic for a London alehouse, especially in that country accent, with broad vowels and a roll to the 'r'. It didn't matter, because the man, this man, was *talking* to him.

He managed a smile that he hoped didn't look too idiotish. "I beg your pardon, I was in a brown study. I'd love company, if you'd like to join me."

The man took a stool. "I will, en. What's your name?"

Gareth winced. "Uh. Um, I don't usually, here—for discretion, you know—"

"No names? Got you, beg pardon. I'm Kentish."

"Well, hello, Kentish," Gareth said, pure instinct. At least part of his brain was still working.

The man's eyes crinkled responsively. "*From* Kent. I meant, we're friendlier down there."

"I don't know. Londoners can be quite friendly, in the right circumstances."

"I bet you can." He smiled, and the dazzling force of it close up rocked Gareth in his seat. "You're London, then? Nice to meet you, London."

Gareth smiled back, hopelessly enthralled. "You too, Kent."

They'd left the question of names there; they'd had better things to do. Kent had obtained the luxury of the upstairs room—private, comfortable, no unexpected puddles of stale beer, drain-water, or worse—in about five minutes, and Gareth had been naked for him two minutes after that. Naked and delighting in it, as though Kent's physical confidence and frank enjoyment were contagious.

They *were* contagious. He rejoiced in his own body and in Gareth's. He laughed, he set out to please them both without shame, or fear, or second thoughts, and Gareth, who was usually consumed by shame and fear and second thoughts, all but forgot them in Kent's company.

They'd met every night since and it had been the most joyous week of his life, this unexpected, gleeful, frank pleasure. Kent's admiring looks, his capable fingers and strong arms. His smile.

Gareth stood now, bare and erect, as Kent stroked and kissed him till his prick was leaking and his knees were weak. He undressed Kent with shaking fingers, in awe of the magnificent solid muscle, loving the rich look of Kent's warm brown skin against his own city pallor. He went to his knees on the bed, and cried aloud as Kent held his shoulder and fucked him with little urgent whispers—"You're lovely, London, so lovely"—and when it was over he buried his face in the rough mattress to hide his sudden urge to weep.

Kent's arm came over his waist. "You all right?"

"Yes. It's—I'm very well."

Kent stroked Gareth's spine. "You've a nice back. Nice arse, come to that."

"Well, you certainly came to it."

Kent chuckled. "So I did."

Gareth stretched luxuriously. Kent's breath came hot against his back in an exhalation. "London?"

"Mmm?"

"I've got to go."

Gareth's stomach plunged. "Already?" he said, and hated the plaintive note he heard in his own voice. "Sorry. Of course. It was my fault for being late."

Kent gave him a little squeeze. "Not right now. I meant I'm going home."

Gareth's eyes snapped open. He stared at the wall. The heat of rutting was fading from his skin and he felt quite suddenly sore, and sticky, and stupid. "To Kent?"

"To Kent. I've finished my business here, and I've a lot to do there that won't wait."

Of course he did. Of course he was going back. Gareth could feel his cheeks heating, not so much at Kent's words as at his own foolishness in not anticipating this. He'd lived in a continuous present of *see you tomorrow* without thinking about when it would end—how had he not thought about when it would end?—and of course that wouldn't carry on. Of course Kent had been planning to walk away all along.

"Yes, of course you must. Have a safe journey. It was good to know you."

The words were well enough, but the tone sounded horribly false in his own ears. Kent, lying against his back, went still, and then took hold of Gareth's shoulder and tugged until he was forced to roll over and face him. "Good to know me? What's that mean?"

"Well...goodbye? Isn't that what you were saying?"

"I was saying I've got to get home. Doesn't mean I can't come back. I have business here, regular-like. I'll be back in April, reckon." He brushed a finger over Gareth's cheek. "Wondered if you'd care to meet again."

Gareth's chest clenched tight. "Meet? What do you mean? How?"

"The usual way? You tell me your name and how I reach you. I write you a note and say I'll be here on such-and-such a day. You turn up. I turn up. Maybe we make a bit more time for a drink and a talk first. Have a bite to eat." He cocked an eyebrow, lips half smiling, eyes full of easy confidence: a man who absolutely expected his week-long lover to be waiting for him in two- or three-months' time.

The enraging thing was, Gareth wanted to. He could already imagine the heady anticipation as April approached, the thrill of unfolding a note with shaking fingers and walking into the Ducks to the greeting of "Watcher, London"...

That was easy to imagine. Fantasies always were. But he could also imagine the slow-dawning realisation as April ticked into

May and no note came, or ever would, because Gareth might have amused Kent for a week but that meant nothing. He wouldn't write; he wouldn't come, and Gareth didn't wait for anyone any more.

"I don't wait," he said aloud.

Kent blinked. "I didn't mean you should save yourself for me. Just, if you wanted to meet again, I'd like to see you."

"Why?"

"Acause we get on? Or I thought we did till about two minutes ago. There something wrong?"

There was everything wrong. Gareth could feel it building in his gut. He knew this dance, being constantly put off by assurances of a future that would never be fulfilled, where he'd plead and cajole for scraps, crumbs, any attention at all, and it would never, ever come.

He was being pushed away with promises again, told to wait for a little while that meant forever, *again*, and his stomach knotted on the thought.

"I don't think so." The words came out hard and clipped, but not needy. He *wasn't* needy. He didn't need this.

"Don't think—?"

"I don't think we should meet again. This was all very enjoyable but we both have things to do." He sat up, swinging his legs over the side of the bed, turning away.

The mattress shifted under him as Kent moved too. "Enjoyable? London—"

"That's not my name."

"You didn't want to tell me your name," Kent pointed out. "I asked."

"Yes, well, perhaps you should take that as a hint." The roiling in his gut was getting worse, and he needed to leave. Leave, not be left. He rose and reached for his clothing. "I didn't tell you my name then and I don't intend to now. I doubt we'll be crossing paths again, so thank you for a very pleasant week's diversion. Let's leave it at that."

"Hold on. Wait. You mind telling me what's got you in a twitter?"

A *twitter*. The word sounded belittling, as if Gareth was making a fuss about nothing. "I am not—whatever that means."

"You seem middling upset to me. What's wrong?"

He sounded as if he meant it. As if he didn't understand what he'd done and wanted to make things right, as if Gareth could sit back down on the bed and explain it all, and give him his name and tell him about today—

No. Absolutely not.

"I'm not upset," Gareth said. "Why would I be upset? I'm leaving, and so are you, so there's nothing more to be said."

"Is this acause I said I had to go back? London, if I've put you in a dobbin—"

The betraying blood rushed to Gareth's cheeks, bringing anger with it. How *dare* Kent assume his leaving would upset Gareth? Who the devil did he think he was, the cocky swine? And if he thought that, could he not have the decency to keep it to himself instead of piling on added humiliation by making a great fuss about it? "I have no idea what that word signifies, and it might be easier if you spoke the King's English. I am leaving, since you ask, because your proposal of exchanging names—rather, my trusting you with my identity—isn't terribly appealing and I consider matters are best left here. I'm trying to do this without causing offence," he added, in the coldest tone he could manage, "so I'd prefer not to spell it out further."

He heard the thump of Kent's feet hitting the floor. "If that's you trying not to cause offence, I don't want to see you pluck a crow. What the blazes do you mean, trusting me with your identity?"

Gareth pulled his trousers up with a jerk and fastened them with shaking fingers. "All I want is to leave without any more trouble."

"Who's making trouble?"

"Well, I'm not." Gareth dragged his shirt over his head. Putting clothing back on was a lot more troublesome and less enjoyable than taking it off. "So if you're not, there's no more to be said, is there? I hope you have a pleasant journey back."

"You said that already. Are you always this maggotty and you were just keeping it quiet before?"

"There's no need to be rude."

Kent made a choking noise. No, Gareth told himself, not 'Kent'. That wasn't his name. Nobody was called Kent, any more than they were called Somerset or Hertfordshire or Devon. It was a false name, a falsehood, a lie like the whole of the last week had been, and he'd been a fool to name a man whose whole purpose was to be anonymous. No wonder Gareth had let himself care a little bit, giving him a name. That had been his mistake, and he was putting it right. He told himself that furiously, pulling his shoes on with jerky movements, not looking round. Absolutely not blinking anything away.

Hat. Coat. He had all his things and he looked more or less acceptable, if not precisely well turned out, so he could go. "Goodbye," he managed, because he wasn't going to be ill-mannered even if other people chose to be unreasonable.

"You're just going like that," the man said. "Right. As you please."

Some people couldn't part with decency. Gareth straightened his shoulders and left the room. He didn't look back, not even at the last, muttered, angry word he heard as he opened the door. It sounded a lot like, "Arsehole."

Two days later the letter arrived, and everything changed.

Two

GARETH ARRIVED ON ROMNEY MARSH FOUR DAYS AFTER that. It was bleak beyond words.

The stage stopped at a coaching inn, the Walnut Tree, high on a ridge. The land stretched out before them, grey-green, blotched with black scrubby trees, and cut with silvery lines that looked for all the world like streams except that many were unnervingly straight. He couldn't see much in the way of houses on the flat land below, or of anything except the sea beyond. An icy wind whipped up the ridge. He shivered.

He'd taken the Kent coach from Haxells, on the Strand, with buildings all around and above him, a bustle of shouting and curses, rattling wheels, men and horses and vehicles jostling for space. That was London and he hated it. He didn't like the crowds and the shouting; he'd always wanted peace, and greenery, and a bit of space. And now here he was, looking over acre upon acre of absolutely nothing except greenery and space, and he was desperate to go home.

No. He was *coming* home. The fact he'd never been here in his life was neither here nor there.

The road from the ridge took a steep descent to the unfathomably flat land of the Marsh. There were a lot of sheep, Gareth noticed. And there was a lot of water, because the straight lines were indeed streams, except they had to be man-made. Canals? The channels looked steel grey as he passed, like blades cutting through scrubby grass, and scrubby trees, and scrub.

Why had his father wanted to live here? Why would anyone?

The coach traversed a wearisome six miles through nothing, emptiness dotted with sheep and the occasional flurry of cottages huddled against the wind. At last it came to a halt at Dymchurch, his destination. This was a town, though only just, with a squat Norman church and a long high street. The stage passed an alehouse called the Ship and then stopped at a public house halfway down, one that was adorned with a ship's figurehead on its wall but was called the City of London. Someone should have thought harder about that, in Gareth's opinion.

He got out, stretched his aching legs, and looked around. It didn't take long: there wasn't much to see.

He was used to bustling crowds, dotted with bright bonnets and smart coats. Here there was just a handful of drably clad people who looked like they had hunched up against the weather at birth and never quite uncurled again. Farmers and shopkeepers, he vaguely supposed. An elderly gentleman wearing an old-fashioned periwig was speaking to a pretty young woman in a brown skirt and mannish black coat. Gareth noted her thick black hair and light brown skin and found himself thinking again of his week-long lover with a tiresomely familiar stab of guilt.

He'd been an arsehole. He knew it all too well, and wished he hadn't. Kent hadn't deserved his anger, as he'd known deep down at the time. But then, he hadn't been angry with Kent. He'd been angry with his father, his uncle, his day, his *life*, so he'd struck back in revenge for a hurt Kent hadn't meant to inflict and spoiled a perfectly lovely thing for no good reason. He'd been kicking himself since the next morning, for all the good that did.

At least he wasn't kicking himself for missing out on future meetings. They wouldn't have had those anyway, not after the letter. And if Gareth *had* agreed to meet again and then failed to appear, it would have meant Kent sitting alone and wondering why he'd been left. Gareth didn't ever want to do that to anyone, so really, it was for the best. Or if it wasn't, there was nothing he could do about it unless they bumped into each other, both being in the same county now. But Romney Marsh was hardly Kent; it was hardly anywhere at all. The population of the whole place looked to be about thirty, plus sheep. No, the odds were that he would never see Kent again, so Gareth's penance for his behaviour would be feeling terrible about it for the next couple of years, while the man he'd insulted had probably forgotten the whole thing already.

"Sir Gareth Inglis?"

He looked around, not a little relieved at being jolted out of his thoughts. A short, wizened man was examining him with a resigned expression that suggested he was disappointed, if unsurprised. He moved a hand in an abbreviated salute that imitated, but didn't convey, respect.

"John Groom, from Tench House, sir. Here to take you home."

Tench House was perhaps a mile outside Dymchurch. It was a fair size, a recent construction of red brick, with a front garden that was mostly damp brown stems. That might be the natural state of any garden in February, but it wasn't cheering.

A woman greeted him. She was perhaps in her mid-forties,

wearing a plain black dress, brown hair greying, and a tired look to her eyes and mouth. He wasn't sure what to call her.

"Good afternoon," he said. "I'm Gareth. Gareth Inglis."

"I'm Catherine Inglis." She blinked, as if the sound of the name unsettled her. "I mean, Catherine Bull. I'm usually called Inglis, but you might not... Please, come in."

The drawing room was pleasant enough, if dark. A young lady stood in the middle of it, and she didn't look pleasant at all.

"This is Cecilia, my niece," Mrs. Inglis said. "Your half-sister. Cecilia, this is Sir Gareth."

Cecilia, a round-faced brunette, looked to be seventeen or so, and was also in dull, unrelieved black. Colour was supplied by her eyes, red from weeping, and her cheeks, also unflatteringly red. Gareth sympathised. He blushed easily himself and hated the way it betrayed him.

"Good afternoon, Cecilia," he said, and was forced by manners to add, stilted, "I'm very pleased to meet you."

She attempted to say something. Her mouth worked, but nothing came out. Then she gave a single, heaving sob and fled the room. Gareth turned to look after her and heard a wail from the stairs. It could have been unbearable grief, but he couldn't help thinking it sounded a lot like fury.

"I'm sorry," Mrs. Inglis said. "She's upset. Too many bad shocks. Will you have some tea?"

They sat down with tea and a plate of little cakes they both ignored, going through the formalities of enquiry: his journey, the weather, if he'd had a good luncheon. Mrs. Inglis was well spoken, without the broad vowels of Kent. She looked calm, but when she wasn't holding her cup, her hands twisted together in a way that looked painful.

"So," Gareth said at last. "We should probably—"

"Yes," Mrs. Inglis said. "I don't quite know where to begin."

That grated. She *ought* to know. She was the one who'd lived here, while Gareth had been alone and excluded, and now found himself dropped into this household. It was his life that had been upended, twice, and he didn't care to pretend otherwise, and if she wanted him to lay out the situation, she could have that.

"I'll begin," he said. "After my mother's death, my father sent me to stay with my uncle in London while he sold our house and moved here. I was six. He said he would fetch me when he was settled. But a month later he married Elizabeth Bull. He said it was best I didn't attend the wedding, for his wife's sake. A year after that, he wrote to my uncle to say he had a daughter. I never saw him again."

The hostility was audible even in his own ears. Mrs. Inglis swallowed. Gareth watched her face. "I wrote—so many times—to ask to come back. He replied twice and then stopped. I dare say his new family required all his attention."

"Lizzy wasn't like that."

"Oh, please," Gareth said. "There's no point in pretending, is there? She's dead, my father is dead. You might as well be honest. She wanted me gone."

"She didn't," Mrs. Inglis said. "Not at all. Your father decided that. He thought it was for the best."

"Best? Whose best?" Gareth demanded savagely.

"You were settled. Sir Hugo thought it would be wrong to change that. His brother and wife had taken you as their own—"

"Let me assure you, they did not."

Her fingers were tightly knotted together. "Sir Hugo said they loved you dearly, and you them, and it would have been cruel to take you away from your new home. He said his brother would have been sorry to lose you."

"My uncle took me in because my father paid him to," Gareth said. "He mentioned that many times over the years. I *begged* my father to let me come back."

The little colour in her face was all gone. "I—but—It's what he told us," she insisted. "Lizzy said we could give you a home here, and he said you had one already. I promise you, Sir Gareth, she was a kind, good woman and if he had wanted you—"

She cut that off sharply, hand flying to her mouth, but it was too late. The words were out, and the look in her eyes at what she'd said just made it worse.

Because she didn't look triumphant, as though she'd scored off him. She looked horrified, in the way one did when one had blurted out something that should have stayed silent.

"If he had wanted me, Lady Elizabeth wouldn't have objected to him sending for me?" Gareth managed. "How very kind of her, to offer to let me share my father's house." It sounded desperately hollow, even to himself. He felt hollow.

"It was his choice," Mrs. Inglis said quietly. "I'm very sorry, but it was. She would have welcomed you, truly. And you must see it was not her choice to keep you away from your father, because he didn't send for you once she died and there was nobody to object."

"You. You could have refused, or Cecilia—"

"I was—his housekeeper," she said, voice flat. "I had no rights here. Cecy was two when Lizzy died. What kept you from your father was his own will."

Gareth hadn't wanted to believe that. He'd told himself otherwise as hard as he could and held onto the idea of a wicked stepmother, although it had become very threadbare over time, worn away by unmet promises, unanswered letters, silence. He wished he could believe it now, because the truth was acid in his throat.

It was your father. You always knew, really.

"If he had wanted me," he said again. "But he didn't want me, and he didn't send. He lied to you rather than send?"

"I'm sorry," she whispered. "I truly am."

"My uncle didn't ask for me: he never wanted me at all. My father foisted me on his household, and never troubled to think of me again." His jaw ached, saying the words. "He thought only of his new family—"

"Did he?" Mrs. Inglis said. "Did he think of Cecy? Can you say that?" Her knuckles were white on the cup. "He left you everything and made no provision for his daughter. No marriage portion, no settlement, not a single penny or a line in the will, nothing. She had his presence in life, for what that was worth, but now everything goes to you, *everything*, and we are left paupers!"

Her voice rang off the walls. They stared at one another.

"Look, he must have made another will," Gareth said after a moment. "Surely."

She shook her head. "He used the same solicitor for all our time here, and there is only one in Dymchurch. He didn't make a new will."

"But when he married Lady Elizabeth, the settlement—"

She made an impatient gesture. "She was just eighteen when they married, and our father was dead. What did she know of settlements? She trusted him to do right by her. *I* trusted him that far, even after twenty years of knowing him. The more fool I."

Gareth hadn't believed the lawyer's letter when he'd opened it. He'd assumed his father would leave his new family everything but the title, and that would only come to Gareth because it couldn't be given elsewhere. He hadn't expected to find himself a man of substance, and certainly not at his half-sister's expense.

"Did Lady Elizabeth bring a portion to the marriage?" he asked.

"Fifty pounds, long spent. Cecilia has nothing at all." The anger rang through her quiet voice. "She is seventeen, she has her future to consider, and he didn't think to provide for her. In all that time, he never once thought!"

"He didn't think of me, either," Gareth said. "That will was made before I was born."

The late Sir Hugo Inglis had made a very brief testament on the occasion of his first marriage, spelling out the provisions for his then wife, and leaving everything else to his eldest son, with no indication of what should happen if he had other children, or none. It was the kind of careless document that a few years in articles had taught Gareth to despise. The idea that Sir Hugo hadn't updated it on his second marriage, let alone the birth of a daughter, was appalling.

"He never cared to be troubled," Mrs. Inglis said. "A grieving boy who had lost his mother must have been troublesome, so he sent you away. To introduce you to a stepmother would be troublesome too, so he didn't bring you back. And drawing up a new will for Cecy's sake? Far too much trouble. He preferred not to be inconvenienced." She bit the last word out.

"It sounds like he was a very poor husband," Gareth said. "Or, uh—"

"Once I understood him, he was perfectly adequate." Mrs. Inglis sounded quite unemotional. "I gave him his comforts and did as he asked. He pursued his interests and left me to my concerns. He sometimes read to Cecilia when he noticed her. He provided a home which I ran. I had no great complaints."

He didn't marry you, Gareth refrained from saying, and felt a brief regret he hadn't known the man, if only to find out what sort of person could make his late wife's sister his mistress. He had a decade's experience in ascertaining whether men might like to indulge in immoral and illegal acts, but he couldn't imagine how you'd go about suggesting that.

"He must have realised Cecilia would need a marriage portion," he said instead.

"I dare say she would have had one if he had lived to see her married. He wasn't a miser, he didn't try to be cruel. He simply didn't think about others. He only considered me and Cecilia when we were under his nose."

"But he wanted Cecilia. He didn't rid himself of *her* when her mother died."

"Because I was here," Mrs. Inglis said. "If he had sent Cecy away, I should have gone with her and he would have had to find a new housekeeper, and a new woman. If there had been a woman available when your mother died, he would probably have kept you."

"I see," Gareth said, through a throatful of broken china.

She gave a tight, entirely joyless smile. "It was never personal. Simply, his greatest requirement of women and children was that we should not be troublesome to him."

"I don't think I was very much trouble," Gareth said, and heard the echoes of boyhood pleas.

"I'm sure you weren't." Her mouth twisted. "But once he'd sent you away, you would be none at all."

"Did you like him?" Gareth hadn't planned to ask that; the words just came out. "You needn't answer that. I beg your pardon."

"I'm not offended," Mrs. Inglis said. "I can hardly be. I... My sister's child was here. I wanted to be with her, I had no money of my own, and his demands weren't excessive."

And this was the home Gareth had spent years longing for. Dear God.

"I think," he said carefully, "I think someone should have given him a lot more trouble. A *lot*. I think it is a great pity you didn't—I don't know. Put frogs in his boots."

She gave a startled splutter of laughter. "Frogs?"

Gareth felt himself flush. "I mean—"

"I know what you mean, but he liked frogs. Teasels in his sheets."

"Cayenne pepper in his food."

"Lots of it. And adders, they bite. I should have *filled* his study with adders while he sat there with his books and his letters and didn't once—he didn't—"

She put her hands over her face. Gareth sat in awkward silence for a moment, then fished out his handkerchief and passed it over.

"Thank you," she said, muffled. "I'm sorry. I'm so very sorry for everything."

"So am I," Gareth said, and found he meant it.

After a few moments, she gathered her composure and wiped her eyes. "And now, where do we stand? Because this is your house, Sir Gareth, and we have nothing but whatever charity you might care to offer us. If you want us to leave, that is your right, but—but Cecilia is only seventeen, and none of this is her fault."

"I don't know where we stand," Gareth said. "I'm entirely at a loose end at the moment. I was a clerk in my uncle's practice, but we parted ways a couple of days before I learned of my father's death. And in any case I can't do that now. Not as a baronet." The title still sounded absurd applied to himself. *Sir Gareth Inglis.* "I don't know what I'm going to do with any of this—the inheritance, the title, the house." Himself. "I need to see what all this means, and I don't want to rush into any decision."

"No. Do you—will you require us to leave the house immediately?" She managed that very levelly, almost matter-of-fact, but her hands were shaking again, as well they might. He'd be perfectly within his rights to tell them to fend for themselves, and think nothing further of the matter. He'd come here with that thought, if not determined, certainly in mind.

"I think we should all take a little time to come to terms with the situation before we make decisions about the future," he said. "It's been something of a shock for me and must be much worse for you both. His death wasn't expected, was it?"

"No. It was quite out of the blue. His heart." She hesitated. "Sir Gareth, you should be aware that Cecy didn't know you existed. She thought she was his only child."

"You aren't serious."

She made a helpless gesture. "He didn't speak of you, so I didn't either, and—well, the subject simply never came up. We, uh, we—"

"Forgot. You forgot about me."

"Yes," she said. "I'm sorry."

"And nobody mentioned me at all—"

"Until he died and left you everything."

"So *quite* a shock for Cecilia, then."

"Something of one, yes." She grimaced. "She's a lovely girl, usually. But it hasn't been easy for her. So if you could grant us just a little time, I would be very grateful. Or—or if you are prepared to maintain her but not me, I shall not make trouble."

She'd been his father's mistress, cared for his daughter, and was now facing penury because the man who'd used her hadn't valued her enough to write a single line on a sheet of paper to protect her future. Gareth knew dependency all too well, and he saw it now: the ever-present fear of abandonment, the humiliation of being at another's whim, the resentment that had to be stifled because to show it could be fatal.

"We will take as much time as we all need," he said. "But let me say now that I will provide a portion for Cecilia and a sum for you. Nobody will be left penniless."

She looked up sharply. "You—?"

"Of course I will. That was my father's duty, and if I've inherited his wealth, I've inherited his responsibilities. I'm not going to throw you out, Mrs. Inglis."

She set her shoulders, a tiny motion. "You know I was not his wife."

"Then he did all the worse by you on that account. It seems to me that my father did not meet his obligations to any of us. I don't think very much of that."

"No," Mrs. Inglis agreed. The word sounded flat, but Gareth suspected it covered the kind of emotion that others would express with breaking crockery. "No, nor do I. And you are far kinder than I could have hoped, Sir Gareth. Thank you. You'll stay here while you decide?"

"If you've room. And if it wouldn't bother Cecilia."

"It's your house," she pointed out. "You're the head of the family."

He didn't have a family, hadn't since he was six. He wasn't sure how to react. "It's my house but it's your and Cecilia's home, Mrs. Inglis. I'm not going to forget that."

"Thank you," she said again, softly. "And my name is Catherine."

Three

April

THERE WAS A HARE RIGHT IN FRONT OF HIM.

It was not long past dawn. Gareth had woken up in a fit of nerves to see it was a beautiful morning, which made a change after all the rain, and had taken advantage with a walk out along the dyke.

Dyke. The waterways that criss-crossed the Marsh were called dykes, Kentishly pronounced 'deeks'; They ran into sewers which, despite the name, carried clean water to the outfalls, or as the locals called them, the guts. Guts and sewers. A poetical lot, the Marsh folk. He'd been here close to two months, and he was only just beginning to get a sense of what a strange place this was.

They called the Marsh the Gift of the Sea, but it had been taken, not given. Long ago people had built a wall to keep the sea out, as they did in the Low Countries, and called the reclaimed land Romney Marsh. It was now a wide expanse of good grazing land, with a few habitations and a lot of thorn trees: a wide, flat expanse inhabited mostly by sheep; birds and butterflies and beetles; grasses and wildflowers. And a hare.

The creature sat up on its haunches, looking at him, obviously aware he'd seen it. Its ears were held at peculiar flat angles, as if giving a signal, and it was utterly still, all but quivering in its stillness, poised to flee. It reminded Gareth of something, and after a few moments he placed it.

The man in the Three Ducks. Kent. He'd said, *You look like a sighted hare.* Gareth remembered his own wide-eyed alarm and understood now exactly what that had meant. He laughed aloud and sent the hare bolting for cover in a flash of long legs.

London felt a very long way away. These days he was Sir Gareth Inglis, baronet, master of Tench House, mixing with the highest society of Romney Marsh. In practice that meant he'd made the journey up to Lympne Castle to the north of the Marsh, dined with the Dymchurch Squire, Sir Anthony Topgood, and called on the Earl of Oxney, the ancient head of the ancient d'Aumesty family.

Lord Lympne had regarded Gareth with a very understandable lack of interest. Sir Anthony had been loud, bluff, and backslapping; his wife had asked probing questions and proclaimed her daughters' qualities; and the daughters had whispered and giggled throughout the meal. It was very much as though they were all considering Gareth as potential marriage material, which wasn't an experience he'd had before.

At least the Squire's house had been comfortable, unlike Stone Manor, a stately home as decayed as the noble family that inhabited it. The Earl of Oxney had been startlingly rude, regarding a mere baronet with obvious contempt. Frankly, he'd struck Gareth as queer in the attic, although in fairness he didn't see how anyone could be otherwise, living in such a Gothic pile with such a peculiar set of people. He hoped there wouldn't be a dinner invitation.

He preferred his own home, and the little family that was forming there. Catherine, quiet, pleasant, and competent, had set herself to make Gareth comfortable much as she had his father, with one obvious exception. It was perhaps a little odd that she had been his father's sister-in-law, then his mistress, then Gareth's housekeeper, but apparently nobody cared, since she was universally known as Mrs. Inglis. Possibly life was too hard on the Marsh for people to bother themselves unduly about other people's personal business. In any case, he counted her a relative and hoped she was becoming a friend, in her reserved way. He wasn't sure yet what he wanted to do with himself, but she was making Tench House a pleasant place to be while he thought about it.

His half-sister had been less easy. She was still smarting from the discovery that her father had left her penniless, and Gareth couldn't blame her. He knew all too well the gaping hole that had opened up in him as he slowly realised that his father didn't care, and Cecilia had been slapped with that realisation in one single moment when she was already grieving. He'd had to remind himself of the pain she must feel several times, when she glared at him as though any of the situation were his doing or exploded with bitter words he hadn't deserved.

She'd begun to warm up once he'd explained what he was settling on her. Three thousand pounds was a substantial portion, not to say a terrifying sum to a man who'd until recently been paid sixty pounds a year, but he could find it, given a little time. His father had been comfortably off, with no land but several good investments and a surprising amount of ready money, and Gareth wanted to be generous. It was, he had discovered, worth substantial sums to gain favour with the women in his life.

The thought of winning Cecilia's favour led to the reason he was awake at this ungodly hour of the morning. He strode alongside the dyke, looking down its sloping sides. Something moved among the reeds, plopping into the water. A frog, from the sound. He wished it luck, since there was a spindle-legged heron stalking the banks up ahead, its dagger-beak ready to stab.

Cecilia had an understanding with a young fellow named Bovey, a Revenue officer. She was only seventeen, and recently bereaved, but they nevertheless walked out and had tea and so on, which Catherine seemed perfectly happy about. Gareth had a vague idea that a baronet's daughter might be able to look higher for a match, but since he knew nothing about young women, baronetcy, or marriage, he kept his opinions to himself. Anyway, the only well-bred young men on the Marsh belonged to the d'Aumesty family, who were dreadful. A Revenue man sounded preferable.

Gareth was probably alone in that opinion since Excisemen weren't popular on Romney Marsh. They were frequently subjected to resentful looks, mockery, practical jokes, deliberate non-cooperation, and a relentless hostility about which Cecilia frequently came home bristling. Gareth thought Lieutenant Bovey seemed a perfectly pleasant fellow, if dreadfully earnest, and there was nothing wrong with his profession. Nobody liked paying taxes, granted, but governments levied them all the same, and one had to put up with it since there didn't seem to be any way of stopping them. He would never have taken out resentment of taxation on a Revenue man; it was an occupation like any other.

Except on Romney Marsh, where it was akin to a mortal sin, because Gareth had moved into a den of crime.

"It's a way of life here," Catherine had explained, when Gareth found a cask of French brandy and five pounds of tea by the back door. "The free traders bring the things we couldn't have otherwise—not just brandy and lace and tea, but currants and spices and that lovely perfumed soap."

"You make your own lace," Gareth observed. He found it soothing to watch in the evenings as she wound thread around pins, creating the elegant netting. "And they reduced the tax on tea years ago. It can hardly be worth smuggling."

"Yes, but I like the tea they get us."

It was excellent tea, and the soap was a luxurious joy. It was also very clearly French, a fact he had chosen to ignore in the pleasure of soft suds and lavender scent. "But trading with France? We're at *war*."

"This is the Marsh," Catherine had said, and as so often, that was all the explanation there was.

Romney Marsh offered a very long stretch of coast with sloping beaches that were easy to land on and impossible to patrol. Smuggling was an industry here. In the quite recent past there had been outright war between smugglers in gangs of hundreds and the outnumbered and unloved Preventive officers. Revenue officers had been murdered in cold blood, smugglers caught and hanged, people shot, assaulted, or beaten to death in bloody pitched battles. Things were less violent now, but the 'free trade' continued apace, with endless cat-and-mouse games between the law and the lawless.

It was outrageous, really. Yet Catherine assured him that every household up to the Earl of Oxney took its brandy without the taint of duty and that plenty of the goods went straight to London's wealthy elite, lords and Members of Parliament among them.

None of which was Gareth's affair. Smuggling was wrong, but in the scale of the world's problems and his own, it came fairly low on the list of things he would have chosen to worry about.

Unfortunately, it was very much Lieutenant Bovey's affair. He was a stiff-backed young man, very hot on smuggling, and Cecilia had taken up his cause with a passion that caused Catherine's shoulders to sag slightly when the topic came up at dinner, as it did frequently. And that meant it had become Gareth's affair despite his best intentions, because he'd caught a smuggler red-handed.

He hadn't meant to, he reflected as he crossed a dyke, heading down Marshland Gut towards the sea. He'd been out late, that was all. Few people walked late here. The Marsh was a strange and unsettling place at night, with its frequent thick mists, treacherous footing that could go from thick tussocks of grass to water in an instant, and the cries of night-birds—owls, curlews, and the eerie boom of bitterns, like hollow moans from a tomb. Which was all very Gothic, but sinister bird noises held no fears compared to being cudgelled and robbed in a London street, and it had been a bright moonlit night, perfect for what Gareth sought.

So he'd headed down along the dyke, and run right into a string of ponies laden with packs and barrels.

He'd realised at once what that meant. Honest men didn't work at this hour, and he'd heard plenty about smugglers by now. Frankly, he'd assumed they would be cautious, quiet, and easy to avoid. In this case, the train of animals had stopped while two of the smugglers had a blazing row.

Gareth had stepped back behind a thorn tree, not wanting to be noticed, unable to avoid hearing. There had been one loud, deep voice, and another much higher in pitch. Curiosity had got the better of him and he'd peered through a gap in the branches to see the arguing pair: a man with a kerchief tied over his mouth and nose, who, as Gareth watched, reached over and pulled a similar cloth off the other's face.

The second combatant was a slender young person in breeches, black-haired, brown-skinned and handsome. Gareth took a second look and realised that he'd seen the smuggler before, in Dymchurch High Street, wearing a skirt.

A woman dressed as a man. Or a youth who dressed as a woman, or one of those who didn't name themselves according to their body's dictates. However that might be, Gareth had got a good look before he or she snatched the kerchief back with a startling oath and gave a furious command. The train of ponies had headed off into the night. Gareth had gone about his business.

Then Bovey had come to tea the next day and recounted a Revenue encounter with smugglers on the way inland past Orgarswick, and like a bloody fool, Gareth told him all about it.

The Revenue officer had swung into action. He'd identified the smuggler from Gareth's description as Sophia Doomsday, a name so implausible that Gareth assumed it was a nom de guerre, until it was explained to him that the Doomsdays were a smuggling clan who kept an inn on the outskirts of Dymchurch, down towards Globsden Gut. Sophia Doomsday had been arrested and would face the magistrates today, and Gareth was to give evidence against her.

He didn't want to. He was very conscious of the tea and brandy at home, not to mention a litany of illegal acts in London, and he had no desire to antagonise a criminal gang who lived barely more than a mile away. That sounded like a terrible idea. But to catch a Doomsday would be a feather in Lieutenant Bovey's cap, and Gareth's testimony was the key. The Revenue officer had spoken enthusiastically on the subject of integrity and honour, and Cecilia had clasped her hands with admiration and praised Gareth's quick thinking and courage. Gareth had never been admired by a young lady before and found the effect from his half-sister remarkably encouraging. He simply had to go through with it.

He crossed the road outside Dymchurch and ascended the Wall.

It deserved the capital letter. The Dymchurch Wall was a great sloping bank, more than twenty feet high, made of bundles of wood buttressed by shingle, stone, and clay, with the coastal road running along its top. It was an impressive work and it had to be, because without the Wall, at high tide the Marsh would be underwater.

The tide was high now, coming worryingly close to the top of the Wall. The great grey sea filled the world beyond, and the sun rising to the east lit a path on the waves that was almost unbearably bright.

He was doing the right thing, Gareth told himself. Miss Doomsday could suffer the consequences of being caught like anyone else. If there would even *be* consequences. Lieutenant Bovey had spoken bitterly and at length about magistrates in the smugglers' pockets, who thundered from the bench about Revenue overstepping and incompetence, handed down derisory sentences or none at all, and went home to drink brandy that was only less weighed down by duty than the magistrates were themselves. Probably nothing at all would happen and everyone would forget about it very quickly.

All the same, he couldn't help the anxious feeling that had woken him too early. He was new on the Marsh, and it was a strange, isolated place with its own rules. He didn't want to make enemies. But it had taken Cecilia weeks to regard him with moderate equanimity rather than as the interloper who'd stolen her house and inheritance. He didn't want to lose what progress he'd made by failing to support Bovey now. If he could do her intended a service, it would be worth a little awkwardness with the locals. And after all, he didn't propose to live here forever.

He walked perhaps half a mile along the Wall, soothing himself in watching the sea, before descending in order to loop back through Dymchurch. As he strolled along the High Street, he was stopped in his tracks by a cry. "Sir Gareth! 'Scuse me!"

Gareth glanced around. The speaker was a boy of perhaps thirteen, unappealing as only early adolescents could be, with gawky pimpled features and brows like a pair of hairy caterpillars under a mop of bright gold hair. Gareth had never seen him in his life, but the boy called out, "Sir Gareth!" again with total confidence.

Everyone on the Marsh knew who Gareth was. He hadn't realised how much he liked the anonymity of London until he'd lost it. "Yes?"

The lad trotted up. "Message for you, sir."

"Message? You were fortunate to find me here."

"Oh, we know where to find you," said the youth, with casual confidence. "Mr. Josiah Doomsday's compliments." He extended a folded and sealed paper. "He'd like the favour of a private word this morning. Before the magistrates sit."

Gareth didn't take the note. "Mr. Josiah Doomsday. Would that be any relation to Miss Sophia Doomsday?"

"Older brother."

The older brother of a lady smuggler, against whom Gareth was to testify, wanted a private word? "Certainly not," he said. "Good Lord. No."

"It's in your interest, Sir Gareth. I wouldn't advise turning him down. You might be sorry."

"I *beg* your pardon? Is that some sort of threat? And what the devil did you mean, you know where to find me?"

The lad raised his thick eyebrows. "Did I say threat, sir? It's more a favour. Your chance to sort this out easy-like."

He was being threatened by smugglers. By spotty smugglers half his age. Alarm warred with outrage, and lost. "I don't require favours from your sort."

The boy gave him a pitying look. "Yes, sir. Only, you might not know this as outmarsh, but if a Doomsday offers you a favour? You want to accept it."

"You can take your damned favours and keep them," Gareth said sharply. "What insolence."

The boy pushed the letter at him. "Sir, I'm to tell you, this is Kent—"

"Yes, yes, it's Romney Marsh and you make your own laws here and do as you please. I've heard plenty about that, and it's about time the magistrates hanged the lot of you. Get along at once, you little wretch!"

"Well, I asked," the youth said, unabashed, and strolled off down the street.

Gareth returned to Tench House in a state of high dudgeon that rapidly turned into disquiet. He very much didn't like the idea that he'd been watched, or mysterious notes from smugglers, or the vague sense of danger that had come upon him, no matter how often he'd told himself that the messenger was only a boy.

He secluded himself in his study before breakfast, in an effort to shake off the feeling. It was really his father's study, of course, and it bore the stamp of his interests and perhaps his personality still. There was a remarkable collection of books on natural history, in English and Latin; there was a microscope, a fascinating toy which had been disturbingly informative about dyke water; there was a map of the Marsh pinned to the wall, covered in notations as to flora and fauna; and there were the notebooks.

Sir Hugo had filled book after book with observations. He'd written about the plant life of the Marsh, finding a world of variety where Gareth saw grey-green scrub. He'd kept lists of birds, of when the seasonal visitors arrived and departed, of where one might see as well as hear bitterns and how the herons behaved and peculiarities of swallows' nesting habits. Most of all, he'd written about insects.

Gareth had always liked natural history. He enjoyed watching birds, even London's grubby sparrows, and had read *The Natural History of Selborne* and *Mr. Ray's Itineraries* several times over. He'd never taken any particular interest in insects except the ones that needed squashing, but his father had observed them, drawn them, learned about them. Loved them.

All along, his father had had so much time and interest and attention to give, and he'd devoted it to beetles.

Gareth had read the notebooks from cover to cover several

times over. At first he'd had some idea that he might learn something of his father. Perhaps he'd hoped that there might be personal reflections, a diary, even a note of regret. *Saw a swift feeding its young. Remembered that I threw my own chick from the nest.*

Hardly. There was nothing at all in the notebooks to suggest the man beyond the naturalist, but Gareth had kept reading anyway because the books were there and his father was not. He'd even gone into the garden and found the rotten tree-stump on which his father had spent hours and pages, just to see what it was that had caught the man's interest in the way his son had failed to.

Two hours later, his knees had been stiff as boards but he'd identified seven kinds of beetle, and when a glossy speckled slow worm had emerged from a hole between the roots, he'd thrilled with excitement. Since then, his fascination had only grown. He wanted to see more, know more, explore the details of the tiny world of insects in the tiny world of Romney Marsh. He wanted to cry out to his father, *If you had let me stay, we could have shared this.*

Too late for that. All the same, the study was his refuge now, a place of connection that offered Gareth a chance to explore his father's world, and it invariably made him feel better. He spent an hour reading about frogs before breakfast and emerged feeling a little bit steadier about the day ahead of him.

That lasted for a full five minutes, until he described the morning's encounter to Catherine.

"Golden hair and pimples?" she mused. "That sounds like Elijah Doomsday's boy, poor thing. I wonder if Sybil has tried witchhazel. Cecy suffered dreadfully and I had an excellent preparation. I should send it to her."

Gareth didn't feel able to concern himself with adolescent skin troubles. "Elijah? He said Josiah."

"Yes, I dare say. Joss Doomsday is..." She waved a hand for the word she wanted. "If Sybil Doomsday is the queen mother, Joss is the crown prince. I wonder what he wanted to say to you."

"I don't suppose he planned to thank me for upholding the law on his sister."

"No," Catherine said. "They're very close and he looks after her."

Gareth fiddled with his teacup. "I couldn't possibly listen to whatever it was this man had to say. He clearly intended to suborn a witness. It would have been quite improper." He looked to Catherine for agreement, which she notably failed to offer. He scowled at his plate and began buttering a slice of toast he didn't want. "You think I should have spoken to him?"

"If Joss Doomsday went to the trouble of sending for me, I'd hear him out. I don't know, Gareth. I will say that if you intend to testify against Sophia Doomsday, you oughtn't speak to Joss. Because if you do, I doubt you'll be able to testify afterwards."

Gareth fumbled the butter knife. "You mean it *was* a threat?"

"Oh, I shouldn't think so. The Doomsdays aren't like the Hawkhurst Gang. They wouldn't cut your throat—"

"Cut my *throat*?" Gareth yelped. "Nobody said anything about throats!"

"I said they wouldn't," Catherine told him patiently. "Joss Doomsday usually gets his way, is all I meant. He knows what people want, and he can charm the birds out of the trees."

"I don't imagine I'd be charmed by a criminal," Gareth said stiffly.

"Of course not." He recognised the soothing tone from her conversations with Cecy; he suspected she'd used it a lot with his father. It meant *You're wrong but I'm not going to argue.* "Only, you know... Cecilia will be furious if you don't testify, but she's not the be-all and end-all."

"Is she not?"

Catherine gave him a wry smile. "To me she is, but you live here too. And the Doomsdays are—well, they're the *Doomsdays*. A lot of people do very well out of them. Sophy is wild but everyone is fond of her, and nobody likes an informer. If you want to stay on good terms with your neighbours—"

"I don't count criminals as my neighbours," Gareth said, and resented that this made him feel priggish. "And I don't care to have smugglers as acquaintances."

"Then you won't have many acquaintances."

"I'm a baronet!" That sounded ridiculous, even to himself. "Not to stand on my dignity, but honestly—"

"You are a baronet, but you're also outmarsh. People won't like this. I can't say I do. I dare say the case will be dismissed, but if it isn't—ugh. I truly wouldn't think worse of you if you changed your mind. You aren't obliged to mix yourself up in Doomsday affairs because Cecy's walking out with a Preventive."

That was exactly what Gareth had hoped to hear earlier. He'd wanted nothing more than a way to avoid this highly uncomfortable situation, and it was enraging that when it was finally offered he didn't feel he could take it. "I might think worse of myself," he said. "I won't be bullied, Catherine. I've had enough of that, and I don't care to be told what to do by criminals, and—I promised Cecy."

"I know. And it's up to you." Catherine rose to clear the breakfast things. "But I wish you'd talked to him, all the same."

The magistrates' hearing was held in the New Hall in Dymchurch. It was a large, panelled room with benches at the front, chairs for some of the spectators, and many more on their feet. The room was packed full, including Revenue officers standing meaningfully at the doors.

If Sophia Doomsday was committed by the magistrates today, she would be detained for the next Assizes. There, if convicted, she would be transported, or even hang. That wasn't a pleasant thought. Gareth's law career, such as it was, had been entirely concerned with property. He didn't like the stakes of a criminal trial. He didn't want to consider what abuses might be visited on a gaoled woman, let alone a young, pretty one on a convict ship to Australia. He very much didn't want to be responsible for an execution.

The truth was, now he was here and facing the reality, Gareth had a profound reluctance to throw anyone at all into the savage jaws of the law. After all, he might have been the one accidentally seen by a busybody, the one in the dock. He wished to God he'd kept his mouth shut.

Not my decision, he told himself. One couldn't ignore criminal acts just because one felt sympathy for the perpetrators. Well, he could when they were his own, but that did no harm, whereas smuggling was certainly harmful. He wasn't sure it was sufficiently harmful to merit the twin horrors of transportation or execution, but that was the law, it was out of his hands, and if one didn't like it, one oughtn't smuggle.

In any case, there was nothing he could do about it now. The law would take its course, and since it sounded like that course was highly erratic on Romney Marsh, Sophia Doomsday would probably walk away scot-free. He very much hoped so.

To his dismay, the magistrates didn't look as amiably corrupt as he'd been led to expect. There were three of them: two grim-faced men from Rye and Hythe respectively, as well as the local squire Sir Anthony Topgood, who boasted the medieval-sounding title of Lord of the Level and seemed in a mutinous mood. Gareth, eavesdropping frantically, heard mutterings to the effect that the Revenue had insisted on the panel including magistrates who weren't local men.

"That Hythe man ain't a friend to the trade," someone murmured.

"Rye fellow don't care for Dymchurch, either. I hear he's an anointed arbitry sort. Young Sophy will be in a peck of trouble if she's sent to the 'Sizes."

"Squire will look after her," someone else put in behind him.

"Two against one. What if he can't?"

"Then we know who will," another voice replied, and there was a quiet ripple of laughter.

It was close in the room, with so many people. And they all knew who Gareth was, he could tell. He could feel himself being looked at, heard the words "King's evidence" whispered in a way that didn't suggest they were particularly fond of the King. *Snitch,* he heard. *Nose. Informer.*

Someone tapped him on the shoulder. Gareth looked round and saw the golden-haired boy again. "What—"

"Last chance," the boy murmured. "Read the letter. Change your mind."

Under the magistrates' noses. The sheer bloody nerve of it. "How dare you?"

A hubbub erupted. Gareth looked around and saw the officers had brought in the prisoner. When he turned back the youth had melted away.

He was feeling decidedly sweaty around the neck now.

Sophia Doomsday was dressed in women's garments and looked rather grimy, but still notably pretty. She was no more than twenty, a striking woman with dark eyes. Now he saw her properly, in the light, she looked oddly familiar. Gareth had a sudden, unsettling flash of half-memory he couldn't place, and which went right out of his mind as he met her openly hostile gaze.

They were called to rise. Lieutenant Bovey made the Revenue case on the illicit transport of contraband goods. It was somewhat complicated, since the Preventives had been given the runaround by a decoy string of ponies carrying nothing but hay. Two officers who'd got lost on the Marsh had stumbled across the real transport, and though they hadn't caught any of the perpetrators, they had managed to seize one stray pony laden with brandy kegs.

"And will you put the pony in the dock, sir?" Sir Anthony interrupted at this point, to raucous laughter from the crowd. "Where is the evidence against the prisoner?"

"The run was seen earlier in the night by Sir Gareth Inglis, Sir Anthony. He is able to identify the prisoner as its leader."

Gareth was called. He stood, ignoring Miss Doomsday's resentful gaze. The atmosphere in the room was expectant and decidedly unfriendly. Someone hissed. It didn't help that the door opened and a late spectator made his way in against the objections of a court official. That set off quite a lot of murmuring in the crowded room which had to be quieted, the delay ratcheting Gareth's nerves up another notch.

He gave his name and made his oath, trying his best to keep his voice level.

"Well, Sir Gareth?" asked the man from Rye. "Tell us what you saw that night."

"I went for a walk about eleven o'clock—"

"Why?" Sir Anthony demanded. "What sort of time is that to be wandering about, eh?"

Gareth had no intention of admitting what he'd been doing. "I couldn't sleep. There was a full moon, so I thought I'd take some air and tire myself."

Sir Anthony snorted. "Better if men stay abed when they're supposed to."

"Let him talk," the Hythe magistrate snapped.

Gareth explained where he'd been and that he'd caught sight of a convoy of ponies. "I stayed in the shadow of a thorn tree to let them pass. I thought it was probably smugglers and I didn't want to be seen. I didn't want anything to do with it," he added wholeheartedly.

"Who did you see?"

"They almost all wore cloths over their faces." Gareth took a deep breath. "But I saw a lady in breeches at the head of the procession. She seemed to be giving orders. And one of the other smugglers pulled the cloth off her face. I saw her plainly for a moment."

Sir Anthony scowled. The Rye magistrate's mouth curved unpleasantly. "And do you see that woman in court today, Sir Gareth?"

"No, I don't reckon he does," said a clear voice from the back of the room.

There was an instant uproar. All the spectators turned to see, voices rising with excited speculation; the magistrate from Rye let out an angry demand as to what the devil this was; a couple of Preventive officers stepped forward belligerently, raising their muskets.

Gareth just gaped. Because he knew the voice, knew it with instant recognition that rang through his nerves and skin even before he saw the man's face.

It was Kent. His warm, laughing Kent from the Three Ducks, and Gareth had a split second of pure joyous thrill—*him, here, close*—before reality crashed down on him.

Because Kent was objecting to his testimony. Kent, who had been accompanied by that very pretty dark-skinned youth in the Three Ducks, and dear sweet Jesus, *that* was where he'd seen Sophia Doomsday before. Kent, who was, had to be—

Oh God, no.

Kent had made his way to the front the crowd. He looked travel-stained, windswept, and mud-splattered, but he sounded as confident as ever. "My name's Josiah Doomsday, my lords," he told the magistrates. "And I'm sorry to interrupt, but I couldn't let Sir Gareth here make a mistake on oath, which is what he's about to do. Pretty bad mistake too."

Gareth's mouth went dry, instantly and horribly. Sir Anthony said, "What mistake is that?"

"Sir Anthony! Sir Gareth is giving evidence! This man is not sworn!"

Kent—Doomsday—met Gareth's eyes. "My sister was at home in bed that night. Reckon you mistook her for someone else. And you don't want to say otherwise."

The magistrates were all shouting at each other. Gareth couldn't stop staring. Josiah Doomsday, the crown prince of the smugglers.

Was it a threat? Of course it was. Doomsday's very existence was a threat to Gareth, if he chose to make it so, and here he was in the court, telling Gareth what to say. Gareth's blood was thumping. He wondered distantly if he was going to faint.

"Sit down and be silent," the Hythe magistrate snapped. "Continue your testimony, Sir Gareth."

"I—" He could feel Lieutenant Bovey's gaze boring into him. "I, uh. If I'm wrong, I'll say so. I'm not sure—"

Doomsday was giving him a steady look. Gareth had lost himself in those deep golden-brown eyes before. "I don't doubt you saw someone, sir." Incredibly, enragingly, he actually sounded sympathetic. "But there's plenty of people up to no good on the Marsh, I'm sorry to say. With only moonlight to see by, and for just a few seconds? Far more like this whole thing's a misunderstanding and you saw some foreign lad, than that a decent girl was running about at all hours like some goystering wench. Don't you reckon?"

"Get him out!" the Rye magistrate bellowed.

None of the Preventives or the courtroom staff seemed in a

tearing hurry to manhandle Joss Doomsday. He raised both palms in a peacemaking gesture that appeared at once quite sincere and a shameless mockery. "Beg pardon if I've offended your lordships. When a man's sister is in trouble, he can't let it go, can he?" His eyes met Gareth's again. "Honest mistake, sir. No hard feelings."

"Silence!"

Doomsday bowed respectfully and retreated, without taking his eyes off Gareth. That meant walking backwards as though he was quite sure the crowd would part for him, which it did. When he reached the door, he propped himself against the wall in a listening pose.

"And no more interference, Doomsday," Sir Anthony said sternly, as though he'd had something to do with the retreat. "Now, Sir Gareth. What were you saying?"

"Sir Gareth was about to identify the prisoner as the woman smuggler he witnessed." Lieutenant Bovey's voice was hard and uncompromising.

Everyone was looking at him now, but Gareth could only see Joss Doomsday watching. His level gaze felt like a warning.

What would he do if Gareth ignored that warning? It almost didn't matter. He had no idea what Doomsday would do, but he knew what the man *could* do, and that was enough.

He swallowed. It felt as if his throat was full of thorns. As if all Romney Marsh was waiting for his response. Sophia Doomsday stared ahead, lovely face serenely unconcerned, but there was a tiny smile tugging at her mouth because she knew she'd won. She'd won and Gareth had dreadfully, catastrophically lost.

"I..." He had to stop and lick his dry lips. "I may have made a mistake."

Four

Cousin Tom raised his mug. "To Sophy!"

"To Sophy!" came back a roar from the assembled Doomsdays. Joss raised his own tankard but didn't shout. He didn't feel like celebrating.

Graveyard slapped him on the back. The shock sent a wave of ale splashing out of the tankard to the table. "Good, Joss. Good." He must be delighted; that was the longest speech Joss had heard from him in a while.

They were all delighted, and right to be. Sophy had been in bad trouble. Joss had had an urgent problem and limited time to solve it. And he'd tried to be fair. He'd warned the man, and it wasn't his fault if Sir Gareth Inglis, baronet, hadn't cared to listen.

"How did you do it?" Uncle Elijah demanded. "What have you got on him, boy?"

"Aye, what was that?" Matt Molash added. "Fellow looked like a startled hare!"

"Like a frightened mouse, more like. White rat of a man."

Joss couldn't deny it. Sir Gareth—the baronet—had looked

terrified, and he'd had every reason to be. That didn't mean Elijah, nobody's prize himself, had any right to sneer. He didn't have any right to know Sir Gareth's business either, even if the man was an arsehole.

Why the blazes had he not listened? Joss had written, he'd sent a verbal message: he couldn't have made himself clearer short of being there in person, and he'd done his best on that. Wasn't his fault he'd been delayed in London and then had not one but two horses cast shoes on the way back. Why had Sir Gareth forced him to play his hand in public? What had he thought would happen?

Granted, it would have been a shock. Joss had had a nasty shock himself all those weeks back, when Sophy had returned from Dymchurch grinning like a witch and said, *You know the new baronet? Sir Hugo's long-lost son? You'll never guess...*

Just bad luck, for Sir Gareth and Joss alike. Joss had wondered at the time whether to introduce himself and assure the man he had nothing to fear, then decided against it. Telling people they had nothing to fear tended to make them nervous. Anyway, Sir Gareth wasn't a Marshman and everyone knew he'd inherited all Sir Hugo's money as well as his title. He'd go back to London soon with its sophistications, its playhouses and tailors and the pleasures of Vere Street. Joss could take or leave what the city had to offer, since the Marsh was the only place on earth that mattered. He doubted the man he'd called London shared that view.

Sir Gareth (baronet, God rot it) probably wouldn't lower himself to speak to a smuggler, and Joss didn't feel any need to talk to him either; he'd heard quite enough at their last meeting. So he had made himself scarce in Dymchurch and waited for Sir Gareth to go away.

But he hadn't gone. He'd stayed, settling in with Cathy Inglis and her Preventive-loving niece, and then he'd seen Sophy at the wrong time, thanks to Elijah, plaguesome chucklehead that he was. So Joss had ended up crossing the Marsh at a flat gallop and forcing Sir Gareth to back down in public, because he'd had no time to do anything else. Considering how much effort Joss had put in to avoid crossing the baronet's path, he felt rather hard done by about the whole thing.

"Oi!" he called. "Goldilocks!"

His youngest cousin was lurking with the other young 'uns, Emily and Isaac, on the other side of the Revelation's parlour, but there was no hiding that hair. He slouched reluctantly over. "Yes, Joss?"

"You gave Sir Gareth my message, right?"

"I conveyed the verbal communication with multifarious compliments." Goldie sketched a bow. Elijah's hand swung out with force; Goldie ducked so the blow just skimmed his hair.

Goldie was a bright spark, not to say smart-arse. Granda had been teaching him for years and, unfortunately, the education seemed to be sticking. "You gave him the message and the letter?"

"I gave him the message. He wouldn't take the letter."

"Didn't take it? Why didn't you tell me?"

"When?" Goldie demanded, not unreasonably. "You weren't there. He didn't want it. He said it was insolence and interfering and whatnot and the magistrates should string us all up. Serves him right, if you ask me."

"Nobody did, bettermy," Sophy said. Goldie stuck his tongue out at her.

Joss snapped his fingers. "Give."

Goldie produced the paper from a pocket. Elijah snatched it from his hand with a laugh, which turned into a shout of anger as Graveyard grabbed his wrist. "Get off, you lunkhead!"

Joss retrieved the letter with a nod to Graveyard and checked the seal was intact. "Next time I give you a letter, you deliver it, or you tell me if you don't."

"Yes, Joss. Sorry, Joss."

"It makes no difference," Sophy said as the boy lurked away again. "You tried to get him out of this peaceful-like, and he didn't want to hear it. He brought it on himself."

"No, you brought this on all of us," Joss retorted. "You were leading the run. That makes everything that happened your responsibility."

She nodded reluctantly. "Yes, Joss."

"And you, Elijah. You won't be on a run again if I can't trust you not to wreck it."

Elijah's face darkened. "You don't tell me what to do, boy."

"That's 'gaffer' if you don't want to use my name," Joss said. "And I won't have any more runs spoiled or people arrested acause you're in a dobbin at taking orders."

Ma coughed meaningfully from the bar. "Give over, Josiah. We'll talk about it later."

Elijah smirked, as well he might. Ma wouldn't tolerate Joss dressing down her little brother in public, but the problem was she didn't want it done in private either. That was something they were both going to have to face another-when. For now, there was the immediate tidying-up to be done. He rapped the table. "Right. Sir Anthony won't have liked any of that. Finty! An extra cask of wine on the next run for the Squire, something middling special. Lace for his lady, gloves for his girls."

Finty made a note. "Yes, Joss."

"We'll have the Preventives buzzing round us like an overset hive for a while. They'll have something to prove when it comes to the next run. We can use that. Get 'em worked up, so they make mistakes."

Finty's chalk scratched on slate. "Yes, Joss."

"The new magistrate from Hythe was a lot too keen. Someone find out about him, what he wants. Emily, get up there and ask questions."

Cousin Emily beamed. She was seventeen, easily overlooked, and becoming a very useful intelligencer. "Yes, Joss!"

"What about Sir Gareth, Joss?" Finty asked.

Sophy shrugged. "What about him? He's outmarsh."

"But he's here," Joss said. "And a baronet, and his half-sister all but engaged to a Preventive."

"If this new man is for the Preventives, he needs to know better, and seems you taught him that today." His mother's voice came firmly from the bar. "If he doesn't like how we do things on the Marsh, he can go back to London and we'll be well shut of him."

Everyone nodded. That was as it should be. Joss knew it as well as anyone. He just wasn't terribly happy about this particular case.

He'd been in London when he heard of Sophy's arrest, and that Sir Gareth Inglis, once *his* London, was the Preventives' witness. Joss wasn't much of a writer, but he'd worked hard on a note to ask Sir Gareth for a hearing, even copied it out three times over to make sure his hand didn't shame him. That was an irritation in itself because he oughtn't give a curse if some bettermy baronet sneered at his penmanship. He'd sent his cousin Isaac back with it in a tearing hurry and followed himself as fast as he could. Sir Gareth should have had every chance to pull out of the trial, and if he'd lowered himself to read the letter Joss had sweated over, none of the morning's events would have been necessary.

It had not been his fault, Joss told himself again, but he couldn't get Sir Gareth's face in court out of his mind. He'd liked that face a lot, once. Not everyone would call him handsome, with those pale eyes and thin features, but there was something about him that Joss had clocked the second he'd walked into the Ducks. He'd seen the man staring at him, the longing clear, and he'd thought, *You, me, now.*

Maybe it was how readable London's expression was. Unguarded, vulnerable, betraying his thoughts so easily. That had gone straight to Joss's balls; why, he couldn't say. Only that he'd felt the urge to know more. That he'd wanted to see a smile, and liked it when it had come.

Sir Gareth hadn't smiled in front of the magistrates. In fact, when Joss had walked in and laid down a threat no less real for being unspoken, he had looked terrified. He'd looked like a man living a nightmare, and Joss had put that look on his face.

Usually if Joss caused inconvenience, he made it up with goods. Baccy, brandy, laces, and silks: they soothed ruffled feathers and guilty consciences alike. But he remembered the stark horror on Sir Gareth's face, and the dull red flush as he choked out his unconvincing denial—*might not have been this lady, it was dark, can't be sure*—and the ripples of contemptuous laughter from the crowd, and he didn't think a pound of tea would do the trick.

Joss slipped out of the Revelation Inn that evening. Most of the Revelation's patrons were free traders, all of them fond of Sophy, and the mood was celebratory, not to say raucous. There was singing and cheering. He would have liked to sing and cheer. He should have been able to. He'd pulled the Preventives' rug from under their feet and showed Romney Marsh once more that the Doomsdays were a force to be reckoned with. Everyone who'd witnessed that, and everyone who heard about it, would be aware that Joss Doomsday had made the new baronet dance to his tune. That was his duty, to look after the Doomsdays and their place and their people, and he'd done it as best he could.

Still, he drifted outside, breathing in the Marsh air with its salt and green. He'd thought he might go and watch the night sea, but instead found himself following the smell of tobacco to where his grandfather sat with a pipe.

"Josiah."

"Granda."

"A good day's work today?"

It was a question. It was always a question. Asa Doomsday rarely judged: he just put you in a position where you couldn't help but judge yourself.

"Good day's work, Granda. Got Sophy off that charge."

"I heard."

Joss tipped his head back to look at the stars. "She wanted to lead the run. She's capable of it. It was just bad luck."

"Is that right." Asa puffed on his pipe. "Luck, you say."

"No such thing," Joss allowed. It was an old lesson, and a hard one. "It was Elijah's fault, is what it was."

His grandfather grunted. Joss would have liked to see his face, though it wouldn't give much away unless Granda wanted it to. Asa Doomsday had learned to control his expressions in a hard school. "And?"

"I need to do something about him. He's drinking more, he's causing trouble, and Ma won't let me act."

"Won't let you," Asa repeated.

Joss sighed. "I don't want to fight with her, Granda."

"Then you'll have to persuade her or obey her."

The former of those was laughably implausible; the latter was most people's choice since Sybil Doomsday was a force of nature, but Joss was running out of rope on this particular subject. He stuck his hands in his pockets. "I've got to do something. Sophy could have hanged acause that chucklehead can't take an order."

"Yes," Asa said. "You don't need me to tell you so. Is that what you came out here to talk about, when everyone's celebrating in there?"

Joss seated himself on the porch by his grandfather's feet, dangling his legs over the edge. He listened to the distant croak of frogs for a few moments, then let out a long breath. "I don't like how I won today, Granda."

His grandfather waited. He wouldn't ask. Joss could tell him, or not. "I used a man's trust against him. Sir Gareth. He put faith in me, and I used it to have my way."

"Did you have to?"

Joss wanted to say he'd had no choice, but he couldn't be sure that was true. "It was all I could think of. They had two hostile magistrates in there, and he's a baronet. If he'd given witness, they'd have committed Sophy for the Assizes, no question, and you know how that would go." He'd pictured it in his head all too clearly. Sophy gaoled for months, perhaps in Rye, maybe even further afield, out of Joss's domain. Gaols weren't kindly places for anyone, certainly not women, and the idea of his sister on a gallows or a convict ship was unbearable. He'd have had to get her out at any cost in money or life, which would only have caused more heartache for more people. The consequences spooled out in his imagination, none of them good.

"I had to stop it," he said. "And I tried to talk to him before and deal with it friendly-like, but he wouldn't read my letter, and I only got to the New Hall when he was already being sworn in. What else could I have done?"

Asa blew a cloud of fragrant smoke in lieu of response. Joss glared at his boots, barely visible in the darkness. He was starting to feel the night chill. "It was a low blow. I *know* that. It was the only one I could land."

"Sounds like it couldn't be helped, then," Granda said, and added, "The way you tell it, anyway."

He always knew where to put the knife in. Joss set his teeth. "No. Only, he hurt my pride a while ago. And now I'm wondering if I maybe wanted to hurt him back."

"Dangerous game, hurting a man's pride."

"And he did it in private. I did it in public."

Asa clicked his tongue. "You have to be fair, Josiah. Injustice is bad tactics. People remember it. They watch it done and wonder when you'll turn on them. Treat people fair for good or ill and they know where they stand. Your mother will tell you that."

Joss, the recipient of many 'what did you let your sister do?' beatings over the years, would not call Sybil Doomsday fair, as such, but it was her iron law that the Doomsdays settled their debts. Generosity was a more effective tactic than riding roughshod, as other smuggling gangs were prone to do. If they caused harm, they paid for it with open hands; if someone caused them harm, they paid that back too.

"Sophy thinks we were fair," he offered. "She says he caused me hurt and went after her for no good reason. And I truly did my best to give him a way out. Not my fault he didn't take it."

"Then why are you asking me?"

Joss sighed. "Acause it wasn't right, what I did. Might have been needful, but it wasn't right, and that's all there is to it."

Asa leaned forward to put a warm hand on his shoulder. "Well done, Josiah."

"For what?"

"Thinking." His grandfather gave the shoulder a comforting squeeze. "If you've done wrong, you'd better make amends, hadn't you?"

"Yes, I had." He'd have preferred absolution, as if he'd been likely to get any such thing. "Thanks, Granda."

"Didn't tell you anything you didn't know," Asa said, and settled back with his pipe.

Joss was up early the next morning, a fine bright April day. He stepped out of the Revelation, inhaled the clean, damp air, smelling of wet grass and the sea, and got a lungful of his grandfather's pipe smoke.

"Morning, Granda."

"Joss." Asa nodded. "I hear Sir Gareth Inglis went walking along the Wall earlier. Face like thunder."

Asa barely left his rocking chair outside the Revelation, weather permitting, which meant that the Doomsdays' many eyes and ears all reported to him as a fixed point. Joss wondered when he'd put the word out about tracking Sir Gareth's movements. "Thank you kindly, Granda."

He took himself up the path to where the Wall rose, walked a little way past the turning you'd take for Tench House, then sat, knees against his chest and back against a post, looking out to sea. He loved the Marsh with a profound and unreasoned passion in all its bare, stubborn, trammelled nature, but the flat land didn't offer much of a view. He watched the few brave sails instead, the sun's bright path on the glittering, shifting waves that had taken his father and brother among so very many. He was still watching when the scrape of footsteps told him someone was coming.

Sir Gareth had the sun in his eyes. He was squinting against it, but Joss didn't think the light was why he looked so tense. He waited and watched until Sir Gareth was close enough to notice him, and saw the recoil of shock and alarm.

That was nice to see, on the face of someone he'd once been taken with. Lovely.

"Watcher," Joss said. "I was waiting for you."

Sir Gareth stopped for just a second, then angled his face away and walked on.

That was what hoity-toity types called the cut direct. If you were both gentlemen it would probably land you in a duel or some such. Good thing Joss was only a free trader.

He scrambled to his feet as Sir Gareth stalked past. "Hold on. I want a word."

Sir Gareth didn't look round. "I have nothing to say to you."

"Bet you do, en," Joss said, catching up. "Will you let me talk?"

"Do I have a choice?" Sir Gareth's gaze was fixed fiercely on the path ahead, as if he was holding on to his composure that way. "What threat may I expect if I don't do as you say?"

Joss bit back a word of irritation. "I was *asking*. Of course you've a choice."

"Then, no," Sir Gareth said, and kept walking.

Joss stared after him. Probably he should take the hint—the many hints, really, starting back in the Three Ducks—and leave the man alone. Except Sir Gareth had looked wretched. He'd carried himself bravely enough, no backing down, but the tremor of fear in his voice had been audible and he'd been braced as if for a blow.

He looked like a man used to taking blows, always had. That didn't make much sense to Joss. Baronet for a father, title fallen into his lap before he was even thirty. What had he to trouble him in life?

Only, he hadn't seemed like a baronet in waiting back in the Ducks. He'd seemed nervous, a little vulnerable, taking a kind of startled joy in how well they'd suited each other. And eager, with a wicked sense of humour when the nerves had subsided, and an absolute joy to fuck. The way he'd gripped Joss's arms, the way he'd wrapped his long legs round him, and his pale skin flushed pink—

If Joss was going to leave him alone, this wasn't a very useful line of thinking.

Well, he wasn't going to, at least not yet. He had an apology to make and an explanation Sir Gareth needed to hear, and too bad if he didn't want them. He might be a baronet, but nobody ignored Joss Doomsday on the Marsh.

Joss wanted to find Sir Gareth on one of his maundering walks, somewhere they could have a conversation without being seen or heard. The baronet took a lot of those, heading along the dykes and through the fields, stopping for no obvious reasons. Same as his father, who had been a regular sight with his big bag, turning up in all sorts of unexpected places. They'd all assumed Sir Hugo was a surveyor or a bailiff or a Preventive at first, but after a while, it had become clear he just wandered around looking at things.

Unfortunately Sir Gareth didn't leave Tench House that day, or the next morning. By then Joss was fed up of waiting, so he strolled round to the garden wall behind the house and scaled it.

Sir Gareth was in there, on his knees, pulling something out of the vegetable beds. There was a pile of sad-looking leaves and long spindly roots beside him. He seemed entirely absorbed. Mind you, he'd always seemed pretty intent when Joss had him on his knees before.

Not helpful.

Joss whistled quietly. Sir Gareth didn't so much as look round, so Joss did it again, this time loudly.

Sir Gareth glanced up, saw him sitting on the garden wall, made a valiant effort to spring to his feet, and more or less fell over. Legs stiff, Joss assumed. He jumped down from the wall and came over to offer a hand.

Sir Gareth ignored it. He managed to straighten up without grunting, which probably took an effort, and brushed dirt off his knees. "What are you doing in my garden? This is private property."

"I need to speak to you."

"I told you—"

"Yes, you did. But there's something you need to hear anyway."

"So when you said I didn't have to speak to you, you meant that I do, whether I like it or not. I see."

"London—"

"My name is Sir Gareth Inglis. As you know."

Joss stuck his hands in his pockets and tipped his head back, searching for patience. Sir Gareth had that hostile, mulish expression on, the one he'd worn that night in the Ducks when Joss had been trying to tell him—well, things he was glad he hadn't got out, because what he'd offered and had rejected was quite enough. "Sir Gareth, then. Will you listen to me?"

"I don't see why I should."

"Acause I'll go away and stop bothering you. And also it might help you sleep better."

"You don't know how I sleep."

"It's written on your face." It was too: dark rings bruising his pale skin under the pale eyes. Joss lifted a hand to indicate, and Sir Gareth jerked his head away, for all the world as if he'd thought Joss was going to touch. "Mate—"

"*Sir Gareth.*"

"Your majesty," Joss said, because his patience wasn't inexhaustible. "You don't have anything to fear from me, all right?"

Sir Gareth gave a sharp, incredulous laugh. "What?"

"That business with the magistrates—"

"You threatened me," Sir Gareth said, low and savage. "You used—what we did." He whispered that last. "You had the *gall* to get on your high horse before because you thought I'd called you a blackmailer, as if I had no right to be afraid of that, and then you turned round and damn well blackmailed me, and now you say I've nothing to fear? Go to the devil. Get off my property!"

"I know. I'm sorry for it. I didn't want things to go that way. I wanted to speak to you earlier, in private, but I'd ridden back from London overnight, and both of the horses cast shoes, and I barely got there as it was. And Sophy's my sister. I wasn't thinking about what was fair or right by you: I was thinking about her going up to the Assizes."

"I understand that perfectly," Sir Gareth said. "You wanted to save your sister, so you humiliated me in front of a crowd, made me an object of contempt to what passes for decent society in this place, and ruined my relationship with *my* sister. Am I supposed to say I don't mind?"

Joss rubbed his hands over his face. "No. I'd like to tell you I'm sorry—"

"What possible worth is an apology when the damage is all done? I dare say it might make you feel better; it's no damned good to me."

Joss couldn't argue with that, in truth. He'd done badly by the baronet, and he knew it. "As you please. But I am going to tell you you've nothing to fear from me. Nothing more," he added before Sir Gareth could. "If you're worried I'll hold how we met over your head, don't be. You've my word on it."

"Your word as a smuggler?"

Joss stiffened at that, couldn't help it. "The Doomsdays keep our word and pay our debts. Ask anyone. And I'm telling you, on my word, you don't have to fear any keg-meg about you. Gossip, I mean."

"What do you mean, I don't have to fear gossip? You forced me to retract my statement in front of fifty people! Of course they're bloody gossiping!"

"I'll wager they're not," Joss said. "You're on the Marsh, Sir Gareth. All anyone will say is you decided not to make an enemy of the Doomsdays. Nobody thinks worse of you for it."

"The magistrates do, and Cecilia, and Lieutenant Bovey!"

"Who cares for Preventives? Sir Anthony didn't want to commit Sophy: he's a Marshman for all he's the Squire. And I'm sorry for your trouble with Miss Cecilia, though if she will walk out with a riding officer—"

"My sister will do as she damned well pleases and not be bullied for it," Sir Gareth said in a vicious hiss. "And I don't want your apologies or assurances. I don't accept them."

"You can at least know you don't have anything more to fear—"

"Until I cross you again. Or are you telling me that if I see your sister smuggling on another moonlit night, you won't stop me testifying?"

"If you see her again, I'll hang her up by her ears," Joss said with profound sincerity. "And no, I'm not telling you that. I can't. I look after my people."

"So I don't need to fear you threatening me, unless you want to do so, in which case you will. Is that what you're saying? Because I really don't see that was worth climbing a wall for."

Joss had felt a distinct protective instinct towards London, his tentative, nervy lover. Sir Gareth Inglis, on the other hand, was like talking to a spitting cat. He exhaled hard in an effort to keep his own temper. "If anyone goes up against my people, I'll act. But I tried to give you warning—"

"The devil you did!" Sir Gareth sounded genuinely outraged.

"You got a message, right? Carried by a yellow-haired brat?"

"There was an insolent little swine with ghastly spots who threatened me, if that's what you mean."

"He was supposed to give you a letter from me. He said you refused it."

"Of course I did. Why would I take a letter from a smuggler when I was about to testify against one of your family?"

"Acause it was from me! You know, me, the man you'd—" *Do not say fucked, not in his back garden.* "Met."

"The man I'd 'met'," Sir Gareth said, with heavy sarcasm. "How the devil was I supposed to know someone I'd 'met' in London was living less than a mile from me, a fact you hadn't troubled to communicate to me in the entire time I've been here, and called Josiah Doomsday of all things? Why would I imagine *anyone* would be called that?"

"It's a perfectly good name," Joss said, stung.

"It's an utterly ridiculous name. It sounds like a Gothic villain."

"Does not. Parson says it goes back a dunnamany years on the Marsh."

"Nonsense."

Joss got a grip on himself. "There's nothing wrong with my name, but in any case, I *didn't* expect you to know it. I was trying to keep out of your way acause you'd made it middling clear you didn't want to see me again."

Sir Gareth went bright red at that, but he came in hard. "And I said so just the other day, but here you are."

"And wishing I wasn't," Joss snapped. "You should have been given a message from Kent, all right? If you weren't, I'll hold my hands up and wring the little wretch's neck with 'em while I'm about it, but that's what I ordered, so—"

Sir Gareth's mouth had opened slightly. "Ah."

"What?"

"He, the boy, he did say Kent," Sir Gareth said reluctantly. "'This is Kent' or something like that. I thought he meant the county. I didn't let him talk. He was annoying me."

Joss had to admit that was reasonable. "Plaguesome brat, that one. Ma says I was as bad at his age, but I don't reckon that's possible. And you were meant to read the letter so you'd know where things stood and have a chance to think about it. Here." Joss extracted the now rather battered note from his pocket and held it out.

Sir Gareth didn't take it. "All right, I accept you wanted to speak to me first. And what? Blackmail me into silence privately?"

"Talk to you. Ask you to drop the testimony, and find a way to do it that wouldn't cause you trouble."

"You seem to think all this is some sort of unfortunate accident that could have been avoided," Sir Gareth said. "It isn't. I saw your sister engaged in a criminal act! I did nothing but tell the truth—"

"You informed. I'm not holding it against you—you're outmarsh, you don't know how we do things—"

"You really don't think you did anything wrong, do you? You actually believe that if you'd forced me to withdraw my testimony in a less humiliating way, it would have been quite reasonable. My God, you Marsh people."

Joss bit back his instinctive reaction. "If I was you, I'd learn a bit about where you live before you start laying down the law."

"The law *is* laid down," Sir Gareth hissed. "It says that smuggling is illegal. It says so very clearly."

"Devil fly away with the law. This is Romney Marsh, and if you don't like it, there's a coach back to London."

"This is my house. It was my father's house. I have a *right* to live here!"

Sir Gareth's cheekbones were blazing red. Joss was in something of a pucker himself, come to that. He'd tried to apologise, he wasn't being heard, and the anger and contempt in Sir Gareth's voice was making him feel like a villain. He didn't have to waste his time on people who were too well-bred and high-strung to listen to a perfectly reasonable explanation.

"You can do what you want," he said. "You can set yourself up against your neighbours and trot out a lot of Preventive rubbish as you choose, but you can't expect to make friends that way. Acause what you are, Sir Bettermy, is outmarsh, and outmarsh doesn't thrive here. We look after our own."

"And I'm not 'your own' so you're going to threaten me whenever I inconvenience you, which is exactly where we started this conversation. Christ. If I'd known what you were—Be damned to you. Get out of my garden."

"Right. I've tried to make amends, you don't want it, that's fine. Your choice. Enjoy the weeding." Joss turned on his heel, stalked to the wall, and vaulted it. He didn't look back.

Five

TWO DAYS LATER, GARETH WASN'T FEELING ANY BETTER about things. Nor, it seemed, was Cecilia.

That dreadful day in the courtroom was still seared on his mind. Gareth hadn't been a particularly good articled clerk, and he would never have succeeded as an attorney, but he well understood the seriousness of recanting testimony and lying on oath. The backwash of guilt and repentance would have been bad enough if only he knew of his shame.

Sadly, it had been obvious to everyone. The magistrates had made numerous pointed remarks as they discharged Miss Doomsday, which was an absurd name no matter what anyone said. Lieutenant Bovey, bright red in the face, hadn't even looked in Gareth's direction, but stalked off, doubtless to be reprimanded by his superiors for the collapse of his coup, after which he'd let Cecilia know that Gareth had made him a public laughing-stock. She'd taken it as well as might be expected, which was to say that, scarlet-cheeked, tearfully furious, and, worst of all, looking at him with bewildered hurt, she'd repeated that he'd *promised*, that he'd *said*, that if he'd meant to let them down he didn't have to make fools of them all. *Why?* she'd demanded, and Gareth had no answer to give.

She wasn't speaking to him now. Gareth didn't blame her.

The fragile bubble of peace that was Tench House had been ruined because Joss Doomsday was a treacherous backstabbing smuggling swine, and Gareth Inglis was a fool and coward who'd let himself be bullied again. To think he'd regretted his rudeness to Kent, and even intended to apologise for it. He'd ruined his reputation with the decent, honest people of the area, assuming any existed, along with his relationship with his half-sister, and achieved nothing by it except to make himself the enemy of a smuggler who needed only to drop a few hints to destroy him.

Maybe he should go back to London. Take the money—sell the house, he thought vengefully, though it wasn't Catherine he wanted to revenge himself on but the whole bloody Marsh—and leave. He could do that. He could go anywhere. He just wished he knew where.

He'd lived in his uncle's house since he was six, been an articled clerk in Farringdon since he was eighteen. He had no idea of how to go about being a baronet; he'd been so comprehensively cut off from his father that he'd all but forgotten he would be one someday. It was something he'd thought might happen when he was old, after years of drudgery, until his father had once more changed his life, this time by dying.

Gareth was sick of being batted around by his father's whim. Not that death was a whim, precisely, but it felt that way. He was sick of being at people's mercy. He did not want to be at Joss Doomsday's mercy, with the man doubtless gloating that he had Gareth in his power and could make him do God knew what.

It probably hadn't been wonderful tactics to refuse Doomsday's— whatever it had been. Apology? Hardly that, when he'd seemed to believe he was entirely in the right. Maybe he'd just believed Gareth could be sweet-talked back into bed, that he could flash that smile of his and make Gareth go to his knees again. Well, he couldn't, not that the smile had been in evidence anyway. Joss Doomsday could go to the devil, and he could damned well leave Gareth alone from now on. He'd made that clear, and if Doomsday didn't respect it, he'd find out exactly what power a moderately wealthy baronet could wield on Romney Marsh.

Just as soon as Gareth found it out for himself, because frankly he had no idea.

He didn't speak about any of it with Catherine at first. She didn't raise the subject, and he didn't want to, but as time passed the great gaping hole was becoming too obvious to tiptoe around any more. Gareth knew he'd have to talk to her, and therefore went for a long walk to put it off.

It was the first walk he'd taken in days because he'd dreaded being seen by anyone. His imagination had conjured crowds of hostile, mocking eyes, but the absurdity of that became apparent on his way to Blackmanstone, when the only sign of human life he saw the whole way was a single distant shepherd—*looker*, they called it here—watching his flock.

He nearly missed his destination. Blackmanstone had been named in the Domesday Book, according to his father's notes, but if it had ever been a thriving settlement, there wasn't much left of that now. There was a looker's hut, a squat brick building, and a few scattered stones, plus the grey ruins of a presumably Norman church. It didn't have quite the melancholy feel of lost hopes and the futility of human endeavour that would have suited his mood, but it was still moderately picturesque. It might even have been Gothic, if you could have Gothic in such an utterly flat environment with not a towering mountainous crag in sight.

The day was steel-grey, promising rain. Romney Marsh often did so, and always kept that promise. The air was cool and wet on Gareth's skin, with drifts of mist billowing gently over the stands of rank grass, softening the black spikes of distant thorn trees. He could hear the high cries of a bird of prey above him, and after a little while he spotted it, a red kite, circling in and out of low cloud.

There were smaller birds, too, ones that hopped on the broken walls: sparrows, dunnocks, coal tits, a pied wagtail living up to its name as it strutted over the ground. A slim, rusty orange centipede two inches long wriggled by his boot, and he watched its complex movement until his eye was caught by a beetle an inch and a half long, its black casing shot with dark yellow, which he followed to a pile of sheep droppings. A dung beetle. His father had written many pages on those in his notebooks, and Gareth crouched to watch it work, while all around him the quiet hum of insects rose.

There was an entire busy, thriving world out here in what looked like a dead land.

He was so absorbed in woodlice munching on the moss that covered the church's ruins that he didn't even notice the man approach until a voice behind him said, "A'ternoon."

Gareth jumped a foot and put his hand to his heart in a mime of shock. "Good afternoon."

The new arrival was roughly dressed, with a shapeless hat, a curious expression, and an accent so thick it was barely comprehensible. "You be the new squire?"

"I'm Gareth Inglis, yes."

"Looking for something, are 'ee? Been here a little moment."

Gareth had no idea what to say to that. If he explained he'd been fascinated by invertebrates, Lord knew what the fellow would think. He didn't much want to add 'eccentric' to his reputation here, to go with 'informer' and 'bullied by Joss Doomsday'.

"Nothing at all," he said stiffly, in lieu of better ideas. "Merely taking the air. Good day."

He shouldered his bag and marched off, taking one of the surprisingly well-trodden grassy paths more or less at random, since he didn't want to give the man an excuse to follow. The misery he'd forgotten about in his absorption came roaring back, with extra force for having briefly lost its power.

All he wanted was to roam around the Marsh, to have time to himself, to watch what was out here and see this small world through his lost father's eyes. But he couldn't even have that, because he'd been made an object of vulgar fascination and contempt, and he resented Joss Doomsday all the more for taking this last little pleasure from him.

He waited to talk to Catherine until they sat down for afternoon tea. Cecilia was out visiting, which was a relief; Gareth had had enough reproachful glares.

"Do you know what people are saying?" he asked as Catherine poured.

She didn't pretend not to know what he meant. "Have you heard anything?"

"Not as such. I... There was a man." He told her about the fellow at Blackmanstone. "He knew who I was, he was watching me—"

"Well, he would," Catherine said. "You were two hours poking around Blackmanstone Chapel?"

"I was making observations, not 'poking'. Why should I not?"

"Because it's a hide," she said patiently. "A place where the free traders leave their goods. You must have noticed the paths are well trodden there for a lost village."

"Oh. You think that fellow was a smuggler?"

"I dare say he's involved: most people are round here. And if you inform on Sophy Doomsday and then start poking—looking—around a hide, you can't expect people not to wonder what you're up to."

Gareth stared at her in horror. "This is appalling. I don't have the slightest interest in smugglers. I only wanted some peace and quiet! And really, hiding contraband in a chapel, even a ruined one—"

"They use all the churches," Catherine said. "You'll hear many a sermon preached on *Thou shalt not* this or that with kegs stacked in the vestry."

"You aren't serious."

"My father was a curate here. He wasn't a friend to the free traders, but didn't care to make himself an enemy either. When you're asked, you close the church and preach somewhere else that Sunday." She gave a little shrug at his doubtless stunned expression. "It's how it is."

"So everyone will think I'm an informer and a Revenue spy now?"

"I doubt that, after—" She stopped.

"After my performance the other day?" Gareth could feel himself flush. "No, I don't suppose anyone will really imagine me setting up in opposition to the Doomsdays."

"That's no bad thing," Catherine said. "You really don't need to feel shamed, Gareth. Joss Doomsday got his way, that's all. He mostly does. Doing what he wanted only makes you like everyone else on the Marsh."

"I dare say." Gareth prodded a teacake. "But I'm not. I'm a baronet, and that sounds ridiculous but surely it ought to mean something. I ought to uphold the law. Set an example. Aren't I obliged to do that?"

"Your father didn't. Sir Anthony has all his brandy from the free traders."

"Sir Anthony was ready to sit in judgement on Sophia Doomsday."

She didn't scoff, because that wasn't her way, but the lift of one brow gave Gareth a distinct impression of scoffing. "He had to as Lord of the Level, but he will be very grateful indeed you changed your testimony. If you hadn't, with the two other magistrates there, he'd probably have had to commit her for the Assizes, and then he'd have had to explain himself to Sybil Doomsday and he wouldn't have wanted to do *that*. If he'd been on his own, the case would have been thrown out, believe me."

"Are you saying he does what the smugglers tell him?"

"Let's say the Doomsdays respect the Squire, and the Squire doesn't do anything to make them disrespectful."

"This is outrageous," Gareth muttered.

"Is it? Perhaps."

"But you don't think so, because this is the Marsh and it's how things are done, and I'm outmarsh. I *know*. People keep telling me."

"Well, you are," Catherine said. "And if you don't like how things are done here—"

"I should leave?"

"I didn't say that. I'd be very sorry if you left."

That stopped his unpleasant thoughts in their tracks. "Really?"

"Very much so. What I was going to say was, it would be a great pity if you can't accustom yourself. Your father loved this place, you know. I don't know if he was a Marshman, but nobody would have called him outmarsh. He knew every inch of it. He belonged here."

Gareth had seen the evidence of that in notebook after notebook full of pencil drawings and observations of the Marsh's plants, birds, insects, all carefully coloured. He felt a stab of envy. "Was he writing a book, do you know?"

"I don't know what he was doing. He didn't talk to me about it. I assumed his work was for his own interest; most things were." She said that without particular judgement. "He settled here and liked it, and I think you might too, but you can't impose yourself on the Marsh and expect things to change for you. We build walls here, Gareth, walls that keep the sea out. We have to."

"I see," Gareth said, not at all sure he did, but clinging on to that *very much so.* "But even so, to let smugglers rule the roast—"

"You did what Joss Doomsday wanted," Catherine said. "I'm not going to ask why: it's your business and I'm sure you had your reasons. Only, so does everyone else. My mother was a Molash, from Burmarsh. Her brother hanged for smuggling twenty years ago, left a widow and four children. They had nothing to live on, and my father wouldn't help. He couldn't afford the extra mouths, and in any case didn't want in to take in a smuggler's brood. So the Doomsdays looked after them. They made sure my aunt kept her cottage, found her work, fed her family. My cousin Matthew is one of Joss's hands now, and proud to be. So you may see this as between right and wrong, or law and crime, and perhaps that's true, but for some of us, it's between the people who feed fatherless children and the people who'd let them starve." That last came out with an edge to her voice he'd never heard before.

Gareth stared. "But—Does Cecy know you're related to smugglers? Does Bovey?"

"You won't find many on the Marsh without connections to the trade. Cecy is an Inglis, no need to recall her grandmother was a Molash. Though I will say, if you'd thrown us out when your father left us penniless, I've no doubt that Sybil would have lent a hand. Sir Hugo Inglis might forget about his dependents, but the Doomsdays don't."

"No," Gareth said. "He told me they look after their own. Joss Doomsday, I mean, he said that."

"They do, yes."

"And what if you're not their own?"

"Then you aren't looked after," she said simply. "More tea?"

She went off to deal with dinner. Gareth settled in the study and read through his father's notebook on dung beetles, with the relevant volume of Donovan's *Natural History of British Insects* to hand. It was absorbing stuff and he was deep in comparison of his father's painstaking drawings with the printed description of *Volinus sticticus* when he heard the door clatter and Cecilia's terrified, tear-filled cry. "Aunty Cathy! Aunty *Cathy*!"

Gareth hurried into the hall to see Cecilia clutching herself, arms crossed over her chest. She was dirty and dishevelled, bonnet hanging down her back, tears running down her face. "My God, are you all right? What happened?"

Cecy gave a great lurching sob. She was clutching the bodice of her dress, which Gareth could now see was ripped at the front. His stomach lurched unpleasantly. "Cecy?"

She held out her free arm. He pulled her into the gentlest embrace he could, considering he wanted to grapple her to him and not let go. "You're safe now," he told her, keeping his voice low and steady. "Whatever happened, you're safe now."

That opened the floodgates. She sobbed on his shoulder, hard, and Gareth held on to her, even when Catherine came running. They both encircled her and hugged her, and eventually had her seated on the couch, held close in Catherine's arms.

"Now, darling, what happened?" Catherine asked.

Her voice was calm but there was fear in her eyes, the same fear that was thudding in every beat of Gareth's pulse. "I'll go if you'd rather," he said, as matter-of-factly as he could.

Cecy shook her head. "No, don't. It was two men in the lane. They stopped me."

"What men?"

"I don't know. I've never seen them before. One small and one huge, a great hulking brute. I didn't look at first, but they said, 'Miss Cecilia?' and I said yes, and they—they accosted me. They pushed me against the wall. The big man had his hand over my mouth and I couldn't scream. I tried." She was doing bravely but her voice was shaking hard enough that it was difficult to make the words out. "They said—they said we Inglises had better think about the company we keep. Me, and Gareth. They said I'd mind who I walked out with if I knew what was good for me, and my brother should learn to keep his mouth shut."

Gareth felt a wave of nausea. "I," he began, and didn't know what to say.

"The Doomsdays have a big man." Catherine's lips were pale. "John Graves, his name is. Bald. Goes about with a foreigner from Hastings, a little one. Was that them?"

"I don't know. I didn't recognise them. He wore a hat. And the little one looked like a rat, and—and he said he'd make me remember and he *touched* me, Aunty Cathy." Her arm came over her chest again, defensively. "He put his hands—and the big one, he grabbed—he tore my dress, and I bit him so he pulled his hand away, and I screamed, and he pushed me so I fell. I thought—I thought—and I got up and ran and they were *laughing*—"

"Where was this?" Gareth demanded. His voice didn't sound quite right to himself.

"In the lane, outside. Globsden way."

"Right. Well. I'll just go and have a look, then."

"Are you sure, Gareth?" Catherine asked, sounding a little worried. "At least take John Groom."

"He's about eighty. Look after her. Bolt the door behind me."

He stalked out, pausing only to grab a walking stick with a heavy metal knob to it, and strode down the lane.

He was furious, and also terrified, so much that his legs shook and his knuckles were white on the stick. He wasn't sure which emotion he felt the more strongly. The last thing he wanted to do was encounter two violent thugs, and he prayed wholeheartedly they weren't lurking and waiting. But he couldn't just sit there, not with Cecilia crying and that torn dress. If he didn't act now, she'd never believe he'd try to keep her safe, and, at this moment, making his sister feel safe was more of an imperative than doing the same for himself.

He went up and down the lane, stick gripped hard, jumping at every bird-call and rustle, fearing every turning. He circled around the whole of their property, saw nobody at all, and returned home feeling a little braver for not having had his bravery tested.

"It's me," he called at the door. "There was nobody there."

Catherine let him in, with visible relief. "That's something. She'll be glad to know they've gone. Thank you for doing that, Gareth."

"Where is she?"

"Washing."

"Did they hurt her worse than she said?" he asked quietly.

"No. It was—fondling." She said the word with distaste. "I don't mean to say that wasn't bad enough, but it wasn't worse."

"It is quite bad enough and I will not stand for this. My sister assaulted outside her own home—how *dare* they? How dare these people do this? How dare some brute presume to dictate who she walks out with—" He stopped dead.

If she will walk out with a riding officer...

He didn't want to be right. He couldn't believe that Kent, the joyful lover who smiled like an angel and told him he was beautiful, had sent violent men to threaten a lone girl. That wasn't possible.

But Kent had never existed. There was only the hard-eyed man who had held the spectre of destruction over him like a sword, and that man might do anything.

"Gareth?" Catherine said.

"I know who did this. Or ordered it done, anyway."

He marched into the hall, the balance very much tipping to anger now. She followed as he took down his coat. "Where are you going?"

"The Revelation Inn. I want a *word* with Joss Doomsday."

Six

THE SIR GARETH PROBLEM WAS STILL NAGGING AT JOSS.

It oughtn't be. He'd said his piece and done his best, and Mr. La-di-da Baronet had made his feelings quite clear. He hadn't wanted Joss's company or apology or amends, so there was no more to be done.

Sir Gareth didn't need anything done anyway. He was a bar-onet, even if he wasn't a red-faced, gout-ridden, heavy-drinking hunting man. The Squire, now, he was Joss's idea of a proper Sir Someone: all bluster and damn-your-eyes. He sat in judgement on free traders, found reasons not to convict them, and took delivery of a lot of French goods at his back door like a reasonable man. Evidently that wouldn't be Sir Gareth's way. Him with his cutting words and his title, and that expressive, unhappy face, and those eyes that were bleak as the Marsh in winter.

Joss had put some of that bleakness there, and he didn't like knowing it. He looked after people where he could. Not that Sir Gareth was one of his to look after, but he'd far rather have got his way with kindness, not force. Their previous acquaintance would always have been a problem but Joss could have let Sir Gareth believe he had a choice what to do. Instead he'd made an enemy, and of a man who hadn't looked happy even before Joss had given him more reason to be miserable.

What had he to be miserable about, anyway? If Joss had a title and money and a big house on the Marsh that he didn't share with his entire family, he reckoned he'd be pretty nigh content with his life. Not to mention Sir Gareth didn't have work to do, runs to manage, or anyone but Catherine Inglis and Miss Cecilia depending on him. Lucky Sir Gareth.

It wasn't a busy evening for custom in the Revelation. It rarely was, since Globsden Gut didn't offer much in the way of passing trade. Good thing they didn't depend on the inn to pay their way. He and his lieutenants were planning the next landing, which Joss would lead. Sophy wouldn't have another chance at that for a while. Joss had said severely *until I can trust you not to make a mull of it*, but what he really meant was *until I deal with Elijah*. To her credit, she wasn't sulking about it.

"Little Stone," she said. "With a decoy north of Marshland Gut to draw the Preventives off."

"Sir Gareth saw you at Marshland Gut, or near enough, last time," Goldilocks observed from the next table, where he was eavesdropping.

"Nobody asked you, bastard," Elijah said. "And who gives a damn for that lanky streak of piss?"

"Goldie's right," Sophy said. "He did see me at Marshland Gut. That's the point. Everyone knows we were there."

"Eh?" Tom said. "So why go back now?"

"Acause they won't expect it. It's a double bluff."

His brow furrowed. "But you said decoy. We *ain't* going back there. Are we?"

She sighed. "Triple bluff."

Finty made a pained noise, chalk hovering over the slate. Matt Molash said, "Marshland Gut for the decoy's a good idea but we bring the goods in at Seeds Gate and up the Kent Ditch, get over the canal at High Knock."

"Sweetwaters are liable to run up that way," Joss said.

"So?"

"So if the Doomsdays and the Sweetwaters start brawling, the only one to win will be the Preventives."

"And what, we'll let them crowd us out of Walland Marsh?" Sophy demanded. "Are you telling Ma that?"

"What's that, girl?" Ma demanded, emerging from the beer cellar. Joss had once seen a pantomime in London where the Demon King had risen through the stage on a trapdoor. The memory returned quite often.

"We're not going to do that, but we're not going to start a fight either," he said. "Especially not with having just kicked over a hornets' nest with the Preventives. What I say—"

There was a whistle from the door. Finty whipped the slate and chalk off the table, and they all relaxed into their ale, just a friendly group. Joss glanced over his shoulder as someone came in and almost dropped his tankard.

Sir Gareth was at the door. His mouth was set, his cheeks were red, and his pale eyes were snapping with fury. "Doomsday!" he said sharply.

Every Doomsday present—Joss, Sophia, Elijah, Tom, Isaac; Granda and Uncle Thaddeus playing chess in the corner; Goldie and Emily sharing a newspaper; Ma at the bar and Aunt Mary coming out from the back room—turned at once. It was a showy way to go on, but it wasn't half effective, and it worked now because Sir Gareth's eyes widened with the realisation that he was seriously outnumbered.

"Doomsday," he said again, albeit slightly less order-like. "I want to speak to you. Now."

"That'd be me?" Joss enquired.

"Yes, you! What the devil are you playing at?"

Ma loomed behind the bar like an ominous moon. "Sir Gareth. We're honoured by your custom. Draw you an ale?"

"I came to speak to Mr. Josiah Doomsday," Sir Gareth said tightly.

"Do that over an ale. Home brewed by my own hands, and on the house, sir. Get Sir Gareth a chair."

"I don't want to sit," he bit out.

"Get Sir Gareth a chair, Josiah."

Joss indicated an empty chair. Sir Gareth glared at him. "I have no interest in drinking with you. I want to know why you attacked my family!"

That was so entirely out of nowhere that Joss could only gape for a second. "Me? What? When?"

"Just now! This very evening!"

Joss gave Ma an accusing look, which she gave right back, with second helpings. They both turned to Sophy, who said, "I did not," with some indignation. Joss glanced around the room for guilt. "All right, who's been playing the fool? Come on, out with it."

Blank faces. He looked back at Sir Gareth. "Wasn't us."

"You expect me to believe that?"

"What happened?" Ma asked.

"My sister, Cecilia, was assaulted and threatened by two men in the lane by our house." Sir Gareth's face tightened, and he glowered across the room at Joss's crew. "By one very large man, and one small one."

Graveyard looked around behind him to see what the baronet was glaring at. Finty, quicker on the uptake, said, "Weren't us."

"Wasn't them," Joss agreed.

"Forgive me if I don't believe you," Sir Gareth said viciously. "My sister was attacked, damn you! Her—her person was *abused*, and if you think—"

"I knew Lizzy Bull very well before she married," Ma said over him, pitching it loud. "I knitted her girl a cap at her birth. Cecy Inglis was a little madam then and she's one now, and as for walking out with a Preventive, the less said the better. But anyone who troubles that girl will account to me, and if someone in this room did that or knows who did, you'll say so now or by my oath I'll make you sorry for your silence. *Well?*"

Her volume had been increasing steadily, and the echoes of the last word rolled through the air like thunder. Nobody spoke. Sir Gareth opened his mouth and, wisely, shut it again.

Ma gave it a moment. "Find out what this is, Josiah. Put it to rights."

Joss scooped up his tankard and went to the bar to collect Sir Gareth's, then headed over to a table in the far corner. "All right, you lot, talk among yourselves," he told his family, and then, once the murmur of conversation rose, "Sit down."

"I don't want to drink with you."

"Then don't drink it," Joss said. "But you don't come into the Revelation throwing blame around like that and then maunder off. Sit."

Sir Gareth didn't sit. He leaned in, so their faces were close, and spoke very low. "Understand this. When you threatened me before, and manipulated me in front of a crowd? Two can play at that game. I *will* not hesitate to use what I know against you in front of your whole family, just as you did to me. So bear that in mind before you attempt to intimidate me now."

The urge to strike was instant and overwhelming. Joss wanted to put the heel of his hand in the baronet's face. Break his nose, put him on the floor, teach him who was master on Romney Marsh, and that you never, ever threatened a Doomsday, and absolutely fucking not in his own fucking home.

You did this to Sir Gareth in the courtroom, in public. No wonder he didn't want your apology.

He breathed out, forcing the hot red instincts down. "You've reason to be in a dobbin, so I'm going to let that pass. Once. Don't ever say it again," he couldn't help adding.

His voice must have carried his feelings, because Sir Gareth's eyes widened with alarm. Joss dug his nails into his palms, for calm, and went on. "Now. Did you come here to fight with me, or to find out who bothered Miss Cecy?"

Sir Gareth's mouth tightened. "The latter."

"So sit down and talk like a civil man." He pulled out a chair that put Sir Gareth's back to the rest of the room, hopefully hiding his excessively expressive face, while Joss would be able to see who was listening, then seated himself. Sir Gareth hesitated a moment, then also sat.

It was a start. "All right, what's this about?"

"You know what. You, your men, threatened my sister!"

"I didn't. No reason I should. What happened?"

"Two men stopped her in the lane that runs out to Tench House." He glared over at Finty and Graveyard again. "They took hold of her, manhandled her. Told her she'd better think about the company she kept, and that I should learn to keep my mouth shut. They laid hands on her, tore her dress, pushed her to the ground. She was terrified. I will have the *law* on whoever dared do this."

His voice was vibrating with rage, and Joss couldn't blame him. "Did she recognise these fellows?"

"No."

"Graveyard's Dymchurch born, Finty's been here five years. She must have seen them otherwhiles, even if she doesn't know them by name. We're not more than a mile away from Tench House here." He saw that register. "I reckon she'd know most of my lot by sight, come to that. When did this happen?"

"Less than an hour ago."

"Those two have both been sat in here with me for the last two hours. It wasn't them. I can't swear hand on heart it wasn't any of my lot, but whoever did it wasn't acting under our orders. You heard Ma."

"Your sister—"

"If Sophy wanted to quarrel with Miss Cecilia, she'd do it herself."

"So you say. But I will observe that the only two people on the Marsh with a grudge against me are your sister and you."

Sir Gareth's face was tight with anger. Nervous, too, but mostly hostile and resentful. It didn't suit him. Joss took a calming breath. "Just listen to me a moment, will you? All right, you informed on Sophy, but you paid a hard price and it's done with on our side. We've no reason to pluck a crow with you, or the Preventive officer either, still less Miss Cecy. We don't work that way."

"No?" Sir Gareth sounded sceptical.

"I'd rather make a friend than an enemy, believe it or not. Threatening Miss Cecy makes an enemy of you, and her, and Mrs. Inglis and Lieutenant Bovey too, and for what? The only person still angry about that business is you."

"Me?" Sir Gareth said in a tone of stifled outrage.

Joss shrugged. "Not saying you shouldn't be. I did you a bad turn, and I'm sorry for the harm I caused you, and the hurt too."

"For the harm you caused. But not, I notice, for doing it."

"I'm sorry for how I did it," Joss said steadily. He usually found it easier than this to win people over. Sir Gareth was a middling obstinate fellow. Or maybe Marsh folk let the Doomsdays get away with things easy-like because they knew they'd have to sooner or later, and there wasn't much point in holding out. He didn't want Sir Gareth to hold a lifelong grudge, or himself to feel a lifelong guilt. He didn't want him as an enemy, and especially not now, like this, sat opposite one another at a table in an inn. He'd daydreamed of this situation a few months ago, only in his thoughts they'd both been enjoying it.

For a start, they should be drinking. "Try the ale," he said. "It's good."

"If I drink it, will I be accused of taking gifts from free traders?"

"If you don't, you'll offend Ma."

Sir Gareth took a reluctant sip, then another. "That is good," he admitted. "Look, Doomsday—"

"Joss. Everyone calls me Joss. There's a lot of Doomsdays."

"Your mother called you Josiah."

"That's for when I'm in trouble."

"How often is that?" Sir Gareth retorted.

"About every day of my life," Joss said, and felt unreasonably pleased at the little choke of responsive laughter that he got before Sir Gareth's expression tensed again.

"You're claiming that the business with your sister is over."

"It is, as far as I'm concerned. Which means her too."

"Very well." Sir Gareth's voice dropped low. "Then the only other person I've wronged on the Marsh is you."

"Eh? When did you wrong me?"

Sir Gareth set his teeth. His cheeks were red. "In London."

Joss hadn't expected that. He hadn't thought Sir Gareth regretted it. "Right. That. Well, you weren't pleasant, but why would I go after Miss Cecy over it? I'd have said something to you if it bothered me."

"It sounded like it bothered you." He was watching Joss, something in those pale greyish eyes that Joss couldn't quite read.

And maybe Joss owed him something here. Maybe, even, he needed to say it for himself. "All right, en. I won't say you wronged me, but you hurt me. I was...partial to you, and that wasn't a kindly way you turned me down." The colour flamed up into Sir Gareth's cheeks again; Joss was grateful his own complexion wasn't quite so revealing. "But that's between you and me. Always was. You think I'm the sort of man who'd have a girl threatened because her brother did me wrong?"

Sir Gareth's lips parted, then he shook his head, such a tiny movement Joss wasn't sure if he was even aware he was doing it. "No. I wouldn't have said that—before."

Before. When they'd liked one another; when Joss hadn't threatened his home and family. "Well, I'm not," he said. "And anyway, this fellow who threatened Miss Cecilia, the message wasn't *Sir Gareth should mind his manners*, was it?"

"It was to think about the company we keep. That she should mind who she walked out with, and I should learn to keep my mouth shut. You've already made the latter point to me very clearly."

"Why would I make it again, then?" Joss asked. "And why would I give tuppence for Miss Cecy's friendships?"

"You said *if she will walk out with a Preventive!*" Sir Gareth retorted indignantly. "You *said* that to me."

"Did I?" If he had, Joss had entirely forgotten. "Well, I dare say most people would think it a shame to see a good Dymchurch girl with a Preventive. But it's not my concern and I should have kept my thoughts to myself. I truly don't care. And if I *did* want her to stop seeing the fellow, I'd say *Don't walk out with that Preventive again.*"

"That's the same thing."

"It's not. If I tell you to think about the company you keep, and you think about it and then carry on keeping it just the same, you've done what I asked."

"That obviously isn't the intended meaning of the expression."

"What I'm saying. Meanings and hints are a lot of bother. When I want something, I say so."

Sir Gareth gave a tiny intake of breath. If he hadn't, they could maybe have both pretended there was no other sense to the words, but he did, and all at once Joss's mind was full of doing exactly that.

Come here, London. Strip bare for me. I want to see you.

"Uh," Sir Gareth said, and apparently had nothing else to add. He took a gulp of ale to cover it.

Joss didn't rush to fill the silence. For one thing, he wasn't sure what to say himself; for another, you got more by waiting. Sure enough, after a moment's silence, Sir Gareth looked up from his drink.

"Please," he said, voice very low. "Please just tell me, is that the truth? It wasn't you or your people?"

"I swear to you, on my life, it wasn't me," Joss said. "And to my knowledge those weren't any men of mine, and if I find it was I'll skin 'em. My word on it."

Sir Gareth's shoulders sagged slightly. "I—thank you. I assumed—"

"You were angry. I'd be angry in your shoes, sounds like."

"Yes. Well. Good." Sir Gareth pushed the tankard away and rose. "In that case—"

"Oi. Where are you going?"

"Home."

"Sit. We're not finished."

"We aren't?"

He sounded quite alarmed, but he sat. Joss said, "No. You said someone threatened Miss Cecy, and it wasn't us. So who was it?"

"That's what I need to go home and find out."

"How?"

"I don't know. I assume Cecy must have some idea."

"You didn't ask before?"

"Of course I did. She said she didn't know who it was, and I assumed that *I* knew. But if I was wrong, then she must have an answer."

Joss scowled. "To think about the company she keeps, and you to keep your mouth shut, you said. The company is the Preventive, right? What other company does she keep?"

"None I know of."

"Might there be someone else? No offence meant," he added hastily. "I've nothing to say against Miss Cecy. But I've got a younger sister and a lot of cousins, and they don't always—" If he suggested Miss Cecy was telling falsehoods, Sir Gareth would probably get upper-class on him again. "Young 'uns might not want to tell all their business—"

"They lie like stink," Sir Gareth said. "I certainly did at her age, but I don't think she's hiding anything."

"The Preventive, then. And you to keep your mouth shut. About what?"

"I've no idea. Well. I was at Blackmanstone earlier today, and someone asked what I was doing there and I have been informed it's used by, uh, certain persons for certain activities..."

"What were you doing there?"

"Nothing. Just walking. Looking at the ruins. I had absolutely no idea it was used by smugglers. I don't *want* to encounter smugglers. If I never heard of a smuggler for the rest of my life, I'd be overjoyed."

Joss didn't point out he was in the wrong alehouse for that. He also knew very well there was nothing cached at Blackmanstone, and he had no plans to use it in the near future. "Just walking by doesn't seem enough reason to send men after your sister. And I don't much like that they'd bother her, not you. Seems more like..." He tailed off, thinking.

"Like what?"

"Well, if someone wanted something from you, they might start off by threatening your family. Soften you up so you're ready to say yes to whatever they want. I don't know, I'm just thinking aloud. Is someone asking you to do anything? You refused any offers recently?"

"Chance be a fine thing."

The response came instantly, as if he hadn't thought about it and his tone was—well, not baronettish. He'd spoken very much in the way a man might say such a thing at the Three Ducks, with a bit of eye contact to boot, and suddenly every hair on Joss's arms and neck was tingling. There was a glinting second of pure stillness, and then Sir Gareth said, stifled, "That is—I mean, no. Not, uh, about smuggling. Or anything else. No."

"No," Joss said, and had to scrabble for what he'd last said. "Uh—watching the company she keeps. Hmph." He drummed his fingers on the table. "Likelihood is, this is just some interfering so-and-so telling a Dymchurch girl who to court. Tell you what, I'll get young Emily to have a chat with your Miss Cecy. Ems won't tell me anything that isn't my business to know, don't worry." That sounded like a reassurance that he wouldn't be spying on girlish confidences, although in fact it was his business to know everything so he'd expect to be told most of it. "She might recognise a description. And if anything else happens, come and tell me."

"You?" Sir Gareth sounded uncertain. "Why?"

"You heard Ma. I'm to deal with this."

"I don't answer to your mother," Sir Gareth pointed out, although he glanced warily towards the bar when he said it.

"Yes, well, I do. And I did you an ill turn before, and the Doomsdays pay our debts."

"Pay or put people in? I don't choose to be beholden to smugglers for favours."

Sharp fellow, the baronet. Joss sat back, sipping his ale. "You don't have to count me a friend, Sir Gareth, but I'd rather you didn't count me an enemy. We both live here." And a middling pity that was, because he'd preferred things the way they'd been in London. "Look, you want Miss Cecy safe, Ma wants your problem dealt with, and I'd like to put things to rights between us, since it was me put them to wrongs."

"It wasn't only you," Sir Gareth said softly.

A bit of an acknowledgement, not quite an apology. Still, it felt as if—Joss wasn't sure what. As if they were talking again, proper-like.

"Between the two of us, we've made a middling bad fist of things all round," he said. "I'd like to make amends, and I'd like you to let me, because I don't care to be beholden either. Suppose we do that, and call it quits on both sides. No obligations, no grudges. Fair?"

Sir Gareth considered that for longer than Joss would have liked. Most people jumped at the chance to have their problems taken off their shoulders. Wasn't as if he could deal with it himself, him on his own and outmarsh, and he didn't have the body of a fighting man: Joss had looked at him long enough to see that. But he still couldn't stomach Joss's help?

He bit back persuasive words with an effort, and waited until at last Sir Gareth looked up, with reluctance. "All right." He paused, then added low, "Thank you."

Seven

GARETH PUT AWAY HIS NOTEBOOK, STOOD FROM HIS POSITION by a dyke, and stretched, working the kinks of long sitting out of his back. The light was fading to evening and he ought to make his way back home.

It had been four days since the business with Cecy's attacker, in which nothing much had happened. There had been more people in the lanes around Tench House than usual, but all from the Revelation Inn: the big bald man with hands like hams, the small, wry-looking person, a youth who Catherine identified as Isaac Doomsday, and a sharp-faced fellow who she had invited in for tea, albeit at the kitchen table, because he was her cousin Matt Molash.

Catherine had been quietly pleased by Gareth's report of his encounter with Joss Doomsday. "He'll find out what that was about," she said with calm faith. "And it's very good of Sybil. I'll send her that witch-hazel preparation for Elijah's boy. I'm glad you're settling in, Gareth."

Gareth had bristled slightly at that. "If 'settling in' means being on terms with smugglers—"

"This is the Marsh," Catherine said, serene as ever.

Cecilia wasn't settled in by that definition, Gareth couldn't help noticing. She'd been unconvinced by Gareth's report that the Doomsdays had denied all knowledge, though she had admitted that the culprits had not been the pair called Graveyard and Finty. She'd also been highly unwelcoming when Emily Doomsday had come round to ask about the incident, saying that it was cheek. Catherine hadn't commented at the time, but she'd sighed. "Cecy used to play with Emily when they were small. I know she's fond of William, but it's a pity."

Gareth also felt Lieutenant Bovey was a pity. He had called twice since the Sophia Doomsday business, both times treating Gareth with a punctilious courtesy that made him want to curl up in a corner. Cecy had of course told him about the assault, and he'd reacted with very natural anger and protectiveness, unfortunately expressed by leaping to the conclusion that the Doomsdays were the culprits, since they were lurking about the house. Catherine had tried to explain the situation; Lieutenant Bovey had been outraged that they would accept the protection of free traders rather than his own, while being unable to explain what protection he could actually provide. A pretty row had sprung up in which Cecilia had switched sides with gay abandon, both objecting to the presence of Doomsdays and taking offence at Bovey's objection. Gareth had spent most of the last two days outside in self-defence, despite the persistent light mist and drizzle. He was beginning to feel that country life was bad for the nerves.

Not that he was quite sure what else he might do. He thought about it as he walked, cutting at an overreaching stand of early nettles with his stick.

The obvious course would be to return to the city. Visit a better tailor, claim his place as one of the Upper Ten Thousand, go to gaming houses and clubs and balls. Become Sir Gareth Inglis, Society gentleman.

The idea had little appeal. It wasn't his world. Gareth had grown up the cuckoo in his uncle's nest, never feeling or invited to feel that this was home, unable to summon up any enthusiasm for life as an attorney, still less as a clerk. The society he'd most liked in London had been in Vere Street, with its secretive company and illicit pleasures, and that was a constantly changing place where people appeared and disappeared without warning, always threatened by the law. He'd never had a settled place that felt like home, not since his mother died. He didn't have one here either, in this peculiar enclave of smuggling that had already proved so treacherous, where he was firmly marked as outmarsh and kept outside the wall. But he liked Catherine very much, Tench House was comfortable, and he was finding himself more and more interested in his father's notebooks and the natural world of the Marsh. He had no pressing urge to return to the frenetic world of shouting and crowds and hurry. He did, quite strongly, want to see a great diving beetle hunt minnows.

He could happily have spent a couple of months more on the Marsh before making any decisions, exploring this odd place and easing into his new family, if it hadn't been for all the rest. The threat against Cecilia. His public humiliation in front of the magistrates, still raw enough to make him flinch when the memory hit him. Joss Doomsday.

He hadn't quite come to terms yet with Kent living a mile from him, let alone that he'd concealed it in the hope that Gareth would go away. His London lover had been so warm, so exhilarating, but on Romney Marsh those golden-brown eyes held little hard flashes like sparks struck from flint, and Gareth hadn't seen that glorious smile once.

He wondered which of them, Kent or Joss Doomsday, was closer to the truth. He wondered if he could really believe the casual promise of help for no better reason than that Mrs. Sybil Doomsday had asked it, although in fairness he wouldn't disobey her either: the woman had the kind of presence that reduced grown men to terrified seven-year-olds. He wondered if he'd imagined those little moments with Joss in the Revelation when they'd felt like friends talking, or that tingling moment where they might have been more than friends.

When I want something, I say so.

Joss Doomsday was unlikely to want Sir Gareth Inglis, and even less likely to say so given their recent history, and that was how it should be. Perhaps they couldn't immediately forget the past, but it had to be ignored in the interests of both safety and sanity, not to mention the dignity of Gareth's position. Joss was a smuggler, Gareth a baronet, and neither of them really knew the other at all.

Only, it felt quite unfair to have met such a perfect man, one who laughed and fucked and held him with such care, and then to discover he was an entirely different person. Gareth wasn't quite sure what he'd done to deserve that.

He was still thinking about Joss Doomsday when he turned into the next lane. He'd have been better off paying attention, because quite suddenly there was a looming form in his face, a hand at his throat, a bewildering rush of movement, and Gareth found himself slammed against a wall. His shoulders and head bumped hard against rough brick.

"What the—" he managed, and a dirty hand pressed over his lips. He made a sound of panic and revulsion, and got a jab in the side.

"Shut your face," his attacker snarled. Big man, square face, with a dirty red neckerchief. He was a stranger, but Gareth knew exactly who he was. And—Christ—there was a second man at his side, this one smaller and ratty-looking, and he had a knife.

A *knife*. Gareth's lungs seized up.

The smaller man clearly saw he'd got Gareth's attention. He grinned unpleasantly and raised the blade, holding it poised a few inches from Gareth's face. "Evening, Sir Gareth. I don't think you listened to our message before."

Gareth attempted to cry out. The big man pushed harder against his face, and his hair grated against the brickwork.

"We told your pretty little frigate that you Inglises needed to watch the company you kept," the ratty man said. "And what have you done? Filled the house with Preventives, and gone running to the bloody Doomsdays."

Gareth made a noise, attempting to convey—something, apology, intention to obey. The hand over his mouth didn't shift. It was hard to breathe.

The ratty man moved the knife point a little closer. "We told you, and you didn't listen. You'll take orders when they're given, hear me? Keep a still tongue in your head, or we'll cut it out."

Gareth stared at him. The man's nostrils flared. "Bloody outmarsh. Why don't we teach this one a lesson, Bowring?"

The big man grinned, an expression of stupid, gleeful malevolence. The ratty one's lips came back over his teeth. "This is just a taste for you, Sir Gareth. Little reminder of what you'll get if you don't keep your trap shut about our business."

He lifted the knife. Gareth tried desperately to twist away but the big man's other hand caught him by the throat, palm over his windpipe, fingers and thumb pressing frighteningly hard into the soft tissue under his jaw. He struggled, trying to force his head back, on his toes, but the hand pressed sickeningly hard and he was panicking now because he couldn't breathe, he couldn't *breathe*, and all he could see in the whole world was the gleaming blade and the ratty man's eyes, bright with spiteful pleasure.

There was a hard, dull thud. Those malicious eyes boggled wide for a second, then the ratty man doubled over with a strange keening noise.

Because Joss Doomsday was there behind him. He stood foursquare, fists ready, and there was nothing at all of friendly, smiling Kent in his expression now.

Bowring released Gareth's neck and swung round with a roar of fury. Joss easily sidestepped his lumbering attack and lashed out sideways. The blow landed with a thud that Bowring ignored. He swung a huge fist at Joss, who ducked and kicked, catching him on the kneecap. The big man staggered at that, and Joss kicked him again in the same place. He looked fluent, and strong, and about half the size of his opponent.

Bowring swung again. Joss twisted, so the blow just glanced off his shoulder, but it still sent him stumbling back. "London, run!" he snapped.

Gareth would have loved to run. He could scarcely stand. The bewildering morass of panic and airlessness held him frozen and he could only suck in great, desperate breaths, clinging to the wall to stay upright.

As he stood gasping, the ratty man straightened, face twisted with vengeful intent. He still had the knife in his hand, and as he turned to Joss, whose attention was entirely on Bowring, he bared his teeth in a savage grin. His arm came back, readying to strike. To stab. To stab *Kent*.

Gareth smashed the end of his walking stick on the fellow's hand.

It was the one with a solid brass knob, excellent at pulping nettles and, it turned out, good at fingers too. The ratty man yelled in pain, and the knife went flying. He lunged after it, and Gareth, a phantom palm still pressing on his windpipe, raised the stick in both hands and brought it down on his skull. The sound of impact on bone was almost as unpleasant as the jarring shock it sent up his arms.

The ratty man went down to the ground. Gareth stared at what he'd done, wondering if he ought to hit him again and, if so, how hard. He looked up in hope of help, and saw Joss grappling at close quarters with the big man. He didn't look like he was winning.

Gareth ran and swung with all the force terror could give him. The stick landed on Bowring's shoulder with a dull thud that had nightmarishly little effect, except that he turned with a bellow of anger. Gareth recoiled in alarm, and Joss's knee went up, hitting hard between his opponent's legs. The big man gave an explosive grunt; Joss kneed him again, even harder, then grabbed his hair and put three fast, sharp punches into the underside of his jaw.

Bowring went down to his knees, eyes clouding. Joss stepped back, shook his hand as if it hurt, and reached towards Gareth. "Borrow your stick?"

Gareth extended it. Joss took it, turned back to Bowring, and jabbed him in the throat with the force and accuracy of a butcher spearing a pig.

"Dymchurch!" he shouted, as the big man hit the ground, face purpling. It wasn't immediately clear if that was a battle cry, a call for help, or an oath. "In flaming Dymchurch!" He kicked Bowring very hard in the ribs, then stalked over to the ratty man and hoisted him off the floor by the hair. "You, ratface, I know you. Nadgett. You listen to me: this is my land. These are *my* people, this is *my* place. If you touch this man or his household ever again you're touching *me*, and you do that, I'll shove your head up Nate Sweetwater's arse sidewise. Sidewise!" He took a sharp breath, visibly calming himself. "So you'll go tell Nate that, and take your dancing bear with you. Show your face in Dymchurch again, either of you, and I'll leather it off your heads. Hear me?"

Nadgett looked dizzy, but he managed a vague nod. Joss dropped him and took a pace back. "Right. And this is to help you both remember." He swung the stick, hitting Nadgett hard across the back, three savage blows. The little man jerked spasmodically at each and lay still. Joss turned, took a couple of steps run-up, and put another kick in Bowring's ribs, hard enough to make the recumbent body jolt.

"Um," Gareth said.

Joss was breathing hard. "That should keep 'em down. Right, Sir Gareth. Let's get you home."

He gestured. Gareth followed, more than a little alarmed but aware that he'd still prefer this company to that of the two men behind them. There were a lot of questions he wanted to ask. The one that came out first was, "How were you there?"

"Luck," Joss said briefly. He still had Gareth's stick, held as weapon rather than walking aid, and was clearly better qualified to use it. "I was on my way to Orgarswick."

Gareth had been to Orgarswick, if you could say that, since there was nothing there to merit a place name except a single building and a few stones. It didn't have so much as a hedge. He had no idea why anyone would go there and decided, firmly, not to ask.

Joss looked round at him. "You all right?"

"No. Yes. I think so. Who were they?"

"We'll talk about that. Let's make sure all's to rights at home first."

"What?"

Joss didn't reply, but he was walking fast, and his face was rather tense. Gareth deployed his longer legs to keep up. "What did you mean about my home?"

They turned the corner to the lane where Tench House stood,

and Gareth made out a hulking human form. He sucked in an alarmed breath, and then remembered that Joss had left the big man choking on the ground behind them.

"Oi!" Joss called. "Graveyard!"

The bald man was lounging against the wall. He straightened with an interrogative grunt.

"Everything all right?" Joss asked. That got a positive grunt, followed by a cocked head and a frown.

"Run-in with a couple of Sweetwater boys," Joss answered, jerking his thumb over his shoulder. "I'll just have a word indoors. Wait for me. Don't let anyone come in."

"Yes, Joss."

"Right." Joss turned to Gareth. "We'll check your ladies are safe and well, a'right? Then you and me need a talk. And—" He pushed the stick back at Gareth, whose hands came up instinctively to grasp it, which meant he had none to spare for fending off when Joss calmly reached over and rearranged his cravat.

He couldn't find a response. They were standing in the open air, under the eye of one of Joss's men, right outside Gareth's house, and Joss, who had just administered a savage beating to two bravos, was tweaking Gareth's neckcloth as though there were nothing remarkable in the casual intimacy. As though it meant nothing, he felt nothing, to have his hands at Gareth's neck, close to his skin.

"Marked," Joss said, stepping back. "You did well back there. Come on."

He headed for the door. Gareth followed, bewildered. Catherine opened it, letting the candlelight spill out. "Hello—Joss Doomsday? *Gareth?*"

Apparently Joss hadn't hidden all the evidence of his experience. Gareth cleared his throat. "The men who attacked Cecy." His voice was croaky.

Catherine put her hand to her mouth. "What happened?"

"You had any trouble, Mrs. Inglis?" Joss asked. "No? That's good. Couple of fellows making a bother of themselves down the lane. So I'm going to leave Graveyard out there a while longer and call Matt Molash here to keep an eye as well. Just to be sure."

Catherine's eyes widened. Gareth could well imagine why. Tench House stood a quarter of a mile from the nearest inhabited building. On Romney Marsh, nobody would hear you scream. He felt a sudden urgent longing for the crowded, thin-walled house he'd shared in a London street that never entirely slept.

"I'll be here," he told her. "Everything will be very well."

Joss gave him a swift, assessing look. "You go tidy up, Sir Gareth. I'll send Graveyard for Matt and we'll both wait here till he's back, a'right?"

"Thank you, Joss," Catherine said, her voice shaking a little.

She seemed reassured by his presence, so Gareth headed up to his room. Cecilia came downstairs at the same time, and gave a little shriek. "Gareth?"

"Look, don't worry—"

"It was those men, wasn't it? Did they come back?"

"They did but all's well. Joss Doomsday is downstairs—"

"What?"

"He chased them off," Gareth said. "I helped. I need to wash."

Cecy stared at him a second and then ran downstairs. "Aunty Cathy!"

Gareth made his way to his room, where the glass showed much what he'd expected: a pale, sweaty, staring man with dishevelled hair and ugly red marks on his neck. He did what he could about that, brushing his hair and washing his face, the latter rather firmly. He rinsed his mouth, too, spitting away the taste of dirty fingers pushing against his lips, and then had to sit down for a moment and recover himself at the sudden flood of memories. Intruding fingers, the glint of fading sunlight on a knife blade, the sound of his stick on Nadgett's skull. Joss, foursquare and threatening, with no humour at all in his face.

Gareth breathed in and out until he felt less sick and dizzy. He attempted to retie his neckcloth properly but the sensation of pressure round his throat was unwelcome. In the end, he knotted it as loosely as he could and went downstairs.

Cecy was in the drawing room, on her own. She looked up as he poked his head in. "Gareth! You look dreadful."

"Where's Catherine?"

"In the kitchen with *that man*." She shuddered, making something of a performance of it, in Gareth's opinion. "Why is he here?"

"In case the other ones come back."

"He's a smuggler!"

"I know. I don't know anyone else around here I can ask to help."

"We could send for the constables in New Romney."

That seemed like an excellent idea, until Gareth considered the practicalities. "Do they work at night? Who could we send? Will they stay here?"

She scowled. "William, then."

Gareth didn't particularly want Lieutenant Bovey's judgemental glowering. "He might be working."

"Not if Joss Doomsday isn't," Cecy said sourly, and probably fairly. "I don't want him here."

"I dare say not, but—I don't think I can do much about those men on my own. I'm sorry. I wish I could but that was terrifying, Cecy. If he hadn't come by—" His voice cracked a bit.

Cecy's face crumpled, making her look very young. She was objecting to everything because she didn't want this to be happening, Gareth thought, and felt entire sympathy. Her voice was a whisper when she said, "Will they come back?"

"Not tonight," Gareth assured her. "Doomsday..." He searched for a verb to convey what he'd done without shocking feminine ears. "Won. The fight, I mean. He had a fight with them and won. Convincingly."

"This is dreadful," Cecy wailed. "What do they *want*?"

"I don't know. They wanted me to keep quiet, which I'd be delighted to do if I had anything to be quiet about in the first place!" He was exhausted, he realised, and suddenly painfully hungry, dizzy with the need for sustenance. "I need something to eat. I've got to go."

Joss and Catherine were in the kitchen. Gareth didn't spend much time in there, because it was Catherine's domain and he didn't want to stamp his ownership on it. He knocked, therefore, and came in to see her at the table. She was smiling, properly smiling as though she meant it, and Joss was grinning at her.

Oh Christ, that grin. Gareth had told himself he'd exaggerated it in his memory, that the whole thing had been nothing but a brief madness which the passage of time would show up as delusion and infatuation. That Joss was no more than ordinarily handsome, and his smile just a smile.

He'd been wrong. Joss was smiling at Catherine like he'd used to smile at Gareth, like sunshine and birdsong, and Gareth's heart cramped in his chest at the sight because it wasn't for him.

Perhaps he made a noise, because Joss looked swiftly round. "Oh, Lo—lumme. Sir Gareth." He stood, just as a respectful man should do in the presence of his betters. "You all right?"

"Yes. Yes, thank you. Catherine, could I have something to eat? Bread and cheese? I'm very hungry, somehow."

She brought out a cold pie and pickles along with bread and

cheese. Joss, pressed, agreed he wouldn't say no, and Gareth found himself eating ravenously, at a table with Joss. They'd never shared a meal before.

They didn't speak, which was good because Gareth had no idea what to say. He just concentrated on the food, and trying not to let his hand shake as he ate.

There was a knock at the back door as they were finishing. Joss went to answer it and let a sharp-faced man in. "Matt Molash, Sir Gareth, think you've met. He'll stay in the kitchen till you're back, just to be sure, with Graveyard out the front. That suit everyone?"

"Till I'm back? Where am I going?"

"Talk," Joss said. "You done here? Come on, en."

Eight

SIR GARETH WAS A BIT UNSTEADY ON HIS FEET.

Joss couldn't blame him. A turn-up wasn't much fun for men who weren't used to fighting, or even those who were. Joss was used to it; Sir Gareth clearly wasn't. But he'd shouted at the man to run, and he could have, and instead he'd put Nadgett on the ground and come at Bowring too.

That wasn't the cleverest thing Joss had ever seen, because Bowring was a notorious bruiser, even taller than Sir Gareth and three times his weight. Come to that, tackling him alone wasn't the cleverest thing Joss had ever done, but he'd had Sir Gareth against the wall, by his neck, *in Dymchurch*, and that offended Joss's sense of what was right on a number of levels.

Sir Gareth had stood and fought, and he hadn't done it for Joss, but he'd still helped when he hadn't had to, and that was...well. Pleasing. There was no shame in it if he felt the reaction now.

So Joss took it slow, leading Sir Gareth up the lane, onto the fields, and a little way along a dyke to where some past Marshman had put a couple of slabs of stone by the edge.

"Want to sit?" Joss did so himself, dangling his legs over the black water. Sir Gareth hesitated, then lowered himself down. He reminded Joss of a father-long-legs, one of those flying bugs that was all spindly limbs and sharp angles.

"Why are we here?"

"We need to talk, and I'd rather not be overheard." And Sir Gareth liked sitting by dykes, so Joss had thought it might calm him down. Not that you could see much, since night had well and truly set in. Joss, well used to moving around the Marsh at night, hadn't brought a candle and suddenly wondered if that was a mistake. "Are you all right without light?"

"Very well. It's quite bright with the stars."

The baronet was a night-walker himself, of course: that had become notorious. "What were you doing that night?"

"Which—When I saw your sister?"

"Mmm."

There was a long pause. "Tell me something," Sir Gareth said at last, instead of answering. "In the courtroom. What would you have done if I hadn't retracted my statement? Would you have— have exposed me?"

"I don't know what I'd have done. Didn't think about it. Didn't think I'd have to."

"And, indeed, you *didn't* have to. Because you always get your way."

"Mostly," Joss allowed. "And I needed to get my way then, with Sophy at hazard. But if you'd stuck to your guns and given your account, it would have done no good to make trouble for you after. That would have just been spite."

"Or revenge," Sir Gareth said. "You said I hurt you."

"Not to ruin you for it."

"So it was a bluff?"

"Pretty much," Joss said. "Sorry."

Sir Gareth sighed. "I'm sorry too. About that evening in the Ducks, I mean. I was grossly rude for reasons that were nothing to do with you, and I should have apologised earlier. I would have done, only—"

"Hasn't been the chance, has there?" Joss would have very much liked to know those reasons. Very much liked, also, to ask *so would you have wanted to see me again?* But that had been London, and this was Sir Gareth, baronet, and he needed to tread carefully. "Thank you for saying it now."

The night closed around them. He could hear Sir Gareth breathing.

"I was beetle-hunting," he said at last.

Joss blinked at the darkness. "Sorry?"

"When I saw your sister. I was looking for a beetle."

He surely couldn't mean one particular beetle. Unless it was a pet one, maybe, like you'd seek a lost dog? "What beetle?" Joss was forced to ask.

"*Dytiscus marginalis*, the great diving beetle. They fly at night. They use the reflection of moonlight to find water, you see, and it was very bright."

"Right," Joss said. "Beetle. Right. Why?"

This time Sir Gareth was silent long enough Joss wasn't sure he'd get an answer, but finally he spoke. "My father was a naturalist, studying the Marsh. He filled notebooks with observations and drawings and records of what he saw. Do you know the natural history of Selborne?"

"Where's that?"

"It's a book. *The Natural History of Selborne*," Sir Gareth said, and this time Joss heard the capitals. "By a clergyman who wrote about his parish in Hampshire. It describes the land and the things he saw there, with pictures, in the most glorious detail. He understands the place deeply, its plants and creatures. He talks about the weather, how the seasons change. It's a wonderful book. I've read it a dozen times. It's sold ever so many copies. Probably thousands."

Joss didn't know how many copies books usually sold, but that sounded like a lot. "Why would a dunnamany people read about a parish in Hampshire?"

"Because he makes it interesting. He looks closely and sees the place for what it is and writes about the tiny details of life there, the birds and the seasons and the landscape. He cares about it. It's his place." He sounded—something. Wistful, maybe. "I think my father was planning to write a book like that."

"A book about the Marsh?"

"One that looked at the Marsh closely and really saw it and told other people what it's like."

"A book about the Marsh," Joss repeated, with a fierce stir of pride. "Sounds like someone should. I don't know this Selborne place but I doubt it's got anything the Marsh doesn't."

"Scenery?" Sir Gareth suggested a bit drily. "Fossils?"

"What's that?"

"It doesn't matter. Anyway, my father wrote a great deal about the Marsh, especially its insects. I've been reading his notes, and I wanted to…follow in his tracks, I suppose. See what he saw. Maybe understand him a little more by understanding what he cared for. That's all."

"That's what he was up to, maundering all over with his bag and his papers," Joss said, the realisation slotting into place. "And it's what you're doing, poking around places and watching on the dykes. You're looking at bugs."

"I suppose I ought to expect you to know exactly what I do," Sir Gareth said sourly.

"Well, people notice. Most of us have things to do all day. Or if we're walking the Marsh, it's usually for a reason."

"I've got reasons. They just aren't the same as yours."

"Fair enough." Joss wondered if Sir Gareth was going to write his father's book. He wasn't much of a reader, though he had his letters well enough, but he'd read that. "Those great beetles—do you mean the big swimming ones? Dark, with yellow trim and a yellow belly, an inch or so long?"

"That's right."

"I know those. They catch minnows sometimes."

"Yes!" Sir Gareth sounded unreasonably excited. "Do you know where I can see them?"

"There's a pond where me and my brother used to act about. We called 'em bobbers. I'll take you if you like."

"Oh, yes please," Sir Gareth said instantly, and then, "That is, uh, there's no need to trouble yourself. If you could give me directions, that would be very kind."

That sounded like a polite refusal, but he'd accepted first, and anyway Joss wanted to know what it was about bobbers that would make a fellow stay up all night, still less write a book. "I'll take you, no trouble. We ought to talk about what happened."

That, as intended, cut off any further argument. "Oh," Sir Gareth said. "Yes. Do you know, I forgot for a moment. How peculiar."

That was reaction, too. Joss hadn't forgotten any of it, but he'd put it to one side in the enjoyment of a conversation with Sir Gareth where nobody was shouting. "So, those fellows—"

"Who were they? You knew them."

"The fellow looks like a rat is a Nadgett and the big lunk's called Bowring. They're from Camber, near Rye. They both work for Nate Sweetwater, a free trader on Walland Marsh."

"What were they doing here, then?"

Joss would like to know that too. Dymchurch was Doomsday heartland. "What did they say to you?"

"They told me what they told Cecy. About the company we keep. No Preventives, and no Doomsdays, they said. They kept telling me I should keep quiet about their business, but I couldn't talk about it if I wanted to. I don't know anything!" He sounded close to tears. "Why is this happening?"

"Don't know," Joss said. "I'll ask."

"Ask who?"

"Nate Sweetwater. Seems the easiest way to go about it."

"*What?*"

"Why not? He's got some idea about you, seems like. Best thing is if I go tell him he's wrong. Any reason I shouldn't do that?"

"But is that safe for you?" Sir Gareth demanded.

Joss couldn't help grinning and was relieved Sir Gareth couldn't see it. He wouldn't want to seem mocking; that had sounded like honest concern, which was nice to hear, if entirely unnecessary. "You don't need to worry about that. I can handle Nate Sweetwater. Long as I'm telling him the truth, that is. Tell me again: you don't know what this is about?"

"No!"

"You don't mean to inform on him?"

"I've nothing whatsoever I could say about him if I wanted to, which I do not. I never heard of him until today."

"Your old man didn't have any dealings with him?"

"I beg your pardon? My father? Dealings with *smugglers*?"

He sounded—well, offended, really, and incredulous. Like there was no way a baronet might have dealings with a free trader. Like he wasn't sat here on a stone, so close to Joss that a shuffle of two or three inches would bring their shoulders together. "Don't ask me," Joss said. "Wasn't my father. You don't think so?"

"I—" Sir Gareth began hotly, and then his voice dropped. "Actually, I don't know what he'd do. I didn't know him at all."

And there was something else Joss wanted to ask: why Sir Hugo had lived on the Marsh for nigh on twenty years and nobody ever heard of or seen a son before. Why Sir Gareth thought looking at bobbers could tell him anything about his father. "Would Mrs. Inglis know?"

"I can ask her. But as far as I'm aware, our tea and brandy comes from you."

"It does. All right, I'll go let Nate know what I think of him acting like he rules the roast in Dymchurch. I won't have my people touched."

"Your people," Sir Gareth said. "You said that. You said if he attacked us, he was attacking you. Why did you say that?"

"The Doomsdays look after Dymchurch."

"You don't look after me. Us. My family."

"Ma said—"

"She didn't tell you to start some sort of war with a rival gang. I don't want to owe you this."

His voice was thin and strained. Of course Sir Gareth, baronet, didn't want to be beholden to a free trader. Joss didn't want him feeling beholden either: that wasn't the footing he wanted to be on in the slightest. Pity he wasn't quite sure what that footing was, let alone how to get there.

"Nate Sweetwater's got no business in Dymchurch," he said firmly. "Give that one an inch, he takes a mile, so I've to stamp on that, which is nothing to do with you. I'll deal with him, and it'll all be over."

Sir Gareth didn't answer. Joss couldn't see his face, but he had a distinct feeling he was getting it wrong, all the same. "What else do you want to find?" he asked, switching subjects again since it had worked before.

"I beg your pardon?"

"Creatures. Bobbers and bugs and the like. Are there others you're looking for?"

"Oh. Er. Well, *Triton cristatus*—No. Look, you don't have to do things for me. I don't *want* you doing things for me."

"Is that, you don't want favours from the Doomsdays?" Joss said. "Or from me particularly?"

"I don't want to owe you, or anyone, anything," Sir Gareth said with precision. "I don't want someone else taking charge of my affairs, my life, and telling me to be grateful for it. I'd prefer not to be dependent now that I don't have to, and I shan't put myself in anyone's hands, given the choice."

Well, that said plenty. Joss wasn't sure how to reply. Sir Gareth started moving, getting up, and Joss put his hand out without thinking and grabbed his arm. "Wait."

Sir Gareth froze. Joss could feel his arm, rigid under the fine cloth of his coat. "Wait," he said again. "Please?"

Sir Gareth lowered himself back down. Joss couldn't see his face but the movement felt cautious. "What is it?"

"You don't want to owe anyone, and you don't want to depend on anyone. That suits me. Everyone else wants their problem solved and their rent met and their wool brought out and their brandy brought in and their boy given work. You'll be about the only one in Dymchurch I won't be responsible for."

"You *said*, if they touched me or my household—"

"Yes, and I also said to run, and you didn't. You could have, and instead you took on a bloke with a knife when I was in a tight corner."

"You'd kicked him in the balls already," Sir Gareth pointed out. "It was hardly a fair fight."

"Never fight fair, that's how you lose. And you came after Bowring too, when you didn't have to."

"You came to help me first!"

"This is stupid," Joss said. "We're going to sit here tithering about who did what? You'd have been in trouble without me; I'd have been in trouble without you. I don't *want* you feeling beholden to me, understand? I really don't. I can't have Nate Sweetwater push Dymchurch folk around, so I'm going to stick my oar in there, like it or not. But that's not about you." Much. Joss wasn't soon going to forget Sir Gareth teetering on his toes, Bowring's hand on his neck, the fear on his face. "I'm not sure what use you think I've got for you."

Sir Gareth gave a tiny, sharp intake of breath. Joss grimaced. "Uh. That came out wrong."

"In what way?"

"I meant to say—look, you're not a magistrate, right? You've no influence over the Revenue, except maybe by way of Miss Cecy's beau, but if I wanted to influence a Revenue officer I'd start higher than a lieutenant. You're outmarsh. I don't *need* you in the Doomsdays' debt. Ma wants to help Miss Cecy acause she liked Lizzy Bull once, and I have to put Nate Sweetwater in his place. That's all."

"Then why did you ask me about great crested newts?"

Joss had to take a second on that. "I…don't think I did?"

"*Triton cristatus.* Great crested newts. You asked me what other creatures I wanted to find and I said—"

"Right. Got you."

"And you didn't offer to show me newts, or beetles either, on Mrs. Doomsday's orders or because of Sweetwater. Why did you do that?" He sounded demanding, a bit aggressive maybe, but there was a hollow sound to it that betrayed raw feelings underneath.

To blazes with treading carefully. Joss took a deep breath. "That might have been me wanting to spend a bit more time with you."

Silence. His hand was still on Sir Gareth's arm. Someone's pulse was thudding fast through Joss's fingertips; he wasn't quite sure whose.

"Not to press you," he said into the dark. "Not about making anyone do anything. Just, I'm sorry things got so wrong. That I made them so wrong. I liked it better when it was London and Kent."

"So did I." The words were barely audible, breathed out. "But it isn't any more. It never was, really, because that wasn't who you are. Who either of us is."

"It was another-when and otherwhere. I know that. I still liked it."

"Yes."

"I'd like it here and now."

Sir Gareth's breath caught. Joss could feel the quivering stillness next to him. A sighted hare.

"We can't," Sir Gareth said at last.

"Why not?"

"Because you're a smuggler and I'm a baronet. You're Joss Doomsday and I'm outmarsh. I informed against your sister and you blackmailed me in public!"

One argument might have been convincing; three was the opposite. Three was encouraging, even. "Eh, details," Joss said. "You still haven't given me a good reason."

"Have I not? What, exactly, constitutes a good reason to Mr. Josiah Doomsday?"

"'I don't want to.' You tell me that and I'll take it."

Another silence. After a moment Sir Gareth said quietly, "Not fair."

Maybe it wasn't, at that. Joss let go the wrist he held. "I'm not pressing you. Only, this is just you and me, understand? Nothing to do with Sweetwater, or those plaguesome fellows earlier, or Miss Cecy. You can say no and I'm still going to sort this business out like we agreed before."

"I didn't think otherwise," Sir Gareth said. "I don't think you're a villain."

"So can I show you the beetles?"

Sir Gareth made a strangled noise. "Why?"

"Acause I'd like to. As—" He was going to say *friends*, but that seemed an absurd leap. Far more to ask than *lovers*, even. "As Chief Beetle-Hand of Romney Marsh."

A choke of startled laughter. "What?"

"Well, nobody else is, so that usually means I'm doing it," Joss said. "Unless you want to. Someone's got to be in charge of beetles, right?"

Pause. "What about newts?"

"Newts if you'd rather. Newts *and* beetles. I'm not particular."

"I gathered that," Sir Gareth said, and there was a quiver in his voice, a ghost of a laugh that made Joss's heart jump stupidly. "I can see why you always get your way." He gave a sudden yawn, the jaw-cracking kind. "Sorry. I'm dreadfully tired all of a sudden. I... don't think I can think about this now."

"Fair enough," Joss said. "That sort of thing takes it out of a man. Let's get you home."

He unfolded himself from the stone. Sir Gareth accepted his hand up, and let it go when he stood, but said awkwardly, "Joss?"

"Yes?"

A tiny hesitation. "I think I would like you to show me great diving beetles. Please."

"I'll do that, en," Joss said, and couldn't help the grin that crept on his face, under the starlight.

Nine

THE NEXT DAY IT RAINED. THERE WAS A REMARKABLY PERVA-
sive quality to the rain on Romney Marsh, as if the sky had chosen
its side in the precarious balance between land and sea. Everything
felt damp, even indoors. Catherine said it was raining heavens-
hard, a phrase Gareth committed to memory. Not that he felt
obliged to acquire the local vocabulary, but it would be useful not
to always need translation.

Another-when and otherwhere. That just meant another time and
somewhere else—he'd asked Catherine—but the words felt like
poetry, especially in Joss's voice. Especially with the meaning they
carried.

London and Kent might have had something, another-when
and otherwhere. He was not going to think about Gareth and Joss,
here and now.

Joss had predicted the rain, and said they'd go beetle-hunting
on a finer morning. Gareth would have rather liked to spend a few
hours reading up about diving beetles but there was, unfortunately,
something he had to do first.

He gathered Catherine and Cecy in the morning room accordingly, told them what the attackers had said, and asked what they knew.

"Your father?" Catherine said, sounding blank. "Dealings with smugglers? None at all that I know of. Well, beyond the brandy and so on, but everyone does that."

"Do you know anything at all about his affairs?" Gareth asked.

"Not really. He wrote lots of letters. He went to Rye reasonably often, but I don't know what for. And the trips to London of course, to discuss business with his brother."

Gareth stared at her. Catherine looked faintly puzzled, then shut her eyes in momentary horror.

"He came to London," Gareth repeated. "He visited Uncle Henry? While I was there?"

Catherine gave him a stricken look, then simply nodded. Gareth opened his mouth and shut it again. There was truly not much to be said. "Well. So. Rye. That's a hotbed of smuggling, isn't it?"

"You don't think Papa was involved with those people," Cecilia said. "Surely not."

"I don't think anything, but Joss Doomsday asked and I'd rather be sure. After all, those people seem to think they have dealings with us. You've really no idea what they might mean, either of you? No mysterious men or unexplained packages or large sums of money you know of?"

Catherine shook her head. "He didn't tell us much of what he did, but I don't think that he was keeping secrets. He just felt no need to inform us. There were the deliveries from London, I suppose—"

"Those were books," Cecilia said. "It was always books, unless it was scientific instruments. I don't know how he had time to read all those books, and I don't see what business it is of Joss Doomsday's."

"He's going to talk to Sweetwater on our behalf."

"On our behalf!" Cecy said. "And him sitting in our kitchen drinking tea, before! Goodness knows what William will think about this."

"Do you have to tell him?" Gareth asked.

She gave him a look. "He'll find out. I dare say everyone knows already. Joss Doomsday of all people coming to dine—"

"He didn't *dine*, Cecy," Catherine said. "He just ate."

"He saved me from a very unpleasant situation," Gareth said as calmly as he could. "I realise you don't approve of smuggling, and I don't either, but I do approve of people who prevent other people from strangling me. And I for one slept better last night knowing we had that enormous man outside in case the Sweetwater people came back."

"So did I," Catherine said. "That's quite a favour from the Doomsdays."

"Joss said that he can't let Sweetwater bully Dymchurch people."

"So we're to make the Doomsdays look good?" Cecilia said shrilly. "The Inglises go cap in hand to Joss Doomsday for protection, like everyone else? Marvellous."

"Cecy—" Catherine began.

"I don't want to hear. William will be furious. This is making him a laughing-stock at work."

"He's welcome to send his own men to protect us," Gareth snapped. "What would you rather we do? I can't fight those men. I can go and alert the constables in New Romney for all the good it will do, but I doubt they'll station men outside as long as we might need them."

"So we have smugglers instead! This didn't happen before you came!" Cecy shrieked.

"Cecilia!" Catherine's voice was startling in its rebuke. "That is not fair!"

"*This* isn't fair!" Cecy whisked up and out of the room. Her footsteps pounded up the stairs.

"Oh dear. I'm sorry," Gareth began, but Catherine waved it off wearily.

"It's not your fault. She and William quarrelled badly when he was last here. He was rather cross and disobliging, and brought up the Sophia Doomsday trial again. Cecy defended you, so naturally she's angry about it now."

That didn't make entire sense to Gareth, but Cecy rarely did, and to know she'd taken his part was rather warming. "I didn't know. I'm sorry they've fallen out."

"He has very strong views and expects Cecy to share them. And she has very strong views too, but they tend to change a lot. She'll settle down soon enough." Catherine sighed. "What now?"

"I'm going to look through my father's accounts, just to be sure. And if I don't find anything peculiar, we'll have to conclude there's nothing to find."

The rain kept up for another two days, during which there was no sign of smugglers of any allegiance. On the second evening, a note from Joss came through the door. It was in a round, evidently unpractised but determined hand, announced that the next day would be fine, and suggested they meet at the Revelation in the morning.

Gareth set off bright and early. The day was sunny and clear as predicted, the air washed clean and smelling pleasantly green and springlike. The lanes had bloomed aggressively pink with valerian flowers, and as he walked along to Globsden Gut, the sides of the dykes were misted with bluebells.

Joss was sitting on the steps of the Revelation, chatting to an elderly gentleman, much darker-skinned than himself, in a rocking chair. He rose as Gareth approached, an easy movement of casual strength. "Watcher, Sir Gareth. My granda, Asa Doomsday."

"I'm glad to make your acquaintance, sir." Gareth gave a bow.

The old man inclined his head without rising. "Forgive my sitting, Sir Gareth, I've old legs. Sir Hugo's son? You don't take after him." He had an unusual accent that Gareth didn't recognise, drawling even by local standards.

"I favour my mother."

"Fortunate for you. This one favours his father." He nodded at Joss. "And his sister's got her father's looks and her mother's temper, and there's a combination. Get about your business, Joss."

Joss saluted his grandfather affectionately. "Ready, Sir Gareth?"

"Of course. Where are we going?"

"The Warren."

That was a particularly waterlogged area down the coast towards Romney Sand, very much suspended between land and sea. Gareth was grateful he'd followed the note's instructions to wear stout boots.

"I've scran," Joss added, hoisting a bag. "Bread and cheese, if that'll do."

"That would be very welcome." Gareth felt suddenly tongue-tied, unsure what to say. If this was just a natural history expedition he should talk about beetles or some such, except Joss doubtless wouldn't care. Joss, who called him Sir Gareth. That was his name of course, and only proper, especially with an audience, and yet it felt increasingly uncomfortable. *Call me Gareth*, he wanted to say, but the intimacy that suggested was a little bit frightening.

"Don't mind Granda," Joss remarked, apparently also wanting to fill the silence. "He's plain-spoken."

Gareth cast his mind back. "That remark about me looking like my mother? I believe I do."

"Wasn't too polite about your father, though."

"I'm not really sure what he looked like," Gareth admitted. "I last saw him when I was six."

There was a tiny silence. "Six?"

"He sent me to London after my mother died. He moved here and remarried. I stayed there."

Joss was staring at him. "Where did you live?"

"With my uncle Henry and his son, Lionel. He's an attorney. Lionel's a partner now. I was a clerk."

He thought he'd said all that easily enough but Joss was still looking at him. "But why did you not come to be with your father? He had a wife here, and the little one."

"I couldn't say. Catherine says her sister wouldn't have objected." He hadn't quite meant to say that last. It came out anyway, propelled by—not distrust of Catherine, but a desire to be sure. If anyone knew, Joss would.

He was frowning. "Well, no. From what Ma says, I don't think Lizzy Bull objected to anything in her life, the poor blood. And he left you with your uncle. Did you want to be there?"

"Nobody asked me," Gareth said, realising too late he sounded perhaps a bit short. "It's not that unusual, really. If a parent dies, if there's a child that needs to be dealt with—"

"My uncle and father died and left five little ones between them, and nobody sent anyone away," Joss said. "But we're not Quality. You didn't exactly look plump in the pocket when we met."

Gareth blinked. "No, well, I wasn't. Clerks aren't well paid."

"But you were your father's heir. His only son."

"I don't suppose he expected to die for many years. I didn't expect him to."

"But—"

"He didn't give me an allowance," Gareth said, because that was clearly the question. "He didn't treat me as his son and heir in any way. He didn't write to me, he didn't send for me, he foisted me on my uncle who didn't want me either. I don't know why, and now I never will. Catherine says he was a selfish man who didn't want to be troubled, and I dare say she ought to know. That's all."

Joss shoved his hands in his pockets. He was wearing his long leather coat, the one he'd worn when Gareth had first seen him, and Gareth could not avoid noticing that he wore it well. "I'm sorry. That's a dismal way to treat a child."

"Yes," Gareth said. The lane pulled right in front of them, with the rank grass and standing water of the Warren on the left towards the coast. "Here?"

"This way." Joss walked with certainty, boots seeming to find tufts grounded on solid earth where Gareth's all too often went through the long grass and plunged into unexpected and unseen water. Some very bent trees grew out sideways over the pools, alive but rotted black with the eternal damp and thick with moss.

There was a fallen log by the edge of the pond. Joss gestured to it. "Take a seat. This is where we used to catch 'em."

"They're fresh-water beetles. Does this part not flood?"

"Mostly from the landward side."

Gareth fixed his eyes on the edge of the pond. Joss sank into a graceful squat, leaning his back against the log, and took out a loaf, a hunk of cheese, and a very sharp-looking knife, using his satchel as a makeshift cutting board. It was the sort of operation Gareth had not yet managed without fumbling.

"Do you know anything about my father?" he blurted.

"Not much." Joss didn't look round. Maybe he'd heard the tremble in Gareth's voice, or maybe he didn't want to risk cutting himself. "Wasn't a popular man. Not one for company. Kept himself to himself, and Marshfolk have no trouble with that, but Ma didn't think much of him."

"No?"

"Lizzy Bull was barely eighteen when he married her, and her father only in the ground two months. And she wasn't born a lady, so the marriage left her neither flesh nor fowl. Ma said Sir Hugo had no business stranding her like that. She was cut off from her own sort and he didn't trouble with friends, so she was on her own except for her sister. Then she died and your father set up with Cathy Bull instead, and no offence but if that's the gentry way—"

"If it is, it oughtn't be. And that's no reflection on Catherine. She is an excellent woman."

"Not fair on her or Lizzy, Ma said." Joss handed him a slice of bread and cheese. "And what with how he treated you..." He puffed out his cheeks. "Sorry to say it, but from what I hear, your father was a middling arsehole. No offence."

"You can't just say something offensive and add 'no offence'."

Joss cocked an eye at him. "Are you offended?"

"No," Gareth admitted. "I spent years wondering why my father didn't want me and thinking of what I might have done to deserve it, or coming up with explanations—romantic ones about being a lost heir, or awful ones about horrible secrets. But the more I learn, the more I think that, actually yes, he was an arsehole. I wouldn't say middling either."

"No?"

"No. Frankly, I should say *utter*."

"That's what I meant," Joss said. "Middling is...you know. A lot of something. Or not much of something, sometimes. Depends how you say it."

Gareth attempted to make sense of that. "What?"

"Your old man was a middling arsehole and a middling father. Meaning, a right arsehole and not much of a father."

"So it means bad?"

"Course not. It's a middling nice day now, with but middling chance of rain. You'd understand me if you were Kentish."

"Yes, but I speak English," Gareth said. "And as such, I'm wondering which of us has gone mad."

Joss gave him a sideways grin. "Wouldn't like to say."

They ate companionably. The bread was fresh-baked, still a little warm, coarse but good. The cheese was sheep's milk, and excellent. Gareth swallowed a mouthful. "Can I ask you something?"

"Go on."

"Your grandfather. Your father's father?"

"That's right."

"And a Doomsday. But only you and Miss Sophia are his colour?"

"Yes? Oh, I see. No, he took the name when he married my grandma, who was a Doomsday born. He had no attachment to his other."

"That's unusual."

"He came from Georgia. That's in America. Born and raised a slave, and named to show who his master was." Joss's voice had a bite in it. "Why would he keep that as a free man, when he could be a Doomsday?"

"I see. Of course."

Joss cut another slice of cheese. "Grandma wanted to stay a Doomsday—there was a woman knew her own mind—so it suited her too. Ma as well. She and my pa were cousins and she used to say she only married him so as not to change her name." He smiled, a little private expression that made Gareth's heart twist. "They were happy enough, but she does talk."

"Your father passed on?"

"The sea took him when I was twelve, along with Sam and Bart. My uncle Samuel and my older brother."

"I'm so sorry. That's dreadful."

"It was hard." Joss sounded contemplative. "Left a bit of a mess, to be honest. Five fatherless children, two widows. Ma kept the family and the work together, mourned her son and her brother and her man, and raised me and Sophy, all at once. It wasn't easy for her."

"No. She must be very strong."

"Well, you met her."

And Joss, the crown prince, doubtless taking on whatever responsibilities a young smuggler should. Taking care of his little sister, Gareth supposed, and growing up to be a man who took care of his people, albeit in a thoroughly reprehensible way. Gareth opened his mouth to say something, and never found out what, because Joss said, "Bobber."

Gareth leaned forward, following the pointing finger. "Where?"

"There. Sticking its arse out of the water. They do that, goodness knows why."

"It's collecting air. They have no gills—can't breathe underwater—so they come up for air and store it under their wing cases for when they go down again."

"Oh," Joss said, sounding a bit surprised to have an explanation. "Well, I never. There's another."

"Good Lord, they're large." Gareth leaned over the edge of the pond to watch, kneeling on the wet grass, careless of the damp. Joss shifted into a squat beside him. "That's a male. See those pads on its front feet? They use those to grip the female when they mate."

"Hmph. Could just say please."

"I don't think they have very good manners. Apparently they exude a foul liquid from the anus when they're frightened."

"Don't we all," Joss said, and Gareth almost lost his balance laughing.

There were great diving beetles everywhere, once he knew how to look for them. He and Joss roamed the Warren and watched males and females, and saw the larvae too, monstrously jawed, terrifyingly oversized monsters that looked like pallid devil's coach-horses. Joss hadn't known they were two forms of the same creature, and Gareth basked in his admiration. Then Joss spotted a beetle tussling with a silvery minnow and they both watched with appalled fascination as it dispatched the fish, decapitating it with the enthusiasm of a French revolutionary in just a few powerful chews. They followed a heron stalking the pools, and found a train of orange and brown fox moth caterpillars, which Joss, delightfully, called measuring-bugs. It was the best morning Gareth had had since... In fact, he couldn't remember a better.

They found a convenient, and drier, log once the sun was high in the sky and sat, enjoying the warmth and finishing the bread and cheese between them.

"So," Joss said. "Happy with the bugs?"

"That was marvellous. Middling good?"

"Middling," Joss agreed, and there it was, that glorious smile for Gareth at last, brightening the sunlight.

Gareth couldn't have stopped himself smiling back for the world. "Thank you for showing me."

"Other way round, I reckon. I've seen 'em all my life and I don't think I ever looked at 'em before today, not proper-like. Great diving beetles on the Marsh." Joss gave a nod of intense patriotic satisfaction. Gareth decided not to mention they were common across Europe. "You want to look for newts another-when?"

"I would love to."

"Same." Joss hesitated, then tipped his head back. "We

probably ought to talk about the Sweetwater business while we're here."

They did have to. Still, it was a grey cloud over the bright day. "Yes," Gareth said reluctantly.

"I went to see Nate."

"Already?" Gareth said, alarmed. "I didn't realise you were going to do that so soon."

"Well, I gave two of his men a leathering. Didn't want that to come back on me. I told him to keep his nose out of Dymchurch, first and foremost, said as far as you were aware, you'd nothing to talk about. I said if he had any problems with your or your family, it should come through me. He allowed that was fair."

"He did?"

"You ask me, this wasn't his doing. If he had a grievance, I'd have heard about it. Not a man to suffer in silence, Nate, so I'm thinking someone else sent those fellows, and I dare say he'll have words when he finds out who. Anyway, he and I shook hands on it, so you shouldn't see any more trouble. If you do, tell me."

"Right. Right. Yes. Good. Thank you."

Joss looked round. "Something wrong?"

"Not wrong," Gareth said uncomfortably. "Only—well, what you said before, asking about my father's dealings. I thought you wanted me to be sure he wasn't involved in anything—I wanted to be sure—so I spoke to Catherine and Cecy. They didn't have any ideas. So...uh." He wasn't quite sure about saying this, but there was nobody else he could ask, or tell. "I looked at where my father's money came from."

There was a frown between Joss's eyes. "Oh, yes? Where was that?"

"He had a substantial amount in the Funds, various invest-ments, and business dealings in London with my uncle. He had some unspecified dealings in Rye which—which I can't find any details of, but which seem to have received excellent returns very promptly." Gareth swallowed. "And he made some losses a couple of years ago but not long afterwards, he started receiving two hundred pounds every four months or so. It came in for the last year and a half of his life, in notes, and I don't know where it came from at all. The money just *appears*."

"He was making a lot of money fast, from nowhere, on Romney Marsh, and you don't know how." Joss's voice was dry as a bone.

"Yes, but—Look, it can't be that. He was in his fifties, a gentleman, a baronet. He can't have been a smuggler."

"Course not."

"He can't! He wasn't making trips to France."

"Not on his own legs, maybe," Joss said. "Do you know how the trade works?"

"I have no idea."

"Sometimes it's barter—we bring over wool to France and exchange it direct-like. Sometimes an innkeeper needs his cellar filled, or a London merchant wants to stock his shop with French gloves, or pepper, or fine soap, so they place the order with us. And sometimes it's speculation. Which is to say, a rich man invests his money with a free trader, who buys and sells as he thinks fit. A while later our gentleman gets his money back and more, and never gets his hands dirty touching the goods."

That last was so exactly what Gareth had feared that he couldn't face it, couldn't hear it. The sheer, shameless *crime* of it all. "You are aware we're at war with France?" he said furiously. "I mean, you do know you're trading with the enemy?"

"Free trading's what we do. I'm not one for politics."

"Politics? This is more than politics. It's more than crime, even. The Continent is supposed to be blockaded, and you're helping the enemy by buying their goods! It's all but *treason*, and you don't appear to give a damn!"

"Hold on there," Joss said. "Yes, there's a blockade. The government set it up, and everyone who lives by the wool trade found themselves sitting on a lot of fleeces they couldn't sell while the French spinners and weavers had empty looms. We've got a dunnamany sheep here and not a lot else, you'll have noticed. How are people meant to live if you cut off their living?"

"It's a war! People have to make sacrifices."

"That right? What sacrifices have you made? The lordships and gentlemen in London, are they running short of food? You think the King's husbanding his coals? Why's all the sacrifice on us?"

"That's entirely specious."

"Talk English," Joss suggested sardonically.

Gareth discovered he couldn't instantly define *specious*. "The argument doesn't hold up. If the nation is at war, trading with the enemy undermines us all. And it's all very well to talk about livelihoods, but whose livelihoods are supported when you import brandy and tobacco and silk? How are those things necessary?"

"They are for the French who make them," Joss said. "People over there are trying to feed their families, just like people over here. And as for whether they're needful here, well, you tell me."

"Me?"

"You're gentry, and it's the gentry who wants those things, need or not. I sell to London clubs and London drapers and who do you think they sell to? The men who make the laws and set the taxes still want their brandy and tobacco, the silks and lace for their ladies, and they buy it knowing where it came from."

"Well...they shouldn't," Gareth said, uncomfortably aware of the lavender soap at home. "And you're still ignoring the fact that we're at war!"

"I don't care."

He sounded like he meant it. Gareth stared at him. "What? How can you not?"

"Lords and kings and emperors fighting about crowns? They aren't my people. George means no more to me than Boney. German or Frenchman on the throne, who cares? We had a dun-namany French kings before."

"When did we—You can't be talking about the Norman Conquest," Gareth protested.

"Got invaded by the French and the world didn't end. What's it to me which rich man runs the country? What difference does it make to Romney Marsh who wears the crown? Or no, I'll tell you what difference: there's no laws against sharing your bed with another fellow in France now. If you gave me a vote, I'd vote for that."

So would Gareth. He struck out for safer waters. "This is all very well, but we're talking about being defeated and invaded! Have you not considered what an enemy army entering this country might mean?"

Joss laughed, but not in a way that suggested humour. "Couldn't miss it, with Martello towers up and down the coast. The invasion will come through here just like last time. That's why they built the Royal Military Canal, to slow down Boney's men."

Gareth knew the Canal, an ugly, wide, straight gash that ran all the way from north of Rye and across the top of the Romney Marsh, just before the land began to rise. "Yes, so—"

"So when these terrible Frog monsters come over here breathing fire and seeking blood, they'll be kept on the Marsh for as long as possible," Joss said. "That's what they built the Canal for: so the Marsh takes the brunt of an invasion. Am I supposed to be pleased about that?"

"Well, no, but... You must see they've got to defend the country."

"Oh, they're going to. You know the other plan? They're going to breach the Wall."

"To *what*?" Gareth felt a spasm of shock. He might be outmarsh, but he knew the Wall was sacred.

"When the French ships land, the soldiers are to set charges, blow up the Wall, and drown the Marsh." Joss's voice was harsh now, almost frightening. "Our land, our home, all gone just to slow the French down for a day or two. Oh, but there's a plan to get the sheep off. Lot of important men own fine sheep here, so they aim to drive them out first. Got to save the sheep."

He spat that out. Gareth stared at him. "Um. I don't... Why is it so bad they want to save the sheep?"

Joss didn't say anything. He just waited. Gareth looked at his face, turned over his words. "There's a plan to get the people out *as well*, yes?"

"Course not. The old, the crippled, the children, everyone with their worldly goods on their backs, we'll all have to fend for ourselves when our own soldiers flood the Marsh, but sheep are valuable. Look, nobody gives a damn for the Marsh except Marshmen. The government and the King don't care if we starve. They put on the blockade but charge their rents and taxes same as ever, and they'll let the sea or the French take us if that preserves their skins for another day. So we look after ourselves. And that means trading, and selling wool—some of it wool off the sheep that are going to be saved when old women and children will be left behind, acause if you think those landowners have given up their income for the sake of the war, you're joking. They want their wool sold, just like the Quality in London want to wear silk and drink brandy, and the merchants want their shelves stocked. We run goods for them, and when they catch us doing it, they hang us for the look of the thing."

Gareth had no idea what to say. He wasn't a political philosopher. He had a vague sort of idea that country, king, and law were the foundations on which the nation was built, while nevertheless acknowledging that he had no intention of taking up arms for the country, the king was a mad German, and he'd spent much of his adult life happily breaking the law. Still, they were principles, even if they weren't his principles. He'd thought this would be an easy fight to pick.

He'd met plenty of radicals in London—men who wanted wealth redistributed, laws changed, the government made representative. Joss Doomsday, fervent patriot of a hundred square miles of marshland, was perhaps the most radical man he'd ever met.

Ten

Joss could have kicked himself. It had been a glorious morning, in ways that were all the better for being so unexpected. He hadn't dreamed he'd be fascinated by beetles. He'd assumed he'd be showing Sir Gareth around, the baronet an invited guest in Joss's place, and instead the lanky outmarsh had made him see his own beloved home with new and sharper eyes. There was a whole world on the Marsh he'd never known and that they'd explored together, alone in their waterlogged Eden and sharing its discovery.

And then Sir Gareth went off in that snappish, condescending tone, just like back in the Three Ducks when it had all gone wrong, and Joss had flown into a dobbin.

Of course he knew they were at war. What was he supposed to do: watch people go hungry as taxes rose and rose? They'd run grain last year, for God's sake. Smuggling grain into a country that should grow plenty, paying a pretty penny for it in France as well, because the harvest had failed and Parliament didn't do a thing about it. Too busy pouring money into muskets and uniforms to be shipped to a faraway country, because God forfend one set of rich men in charge should be exchanged for another.

War and kings and the shuffling of crowns meant nothing to Joss. Of course they meant something to Sir Gareth Inglis, baronet.

Joss forced a tight smile. "You don't agree. You wouldn't."

"I don't know."

He said that so simply, without the hostility, and it took the ground from under Joss's feet. "Eh?"

"I don't know what I think now. I'm not sure I've thought about any of this properly before. And you're quite right: I've been drinking smuggled gin and brandy for years so I've no room to talk. Could I have some time to consider?"

Joss blinked. Sir Gareth gave him a worried look. "I would rather turn this over in my head a little because—well, I think you must be wrong, but I can't put my finger on where. And I'd rather think about why that is and what you said than argue about it."

"Yes, but hold on," Joss said. "We *weren't* arguing before. You started it."

"I know." Sir Gareth's shoulders hunched a little. "And it's not the first time, is it? I was uppish with you because I didn't like where that conversation was going, and it wasn't fair of me." He offered a wary smile of his own, every bit as tentative as Joss's. "I had such a lovely morning, and I didn't mean to spoil it. I'm sorry."

"I don't want to either, but when you go at me like that—" He didn't know how to explain the way it got under his skin, that superior way of talking. Maybe because it was a reminder Sir Gareth *was* superior. Maybe it just brought back that night, and the hurt of it.

Sir Gareth was looking miserable. "I shouldn't have. I really am sorry. I, uh, I don't deal well with difficult situations. It's cowardly, I know it is."

"You walked into the Revelation and faced down my whole family, and then you took on two of Sweetwater's men," Joss said. "I wouldn't call that cowardly myself."

"Starting fights instead of facing problems isn't courage." Gareth sounded a touch bitter. "I'm aware of it and I meant to do better. I *will* do better. I just...ugh. I don't want to believe my father was a smuggler, along with everything else it seems he was. Because whatever arguments you have for your work—and I truly will think about them—I don't think they apply to him. He wasn't in need, his livelihood wasn't threatened. He wasn't helping anyone but himself. And if that's the case, I find it shameful."

"I don't think much of a rich man who sits on his arse and pays other people to do his dirty work," Joss said. "So we're agreed there."

Sir Gareth's shoulders dropped. "We'd probably agree on more than that, if I listened to you properly. I shouldn't have spoken to you like that."

"You're allowed your opinions."

"That wasn't opinions. It was just picking a fight."

"At least you didn't throw punches."

"Well, I'm not a fool," Sir Gareth said. "I would like to talk about this again, more civilly, to understand your point of view. I don't know if I'll agree but I'd rather disagree with more nuance."

Joss hoped *nuance* didn't mean shouting. "I don't expect you to agree. Only, I'm not a fool myself, or a villain either. I stand for the Marsh, that's all. Not England, not France. And you don't see that—"

"Because I'm outmarsh," Sir Gareth said with what sounded almost like bitterness.

"Acause you're a baronet from London and this isn't your life. That's fair enough. You've got reasons for what you think and do. All I'm saying is so do I."

"I wish I had your certainty. And even if I did, in your position I should probably have flown into a fury rather than taking the time to make my case and—thank you for not doing that. Thank you for showing me the Marsh, your Marsh. Thank you for not walking away. I shouldn't have blamed you if you did." He offered Joss an apologetic smile, so cautious and hopeful that it stopped his breath.

"That's all right," Joss managed. London—Sir Gareth, whatever—sitting with him here, with that smile, those pleading eyes, so close. "I'd just rather you didn't think ill of me."

"I don't. Truly."

Joss looked at his face and threw caution to the wind. "To be honest, my nerves are all to pieces having you this close. A whole morning with you right here with me? Can't think straight." Sir Gareth's lips parted soundlessly. "I went off acause you've got me in a merciful twitter. And maybe you don't feel the same—"

"N-no. No, I think that might be something to do with it, now you mention it. Quite a large something. Merciful twitter, did you say?"

There was a touch, light as a butterfly's wing, on Joss's hand, and he looked down to see pale, if rather grubby, fingers brush his. "Merciful," Joss said a little hoarsely. "Acause it's a bit much, being this close to a fellow like you and thinking I can't kiss you." Sir Gareth's eyes widened, and Joss thought, the blazes with it. "Or can I?"

"Can we?" Sir Gareth whispered. "Here?"

Can we. Not 'no', not 'but', just 'can we?' Joss's lungs felt a bit constricted. "There hasn't been another soul by for the last three hours."

Sir Gareth made a little needy noise that sounded to Joss like a yes. He put a hand to his face, London's face, feeling smooth skin barely prickled with beard, and saw the familiar hunger in his eyes, and kissed him.

Just a kiss, just a gentle, reverential press of lips for a few seconds, and then London whimpered in his mouth and snaked a hand up into his hair—Joss wished he hadn't tied it back, he'd missed those hands in his hair—and Joss got an arm to his waist, and suddenly it was wild.

Joss kissed him frantically, blood thundering through his veins at London's response. Christ, the way he responded, all hungry mouth and urgent hands, grabbing each other, so hopelessly wide open, just like before. London was clutching Joss's face, at once reaching for him and bending back under him, and Jesus God, Joss wanted this now. The blood roared in his ears. He wanted to lay the man back on a bed and spend an hour relearning him from crown to toes, preferably with his tongue.

They didn't have a bed. They had a log, though, and Joss eased him back on it. Sir Gareth swung his legs astride, which put one foot on each side to keep his balance and gave a satisfying prominence to the bulge in his breeches. The look in his eyes suggested that was no accident.

Joss leaned over him, thigh to thigh, his own arousal pressing hard against the baronet's. "London," he said, voice hoarse.

"I missed you so much." It was a whisper.

"Same." Joss shifted, got a hand under him, massaging the outline of his prick.

"Oh God, Joss. Please."

His name sounded so good in that soft voice. "Gareth," he tried out. Dropping the title felt almost more of a liberty than delving between the man's legs, but Gareth's lips parted breathlessly and that was what Joss was calling him now, just to see that look. "Hearts alive. Gareth." He fumbled with buttons, needing to touch skin.

Gareth bucked under him, not making it easier. He arched his head back, which let Joss see the bruises on his neck, and he was going to make Nate Sweetwater regret his mother ever bore him for every one of those bruises, but that was for later. Instead he got his other arm under Gareth's shoulders, pulling him up a little, and then he had Gareth's stand in his grip, kissing and stroking him, relishing the abandon. Sir Gareth, baronet, open and helpless in his arms, moaning in his mouth, thrusting into his hand, with the dappled sunlight on them and nothing else but the strimming of grasshoppers, the rustle of leaves.

"Gareth," he whispered. "You beauty. The way you look when I've got your prick. Oh Christ, I want to make you come, I want to watch you do it."

Gareth's arms wrapped around his neck. He moved against Joss with increasingly urgent noises as Joss murmured his desire, and stiffened, and spent in his hand with cries that Joss's mouth muffled, clamped over his.

Joss held him for a second longer, to be sure he was done, and lowered him down as Gareth sagged back.

"Christ. Joss."

"You are so beautiful," Joss said, and the words sounded like talking in church.

Gareth's eyes opened. They looked drugged, dizzy, darkened with arousal, and frankly wicked. He reached down, running a hand over Joss's arse, between his thighs.

"Normally I'd kneel," he said. "But the ground is mostly water, so if you come up *here* a bit and I go down *there* a bit—?"

Joss worked that out and moved as requested, standing straddling the log to let Gareth wriggle under him while he unfastened his own breeches. He leaned forward, taking his weight on his hands as Gareth got his mouth to work. Gareth under him, sucking him, gripping his arse with both hands, using only his mouth. Lips and teeth and tongue, all working to glorious, toe-curling effect. "Oh, Jesus, Gareth. God almighty. Your mouth. Oh God, so good, so good—please—"

He wanted this to last forever but Gareth was sucking him with wild urgency, wet and slick and frantic, moaning pleasure around his prick. His fingers dug into damp bark; he tried to hold off for about five seconds more, gave up the struggle, and came in Gareth's mouth with pulsing, quivery joy.

He rocked forward, bracing himself on his elbows because his strength had failed. Gareth's arms came around his waist and they stayed like that for a moment in silence. Which was fine at first—welcome, even, because Joss's brain had gone white-hot and was only just starting to work again—and then less so, as the world took shape around them once more and he started to wonder what happened now.

"I tell you what," Gareth said, muffled.

"What?"

"Next time a man says he's taking me to look for beetles, I'll know what he means."

Joss choked on laughter and relief. "Could be worse. You could have said newts and then you'd be in trouble."

Gareth gave him a very saucy eyebrow. "Please, I'm not an innocent. We all know 'Hunt the Newt'."

Joss got himself upright, tidying himself as Gareth did the same. "I'll play Hunt the Newt any time you like, London. Gareth."

"I'd like that. You have no idea how often I kicked myself about that last time in the Ducks. I really am so sorry about that."

"You're forgiven," Joss said. "Only, what did I say?"

"It truly wasn't you. Not at all. I was a prick because—well, several things at once, but mostly because I didn't want you to go."

"You had a funny way of showing it," Joss said, and then, "Right. You *do* have a funny way of showing it."

Gareth leaned against him. Joss put an arm over his shoulder, as though it was quite natural, and thought about a motherless boy dumped in an uncaring household, writing letters to a father who never came. Joss knew what it was to lose a parent, but he'd been older, and he'd had Ma and Granda and Sophy. If Ma had packed him off somewhere else after Pa died, sent him off the Marsh and never let him back, probably he wouldn't take parting with grace either.

"Maybe you had reason," he said. "Ah, Gareth."

"It hurt," Gareth said softly. "I'd enjoyed being with you so much, and when you said you were going—"

"I said I'd come back."

"I didn't believe you."

"No. No, I see you might not."

Gareth sighed. "I don't suppose I listened to what you were saying at all, not properly. My uncle had dismissed me that morning. Nine years working for his dreadful tedious business, and he sacked me without notice."

"That same morning? You might have said. What did he do that for?"

"I've no idea. Probably because I wasn't a very good clerk, but perhaps he was just in a bad temper. It became rather unpleasant. He told me to go back to my damned father because he didn't want me. I said nor did my father, and he said nobody did or ever would and I should get out of his sight."

Joss twisted round to stare at him. "What kind of way is that to talk to family? And you don't know why?"

Gareth shrugged as if it was nothing much out of the ordinary. "I was rather upset, and I had no idea what I was going to do with myself, so I made a dreadful scene at you when what I'd meant to say, if I'd just thought, was, yes please, I would love to see you again." He grimaced. "And then two days later I found out my father had died, which I assumed answered the question of what I was going to do, except I'm discovering it doesn't."

"Does it not? You're a baronet."

"That's not an occupation," Gareth said. "I don't wake up in the morning and engage in a spot of light baronetting before luncheon. I don't actually have a great deal to do, but I don't have anything particular I want to do in London either."

"Aren't you supposed to..." Joss had only the vaguest idea of what Quality did all day. "Go to parties? Buy clothes?"

"Again, not an occupation. And I don't know anyone to go to parties with. I dare say it would be easy enough to be invited to things, with a title and a respectable income."

"I'd have thought. Got to be plenty of ladies looking for that."

"Except I'm not looking for ladies, so I'd be wasting my time and theirs."

"But you've got to get married, right?" Joss knew this: he'd seen plays. "You need an heir for the title."

Gareth snorted. "It's hardly worth putting some poor woman through childbirth. I'm a baronet because my great-grandmother tupped George the Second for a couple of years, and my great-grandfather took his cuckolding without complaint. The title was a reward. I'm not sure which of them was supposed to have earned it."

Joss took that in. "Your great-grandma won a baronetcy on her back? She must—" He snapped his mouth shut, too late.

"Must have been good?" Gareth supplied. "Quite. Although I think Charles the Second made two of his mistresses duchesses, so not *that* good."

"Be fair, nobody's so much as given me a knighthood. Yet."

"It's a travesty of justice."

Joss leaned back to have a squint at him. "King's mistress, you say? So, your granda...?"

"Born before the affair. I've no royal blood, and if you ever see a portrait of George the Second you'll share my relief at that. I really do have a title for no better reason than that my great-grandmother was a royal ladybird, and I dare say the same is the case for a lot of noble families but...well. I wasn't brought up to it. I'm a clerk masquerading as gentry, and I dare say I could remake myself as a Society gentleman but I don't enjoy gambling, or sport, and I'm not a good dancer, and I really don't know what else Society *does*. I do realise that there are people who would give their eye teeth to be in my position, but I'm astonishingly poorly fitted for it."

"Squire doesn't go up to London hardly ever, or the earl," Joss said. "They do their gentlemanning here."

"But they belong here. I don't. I'm like Lizzy Bull, neither flesh nor fowl. I don't think Sir Anthony and I are destined to be friends, the d'Aumestys all have rats in the attic, and to everyone else I'm outmarsh. I don't mean to complain. I like Catherine a great deal, I want to spend more time with Cecy, and I'm learning so much. I took up my father's natural history books because I wanted to understand him better, which hasn't come out in his favour, but I'm interested on my own account. I'd like to stay longer. Only it's been made very clear that I don't belong here, and that's rather lonely."

Joss had known Gareth wouldn't be staying forever and he'd have put that as the reason too. He hadn't expected a London gentleman to stay this long. He ought to take today as an unexpected, joyful gift, not be already wanting more. "It's not bustling here, I grant you. I know there's people who find it bligh. Lonely. Dull," he made himself allow.

"I haven't found it dull," Gareth said, with feeling. "The very opposite, frankly. And I like the quiet. London is far too loud and busy. I like having time to myself and I don't need constant people, especially when there's so much to see. But I think always being outmarsh, never having people at all, might become hard too."

"It takes a bit of time for the Marsh to get used to newcomers," Joss said, knowing full well 'a bit of time' might be years.

"Especially when the newcomer informs on a free trader." Gareth sounded resigned. "I don't quite see how I recover my position from that."

"Well, I got over it," Joss pointed out.

Gareth turned to him with a quick smile. "So you did. And I shouldn't complain, when we've had today because it's been wonderful. Only—can we do this again?"

"You want to?"

"It's been one of the best mornings of my life," Gareth said simply. "And I wanted to see you again after I left, so much, and here you are. I'd like to do all of it again, as often as possible. I'm asking if we can."

He reached up, meeting Joss's hand as it lay over his shoulder. Joss took the slim fingers in his. "Why not?"

"Because everyone here knows who I am and who you are. What if you're caught?"

"We won't be caught."

Gareth's brows angled into a frown. "I wasn't asking for reassurance. I said, what if *you* get caught. You, on Romney Marsh, in your home. I mean, do you usually do this here? With men, on the Marsh, where everyone knows you?"

He was pretty sharp. "Not usually," Joss said. "No."

"No. You go to London."

There had been a very charming French brandy merchant in Dunkirk a couple of years back, but Gareth had the principle of it. "Mostly."

"Your whole life is here. I could leave if there was trouble and not look back—not much, anyway—because this isn't my home. But it's yours."

"Is this—" Joss wasn't even sure what to call it. "Are you worrying about me?"

"I'm not *worrying*," Gareth said a bit defensively. "I'm just concerned."

"Hearts alive, London," Joss said, pulled his face round, and kissed him.

They emerged from that after several minutes, with Joss somehow on his back on the log and Gareth's flyaway hair in a tangle and his eyes wide. He looked lovely, if dishevelled. "That was delightful, but you didn't answer the question."

"What—oh, that." Joss clonked his head back on the bark. "Ugh. You're sort of right. I don't want the whole Marsh knowing my business, nor my whole family either."

"No." Gareth shifted off him to sit upright again. He looked nervy discussing this subject, as well he might, a respectable man. Joss knew exactly how he felt about the idea of getting caught: he'd seen, and put, that expression on his face a couple of weeks back. "You have a lot to lose."

"But I've a fair bit to lose if they hang me for smuggling too. You can't just not do things acause of the consequences."

"Consequences are literally the reason not to do things. That's what they're *for*."

Joss grabbed his hand. "Gareth. I want to see you. I've been thinking about you since February, with you living a mile up the road, and it's been driving me to Bedlam. I want more too. I want to see you bare again. I want to go newt hunting, in all the ways you can think of. And I like that you're concerned for me but, not to get all puffed up about it—"

"If you say, 'I'm Joss Doomsday', I will push you off this log."

"I am, though," Joss said, grinning. "And if I can get two hundred kegs of brandy over the Royal Military Canal, I can get my arse into your bed. Give me a chance."

Gareth's cheeks pinked. It suited him. "I have been told you always get your way."

"I do, so you might as well stop arguing." Joss squeezed his hand. "If I work out something safe, will you come?"

"Yes," Gareth said simply, and Joss wanted to take the word and preserve it, put it between the Bible pages like Emily did flowers and press it for his box of treasures at home.

He laced his fingers through Gareth's instead, for the pleasure of it. "Dare say I can organise that, en. I ought to be getting back."

Gareth rose but didn't let go of his hand, and they stayed palm to palm as they strolled at a maundering pace through the Warren. It felt good.

"Joss," Gareth said as they approached the road and reluctantly let go of one another. "This business with my father. I interrupted you when you were saying what you thought, but I'd like to hear if you'll tell me."

"We were at the bit where your father was making money fast, right?"

"And you had a professional opinion on that."

"Thing is, plenty of folk here might hand me ten shillings to buy cargo and hope to get a bit more back. But that's ordinary people. Squire drinks plenty of French brandy but he doesn't fund me to run it."

"No. There's a difference between winking at a crime and actively conspiring to commit it."

"So if your old man wanted to put money in, he probably wouldn't do it at home, in Dymchurch. But you said he had dealings in Rye, and Nate Sweetwater's based in Camber, which is just by. There's a lot of private rooms and closed mouths in Rye."

Gareth made a face. "Do you think that's it? My father was speculating in free trade with Sweetwater, and, what, they didn't want me to kick up a fuss about it?"

"Well, when money turns up on the Marsh, there's usually just the one reason. I'm not sure how anyone thinks making a plague of themselves would help keep anything quiet, but there's some chuckleheaded folk out there. Look, Nate agreed you'd be left alone. Tell me if you're not, and if you do find out anything for sure, don't tell the Preventive."

Gareth blew out a long breath. Joss said, "That a problem?"

"No. It's very much what I'd prefer. If my father was involved in, uh, free trading, I'd vastly rather keep it secret. Only, I can't help feeling rather ashamed of that."

They'd come all the way back and the Revelation was at hand. The lane looked empty of eyes, but Joss knew better than to trust that. Which was a shame, because he'd have liked to touch Gareth now. Grip his hand, kiss him, tell him not to fret. He gave him a reassuring, entirely blameless pat on the arm instead. "Look, we don't know for sure if this is right. But all ways, whatever he did wasn't your fault, and you've Miss Cecy to think of. Let the dead bury their dead, eh?"

"I dare say you're right."

"I am right. Listen, I've got a bit of work on over the next few days. Going to be busy. Uh, don't mention that to Miss Cecy's intended," he added hastily.

"I think I have learned my lesson there," Gareth said, voice a touch dry.

"So don't expect to hear from me a little while, all right? But soon as I'm done, I'll send to you with a place to meet. If you still want to."

Gareth met his eyes on that, a flicker of a look that sent heat spiking through his skin. "I want to. I've been promised newt-hunting, after all."

Eleven

IT WAS A GOOD THING JOSS HAD TOLD HIM NOT TO EXPECT anything for a few days. Otherwise Gareth might well have driven himself to distraction, with his heart jumping at every tread on the path or knock at the door. As it was, he couldn't quash the swarm of butterflies in his stomach, no matter how he tried.

Joss's smile. The way they'd kissed. Even that stupid argument, about which Gareth had given himself some serious talkings-to, because of how Joss had listened afterwards. The touch of his hands, the wonder in his eyes, the astonishing sense of familiarity, as though he and Gareth had somehow slipped past one another all their lives and their meeting was long overdue.

It had felt like that with Kent too, and he'd told himself it wasn't real. Now he'd started wondering if it had been, say, true in outline. As if 'London and Kent' had been a pencil drawing, and now it was being filled in with colours.

He didn't want to make this an ideal. Joss was a free trader, a radical, a ruthless and even brutal man at times. Those were the less attractive tones and shading of the picture. But then Gareth was nervy, snappy, temperamental, too used to being bullied, never able to react as he might wish. One couldn't ask for perfect, he told himself, and decided not to consider if there might be a middle way between 'perfect' and 'professional criminal'.

In fact, Joss was taking up a great deal of Gareth's heart and mind, and if he didn't send, if he decided this had been a mistake after all—

No. Gareth would not anticipate that, and he refused to sour the waiting with worrying. He couldn't entirely stop himself, but at least his efforts to distract his thoughts meant he got plenty of reading done.

He was in his study on the afternoon of the second day when there was a knock on the door.

"Gareth?" It was Catherine. "There's someone to see you."

She sounded rather odd. Joss? He leapt to his feet. "Please, show him in."

"In here?"

"That'll be good, mistress," said an unfamiliar voice, and a large man appeared in the doorway. Catherine gave him an affronted glance and whisked out of the way.

The visitor was not someone he recognised from the Revelation. He was a big, bulky man in his early thirties, perhaps, though his skin had a weatherbeaten look to it, and he moved confidently. "Sir Gareth Inglis," he said with a nod.

"Good afternoon. Are you...?" A messenger from Joss, perhaps? Gareth hesitated, wondering how to phrase it.

"Bill Sweetwater."

Gareth actually found himself thinking for a second *that's a coincidence*, and then realised. "Sweetwater," he repeated, his pulse thudding unpleasantly. He wondered if he could shout for Catherine, if there was anyone in the lane she could run and fetch.

"That's right." The free trader looked around the study with interest. "Lot of books you have here."

"My father's collection. What—"

"This the Marsh?" Sweetwater ambled over to the map on the wall. Sir Hugo had obtained the most detailed map available and covered it in scrawls, noting where particular birds, beetles, or plants might be found. "What's all this, en?"

"Excuse me," Gareth said, more sharply than he'd meant because he was trying not to let his voice shake. "Would you please explain the nature of your call? I was under the impression that the, uh, difficulty had been cleared up."

"My call," Sweetwater repeated. "Aye, well, I *called* on you for a talk, Sir Gareth." He peered again at the map, then turned. "I don't think you've been honest with me."

"I've never met you before."

Sweetwater waved that aside. "You said you knew nothing of Sir Hugo's dealings, had nothing to do with 'em, wanted nothing to do with 'em. We got that message, with Joss Doomsday as your messenger boy. How'd you manage that, eh? Outmarsh, newcomer, and you've got that Joss at your beck and call?"

"I wouldn't say—"

"Overplayed your hand there," Sweetwater went on over his protest. "Think we wouldn't notice? No, I reckon you know just exactly what old Sir Hugo was up to." He looked around, nodding, as Gareth spluttered a denial. "Was he working with you or did he write it down?"

"I hadn't heard from him in years and there is nothing whatsoever—"

"Where's Adam Drake?"

Gareth stopped mid-denial at that abrupt question. "Who?"

"Adam Drake. Where is he?"

"I've never heard of him."

Sweetwater gave him a level look. "You've never heard and you don't know and you've never met. Funny, that. You seem to be making yourself proper comfortable on the Marsh without knowing anything about anyone."

"If you tell me who this person is, I might be able to help," Gareth snapped. "As it is, I am entirely at a loss. I've only been here since February. I don't know anything about my father's affairs or his friends. What do you want from me?"

Sweetwater cocked his head. "Let's not be coy."

"I'm not," Gareth said tightly. "I have no idea what you're talking about. If you explain yourself rather than speaking in riddles, I might be able to help."

"Glad to know you've a mind to be helpful. I don't like unhelpful people."

"You aren't helping *me* very much, Mr. Sweetwater," Gareth said, somehow not letting his voice rise in pitch. "Again, what is it you want?"

"You know what I'm after," Sweetwater said flatly. "And if you don't know, well, I wouldn't want to say. But I think you do."

"You are entirely wrong. Was it you who sent men to attack me and my sister?"

"Attack? Friendly warning, that was all."

Gareth couldn't help lifting a hand to his neck. "Friendly warning?" he repeated. "*Friendly?* Well, I believe Joss Doomsday gave you a *friendly warning* not to trouble Dymchurch people, so—"

Sweetwater's eyes met his, and Gareth recoiled at the look in them, which made him suddenly and horribly conscious of his isolated position. "You're not Dymchurch," the smuggler growled. "You're outmarsh. Joss Doomsday should keep his neb out of our business with outmarsh."

"I don't *have* any business with you." His voice shook, but not too badly. He gripped the edge of the desk for stability. "I don't propose to engage in any. If you want something from me, say so. But I will not have my sister or my housekeeper followed or harassed or assaulted or threatened, do you understand? Leave my household alone!"

"Oh, yes?" Sweetwater said. "And what are you going to do about it if I don't?"

Gareth didn't have an answer, or at least, he only had *I'll tell Joss!*, which didn't feel like it would have much effect in this moment. He couldn't speak, and Bill Sweetwater's grin grew. "Didn't think so." He took a pace forward, rolling his shoulders. He had very large, powerful arms. "So I tell you what—"

There was a knock at the door. Gareth let out a breath that he'd been all too aware he was holding, and called, "What is it?"

It opened. There was a small, wry person there, with a much larger form looming behind.

"Devil do you want?" Sweetwater demanded.

"Watcher, Bill," said the small one—Finty, Gareth recalled. "Seems to be a misunderstanding here. Joss said you was to let these people alone."

"I don't take orders from Joss Doomsday."

"You do from Nate," Finty said. "Or are you saying you do what you please in Dymchurch, regardless of Joss and Nate both? Is that what you mean?"

"Nate said there wasn't to be trouble, that's all," Bill Sweetwater said. "Do you see any trouble? Eh?"

"Joss said," Graveyard growled, in a baritone so deep that Gareth only just made out the words.

"I'm on a friendly visit," Sweetwater returned, lip lifting like a dog's. "Just a little chat with my mate the baronet to sort things out. None of your concern or Joss Doomsday's either."

"Hope you enjoyed it." Finty stepped back from the door. "Reckon you'll be off now, Bill. Reckon you won't be back either, less you want to have it out with Joss."

"Runt," Sweetwater said through his teeth, or possibly something that rhymed with that. Finty appeared unmoved. Gareth would probably be unmoved if he had someone Graveyard's size at his back. "You think on this, Sir Gareth. Give me what I want, and we won't have a problem."

"Off you go, Bill," Finty said. "Joss'll be along for a word, I've no doubt."

The free traders shepherded Sweetwater out. Gareth followed at a safe distance to see him leave the house, then staggered into the sitting room and more or less fell into a chair.

Catherine and Cecy were there, wide-eyed. "Are you all right?" Catherine hissed. "What did he want?"

"He wouldn't say. Why won't they say? How can these people just walk in?"

"I'm so sorry. I didn't know what to do."

"I didn't expect you to stop him," Gareth said hastily. "But to turn up here—What is going *on*?"

Footsteps in the hall, and a knock at the door. Gareth hauled himself to his feet as Finty's head poked round. "Beg pardon, Sir Gareth, mistresses, only I wanted to check there was no harm done."

"None," Gareth said. "Thank you for your intervention. I appreciate it very much. Can we offer you, uh—" A tip? A drink? He had no idea what would be appropriate.

Finty waved that away. "Beg pardon we didn't see him coming, sir. I could send someone around for the night if that'll help put your minds at rest?"

"Yes please," Gareth said wholeheartedly.

"And we'll let Joss know. I dare say he'll have something to say to Bill Sweetwater. Beg pardon."

The henchperson departed. Gareth flopped back into his chair as Cecy and Catherine's voices both rose.

Romney Marsh offered peace and quiet, a house that was feeling like a home, a fascinating natural world all its own, and Joss. All the same, Gareth was very tempted to wish he was almost anywhere else.

Twelve

JOSS SAT ON THE DYMCHURCH WALL AS DAWN BROKE, looking out over the endless sand and endless sea.

He wasn't ready to sleep: three nights' hard work had left him
shivery and wakeful. It had been a big run, and big runs were
difficult now. Once he could have made forty ponies laden with
brandy-casks disappear into the Marsh with no trouble at all. Now
there were Martello towers all along the coast, manned with soldiers ready to be called in if the Excisemen demanded it, and the
Royal Military Canal cut off the Marsh from the outside world for
a twenty-eight-mile length.

They could still slip past the Preventives, of course, and they
had. Tom had taken the lugger in close to Little Stone, where the
goods were loaded into small boats and brought to shore. Joss had
had the land crew waiting, ready to load the kegs and barrels and
bundles onto the horses and ponies they borrowed from around
the Marsh. Sophy had arranged some incautious lights and loud
conversations that brought the Revenue men to Marshland Gut in
force, and led them a pretty chase through the Marsh mist.

The hard slog began after that. It had been a night's work to bring the goods to the hide at Cuckold's Corner and stow them safely, another to load up again and cross the Canal outside Warehorne. They'd run into a Revenue patrol there; fortunately, the men had been amenable to ten guineas each to look away, plus a keg of brandy for the inconvenience. That suited most Preventives better than a fight, and it suited Joss too: he had no desire to break heads. He considered himself an honest trader, apart from the criminal parts.

By far the greatest risk of free-trading came on the water, from the Revenue frigates that patrolled the coast. But the land work was hard physical labour, with a lot of men needed and a long way to travel, and it took a deal of planning and organisation to make each run as uneventful as possible.

Not everyone wanted uneventful. Elijah called him timid, saying they should go out in numbers armed with billy clubs and boat-hooks and frighten off the Preventives by sheer force of arms. Joss called that stupid. He didn't want a war, far preferring to operate by stealth, goodwill, and corruption. If the Revenue called on the soldiery, if Joss's people failed to send the riding officers the wrong way, or an informer chose to claim the lavish rewards on offer, the Doomsdays could find themselves facing a lot of men with guns.

Elijah shrugged at that because he was full of piss and wind, and so did Cousin Tom because he was twenty-two, which was to say the same thing. If they were taken and convicted of smuggling they'd hang or be transported, they pointed out, so what was the point in avoiding a fight? A man might as well be shot as swing.

Joss supposed they had a point, but he wasn't inclined to do either. The Doomsdays had been running rings around the Revenue for years; they knew every inch of the ground, where most of the riding officers and Preventives were outmarsh. Most of all, the Revenue worked for the government, while the free traders were working for themselves, their families, their people. Joss knew which of those he'd risk his skin for.

So they took the goods by cunning routes, nobody got hurt, plenty of people got paid, and the only ill feeling they caused was to the dedicated Preventives, who didn't count. That was how it would carry on under Joss's leadership, and if anyone didn't like it, they could say so.

Elijah was saying so. Elijah had sabotaged Sophy's run and caused that snarl-up with Gareth. Elijah had gone whining to Ma when Joss had dressed him down, and since her sole soft spot was for the ten-years-younger little brother she'd all but brought up, she'd leaned on Joss as only she could. He'd given in, like he always did to her, and let Elijah along on this latest run, and the dratted man had been a menace once again—talking too loud, muttering about every setback, heavy-handed with the casual men whose labour and silence they relied on. Worse yet, he was egging on Tom, a fine boatman but a thick-skulled roistering boy who didn't like taking orders from a cousin just a few years older than himself. Joss had a bad feeling the pair of them were gearing up for a fight.

Not to mention the Goldie problem. Elijah had never been a loving father, but he'd mostly treated the boy with indifference. That had been changing recently, more so since Granda said Goldie should go to a fancy school for a proper education. He thought the boy was a rare bird, with too much brain to waste on free trading. Joss didn't see how that followed, but he trusted his grandfather and had agreed they'd find the money. He hadn't asked Elijah's opinion, not thinking he'd care.

That had been a mistake. Elijah didn't give a damn for his son being sent away, but his fortieth birthday seemed to have started some maggot in his brain about younger men. He'd been increasingly hostile to Joss for a while, and now he seemed to be looking at Goldie with resentful eyes as well.

Elijah had the right as a father to decide Goldie's future. Joss couldn't argue that, but anyone could see his decision was pure spite. His blows were getting heavier, his words crueller. Goldie mostly dodged his father's blows but he came back for more like a kicked dog, as if, for all his brains, he couldn't grasp that Elijah's indifference was turning sour and hateful. It made Joss think uncomfortably of Gareth, talking about his own uncaring father but still trailing after a dead man to look at beetles.

Goldie was thirteen. He was growing, and a mistreated boy didn't take long to turn into an angry, bitter man. Joss needed to deal with that, which meant dealing with Elijah, which meant facing Ma down too. He didn't want to do any of it.

What he actually wanted right now was for Gareth to come along the Wall on one of his early morning walks. He'd arrive, blinking at the sun, and see Joss, and maybe blush a little in the way he did, hopeful and excited. They'd clamber down the seaward side and sit together, and Joss would probably fall asleep on his shoulder right there but that would be all right. They'd share a breakfast somewhere, eating and talking, then use this lovely morning to go find those newts Gareth wanted to see, stopping now and then for kisses, chatting idly about bugs and nonsense and things just for themselves, and return to Tench House in the evening for a leisurely night together.

That was something Joss wanted, had been wanting since February, and he was middling sure Gareth wanted it too. Gareth would strip for him like he had before, and Joss would pleasure him in all the ways he liked, with words and hands and mouth, till Gareth was crying out and begging him never to leave—no, not that. Till

Joss had put that transformed look on his face again, the one he'd got sometimes in the Three Ducks, where he lost the brittle self-consciousness and wasn't fretting or holding back or thinking of anything in the world but Joss. His London, all his, just for a little while.

Joss had never really had much for himself. He was a younger brother to Bart, an older one to Sophy, a big cousin to Tom and Emily and Isaac, a support for Ma. If Pa or even Bart, who'd been sixteen, had survived Uncle Sam's drowning, one of them would have become the Upright Man in his place, the leader of family and gang alike, and Joss would have had time for a life of his own. That couldn't be helped. He'd been born to his work and did it as best he could; he'd never asked for anything all his own except a space to sleep. He worked for his family. It sometimes felt like he never stopped working for them. And now he wanted something just for himself and felt a deep, smouldering anger that he couldn't have it.

He *couldn't* just stroll to Tench House and see if Gareth wanted breakfast. Couldn't share his baronet bedroom now or ever: what a joke. Could probably take him to hunt newts, because if they went off on enough nature-watching walks it would become a thing that nobody thought about; the Marsh got used to odd habits. But that meant being seen, which meant no kissing, no holding hands, and that pissed Joss off so intensely he could feel his eyes prickling, because he wanted those things. And more, of course. He wanted Gareth's mouth on his cock, wanted him on all fours and twisting under Joss's strokes, wanted to find out if he liked it the other way round. But right now he wanted more than anything to interlace his fingers with Gareth's, palm to palm, and walk through the Marsh being told about bugs.

Christ, he was tired.

He needed to sleep. And to find out from Sophy what had

happened in his absence and if she'd organised what he'd asked, to check if any Sweetwater men had showed their faces. To talk to Ma about Elijah, and Granda about Goldie, and there was Isaac chafing to lead the boats...

He should get up and go to bed if he was to stand a chance of dealing with the day, but instead he sat on the Wall, staring at the sea with exhausted eyes, until he heard the crunch of approaching feet. His heart leapt for just a moment, until he realised that they were coming from Globsden Gut way.

"Joss?"

"Sophy."

"What are you doing up here?"

"Falling asleep." He hauled himself onto his feet with some difficulty; he had stiff legs after the last nights' work. "You?"

"Came to find you. All well?"

"Not so much." Joss rubbed his face and took in his sister. She was wearing skirts and a sour expression. "Elijah, the sorry fellow he is. Complained about the way we took, complained about the work, complained about everything."

"He's complaining right now, with Tom. Why I came to get you."

"Don't tell me," Joss said as they set off back home. "He'd have managed it all a sight better. He'd have come mob-handed with batsmen and fought his way across the Canal, and we'd all be sleeping on silk sheets forevermore?"

"About right."

Never mind that the Canal had been built to obstruct Napoleon's entire invasion force. "Run was smooth as glass. No problems to speak of except Elijah."

"That's what Matt Molash is telling 'em, but Elijah's running off at the mouth and Tom's backing him. You're going to have to give him a kicking, Joss."

And who was going to hold Ma back while he did? He sighed. "I know. Did you see about that job for me?"

"The looker's hut? It's yours. Swept out, shutters darked, and the door checked."

He'd asked Sophy to sort that out as a place he could meet Gareth. She hadn't passed comment at the time, but she wore a little frown now. "What is it?"

"Nothing. Or..." She paused, then said in a rush, "I know you were taken with him, Sir Gareth, in London. Only, that didn't finish well, did it? You said he was an arsehole. You were middling cut up about it."

"We talked about that, him and me. He had his reasons."

"And you did him a pretty bad turn in front of the magistrates."

"That was your fault."

She acknowledged that with a shrug. "Just seems to me you're asking for trouble with this one."

"Why so?"

"It's been merciful ill-starred so far," she pointed out, not unfairly. "And he's on the Marsh, so you'll need to look sharp in case of keg-meg, and he's outmarsh, and—Joss, he's a *baronet*. You can't tup a baronet."

"Someone's got to."

"Other baronets! Or baronesses," she added fairly. "Baronetesses? Not you, anyway. He's not like us."

"Why should he be? Jean-Jacques was French."

"In France! They don't mind it over there."

Joss wasn't sure whether 'it' meant Frenchness or sodomy, and was too tired to ask. "What difference does it make? Not like everything would be easy if he was a good Marsh-born free trader, is it?"

"I know. But..." She kicked a stone. "Is this serious, Joss?"

Joss stared ahead at the looming Revelation. He wasn't sure he wanted to have this conversation here, or now, or at all, or with anyone except Gareth. "Don't know. I mean, you're right. He's a baronet and outmarsh, and educated—"

"I didn't say educated."

"I did."

She bristled. "Book learning's not all that counts."

"How would you know? We've neither of us got any. And I wouldn't care for that except—"

"You wouldn't think twice about that if it wasn't for Mr. Bettermy Baronet," Sophy said. "That's what I mean."

"He's not like that," Joss said. "Not much, anyway. But you do notice, can't help it. I don't know, Soph. Maybe I'm making a fool of myself over a pretty face." He ignored the mumble of *not even that pretty.* "And I don't suppose it *can* be serious, considering." He pushed his hands into his hair, remembered how it felt when Gareth did the same thing. "Only, it feels like it is. And I'm not sure I can help it."

Sophy peered into his face. "You really like him, Joss?"

"I really do."

She took a few more steps, then reached for his hand and squeezed it. "I'm sorry I made you problems with him."

"Not your fault. It was bad luck and Elijah."

"Same thing said twice. Right, well. If that's the way, you'd best be sure and look after yourself, Joss Doomsday, hadn't you? Don't take any risks. And tell me when you need cover and I'll have it done, and there's to be no messing about. Got it?"

His little sister. He grinned at her. "Yes, Soph."

Thirteen

Joss had her carry a message to Gareth, in the end. He'd have liked to drop round himself but he had other things to do, like squaring away the accounts of the run, planning the next, having a blazing but inconclusive row with his mother on the subject of Elijah, and eating. He didn't have a chance to speak to Elijah, who'd gone off drinking with his equally worthless cronies, or to Goldie, who had disappeared, but at least that allowed him to snatch a belated few hours' sleep.

He'd sent instructions to meet at the dyke where they'd sat before, after dark, and rather regretted it when night fell because it was a misty one. The air was wet and wispy, the thorn trees witchy shapes in the darkness, the grass sodden underfoot. People got badly lost on misty nights. Joss could find his way across the Marsh with his eyes shut, but he arrived at the dyke fully prepared to head back toward Tench House and work out where Gareth had got lost.

But he was there, a tall, dark shape huddled in a long coat. "A'night," Joss murmured.

Gareth yelped. "God, you startled me. How do you move so quietly? Good evening," he added.

"Practice. Wondered if you'd like to go somewhere a bit warmer. And drier."

"Yes," Gareth said. "Well, anyone would, because this is ghastly, but I'd very much like to be warm and dry—and private?—with you. If it's across the Marsh, please be aware that I'm going to fall in a dyke."

Joss reached for his hand, wrapping his fingers around Gareth's chilly ones. "No, you're not."

It wasn't far, though it was over the fields, which meant tussocks of rank grass, and plenty of sheep treddles squashing underfoot. Gareth stumbled a few times and cursed under his breath, but he held Joss's hand and didn't fall, and they reached the hut without trouble.

"Hold on." Joss took a quick turn around the building to check the shutters and be sure nobody was lurking, then let them in. There was an oil lamp burning, turned very low, and the embers of a fire in the grate.

Gareth looked round, open-mouthed, as Joss turned up the lamp and bolted the door. "Where are we?"

"Looker's hut."

The hut was one of many dotted over the Marsh to provide shelter for the men who watched the sheep. Red brick, a little fireplace where you might cook a simple meal or boil water for tea, a bench with a straw mattress. The mattress looked new, or newish, and the blankets worn but clean. There was also a cask which Joss recognised as one of the Revelation's own and a couple of tankards. Bless Sophy. He threw some coals on the embers of fire and got it going again. "There."

"Is this your hut?"

"It is now. We can use it when we like."

"What if someone comes?"

"Nobody's coming to an unknown looker's hut at this hour. And the shutters are well darked." Light carried a very long way on the flat of the Marsh. "It's as safe as I can make."

Gareth looked somewhat stunned. "You organised this, for us?"

"I wanted to see you."

Gareth strode over, took Joss's face in his hands, and kissed him. His mouth was urgent, demanding, forceful, and at enough of an angle to remind Joss that he was several inches shorter than his lanky lover. He tipped his head back a little, enjoying the sensation of being kissed for a few moments, then went up on his toes, getting his hands into Gareth's flyaway hair, and kissed him right back.

"Mmm," Gareth said when they broke for breath. "You're a genius."

"I just give the orders. Thank Sophy."

"I was going to ask."

"She knows what I like," Joss said. "Well, you saw her in the Ducks."

"She knows and she's on your side?" Gareth's eyes were— hungry, or longing, or something. "You're a lucky man."

"I am that. Come here." Joss seated himself on the straw mattress. Gareth joined him, shuffling close. "A'right?"

"All the better for seeing you. Whereas you look exhausted. Did your work go well?"

"Do you want to know? Only, you might need to swear you never heard anything about it."

"That's the sort of quibble that makes people hate lawyers," Gareth said. "And I've already lied on oath once, so it hardly makes a difference. You're a free trader, and if I don't like that, I oughtn't be here."

"Does that mean you like it?"

"No, it means I oughtn't be here. Unfortunately, I have very poor judgement, and you are unreasonably lovely. Could you take your hair down at all?"

Joss pulled his hair loose, shaking it out as far as possible. It was full of tangles but Gareth got his hands in there anyway, and they were kissing again, rocking together, shifting without breaking apart until Gareth was on his back with Joss sprawled over him. He had one knee on the mattress, the other thigh wedged very comfortably between Gareth's legs, and nothing had felt so good in days. "Ah, God, I wanted this."

"Good." Gareth angled his head up and kissed Joss's ear, getting his teeth gently to the earlobe, nibbling his way down Joss's neck. "I was thinking about you. About the Three Ducks." The words vibrated on Joss's throat. "About me standing there naked while you just looked at me." He tugged at Joss's hair, pulling his head sideways and down, and then his tongue was sliding into Joss's ear, which was wet and ridiculous and painfully arousing. "The way you looked. It made me feel like...I don't know. A courtesan, or a work of art."

"I don't know what the first one is, but the second's about right. Jesus." Joss would have liked to do that now, but it would mean letting go and he didn't want to. He leaned into Gareth instead, wanting to feel every bit of him—his lips, teeth, tongue; his hands in Joss's hair and roaming down his body, glorious and overwhelming. "You're proper beautiful. Eyes like Marsh mist. Oh hell. *Gareth.*" He dived forward and then there was silence in the hut except for the creaking of straw, the rustle and muffled cursing of men trying to get their breeches down without separating too much, the whisper of skin against skin as Joss slid his rigid prick between Gareth's tight thighs, watching his face the while. Warmth, and the gentle friction of his cock against the soft flesh enveloping him, and Gareth's hands in his hair, pale eyes on his face, lips wet and parted. "Ah, Gareth. You feel so good."

"I want you like this," Gareth whispered. "And I want you to fuck me, too, and I want to be naked for you—"

"I want all of that." Joss rocked his hips forward, pleasure spiking through his nerves, riding Gareth and rubbing against his prick at once. "I want all of you."

"But first I want you to come like this, now, because you're so perfect when you come and I need to see it again. God, Joss, *please*."

His hands were tight on Joss's arse. He looked wild and wondering and magical, and Joss threw his head back, biting his lip hard to avoid shouting, thrusting hard as he spent himself between Gareth's legs. Gareth gripped his head and pulled him close as he sagged forward, and Joss let himself collapse. His baronet could take the weight, just for a moment.

"You looked like you needed that," Gareth said softly.

"You've no idea." Joss took a moment to get his breath back. "Been thinking about you too."

"What were you thinking?"

"Lots of things. Getting you naked, that's one."

"We could start—" Gareth squirmed out from under him. Joss propped himself on an elbow and watched as he worked his way out of his clothes till he stood bare, body tinted by the flickering lamplight and the shadows it cast. "There."

"What was it you said you looked like?" Joss asked, voice a bit thick.

"A courtesan, or a work of art."

"What's the first one?"

"It means a kept lady. A very expensive kept lady."

"Like a king's mistress? I reckon I can see that. So can I afford you?" Joss grinned at Gareth's expression. He swung himself off the bench, hitching his breeches up, and prowled round Gareth, so pale and bare and slender. "What do I do with a courtesan, then?"

"Well, whatever you like: that's the point. Although I believe the gentlemanly obligation is to provide a town house and a carriage and pair." He fluttered his lashes.

"I *can't* afford you."

"Or silks and lace? I'm sure that would do."

"Oh, you can have all the silk and lace you want." Joss ran a finger down Gareth's spine, making him shudder. "Cover you in them. You'd look good in silk. Not as good as you look out of it, mind. If you were my courtesan, in my town house…"

"Mmm?"

"I'd keep you naked all the time," Joss said softly. "Just so I could come back and see you like this."

"Oh God."

Gareth had a very substantial stand. Joss brushed his fingertips up and down the smooth length. "Would you do that? Be bare for me, London?"

"Always."

"Maybe not winter," Joss allowed. "But there's furs for that. Furs in winter, with nothing under. Satin in spring, bare in summer. I'd have that." He moved behind Gareth, kissed his shoulder, stroked his stand again with thumb and forefinger. Gareth was trembling, and he was leaking, too, the tip of his prick wet. Joss let his thumb rub over it in light circles, heard him whimper. "And you reckon I look at you like that? Like a lady of easy virtue?"

"Sometimes," Gareth whispered.

"How's your virtue?"

"Couldn't be easier."

"Thank God for that." He pulled Gareth round, getting a

startled grunt. He dropped to his knees, ran his fingertips up Gareth's thighs, still sticky with his own spend, took a moment to appreciate the glistening length of Gareth's cock, standing so hard for him, then leaned in to take it down.

Gareth moaned, winding his hands in Joss's hair, and Joss got his own hands to work along with his mouth, stroking and fondling Gareth's balls, caressing with his lips and tongue. He'd meant to draw it out with long slow licks, but Gareth was panting and this wasn't going to take long. Might as well make a virtue of necessity. He took Gareth deep in his throat, sucking hard and working his fingers, and Gareth keened aloud. "Joss, my God, Joss—*Kent*—Christ!"

He came hard, pulsing in Joss's mouth. Joss rode the waves of pleasure till they subsided, feeling thoroughly smug. He swallowed, licked Gareth's piece clean as he shuddered, and sat back on his heels.

Gareth put a hand on his head for balance. "Just a moment. I think I may have gone blind."

"They do say that happens." He didn't mind swallowing, but you needed to sluice your mouth after. "Ale?"

"Please."

Gareth put a blanket on the mattress and collapsed on it as Joss got the drinks. Joss tossed another one on top of him, slightly regretting the cover but not wanting him to be cold.

"God," Gareth said after a moment. "I wish we could stay here. Could I run away to sea and be a free trader?"

"Well, you could, but I'm a landman. We can always use help to haul the kegs, mind."

"That sounds like hard work. I think I'm more the silks and lace type of smuggler." Gareth propped his head on Joss's thigh. "Can you stay a while?"

"As long as you've got."

"I said I was going to listen for owls and I'd be back late. I've a key for the back door."

"Good. I'm not done with you."

"I should hope not, but I need a moment." Gareth smiled. He had such a lovely smile. "Do you want to tell me about your trip? Or why you look so tired?"

"Well, night-work," Joss said. "And family business. This and that, not worth your time."

"You've listened to my problems often enough."

"You've got bigger problems, sounds like. What's this about Bill Sweetwater?"

"Not yet," Gareth said. "I want to hear about yours first."

"It's nothing. I just had a row with my ma."

"I think most people on the Marsh would call that quite a big problem. What was it about?"

He clearly wasn't going to give this up and, much as Joss didn't need to share his troubles, a sympathetic ear seemed very appealing somehow. "Ah, it's stupid. My uncle Elijah's a nuisance, that's all. Shuckish fellow, which is to say unreliable. A middling arsehole is what he is, but he's Ma's little brother, so we don't agree on what to do about him."

"What's the issue?"

"Well, Ma wants to keep him happy. Whereas I want to send his son off to school against his wishes, give him a good thrashing, kick him out of the Revelation to fend for himself, and tell him when he comes crawling back that the only thing he says to me from now on is 'Yes, Joss'."

"Quite a material disagreement, then." Gareth reached up for Joss's hand, giving it a squeeze that felt comforting. "Who won?"

"Ma," Joss said. "Usually does. Only she's wrong, and we'll all lose if I don't sort this out, acause he's stirring trouble and talking spite. I'm going to have to face her down, and I can't say I'm looking forward to it. Can't be helped; I've let this business go on too long as it is. But she won't be pleased, and it could get nasty."

"Will she side with him against you?"

"If I force her to a choice? Don't know. She feels guilty." He stroked Gareth's hair back from his forehead. "When Pa and Uncle Sam died, Elijah should have become the Upright Man, like we call it, in charge of the free trading and the family. He was what, twenty-six, age I am now, and Sam's younger brother. We needed him to take charge, but he made a one-eyed job of it."

"A...?"

"Careless. Half-hearted. He liked giving orders, and never mind what use they were. He liked a drink even more. Threw his weight around. Bullied the men. Did worse, too." Goldie's mother hadn't wanted Elijah's attentions. She'd abandoned her squalling baby on the Revelation's steps with a note that had, for once, made Ma truly angry at her little brother, then vanished from the Marsh. It was a stain on the family, a debt they couldn't pay. "We had people caught, we lost money and cargo and respect. Things were falling apart. So Ma took over, with me to help her. Not in name at first, course. Elijah sat around being the Great I Am while Ma and I did it all. Only, soon enough she became Ma Doomsday. People did as she said and stopped looking to Elijah for his nod. And I got older, too, and he didn't like that."

"You could hardly help it."

"It's one thing to have a little nephew running around doing errands for your sister, another once he noticed people were taking my orders. Took him a while to realise that, mind. Seems he had this idea I was working for him all along, what with that's the natural way of things, given my colour."

Gareth twisted round to look into his face. "He said that to you?"

"Couple of years ago. We had a row and he came out with that in front of everyone. And I'd have had something to say back but I never had the chance, acause Granda served it to him hot. Never seen him lose his temper before or since, but he hauled himself out of his chair and called Elijah over like a schoolboy. Ripped into him for his idle selfish ways, told him everything wrong with him from head to foot, till Elijah raised his fist to him. A man twice his age, with a gammy leg."

"That's absolutely disgraceful. Shameful."

"Stupid," Joss said, grinning. "See, my granda was a boxer in his day and if you ask me, he was waiting his moment. He cracked Elijah one in the right eye, one in the left, then laid a punch on his jaw like Cribb himself. Elijah went straight down and didn't get up, and that was that. He slunk off after. Nobody saw him for a couple of weeks, then he came back like nothing had happened. But it changed things. I wouldn't take any more nonsense from him—I'd been polite before, but the blazes with that—and Granda had words whenever he opened his mouth, and a lot of people wanted to remind him a man of seventy put him on the floor."

"That must have been humiliating for him," Gareth said.

"That's Ma's view. That me and Granda shamed him, and that's why he's acting about."

"And what about what he said to you?"

Joss sighed. "She reckons he was well punished for it. Only, for me, it's not that he said it once, it's that he thinks it, and always did, and always will. She doesn't see that. Or she's used to people mouthing respect and not feeling it. I don't know. So anyway Elijah's sister runs the family and his nephew runs the business, his son's got twelve times his brains, he's turned forty. He's missed his chances and knows it, so he's in a pucker all the time. Which I wouldn't care, but Ma feels guilty for it."

"Ugh," Gareth said. "Have you given him an ultimatum?"

"Didn't have one lying around."

Gareth batted a hand at him. "An 'or else'. Last chance. He stops making trouble, or you'll give him that thrashing and kick him out, whatever your mother might say."

"I haven't, acause he knows Ma won't stand for it."

"Yes, but does he really know that? Is it a risk he'd prepared to take, if you put it to him directly? If he's aware he isn't invaluable, or even much use, he might be less confident in keeping his place than he pretends."

That was an interesting thought. "Maybe."

"It might be worth a try. People do say that bullies give in when you stand up to them. I wouldn't know, myself."

He said that last with a bit of a twist in his voice. Joss stroked his hair, silky and soothing to his fingers. "You could be right, at that. I'll chew it over. Anyway, enough of Elijah, I didn't mean to jabber on so long. What about you? You sounded a bit fraped. Is that Bill Sweetwater?"

"He paid me a visit, as I'm sure you know," Gareth said. "He wants something—I don't know what because he wouldn't tell me. He said if I didn't already know, he wouldn't want to say."

"Queers me what that might mean. Any idea?"

"No, but I doubt it's anything good. He asked me where Adam Drake was."

"Who?"

"Apparently a man who did some odd jobs for us. Catherine says he's an allworks, is that right? A man my father employed to work in the garden and help repair the stable. She thinks he's from Guildford Level, but she doesn't know anything more. I hoped you might."

"Dare say I can find out. Why did he ask?"

"Again, he wouldn't say. It would have been a very frustrating conversation if I hadn't been continually wondering if he was about to hit me. He didn't touch me," he added, responding to something on Joss's face. "But it was unpleasant and very frightening. He walked into my *house*. And nothing bad happened because your people were there, and I'm immensely grateful to them, but to think what could have happened, or that he could do it again—"

"I'll have a word with Nate." Joss had a word or two in mind already. "I won't have this."

"It would be nice if it went away." Gareth tried for a smile. "I've also been afflicted by uncles, you see. It never rains but it pours. My uncle Henry has arrived for a visit."

"The one that sacked you?"

"The very one. His son, my cousin Lionel, is staying with the Topgoods. It seems he knows their son. Is there a son?"

"Worthless roistering fellow. Went for a soldier. On the Peninsula now, I heard."

"Well, I have no idea how Lionel knows him, but he's visiting the Topgoods, and Uncle Henry is at Tench House. I went out for a breath of air after Sweetwater visited. Uncle Henry arrived while I was out, informed Catherine that he ought to know more of his dear brother's family, and by the time I had come home she was making up a room for him. I dare say he'd have badgered me into letting him stay if I'd been there, so it makes no odds. He is now on a stay of unspecified length. Lovely to have visitors, isn't it? Just when I was complaining I didn't know anyone. He says he's come to restore family relations, which is terribly good of him, but I don't *want* family relations. I lived with him when I had to, and worked with him when I couldn't think of anything better to do, but I really didn't intend ever to see him again."

"Is he bad to you?"

Gareth made a face. "Condescending. Hectoring. He gives orders, which was one thing when I was his unwanted nephew, or his clerk, but—he's in my house. Wandering around poking at things, criticising Catherine's housekeeping, and wanting to handle my father's—my—affairs. He's an experienced man of business, you see, and I was never as diligent or attentive as one might like. Really, it would be so much easier if I put my affairs in his hands." Gareth dropped the pompous voice he'd put on to say that. "What he means is I'm not competent to handle them myself. It makes me feel like a child. The worst thing is I probably would end up letting him do it if it wasn't for this business of where Father's money came from. I'm used to giving in to Uncle Henry, and it's so much easier than having him go on at me, but if he snouted out mysterious sums of money and demanded answers—my God. And then there's Lionel."

"What's the problem there?"

"He's horrible," Gareth said wholeheartedly. "He was *vile* to me when we were growing up. I suppose I can't blame him for not wanting a whining brat around the place, but it wasn't my fault I was there, or that I missed my own family. He wanted me gone and never lost an opportunity to say so. Or to make me look bad to my uncle, not that he needed much help doing that."

"What's wrong with you?"

"Ask Lionel. He'd have a list."

"Well, be rammed to him. You're a baronet now."

"You'd be amazed how little that helps. Actually it makes it worse, because Lionel is furious I finally have something he doesn't have and can't take. He came for tea and spent the whole time making spiteful remarks and flirting dreadfully with Cecy. He's very handsome and older and all that, and I'm quite sure he's just doing it to show that he can."

"Can what?"

"I don't even know. That he can steal her affections from me—joke's on him, half the time I don't think she can bear me—or that he could break her heart if he wanted, and I couldn't stop him. *Something.* Just...power. I feel like I've no power with them, or this Sweetwater business, or anyone, and to be honest, it's awful. God, I'm sorry, Joss. You have quite enough on your plate without me piling all this on you."

"I've plenty. Only that plate's a trencher I share with my family and my people and most of the Marsh." He put a careful hand to Gareth's face. "Whereas with you, that's just for me."

Gareth's lips rounded. "I...I would like to be just for you."

That got into Joss's lungs like Marsh mist, making it oddly hard to breathe. "Tell me something," he managed. "You ever had someone on your side? Really on your side?"

There was a long silence at that. So long he began to think he'd said something very stupid indeed, and Gareth's wide eyes and almost frightened expression suggested as much. Then Gareth shook his head, almost imperceptibly. "Not—not really. My mother, I suppose, but I don't remember."

"Suppose you believed I'm on your side. Suppose you can tell me about the bad days and the blessed awful relatives whenever you like."

Gareth swallowed hard. It looked painful. "I don't want to depend on you, Joss."

"I didn't mean that. Though you're allowed to depend on people—you got any idea how many people I depend on for a run? And we wouldn't have this place without Sophy. But what I'm saying is, I'm here with you. No more or less, just with you." He brushed his thumb over Gareth's lips. "Let me be on your side, London. I want to be."

"Why?"

"Acause... I don't know. Acause I want to watch beetles with you, and you went at two of Sweetwater's men to help me out when you should have run away. Acause you stripped naked for me after five minutes, and you don't care I'm Joss Doomsday, and I wish to blazes you weren't a baronet. I don't know how long we've got, you and me, but I want all of it. I want to talk with you and eat with you and sleep with you. And if you want to send Cousin Lionel out for an evening walk, I'll make him sorry he ever set foot on Romney Marsh, how about that?"

"Joss!"

Joss grinned. "Just something to think about."

Gareth looked at him for a long moment. "On my side. Really?"

"Promise."

Slim fingers interlaced with his. "I'd like that. I'd like that more than I can say."

Joss squeezed back. "Good thing I'm here, en."

Fourteen

"YOUR COUSIN IS COMING FOR TEA."

Gareth was in the garden, taking out his frustration on the ground elder, which was foolish. You had to pull ground elder gently, if firmly, to get all the roots out, or it would come roaring back within days. Tugging at leaves was a futile pursuit, but better than being inside his own house.

And now his uncle had followed him into the garden. Wonderful.

"Gareth! I spoke to you!"

The compulsion to hang his head and apologise was almost impossible to resist. *My house*, he told himself ferociously. "I'm working, Uncle. And I heard you: Lionel is coming for tea. I don't recall inviting him," he added waspishly, and regretted it at once.

"I gave you shelter in my house for twenty years. I believe I may invite my son, your cousin—"

"As you please," Gareth said over him, not caring to hear another speech on what he owed. The sun was hot, for once, and his broad-brimmed hat was making his head sweat. "When is he coming?"

"In an hour."

"Then I have time to finish weeding."

"I see no reason for you to do menial labour. You have servants. I am very concerned you cannot staff the house properly. Really, I wish you will stop this peculiar secrecy about my brother's affairs. I dare say I can have it all in order for you in a few days."

"I would rather handle my own business." Gareth teased a long root loose in the earth, digging his fingers deep. The pallid strings would snap at the slightest encouragement. "I must learn to manage my own estate."

"It is perverse to refuse knowledgeable assistance."

The earth was getting solid. Gareth worked the elder root sideways, tugging gently to see if there was any give, and stifled a curse as the damned thing broke off in his hand. "Anyway, you have far better things to do than worry about my small property, Uncle. I'm sure you'll need to go back to London soon."

"On the contrary. I have been told I require healthy country air."

"Oh, but I cannot recommend the Marsh for that, sir." Gareth sat back on his heels, adopting a look of concern. "You must have heard of Marsh ague? A dreadful affliction caused by the damp air, and it is usually damp here. Not at all a healthy environment."

"Then I cannot imagine why you stay. You were always a sickly boy."

Joss could have him killed and his body thrown into a dyke, Gareth told himself. It was a heartening thought, and one he'd allowed himself to dwell on several times in the past couple of days. "I'm going to go and wash, Uncle. Excuse me."

He went through the kitchen. Catherine met his eyes and said, "I shall bring you hot water."

She came up to his room a little later with a pitcher, let herself in, and closed the door. "Are you all right?"

"He grates on my nerves. They both do."

"I'm sorry. If I had known—"

"Do you think he would have accepted it if you said he couldn't stay? He wouldn't if I said it."

"You could ask him to leave?" she suggested.

"He had me in his house from the age of six and I don't suppose he wanted me there. I can't ask a guest to leave because he has a brusque manner."

"I suppose not." She sounded dubious. "What does he want here?"

Gareth scrubbed at his filthy nails with a brush. "He said he wanted to restore family relations. One might think he'd be a little less abrasive if that was the case."

"Mmm. He asked me for the key to your study."

Gareth had locked it after the second time his uncle had suggested taking over his affairs. That had felt appallingly discourteous and defiant, and his uncle had been furious, calling it an insult and a statement of mistrust. Which, in fact, it was, since Gareth wouldn't put it past his uncle to make himself master of the papers there without permission. The last thing he needed was an attorney knowing about his father's probably dishonest dealings and, no doubt, feeling obliged to report them to the authorities. He'd stood through his uncle's dressing-down reminding himself that the papers, study, and house were his, but not quite finding the nerve to say so.

He glanced at Catherine. "He's very keen to help. Er, please don't give it to him, though."

"I don't intend to."

"You don't like him, do you?"

"No, I don't," Catherine said. "He's rude to you. He makes his opinion of me very clear."

"Has he been offensive?"

She spread her hands, which was enough reply. Uncle Henry didn't need to insult her in so many words, of course, merely to treat her with the distaste her unfortunate position in his brother's household had merited. Many people would applaud him for it. "And I don't like your cousin either. I don't like the attentions he is paying Cecy."

"Does she like them?"

"She's seventeen, he's handsome, and William Bovey is being an obstinate prig. And she's not used to being charmed, Gareth. I don't know what to say to her."

That was probably the most unguarded speech he'd ever heard from Catherine, and betrayed a level of distress he hadn't realised. "I'm sorry," he said. "I'll do something. I can't throw Uncle Henry out but...I'll do something."

She sighed. "I wish you would."

Gareth expected Lionel's arrival to make everything worse, and it duly did.

He was a very handsome man, well built, with light brown hair and manly good looks. A son anyone would be proud of. He was charming too, and knew how to use his charm, kissing Cecilia's hand with a dashing sophistication that made her blush excessively. He focused on her, quite ignoring Gareth. He spoke of balls and parties in London, dropped the names of titled acquaintances, and paid lavish compliments with a lingering gaze, and Cecilia melted like butter in the heat of his regard.

Gareth had no idea what to do. He was well enough acquainted with his sister to suspect that if he attempted to interfere she would fly up in the boughs. He had already taken a great deal from her and impeded her hopes and ambitions; if he tried to stand between her and a handsome, eligible, wealthy admirer, she would not respond well. He didn't want to show Lionel how easy it would be to drive even more of a wedge between them.

So he sat silently as Lionel flirted, and Uncle Henry put in remarks about Lionel's talents, Lionel's social success, Lionel's London ambitions, all of which made it quite clear by contrast how much Gareth lacked of them.

Tea seemed to go on forever. By six o'clock, Gareth was beginning to wonder if he'd ever be rid of the man.

"And what are your plans in Romney Marsh?" he asked his cousin, striving for a pleasant tone that didn't say *when will you leave?* "Do you stay long with the Topgoods?"

Lionel gave him an utterly false smile. "I had in mind a week, but that was before I understood the beauty this place offers." His eyes flickered over Cecilia. "I must say, Gareth, you might have managed *some* praise of your situation. You scarcely presented it as pleasant in your letters."

Gareth had written to his uncle precisely once, a brief note to inform him that he had taken possession of house and title. There was no point protesting: the implication that he had done nothing but complain and disparage the Marsh and his household was firmly made.

"I hope you will stay longer, Mr. Inglis," Cecilia said. "Perhaps you will remain with us for dinner tonight?"

Catherine made a faint noise, cut off almost at once. Uncle Henry said, "An excellent idea. You should be more acquainted with your charming cousin, Lionel. What's the phrase, kissing cousins?" He laughed uproariously. Cecy blushed scarlet. Lionel gave her a look combined of apology and rueful acknowledgement of her charms, which he did very well. "Yes, an excellent idea. You must stay, my boy, and we cannot have you riding back afterwards in this desert of a place. I dare say Catherine will make up a bed for you for the night."

You have no right to make free of her name, or my house. Gareth wanted to say it and didn't dare for fear of the inevitable rebuke—*inhospitable, rag-mannered, jealous.* "I don't know if that—the short notice for dinner—Catherine?"

"The larder is very poorly stocked," Catherine said. "I do beg your pardon. I had intended to market tomorrow."

"I'm sure you'll manage," Uncle Henry told her dismissively.

"I think Lionel should come for dinner another day." Gareth hated himself for the halfway measure as he said it. He didn't want the bloody man in his house ever again, but social obligation and his uncle's expression forced the words from him. "We would be delighted to have you but I'm sure the Topgoods have been looking forward to your presence tonight and I don't dare seem ill-mannered to Lady Topgood by taking you away without notice."

"I think I may judge my hosts' feelings for myself," Lionel told him.

"Of course you should. Aunty Cathy, surely—" Cecy sounded like a child pleading for a treat.

"Lady Topgood is a high stickler," Catherine said in her unemotional way. "And I dare say Miss Topgood is looking forward to Mr. Inglis's company."

Cecilia's eyes widened. Lionel's expression didn't change except for a tiny tightening around the mouth, which told Gareth Catherine had landed a hit. "Then that is decided," he said, rising. "Perhaps you'll let us know when will be convenient for you to dine with us, Lionel. It has been a pleasure to see you again. Pray give my regards to Lady Topgood and the Squire."

"This is very abrupt," Uncle Henry said. "Are you chasing your cousin from the house?"

"It has been a delightful visit and he is welcome to let us know when he will join us next," Gareth said. "I think the maid has your coat, Lionel. Good day."

His uncle walked his cousin to his horse. Cecilia was scarlet. "Aunty Cathy, *why*—"

"He isn't a good man, Cecy," Gareth said. "Very charming, but not at all kind."

"You would say that!"

"Yes, I would, because he was unkind to me for many years. I should be very sorry indeed to see any woman I cared for married to him. In fact, any woman at all. He would not make a good husband—" He stopped there, belatedly noticing Catherine's wincing head-shake, but it was too late. Cecy had gone bright crimson.

"I didn't want—You thought—How dare you! I hate you!" she half-screeched, and fled up to her room.

"That was wrong?" he said, rather hopelessly.

The front door opened to readmit his uncle, scowling. Catherine waved a despairing hand and whisked out of the room. Gareth resigned himself to an extremely unpleasant evening.

"It's been awful," he told Joss later as they were lying together in the looker's hut. It felt safe here, safe enough that they could kiss and talk at leisure rather than snatching hurried intimacy. "For all of us. I can't imagine even Uncle Henry's enjoying himself, unless he takes pleasure in disapproving of me."

"Kick him out."

"I was going to tell him I have other guests arriving next week,"

Gareth said. "Though Lionel will be able to tell him that isn't true, if he stays. But then he might be so offended he never wants to speak to me again, which would be wonderful. How's your uncle?"

"Same as always. I was going to give him a what-d'you-call-it today. That cramp-word of yours."

"Ultimatum?"

"Ultimatum. Only I spent the day doing things a baronet probably doesn't want to know about and I didn't get round to it. Tell you what, how about we both kick our uncles out tomorrow?"

Gareth wasn't sure about kicking, but he needed to act and he knew it. Cecy had been made unhappy and angry, which was exactly the result Lionel had hoped to provoke. Catherine had been driven to actual complaint. He couldn't sit here feeling aggrieved at the mistreatment of his family in his own home and not do anything about it. "We both put our feet down tomorrow," he amended. "I'll tell Uncle Henry to set a date to leave. You tell Elijah to mend his ways or pack his bags."

"It's a bargain."

"I'll feel better," Gareth said. "This whole situation is so peculiar."

"How so?"

"Well, that he's here at all. He doesn't like me and he's not enjoying his visit any more than I am, and he won't leave the house. He just hangs around, poking and prying. Catherine found him in the attic this morning, for heaven's sake. He said he was looking for some chest of oddments from his and my father's youth, but if there's something of my father's he wants, I don't know why he doesn't simply say so. I'd happily give him a vase or a portrait or what-have-you to make him go away. John Groom said he was looking through the stable yesterday, and I've no idea what he thought he might find there. And he's still pressing about seeing my father's papers. Catherine thinks he's after something."

Joss propped himself on an elbow. "Bit of a coincidence, that."

"What is?"

"Bill Sweetwater and your uncle. Both after something, neither saying what."

"Uh," Gareth said blankly. "Yes, but—you can't think it's related. What could my uncle the London attorney possibly have in common with Bill Sweetwater the Marsh smuggler?"

"Your father," Joss said. "That's what they've got in common. They were both working with him, and now Bill's bothering you even when he's been told not, and your uncle's squatting in your house like a toad while he searches it. Your old man was up to something."

"Oh my God." Gareth flopped back on the bench. "Oh God, you're right, aren't you? No, no, no. Good Lord. What is going *on*?"

"I don't know," Joss said. "I'll have a word with Nate tomorrow. If I was you, I'd kick your uncle out and worry about what he's up to later. And if you need help kicking him out, send to the Revelation."

Gareth leaned forward and kissed him, very deliberately, on the nose. Joss's eyes crinkled delightfully. "What was that for?"

"Being on my side."

"Oh, well, then." Joss tugged him closer. "Mph. God, you're lovely."

He was lovely. He was so lovely it constricted Gareth's airways—the eyes, the smile, the thick loose curls spilling over his shoulders, the broad muscles of hard labour. Gareth had no idea why Joss wanted him, of all men, but by some miracle he did, and Gareth Inglis was, at this moment, the luckiest man on Romney Marsh. Possibly in England.

He slid his hand down Joss's side, under his jacket. "I don't know if you've anything in mind for tonight..."

"I had some ideas. You?"

"I would love you to fuck me."

"Great minds." Joss's eyes met his, and Gareth might actually be the luckiest man in Europe, to have Joss Doomsday looking at him like that, so hungry and wondering.

They took their time undressing. Gareth wanted to look his fill at Joss for once. His tawny skin was lit bronze by the light of the oil lamp, his muscles emphasised by shadows. He could have been a statue, albeit not one for public display given the very substantial stand he sported. Gareth kissed his way over those magnificent shoulders, wound his hands in Joss's thick hair. "I love your hair."

"I like yours. Would you wear it longer, ever?"

Gareth had kept it in an unexuberant Brutus for some years. Uncle Henry had not encouraged poetical indulgences in his clerks' appearances. "I hadn't thought of doing so. Would you like it longer?"

"It's your head. But I do like something to get hold of."

He was growing it out, Gareth decided, starting now.

They were standing together in the hut, both bare, Gareth behind Joss, kissing his neck. His own stand was nestled very comfortably against Joss's back, or mostly against his back, and as he realised that, Joss pressed backwards, rubbing his extremely well-muscled arse against the root of Gareth's cock. "Mmm. Nice. You ever take the other part, London?"

"Give, rather than receive? Um, I haven't tried, actually. Nobody ever suggested it."

"Would you?"

Gareth considered Joss's tight, powerful body, tried to imagine it yielding under him. The idea was profoundly implausible. "Do you take it that way?"

That came out sounding a bit more incredulous than he'd

intended. Joss gave him a look over his shoulder. "Otherwhiles. Shouldn't I?"

"No reason why not. I just thought you liked to be in charge."

"It's not about who's in charge, is it? And I don't see anyone needs to be in charge in the bedroom at all. Unless the other fellow wants it, I suppose."

"Well, perhaps not, but you certainly seem to enjoy telling me to strip for you."

"That's not the same," Joss said, sounding faintly embarrassed. "And I like it all ways. Had a French privateer give me what you might call an education when I was seventeen. *There* was a fellow who liked to be in charge."

"You were debauched by a pirate?"

"Might have been? He fucked me six ways from Sunday, if that's what you mean."

"That's roughly the definition, yes," Gareth said, a little unsteadily. "And that was good?"

"Merciful good," Joss assured him. "Talk about sowing your wild oats: I got my field proper ploughed." Gareth spluttered. "He wanted me to join his crew and I might have done, but, well. I'd work here, so I had to stay, and that was that."

Gareth had a feeling he'd be thinking about the youthful Joss in the hands of a dashing pirate captain on solitary nights for the rest of his life. "I'm not sure I can match a pirate."

"Privateer. And I wouldn't want you to. You do me just as you are."

Gareth pressed a little harder against Joss's back, rolling his hips, feeling Joss press back. Maybe he could imagine this. "I think—I think I might want to fuck you, actually. Some time. Maybe not tonight, though?"

Joss twisted round in his arms. "No, I reckon you're mine tonight, London. That what you want?"

"God, yes."

"I had—debauched?—you our first night." He slid his fingers between their bodies, caught Gareth's prick and his own in a callused hand. "Remember?"

"Yes."

"Over the bed in the Three Ducks. I said, could I fuck you, and you said, *yes please*, and I thought, there's manners. Proper breeding, that is."

"I try to be courteous. Could I trouble you to do it again, Mr. Doomsday?"

"My pleasure, Sir Gareth."

Joss had oil. Of course Joss had oil, Joss thought of everything. Or most things; there was no rug on the cold stone floor. Gareth mentally prepared to sacrifice his knees, but Joss pulled him over to the bench and the mattress. "On your back?"

"I'm a bit—" He couldn't think of a tactful way to put it. "Tall for you?"

Joss narrowed his eyes. "Going to pay for that, baronet."

Gareth had never really had this position work before. He *was* too tall. But Joss seemed untroubled by his lanky limbs, and God knew he had the shoulders to bear them, and mostly, any physical awkwardness was washed away in the bewildering pleasure of seeing Joss's face as they fucked. The look of intense concentration as he pushed into Gareth with such tender care; the transported expression, drugged with pleasure, as he moved and thrust; the peculiar helplessness of being on his back, curling up on himself to reach Joss's mouth with his own, clinging on and being fucked and giving himself up to nothing but Joss, and the increasing power and urgency of his thrusts. And they were powerful because God, he was strong, making Gareth cry out with something between pleasure and alarm at the sheer force of the man between his legs.

Joss grunted something and changed the angle of his strokes, hitting the pleasure point. "Oh Jesus," Gareth yelped. "More. That. God."

"Like it?"

"Fuck. Yes."

"Tell me."

"More. I love it, I want it. Fuck me like your pirate."

"I'll fuck you like a king," Joss said, through sharp gasps for breath. "And you—going to come first." He somehow got one hand to Gareth's cock between their locked bodies, holding himself back with gritted teeth. Gareth wailed. "I want to feel you spend with me in you. I want you crying out for my prick."

"Yes, Joss," Gareth managed, and Joss gasped a laugh, and then Gareth couldn't think of anything else at all except Joss's hand and his prick and his face, tense with holding off, watching him. "Oh, oh, Joss. Yes. Yes." He jerked, and then he was spending, thrashing under Joss with ecstatic agony, and Joss was letting go his restraint, head thrown back in rapture. There was nothing at all in the world but Joss Doomsday, in and around and owning Gareth's body, driving hard into him once, twice more. He gave a cry of something like pain and collapsed over Gareth's chest.

His shoulders were heaving. Gareth could barely breathe, for his weight and the faceful of thick hair, and didn't care.

"I'd knight you," he mumbled.

"Duchess at least." Joss sounded light-headed. "If your great-grandma was like you, she got cheated."

"If the king was like you, she didn't mind. Ow, ow, cramp."

"Sorry." Joss pushed himself off and out, and carefully eased Gareth's thighs down off his shoulders, then squirmed until they were lying alongside one another in a tangle of limbs and spend and sweat. "You've got merciful long legs."

"I did say."

"I already knew. But there's seeing a taant fellow, and there's having a mare's worth of leg round my neck." He flashed his glorious grin. "I liked it. Let's do it again."

"So did I. What did you call me?"

"Taant. It's what you say for a ship's mast that's over-high."

Gareth swiped at him. "Thank you *so* much. How do I say 'short-arse' in Kentish?"

"To me? You don't."

Gareth would have protested, but Joss squirmed against him to kiss his ear, which took his mind off it. They snuggled comfortably together, in the sheer simple happiness of contact and intimacy. Joss, by his side and on his side.

"I have to object," he said drowsily.

"About what?"

"'No need to be in charge'? Did you have the gall to say that?"

Joss looked delightfully schoolboyish when you caught him out. "Got carried away. Did you mind?"

"Good Lord, no."

"It's not being in charge, exactly. Just, I'm in the habit of saying what I want, without bark on the word. Doesn't mean you have to do it."

"If you want something, you ask for it. You told me so, before. Is that always how you get what you want?"

Joss shrugged. "You don't get what you want by *not* asking for it."

Gareth contemplated the obvious truth of that statement. "I may have to change my approach to life."

Fifteen

JOSS SLEPT LATE THE NEXT MORNING AND WOKE CURLED IN
his blankets like a cat in a sunbeam.

What a night. He snuggled down and let his mind dance over the
details for a while, remembering Gareth's look and taste and smell.
The expression on his face when he'd spent, with Joss between
and under his long legs. God, those legs. Gareth could wrap them
round him any time.

It all felt implausibly perfect. Joss basked in that feeling because
it was going to go away the minute he got up.

He had to deal with Elijah and for good. No more delays. For
one, he'd said he would and Gareth had heard him, so that was
that. For another, it needed doing. Goldie was looking haunted
these last days. What queered Joss was that the boy wouldn't stay
out of his father's way, as if any attention was better than none.
It made Joss think of Gareth, alone in his uncle's home for years,
which in turn made him want to punch something or someone
extremely hard.

Looked like it was Elijah's lucky day.

He got up on that thought, scrubbed himself under the pump, and stuck his head into the kitchen, where Ma was making breakfast.

"Busy last night?" she asked. "I was looking for you. Parson at St. George is grumbling."

"Ivychurch? Ah, drat. My fault, Ma. I meant to sweeten him up, didn't get round to it."

They'd used the great old church tower to store goods twice in the last month, which required a very blind eye from its clergy. Joss had meant to pay his respects accordingly but it had slipped his mind, what with everything else he had on it. "Drat," he repeated. "I'll have a cask of best brandy left for him."

"And silk stockings. Three pair."

The parson had a decided taste for silk stockings considering he was an unmarried man. Joss counted that none of his business. "I'll get that done today."

"And there's Margaret Broddle fraped about her boys—"

"I don't have time for the Widow Broddle, Ma. I've to ride to Camber today." He hadn't yet confronted Nate Sweetwater about Bill's visit to Gareth, simply hadn't had a chance. That couldn't wait any longer.

Ma frowned. "I want that done. Those boys are trouble."

"You scare them more than I do," Joss pointed out. "And talking of troublesome boys, I want Goldie to go to school."

The frown became a scowl. "This again? It's decided. Elijah's son. His choice. You think I'd have let any of your uncles send you away?"

"Goldie wants to go."

Ma put a plate of ham and eggs in front of him. "The trade a man sets his son to is his business. It's not for you to interfere."

"You had me and Graveyard tell George Banks that we'd bury

him in the sand and wait for the tide to come in if he laid a hand on his wife again. Was that not interfering in his business?"

She glowered at him. Joss speared an egg yolk. "Granda says he's bright, Ma. He could do something more. Have bigger horizons."

"Marsh not enough for you now?"

"It's very well for me."

"You think I should have sent you away to school? Is that what you wanted? To leave us all when your father died and go off to learn Latin—"

"We both know I was born for free trading. Granda thinks Goldie's meant for something different."

"Different." Ma slapped a mug of tea onto the table hard enough to spill. "Why do you need different?"

"I don't," Joss said, a denial that felt not quite true as it came out of his mouth. "We're not talking about me. Goldie shouldn't miss a chance acause Elijah can't bear that his son might be more use than he is."

She swelled. "You're speaking of your uncle, Josiah Doomsday!"

"I am, and I've spoken less about him than I should have. You've seen how Elijah's been with Goldie the last few months. He's holding him back out of spite and knocking him about for no reason. What are we going to do about that, wait for Goldie to be big enough to hit back?"

Her face tightened. "I've spoken to Eli, but it's his right to chastise his child."

"He's not chastising, he's hitting," Joss said. "Goldie deserves better, and Elijah needs to do better. He's too often soused, he's free with his hands, he doesn't do his share. He needs to learn his place."

She slammed a hand on the table. "Place? He's my brother!"

"That's the only reason I haven't kicked him out, and it's not been well done of me. You know it, I know it, and it's time he knew it."

"You're overstepping, Josiah."

Joss stood and met her eyes with a level gaze. He was a few inches taller than her these days, but it never felt that way. "You telling me that, Ma? I'm gaffer here. I've a right to order my men."

"Is that so?" Her voice was low and dangerous. "You're the Upright Man now, are you? The new master?"

"Don't do this, Ma. You'll rule this family as long as you can stand, and I don't want to change that. But it's my job to deal with problems. You know Elijah spoiled Sophy's run. You know he's undermining me, you know it's not right how he treats Goldie. But you haven't dealt with him like you would anyone else, and that's not fair. People *see* it's not fair." That blow landed hard, he saw in her face, and he gentled his tone a little. "I'm doing the job as I think best. That means coming down hard when people do wrong. And if you and I can't agree on what's right and wrong, we have to talk about that."

Another few ticks of the clock, in which he braced for explosion. At last she said with unnerving calm, "You've grown up."

"Long time since, Ma."

"Not in age. In... I don't know. You sounded like your father there."

Joss tried a smile. "Hope so."

"John never had time for Elijah either. He was a lively one, but there was no real harm in him. Boys will be boys. But John wouldn't hear me. He wouldn't give Eli a chance."

Joss kept his thoughts on that to himself. Ma stood for a few minutes, face working. "I don't want him upset."

"No way round it, Ma. Why should we always be caring for his feelings when he doesn't give a curse for anyone's?"

"That's just his way. You know how he is."

"Yes," Joss said. "I know it, and I don't like it. That's how *I* am."

Ma gave him a look. "I won't have you dressing down my brother. I'll speak to him."

"There's been plenty of speaking and not enough doing. He needs to be told right out that he stops acting about or he's gone."

"I said, I will speak to him, Josiah Doomsday," Ma said flatly. "I'm not in my grave yet. *I* will do this. You will give him a fair chance to mend. And if he doesn't..." Her face tightened. "I won't stand in your way."

Joss rode down to Camber after that. It was a long way but his mare, Fleurie, was fresh and he took it at an easy canter, enjoying the breeze and the dappled sunshine.

He'd come alone. Generally he'd bring one or another of his crew to visit Sweetwater: Finty or Matt if he was talking seriously, Graveyard or Sophy if he was looking to make waves. This time he wanted a private chat.

Camber was a tiny collection of dwellings behind the rolling sand hills. Joss rode to Nate's house and knocked at the door. Mrs. Sweetwater, a draggle-tailed woman with a magnificently dirty laugh, rolled her eyes when she saw him, and bellowed, "Nate! Doomsday's here!"

Nate Sweetwater emerged a few minutes later, unshaved, unwashed, and yawning. He was a strapping man, broad-shouldered and muscular, with a bit of a belly and hands almost as big as Graveyard's. "Ah, 's'you," he said. "She calls me like that, I think, 'Is it Joss or am I about to meet my maker?'"

Joss had heard that joke more times than he liked to remember. He chuckled anyway. "I want a word, Nate. Just the two of us."

Nate raised his brows. "What's this about?"

"Take a walk with me."

Nate pulled his boots on and they headed to the path that ran through the sand hills, tramping in silence.

He wasn't the worst man, Nate Sweetwater. Not a friend, didn't run his business in a way Joss liked, heavy-handed and short-tempered. But he was honest by his own lights, adored his sharp-tongued wife, and didn't seek trouble for its own sake. Joss could deal with him.

"So what's the trouble?" Nate asked, once they were crunching over the sandy path.

"Sir Gareth Inglis," Joss said. "I told you to call your boys off."

"You did, and I did."

"Then why was your Bill round Tench House other day making threats?"

There was a tiny silence. Joss cast a glance at his face and saw the unshaven jaw had tightened. "What's that, now?"

"Bill came round to see Sir Gareth, not friendly-like. We talked about this, Nate. What's the game? Was he acting on your orders, or against 'em?"

Nate gave him a vicious look. Joss waved a hand, indicating the empty space around them. This was why he'd made sure there wasn't an audience: he had no desire to embarrass his counterpart. He and Nate were rivals, shouldering one another for space, but they were also two men in the same line of work, both saddled with relatives more trouble than they were worth, and just now and again, that made them allies.

Nate puffed out his cheeks, a silent admission that his brother had crossed him. "I'll have a word with Bill. No offence meant, not on my part."

"Thank you kindly," Joss said. "What did Bill mean by it?"

"Joss—"

"It's the third time of your boys sticking their nebs in to this business, and I want it to be the last. This is about Sir Hugo's dealings with you, right?"

"Course you bloody know," Nate said with resignation.

"Your boys shoved it in my face. Don't blame me for having a look." He took a stab, if not quite in the dark, at least in the mist. "Baronet was playing middleman for his brother, right?"

"Bloody gentry. It's never worth dealing with 'em. Nothing but trouble. Even when they're dead they're trouble."

"Can't say I've tried. What happened?"

Nate shook his head. "Nothing you need to know about, Joss Doomsday. Except," he added, with the fervour of a man holding a grievance, "except turns out Sir Hugo's brother is a bloody latitat! Sir Hugo up and dies on me, and not five minutes after the funeral, there's this Inglis lawyer-fellow round here asking me questions! What's the point of a middleman if he lets both ends meet?"

"None at all." Joss couldn't make sense of this. If Henry Inglis had been prepared to deal directly with smugglers, why involve his brother in the first place? "What was he asking you about?"

"My business."

Joss left that there. "And what about this Adam Drake?"

Nate turned sharply. "Why'd you ask that?"

"Because Bill asked Sir Gareth about whoever he is. One of yours?"

Nate shrugged. "Did the fetching and carrying between Sir Hugo and me. Gone missing. Bill's been looking into what happened to him."

"Why the blazes would Sir Gareth know that?" Joss demanded. "In fact, what's any of this got to do with Sir Gareth?"

"My business, Joss," Nate repeated.

"I don't want to be in your business. Problem is, Nate, you're in mine. Your men—your brother—making trouble in Dymchurch *is* my business. I told you to leave Sir Gareth be."

"The latitat reckons he was in on my business with his father."

"He wasn't," Joss said flatly. "He's got nothing to do with this, and that's the long and short of it. Bill's wasted his time bothering Sir Gareth. More, he's wasted mine, and I'm out of patience. You stop it, or I will."

"Mph. You sure about Sir Gareth?"

"As eggs. Fellow just maunders about looking at bugs. He's harmless."

"You have him under the thumb, don't you? Heard about that."

Joss felt a pulse of alarm before he realised Nate was referring to the magistrate's hearing. He gave a modest little wave. "Do my best. *But*, Nate. He was minded to run and tell the Revenue that his old man was smuggling."

"What's that, now?" Nate's voice sharpened dangerously.

"What the devil did you expect?" Joss demanded. "Bill coming around threatening him, finding out his father was free trading, and his uncle all mixed up in it and mixing him up too. He wanted to tell the lot to the Revenue and let them sort it out."

Nate was swelling visibly. Joss tapped his arm, quite hard. "I talked him out of it. Told him he wouldn't be bothered again and it was better to keep his mouth shut. He agreed, long as he hears no more about it. But that's the agreement, Nate. Leave him alone and he'll keep quiet. But if you bother him or his people again—the ladies in Tench House, I don't care about the lawyer fellow—you'll be making yourself a problem with the Revenue alongside a problem with me. Hear me? Keep your nose and your brother out of Dymchurch, or it won't end well."

Nate's face was hardening. "Don't care for your tone, Joss Doomsday. You're in Camber now."

"I came here civil-like, which is more than your Bill did to my ground. And I'm here to stop trouble, not start it."

He kept his tone relaxed though his muscles were tensing. After a moment, Nate relaxed too. "Fair enough."

"We've both got enough on our plates," Joss added. "Hard enough to make an honest living these days, with the Preventives all over. Last thing we need is Sweetwater against Doomsday. Only winner there is the Revenue."

"You're not wrong. D'you hear about that business on Pet Level?"

They talked shop for a few moments, letting the mood calm between them. Joss would have tried to do that anyway, but the usually belligerent Nate seemed oddly obliging today. Joss thought about that, and back to Mrs. Sweetwater's thick-waisted form in the doorway, and asked, "And how's the missus? She's looking very well, I thought."

Nate's unshaven face split in a huge grin, but he made very sure to sound casual as he said, "Not so bad. Moaning a bit, don't they always. Got one in the basket, see."

They had been married three years with no sign of children before now, and Nate was clearly delighted that his labours would bear fruit at last. Joss slapped him on the arm in congratulations and said all the right things about fatherhood to come, and they headed back to Camber in a state of great friendliness.

Joss returned to the subject at hand as he collected Fleurie. "I don't want to be in your business, Nate, so don't make your business mine. Call Bill to heel and let Sir Gareth alone, and you and I have no quarrel."

"Long as you're not messing me about."

"On my word." Joss spat on his hand and held it out, and after a moment's consideration, Nate shook.

That had gone about as well as might be hoped. Joss hadn't got any answers, but he didn't much care about answers. He wanted Nate to rein his brother in, and that was all.

He rode back at a more leisurely pace, halting Fleurie by Denge Beach in order to walk over the slippery cobbles, thinking of landings, and also plants. There were things growing here he didn't see anywhere else: the sea cabbage and sea peas, neither like their garden counterparts, the hemp-nettles and yellow vetch. Gareth would probably be interested, and have interesting things to say. Maybe he'd know why the tall one with spiky flowers smelled like a wet goat.

None of which was what he was here for, so he set his mind firmly back on work. It was possible to land here, with men wearing backstays under their shoes to avoid turning their ankles on the shingle, but it was a slow business and you couldn't run if you needed to. Still, the area where the shingle beach came up to Great Stone was useful and they hadn't been this way in a while. He planned out the next couple of runs in his head as he rode back, an activity from which he was not pleased to be roused by a shout.

"Hey, there!"

Elijah was standing on the road a little way down from the Revelation. Joss raised a hand in lacklustre acknowledgement; Elijah signalled him to stop. Doubtless he'd spoken to Ma.

Joss repressed a sigh, halted Fleurie, and slid down to the road. "Watcher, Elijah."

"Been looking for you, boy."

"What's the problem, en." He didn't put any enthusiasm into it; he didn't feel any.

His uncle's face, never a pretty sight, took on a rather gloating cast. "Oh, I don't reckon it's my problem. I hear you think you can tell me what to do."

"Talk to Ma, did you? Then she told you what I said, and I dare say she told you I meant it. You need me to tell you myself?"

"Why don't you tell me something else. Tell me..." He drew that out. "Oh, I know. Tell me what you were doing in the Warren."

Joss had learned the skill of plausible denial living with his mother and had plenty of opportunities to practise it with Excisemen. He called on it now. "The Warren? I've been on Denge Beach, working. You've maybe heard of that."

"Not now. Couple weeks back, in broad daylight, in the Warren." He paused, an ugly smirk curling his lips. "With Sir Gareth Inglis."

Joss gave his uncle a long contemplative look, which he hoped disguised the very cold feeling at his neck. "I was showing him bobbers. Great diving beetles, they're called. They trap air under their wings to breathe under the water, which is a good trick if you can do it. So?"

"So beetles weren't all you were looking at, was it?"

"Mostly," Joss said. "Saw some measuring-bugs too, the hairy ones. You care about bugs now?"

"I tell you, I know what you and Sir Gareth were doing in the Warren."

"I just said. Foxed already?"

Elijah's hand came out, hard but not nearly fast enough. Joss grabbed it at the wrist. "Mind yourself. I'm not your son to knock about."

"If you were my son, I'd teach you—"

"But I'm your nephew, and that's the only reason I haven't given you a drubbing and thrown you out before now." He locked gazes with Elijah, gripping his wrist hard. "Don't rely on that."

His uncle's eyes bulged under their thick brows, his only point of resemblance to his son. "I'm your elder! I should be the Upright Man here."

Joss snorted. "You think anyone would trust you to lead a run, let alone the family? The only reason you aren't kicked out of every alehouse in Dymchurch is you trade on our name." Elijah had gone a deep and unappealing crimson. Joss wondered if it was possible to provoke a man into an apoplexy. "I'm tired of carrying your weight. Make yourself useful, or make yourself scarce."

"You don't tell me that, boy!"

"Call me *boy* once more and I'll kick you clear over the Wall. Or shall I get Granda to do that?"

"I'll call you what I like, acause I know about you and Sir Gareth. And if you don't want the rest of the family to know it, you'll show me a lot more respect, *boy*. Starting now."

"Say whatever you want to whoever you like. I've no time for your jibber-jabber." He threw his uncle's wrist down contemptuously and turned on his heel.

"You'll be sorry!" Elijah shouted as Joss remounted Fleurie. He ignored his uncle as he trotted her home, wondering how the blazes to handle this.

Be rammed to Elijah and anything he had to say. Joss knew himself to be well-liked and very good at his work; Elijah was neither. But his uncle hadn't said *I saw you*; he'd said *I know*, and that meant someone else had seen them. Someone quick and quiet who might tell Elijah things in an effort to win favour, and Joss had a very good idea who that was.

The sneaking little wretch. What would he do that for, when Joss was trying to help him? Shocked, perhaps. Or currying favour with his father, or just thirteen and therefore a pain in the arse.

Now what?

Joss considered tactics as he rubbed the mare down. He'd have to outface Elijah and quiet Goldie, and he'd need to do a merciful good job of both. Because if he had to tell Gareth that Elijah was running his mouth...

He didn't reckon Gareth could ignore chatter the same way Joss could. A sensitive sort of fellow, his London, and didn't have Joss's standing, what with being new-come, a nob, an informer, and, fundamentally, outmarsh.

No, Joss couldn't let Elijah talk about Gareth. He'd promised his lover they'd be safe. He'd said he'd take care of things, so that was what he'd do. And since his uncle would take conciliation as a sign of weakness, he'd need to come on strong.

Joss thought about that. Then he stalked into the Revelation and banged the door behind him.

Elijah was sitting beside Tom with a smug smile. Sophy was heads-together with Emily and Isaac; Graveyard and Finty sat in their usual companionable silence; Granda and Goldie were busy with a slate in the corner. Everyone looked up at his dramatic entry.

"Something wrong?" Sophy asked.

"Goldie!" Joss snapped.

Goldie looked round with obvious reluctance, radiating guilt. "Yes, Joss?" he asked in a thread of a voice.

"What's wrong with you?" Sophy demanded.

"Quiet. Goldie, I want an answer on this business of sending you off to school. If you don't want it, there's no more to be said. This is your home and always will be. But if you want to go, let's get on with it."

"That's not up to you, boy," Elijah said.

Joss ignored him. "You decide, Goldie. If you don't know how to decide, go talk to someone who does. Granda, help him with that."

"Yes, Joss," Asa said, voice so dry you could start a fire with it.

"You not listening to me, nephew?" Elijah demanded.

"No," Joss said. "I'm not. Ma warned you this morning."

"And I warned you just now—"

"Shut up. You say one word now in defiance of me, I'm going to

take you outside and give you the thrashing you deserve, and don't
be too sure you'll walk away."

He could hear intakes of breath around the room. Elijah was an
ugly shade of red. Joss stared him down. "Give it a try. You're half-
cut and broken-winded. You're getting *old*, and I've been holding
back for months. Come on, Elijah. Here and now. I dare you."

"You don't want me to talk acause you fear what I'll say."

Joss stalked over, planted his fists on the table, and leaned in. "I
don't want you to talk acause I'm sick of the sound of your flapping
lips. We've all heard how you'd do the runs better, and you'd get
more for the cargo, and you'd marry the King of Sweden's daughter
while you're at it. You've talked enough. Open your mouth again
and I'll close it for you."

"Joss..." Isaac sounded alarmed.

The whole room was staring. It was possible Joss had been shouting: his throat felt a bit raw. Maybe he was angrier than he'd realised.

He turned. "Tom. Hear you think you'd be a better landman
than me."

Tom's eyes widened. "I only said—"

"Show us. You're on the land now, seconding me. Plan one that
we all like, and you can lead it."

"But—"

"I said, you're on the land till I tell you otherwise. Hear me?"

"Yes, Joss," Tom said through his teeth. "But who's on the boats,
then?" He was a born sailor, never happier than on the water.

"Isaac!"

"Yes, Joss?"

"You and Sophy will run the boats over while Tom's on land.
Soph, you parlay French the best and you're a better trader, so
you'll handle business in Dunkirk but Isaac's to lead at sea."

Sophy grinned. "Yes, Joss."

"Yes, Joss!" Isaac echoed. He'd wanted this chance for a while.

"But—" Tom began.

"But what? You reckon you'd do better than me on land, so now's your chance to show us all. Big man like you won't mind hauling kegs," Joss added, since he wasn't feeling kindly.

"And what about Elijah?" Tom demanded, somewhat mulishly.

"Elijah?" Joss contemplated his uncle. "Elijah's not on the runs at all till he learns to take orders and shut his mouth. And that means he'll can pay for his beer from now on, like a customer."

"What?"

"You heard," Joss said. "If you want to drink, you can work for it."

Elijah's face was a mask of incredulous rage. He stood and Graveyard stood too, a threat by virtue of sheer bulk. He was a placid soul, despite appearances, but he dearly loathed Elijah.

Elijah weighed up his chances then stamped to the door, where he turned to stab a finger at Joss. "I'm not done here. I'll have you. I'll *have* you, you bloody molly."

"Oh, piss off," Joss said. "I'm sick of the sight of you."

He waited for the door to slam, then looked around. Everyone was staring at him.

"I said to Ma this morning, I've been patient too long. Well, I've lost my patience for good and all," he told the room. "Granda, Goldie, sort this school business out between you, and give me an answer, quiddy. Only, Goldie?" He waited for the boy to look at him. "Don't worry about what your father thinks. If he gives you any trouble, come to me. Hear me? We'll get you settled, however suits you best."

"Yes, Joss." It was a whisper.

"That goes for everyone," Joss added. "We'll have no more of Elijah's nonsense."

"If he gives me trouble, can I kick him in the balls?" Sophy asked.

"Make it hard."

"Oh, I will," she assured him. "Uh, you've talked to Ma about this, right?"

"And will again." Which was going to go merciful badly, because she'd think he hadn't kept their agreement from the morning, and he doubted he'd persuade her otherwise. "She in?"

"Out visiting."

That was a small reprieve. Joss nodded and headed up the stairs to his room. He needed five minutes' peace.

He reckoned things had gone as well as possible. Elijah might make accusations, but now everyone would think he was only casting about for revenge. If Goldie was as bright as he was supposed to be, he'd take the hand Joss had extended. Elijah had nothing at all in the way of proof against Gareth—

He stopped on that thought. Went faster up the last flight to his tiny room, opened his box of bits and pieces. He didn't have many things beyond clothes, and his collection of treasures wasn't much to show for twenty-six years on this earth. A lopsided dog Bart had whittled for him out of driftwood, a neckerchief his father had worn often, a childish drawing Sophy had done of the whole family together. There was a gold fob watch that had been a gift from Jean-Jacques in Dunkirk, and a garish emerald ring given to him by the French privateer as exchange for his innocence, such as it had been. He didn't wear either of those—the past was the past—but they were good memories to have. One day maybe he'd have something in there to remind him of Gareth, but that wasn't a thought he wanted to entertain now.

Because he'd put the letter in the box: the one he'd written to Gareth before Sophy's trial, that he had refused twice. Joss had kept it safe as proof that he'd tried to talk to him, then it hadn't been needful any more and he'd forgotten about it.

And now it wasn't there.

Sixteen

GARETH HAD ALSO BEEN WOKEN BY SUNBEAMS THAT MORN-
ing. It was the kind of wonderful day that ought to follow a wonderful night, with blue sky and fresh air, and he decided to ride.

He headed across the Marsh in the direction of Appledore, leaving the sea behind him, and rode to the Isle of Oxney. It wasn't
really an island, but a large, long, flat-topped hill to the north
of Rye, with the River Rother running around it, and the Royal
Military Canal a grim, straight line to its east. This was his second
trip up here in the last few days. Partly he wanted to be out of the
house while his uncle was in it, but he was also pursuing one of his
father's very last notebook entries. There was a sizeable colony of
great crested newts in the wooded areas at the base of the Isle, and
Sir Hugo had spent hours observing them, staying nights with the
d'Aumestys at Stone Manor to avoid the travel.

Gareth didn't want to do that: having met the d'Aumestys, the long
journey seemed preferable. It was worth it for the newts, and he spent
a very enjoyable morning fossicking about in ditches and woodland.

His only human encounter was with Pagan d'Aumesty, one of the

Earl of Oxney's more peculiar relatives, who was wandering along High Knock Channel poking vaguely at the sides of the stream with a stick.

Gareth halted. "Good morning, sir."

"Eh? Oh. You're, uh…"

"Gareth Inglis. I came to tea with the Earl in March."

"No. No, that's not it."

"I beg your pardon?"

"I'll have it in a minute. Let me see, you are—"

"Gareth Inglis," Gareth said with extreme clarity.

"Ah, I have it! You are Gareth Inglis," Pagan informed him. "Are you looking for your father? He's just around here, I believe."

"I…I'm afraid he's dead, sir."

"Just around here." Pagan gestured in the vague direction of the Isle. "I saw him—now, was it today?"

"No, because he's dead?" Somehow that had become a question. "He's dead," Gareth repeated more firmly. "He's been dead for months."

"Are you sure?"

Gareth dug his fingernails into his palm against the wholly inappropriate laugh that wanted to bubble up. "Quite sure, yes."

"Hmph. That seems very odd of him."

"I do apologise," Gareth said hopelessly.

"We had been discussing my researches. I wanted to tell him about the progress of the project. I wondered why he had not visited." There was a distinct suggestion that Sir Hugo's death was insufficient excuse. "Really, it is most inconvenient. I wished him to assist in illustrating my theory."

"What theory is that, sir?" Gareth asked, out of politeness that he was very rapidly to regret, and then stood subject to ten minutes of monologue on Romano-British Mithraic mysteries before he was forced to remember an urgent appointment.

He rode home, reflecting that there might be relatives even

worse than his own or Joss's, to discover that his cousin and the Misses Topgood had taken Cecilia out for an expedition. Uncle Henry informed him of this, and added that he had been enjoying his book in the peace and quiet of the Marsh.

"A very soothing place, but I fear I am in search of new reading matter. I should like to look through my brother's bookshelves."

"All his books are here," Gareth said. "His study only has reference works on natural history—"

"That is precisely what I should like to see."

"Have you an interest in natural history, sir?"

"Of course I do."

"Then perhaps I could take you out on the Marsh. You'll agree there is nothing that compares to seeing the reality. It's a beautiful day for a walk." He was thinking of the Warren. It would be waterlogged, and his uncle's shoes didn't look robust.

"I don't want to walk," Uncle Henry said with a snap. "You should go out by all means. Leave me with books and I will be a happy man."

"I know exactly what you want," Gareth said, and saw his uncle's eyes widen sharply. "Uh—my father had a copy of *The Natural History of Selborne*. I believe it's in his study. Have you read it?"

"I have not."

"Shall I fetch it?"

"Yes. I shall come with you."

"Of course," Gareth said. He walked to the study, uncle on his heels, said, "Oh, for heaven's sake," and picked the book off a shelf in the hall, where he'd left it with an idea of giving it to Joss that had foundered on uncertainty about his literacy. "Here it is, Uncle Henry. I'm sure you'll find it fascinating. I must speak to Catherine about dinner, do excuse me."

He left his uncle behind in a couple of swift strides and found

Catherine in the kitchen, making a raised pie. He shut the door and came close.

"Is something wrong, Gareth?"

"My uncle," Gareth said. "Has he—You haven't seen him—This is something of an odd question, I realise—"

"He was trying to get into your study earlier," Catherine said, calm as ever. "He told me to busy myself in the kitchen once Cecy had left, and I heard the rattle of the door handle. It has a distinctive click. I've been coming out on errands and I caught him twice fiddling with the lock. He shouted at me the second time."

"For God's sake. What was my father *doing*, Catherine?"

"I don't know."

"Whatever it was, my uncle knows and so does Sweetwater. They both want something. Joss thinks it's the same thing."

"I expect he's right. But what is it?"

"Money, I suppose. I don't know. I need to—" He needed to talk to Joss, was what he needed to do. "Think about this. And I don't want my uncle left alone in this house any more."

"Do you want him in the house at all? He—" She stopped, and Gareth heard it too, a faint sound at the door.

He walked silently over, grabbed the handle, and pulled the door open. Uncle Henry, in an awkward stooping posture, all but fell into the kitchen.

"Oh, I'm terribly sorry," Gareth said. "Were you leaning on the door?"

Uncle Henry straightened, face reddening. "I wish to speak to you, at once."

"Yes. I think I should like a conversation too."

"In private. Not in front of this female. We will go to the study."

"Oh, give it up," Gareth said. "You won't be getting into my father's papers, and that's all there is to it."

Uncle Henry's eyes bulged. "I *beg* your pardon?"

"Excuse us please, Catherine," Gareth said. She nodded and went out of the back door. "Uncle Henry, I think it's time you told me exactly why you invited yourself to stay in my house."

"I paid you a visit, as head of the family—"

"I *am* head of the family," Gareth said. "You're absolutely right. Thank you for saying so."

"*I* am head of the family! As your elder—"

"I'm the baronet." Gareth's voice was shaking, but a tiny, detached part of his brain identified that as stemming from anger as much as nerves. "I am the baronet, and this is my house. My father's papers are mine and the property he left is mine. If you've any claim to make on my estate, make it now, in plain words."

"You are ranting, Gareth, and uncivil—"

"No, I am not, but if you find my manner so distressing, I think you should leave. There is an afternoon coach from the City of London in Dymchurch that will take you part way to London tonight."

"You propose to throw me out? I, who took you in out of charity?"

"I didn't want to be taken in," Gareth said. "I had a home. My father chose to leave me with you, and whatever arrangement you had with him is your business, not my obligation. If you didn't want me, you should have sent me back."

Uncle Henry's face darkened. "Your ingratitude is revolting."

Gareth opened his mouth to say *I'm not ungrateful!* and bit it back. He wasn't grateful in the slightest, he oughtn't have to be, and he was tired of pretending. "I'm sorry you think so. You should definitely leave if—*since* you feel that way. I will order the carriage to take you into Dymchurch."

Uncle Henry took a step forward, jabbing a finger. "You owe me ten thousand guineas."

"What?"

"Ten thousand guineas." He said it through his teeth. "Your father owed it to me, *you* owe it to me, and you will give it to me or by Christ I will make you regret it."

"But I don't have it," Gareth said blankly. Ten thousand guineas? He'd have to sell the house, sell out of the Funds; he wasn't sure that all his father's investments together would come to such a terrifying sum, or what he'd live on. He'd be ruined. Cecy and Catherine would have nothing. He'd be dependent and helpless, *again*—

A Kentish burr in his mind: *Sounding a bit fraped there, London.*

He took a deep breath and steadied himself. "That's a great deal of money. How did he come to owe you that?"

"It is none of your concern."

"I think it is. I haven't seen anything about this debt in his papers." The papers Uncle Henry had been so desperate to look at. "He wasn't paying you interest, and I have seen no note of hand. When did you lend him this money?"

Uncle Henry's jaw tightened. "It was a private business dealing."

"Then I dare say you have records of it," Gareth said, skin tingling. "You wouldn't have exchanged that sort of sum on a handshake. If you can prove that he owed it to you—"

"I will take you to court for it!"

"The court will also want proof." His whole body was trembling with tension, and anger too. Bad enough his uncle felt entitled to every penny he had; far worse that he believed Gareth would meekly acquiesce; worst of all that once he might have done so. "Show me written evidence of this debt and we'll discuss it. Until then I must decline to entertain your claim. And if I were you, I'm not sure I'd rush to lay your business dealings with my father before a court. Imagine if you were asked to explain in what trade you were investing."

"What are you implying?" Uncle Henry demanded, as betraying red spread over his cheeks, and Gareth felt a pulse of triumph.

"Implying? Nothing at all, so long as you don't dun me for debts I don't owe. What was my father's is mine now, and I am keeping it."

"It is my money!" Uncle Henry shouted, flecks of spittle flying. "I will have it back and you will do as I tell you, boy!"

"You have no right to give me orders any more," Gareth said. "None."

"I brought you up, you ungrateful, graceless fool. I employed you, when nobody else would have done so. You owe me everything you have. You and your miserable father have stolen from me, and I'll destroy you for it." He jabbed a shaking hand. "Give it to me, damn you!"

Gareth fought a very strong desire to get behind the kitchen table. His uncle's temper had never been kindly, but this was beyond anything. "I should like you to leave my house now. John Groom will take you to the City of London—the inn—and we will send your baggage after."

"You will not throw me out! I will stay here as I please!"

"The carriage is being made ready now, Gareth," Catherine said from the corridor, her tone wonderfully calm. "I shall pack Mr. Inglis's things myself but I should prefer him to supervise. I should be most distressed if he discovered anything was missing after he had left. We wouldn't want him to have to return."

"Quite right," Gareth said. "I'll come with you. Shall we all go upstairs and do that now?"

Gareth watched the carriage go off down the lane, Catherine at his side, and heaved a huge sigh. "Thank heaven that's over."

"I don't know about over," Catherine said. "What about Mr. Lionel?"

"Not welcome for dinner. And Cecy isn't to go on any more expeditions with him."

"She won't like that."

"Whatever Uncle Henry is up to, Lionel is probably in it. I might see about hiring a man with a stick to sit here until they've left the Marsh. I don't suppose you know where one might do that in Dymchurch?" he enquired, for the look of the thing.

"You should speak to Joss Doomsday," Catherine said placidly.

"I'll do that. Er, do you think you should tell Cecy about Lionel? I didn't do terribly well before."

"Not very, no. I'll talk to her."

"You might mention that, if Uncle Henry did succeed in this claim, it would be paid out of the estate and her portion would have to come from anything that was left."

"Yes, I think she should know that," Catherine said. "I dare say it will colour the conversation. Will you go to the Revelation now? I don't expect her back until the evening."

"Good idea. And if Lionel comes with Cecy, don't let him in."

Seventeen

GARETH WALKED DOWN TO THE REVELATION INN AT A CLIP-
ping pace, conscious of his aching thighs from the morning's ride, a
touch of soreness from last night's exertions, and a fine set of jitters
from the backwash of the encounter with his uncle. He wanted to
see Joss, to tell him, *I did it* and *Thank you.*

It was still only mid-afternoon, extraordinarily: the argument
with Uncle Henry seemed to have lasted months. Asa Doomsday
was in his habitual place on the Revelation's porch. He raised a
hand in greeting as Gareth bounded up to the stairs, lightness of
heart only slightly impeded by heaviness of legs. "Good afternoon,
Mr. Doomsday. I'm looking for your grandson."

Asa raised a brow, then his stick. He angled it back over his
shoulder and banged on the window-pane behind him before reply-
ing. "Afternoon, Sir Gareth. Would you be able to spare a moment?"

"Yes, of course. What may I do for you?"

A young Doomsday, possibly Isaac, stuck his head out of the
door. "Get Joss," Asa told him.

"Joss, Great-Uncle? But—"

"Joss."

"But he's talking to Aunt Sybil!" the youth said with an overtone of panic.

Asa rapped his stick on the floor. The Doomsday made a face that suggested the throwing up of hands and disappeared. Gareth couldn't help noticing, while the door stood open, that several people were shouting somewhere inside the inn, all at once.

"I wanted to ask you about my great-nephew," Asa said, ignoring the interruption. "We're thinking of sending him for an education. I wondered if you'd speak to the boy. Tell him where schooling might get him."

"Yes, of course," Gareth said. "It would be my pleasure. I do need to speak to Joss rather urgently now, but I'd be happy to come again, or if you'd like to send the lad to Tench House—?"

"Many thanks, sir. I'm most grateful. He's a clever boy and I want to be sure of his future. His happiness too." Asa met his eye with a steady gaze. It looked almost like a command. "Can I charge you to help him, Sir Gareth, if he needs your help?"

"Well, I'll gladly speak to him," Gareth said, nonplussed. "And I will do what I can to assist, of course."

Asa nodded. "I'll hold you to that, sir, as an honourable man."

Joss emerged at that point, looking nothing like himself. His warm eyes held no laughter, his mouth was set, and he looked, frankly, dangerous. "Yes, Granda?" he said tightly.

Asa jerked a thumb towards Gareth, who said, "Uh."

Joss shut his eyes and breathed in deeply. "Sir Gareth, beg your pardon. Help you?"

Gareth wondered about saying *I'll come back another time*, but that seemed un-baronetlike in front of witnesses. "I was hoping to hire one of your men. There have been developments. But if it's not convenient—"

"It's convenient," Asa said over him. "Go and speak to the gentleman, Josiah."

"Bit busy, Granda," Joss said through his teeth.

Asa lifted his arm imperiously. Joss came over to help him up. "Just a moment, Sir Gareth," the old man said. "Help me in, Josiah."

Joss cast Gareth a look he couldn't entirely interpret, and escorted his grandfather into the inn's interior, shutting the door behind him. After a few moments he emerged, alone.

"I'm awfully sorry," Gareth said. "I didn't intend to trouble you."

"It's not you doing that." Joss started walking, heading down to the sea. Gareth matched his stride, grateful for his long legs since Joss was walking at the pace of an angry man. "And I won't say it's a good time, but maybe it is acause I needed to get out of there. I'm two men just now."

Gareth knew 'two men': it meant *in a ferocious rage*. "Would it help to tell me? Or if you'd rather walk in silence, or talk about something else, or throw rocks at the sea, we can do that."

Joss stooped, picked up a stone, and threw it with the kind of force that deserved a window-pane. "Christ merciful Jesus, I'm going to wring Elijah's neck. Tell me why you're here."

"Joss, what's wrong?"

"You don't want to know."

"Of course I do. You're on my side: why can't I be on yours?"

Joss sent another stone at the water, this one on a viciously low, flat trajectory. It bounced off the surface of the sea five times in a row. Gareth gaped. "How did you do that?"

"You never skimmed stones? I'll teach you. All in the wrist." He breathed out hard. "I told Elijah to go to the devil. Ma didn't like it. We'd agreed he'd have a last chance; she doesn't think I gave him that. And maybe I didn't, but there's always another chance for him and I'm sick to my back teeth of it. They want me to be the gaffer and the allworks together, do every merciful thing going, and when I do, I get treated like the Revenue. Tell me to do everything and whine about how I do it." He scooped another handful of stones and sent them flying, one after another. "Maybe I did go too far. Wasn't like I had a choice. Or—Do me a favour, London?"

"Anything."

"Take my mind off it a minute. I need something else to think about. Is this Sweetwater? Did they come back?"

"My uncle demanded ten thousand guineas, so I threw him out of my house."

There was a short pause.

"All right, that worked," Joss said. "Let's have it."

Gareth plunged into an account of his uncle creeping around the house, listening at doors, attempting to get into the study. "Ten thousand guineas! He said my father owed it to him. I can assure you, there's no such sum around. I told him to come up with proof of the debt, and implied very heavily he was involved in free trading, and he simply—Are you listening to me?"

Joss was wearing an arrested look. "I'm listening. Oh, I'm listening. Guineas, he said, not pounds?"

"Yes. Does that matter?"

"Reckon. You know about the guinea boats, the ones that take coin to France?"

Gareth wasn't sure what that meant. "You mean, to buy goods?"

"No. They take the guineas to sell."

"What do you sell guineas for? Do you mean exchanging English coin for French?"

"Not that. Selling the gold." Joss must have seen the incomprehension on his face. "Look, suppose you have ten guineas in your pocket and you want it in pounds. What do you get for your coin?"

"Ten pounds and ten shillings."

"Right. Only, Boney wants gold so badly, he'll pay more than it's worth in paper to have it. Gold, actual gold in his pocket, is worth more to him than bills on a bank."

Gareth had never had a knack for finance. "Why?"

"To pay for his war. What's an English pound note to a French soldier, more than something to wipe his arse with? Plus, any gold Boney has is gold England doesn't, right? So you take your ten golden guineas to France, and sell 'em to a fellow who gives you bills on a bank that'll give you paper money, and now what you get for your ten guineas is twelve pounds or thereabouts. Thirty shillings profit. On ten thousand guineas, you'd make maybe..." His lips moved silently. "Fifteen hundred pounds. And there's no work or costs to it except the transport. No wages to pay, no raising animals, no loss or wastage or storage. Gold doesn't spoil."

"But..." Gareth stared at him. "No. Joss, *no*. I have listened to what you said about trading and people's livelihoods, I swear, but gold to France, to pay enemy soldiers? You *cannot*—"

"I don't," Joss said. "We're traders, not bankers. Keeping the war going with English gold isn't making a living, it's—" He waved his hand for a word.

"Profiteering." Gareth's lips felt numb. "Treason, even. Exporting gold is against the law."

"We've a dunnamany Marshmen in the Navy, with people waiting for them to come home. I'm not running gold to pay the sailors who fight them. It's not a Marsh business all round: the guinea boats mostly run from Deal and Dover. But you can put a chest of gold on any boat you care to, if you're the sort of man to do it."

"Sweetwater?" Gareth said.

"I had heard chatter he was taking gold. Thought it was idle talk. Ten thousand guineas, though." He whistled. "Your uncle's rich, you said?"

"Not that rich. I have no idea if he could raise that sort of sum."

"Suppose he could. He'd send it to your father, who would pass it to Sweetwater. Uncle Henry funds it, Sir Hugo acts as middleman, Nate Sweetwater ships it over, and everyone gets a cut."

"My father had that series of sums that I couldn't explain. Around two hundred pounds each time."

"Sounds right," Joss said. "Don't know what Sweetwater might do the work for, suppose we say another two hundred. And your uncle sits on his arse in London and makes eleven hundred pounds profit. Not to sneeze at, especially if you're doing it over and over." He glanced at Gareth. "You all right, London?"

"No." Gareth scrubbed at his face with the heels of his hands. "Christ. To think I shouted at you for smuggling. To think my family is involved in this—"

"If we're right."

"It makes sense of everything. When Uncle Henry threatened to take me to court, I asked him if he'd like to explain the details of his trading to a judge, and he looked afraid."

"All right. So what happened?" Joss asked. "'Acause if your uncle wants his money back, it sounds like something went awry."

"My father died," Gareth said. "Might that be it? His heart, nobody expected it. Least of all him, I imagine."

"Suppose he received the guineas but had no time to pass them to Sweetwater—"

"There really are not several chests of guineas at Tench House, I promise you."

"He might have kept them elsewhere. But why wouldn't your uncle come and get them right away?"

"He was furious, in February," Gareth said slowly. "So angry, and he wouldn't say why. He dismissed me and told me to go back to my father. If he'd had bad news of some kind…"

"The boat sank, maybe. Or they got stopped by Revenue cutters and threw the goods overboard rather than be caught. Any man would be in a dobbin about that sort of loss."

"But in that case, why would he be looking around the house and demanding I pay him now? Why would Sweetwater ask me for it if they knew it was on the bottom of the sea? Why are they all accusing me as if I have it?"

Joss stopped dead. Gareth halted a step later, turned, and blinked at the expression on his lover's face. "Joss?"

"I talked to Nate Sweetwater earlier today. Asked if he'd had dealings with your father and he said yes, but he also said your uncle Henry came to ask him questions after your father's funeral. Funny way to go on at his brother's burying."

"I suppose so?" Gareth said warily. "I wasn't there."

"Yes, but—All right, let me puzzle this out. Suppose your uncle was sending guineas down for France. Suppose, the last time, your uncle sent the money down as usual, and your father took it and put it aside. Didn't send it to Nate Sweetwater, just told him there was no shipment this time. And suppose he wrote back to your uncle and said, *Bad news, the gold was lost at sea.*"

"Are you suggesting my father cheated his own brother?"

Joss shrugged. "He didn't have much regard for his own son, or his womenfolk either."

That was undeniable. Gareth would have very much liked to deny it, all the same. He felt the panicked urge to push back, to lash out and make this conversation not be happening by any means necessary. He took a deep breath of the salt air instead, and exhaled with the swish of the waves.

"That's—not impossible. You really think he stole it?"

"I'm just guessing," Joss said. "But imagine he did. He tells your uncle it's gone, hides the guineas—and then his heart gives

out and he drops dead. All the while, the money's sitting somewhere secret. And then your uncle comes down for the funeral. I
suppose your father might have let slip the name of the smugglers
he was working with, or maybe Henry found it in his study, but
either way, he goes to talk to Sweetwater. Probably to discuss
another shipment of guineas, because he'd need to make up his
losses. Only, it wouldn't take long once they're talking direct to
realise they've both been lied to. That your father had kept the
money. That there's ten thousand guineas somewhere for the
picking-up."

"Hell's teeth," Gareth said. "Oh my God."

"That's what they've both been after. And it's why nobody's
saying outright what they want with you. Nobody's going to say,
There's ten thousand guineas lying around here somewhere. They
wouldn't want anyone else looking for it."

Gareth wanted to sit down, or possibly to cast up his accounts.
He wrapped his arms around himself, since he couldn't ask Joss
to hold him out here in the open. "My father stole from my uncle,
while helping him smuggle guineas to Napoleon, and now my uncle
is trying to dun me for the money while a gang of smugglers threat-
ens my family. Dear God. If people find out what he did—I have to
keep this quiet, Joss!"

"You do, and so will everyone else want to," Joss said. "That's
a dangerous lot of money to have around. What about your uncle?
How bad is this for him?"

"I very much doubt he can afford to lose ten thousand guineas.
And I don't know the penalties for exporting gold, but I imagine
they're severe. Not to mention he'd be ruined professionally. Would
you trust your affairs to a lawyer who was trading with the enemy?"

"Not one who got caught at it. Think your cousin's in it too?"

"Probably. If my uncle is ruined, so is his future."

"I don't like this," Joss said flatly. "There's too much at stake. I'll send people over to you and keep 'em there from now on."

Gareth nodded. He felt cold and miserable and rather dizzy, as if the world he'd known was slipping away and anchored only by Joss. Solid, strong, capable Joss, who was on his side. "Thank you," he said, feeling the hopeless inadequacy of it. "I have no idea what I'd do without you."

Joss snorted. "I've no idea what to do about this either. I've just got people who can hang around with cudgels while we work it out."

Gareth held on to that *we* as to a life preserver. "That's a good start. As to what to do… The obvious answers are either persuade Sweetwater and Uncle Henry that I don't know where this damned money is, or actually find it. Only I've been trying to do the first without success, and I've no idea how to go about the second."

"You might want to think about what you'd do if you found it too. Hand it back to your uncle?"

"But if he were to continue smuggling guineas, I'd be complicit. And if Sweetwater learned I had it and didn't give it to them—I don't think I want to find it. I think that might make everything infinitely worse."

"Not sure you're wrong," Joss said grimly. "It queers me what we ought to do here. I've got a bit of a problem myself right now, but suppose we meet this evening to chew this over."

Gareth felt a stab of guilt. "I'm so sorry to be piling my troubles on you when you have your own. Is there anything I can do to help?"

Joss made a face. "Shouldn't think so. I'd rather think about yours, anyway. We should head back." He turned, went still, and said, "Hell."

He was staring ahead. Gareth looked in the same direction and saw a burly man approaching, tramping down the beach toward them, less than a hundred yards away. The set of his shoulders suggested menace. A boy trailed miserably at his side, sun glinting off his guinea-bright hair. "Is that your cousin?"

"Goldilocks." Joss sounded remote. "You need to go. Quiddy, now. I'll send someone over to you as soon as I can."

"What's wrong?"

"Later. Go."

There was something Gareth didn't like in his voice. "I don't work for you, if you recall. What's going on? Who's that man?"

"Elijah. You said you wanted to help me? Then clear off. Now!"

"No," Gareth said. He wasn't even sure why not, except he could feel something was very, very wrong. "For goodness' sake—"

Joss made a ferocious, frustrated noise as the new arrivals came close and snapped, "Keep your head."

The boy looked dreadful. His eyes were puffy from crying, a dark red mark on his cheek suggested a recent blow, and he wore a wretched, fearful expression nothing like his earlier cocky demeanour. He gave Joss a fleeting, desperate look, then dropped his gaze as if ashamed.

Elijah Doomsday was a solidly built man, a little taller than Joss and certainly bulkier, but running to seed. He had the red face of a drinker, with thick brows like his son's. Gareth had a feeling he'd seen the man before, perhaps in Dymchurch, and a stronger feeling that he'd rather not be seeing him now, because his smile was unpleasantly triumphant. Gareth glanced at Joss, whose face was set in hard lines.

"Hello there, Sir Gareth," Elijah said. It was an open sneer.

"Good afternoon, Mr. Doomsday."

Elijah smirked. "Respect. That's what I want."

"Mind your tongue," Joss said, and his voice had a very dangerous note.

"Don't think so. I've got the upper hand now, boy, and I'll be using it."

Joss's fists were balled. "We'll see about that."

"You won't touch me," Elijah said. He grabbed the boy's arm

and shook it. "Reason is, this one told me he saw you two fucking in the Warren."

It was a punch to the gut, knocking the breath out of Gareth's lungs. Joss's face was set, but not shocked, not even surprised. Very much as if he'd known this was coming.

"Aye, he saw you all lovey-dovey, didn't you, boy?" Elijah made an unpleasant slurping noise with his lips. "Seen you sneaking out of Tench House a'night, too. Eh? What about that?"

"I told you," Joss said softly. "You need to stop talking."

"I'm going to talk all I like," Elijah said. "I'll say exactly what my boy here told me. And if you say it ain't true, I'll beat the little bastard bloody for a liar. I'll thrash him till there's not a bone whole in his body." His face was a picture of malevolent triumph. "You'll do as I say, or I'll take him back to the Revelation to tell your ma what he said to me, and if you deny it, you can watch him take his punishment. What's it going to be, 'Yes, Joss'?" He spat the words. "How about you, Sir Gareth?"

Gareth wasn't sure which was the sound of the sea, and which the blood roaring in his ears. He dug his nails into his palm, willing the appearance of calm, because he had no idea what to do and Joss was giving no lead. The boy Goldie's face was white and frightened, pimples standing in ugly relief against his pallid skin.

"What it's going to be is you and me, right now," Joss said. "You're a merciful fool, Elijah."

"You won't lay a finger on me." Elijah sounded too confident. "Think I came alone?"

There were, now Gareth looked, a few people on the normally deserted beach, out of hearing but unquestionably watching. "So?" Joss said. "They can see me leather you and welcome."

"Your ma would like that, wouldn't she? You're going to give me what I want, or either you'll be sorry or he will." He shook his son's arm again. The boy's lips were white where they pressed shut against tears.

"Excuse me," Gareth said. The words came out surprisingly loudly. "Goldie—I'm sorry, is that your name?"

The boy looked at him as if he were mad. Elijah said, "Shut your face."

"Well, it can't be. Nobody is called Goldilocks." Gareth felt rather light-headed. "At least not normally, but your family never ceases to surprise me. What is your name?"

"Luke." The word was a whisper.

"Luke, why don't you and I go away from here? We can go to Tench House. I dare say you know Matt Molash's cousin Catherine? She's a wonderful cook. There's probably cake."

The boy's mouth worked silently. Gareth took a step forward, away from Joss, and held out his hand. "Come with me, Luke. Come away from this. I won't let anyone hurt you."

"He'll do as I say, not you," Elijah snarled.

"You are a vile, worthless coward and you deserve everything I expect is going to happen to you," Gareth said. "Luke, your great-uncle Asa asked me to help you. You can stay with me until you're quite safe to return, and you won't be in trouble. I'll make sure of it. But you ought not be here."

"Go with Sir Gareth, Goldie," Joss said.

"You won't go anywhere, bastard," Elijah spat. "You'll come to the Revelation and say what you saw, or I'll give you the thrashing of your life."

"Pa," Luke said. "Pa, don't make me. *Please.*"

"Do as I say!"

Luke stared at his father. His eyes flicked to Joss, standing tense and ready, then to Gareth's hand, still outstretched to him, then he looked up at his father again. "No."

"What's that you said?"

"No. I won't. I will not." The boy's eyes slid to Gareth, lips distorting in a pale effort at a smirk. "I may have made a mistake. I'm retracting my testimony. You can't make me say it!"

That was a cry of defiance, and Luke wrenched his arm at the same time, attempting to shake off his father's grip. Elijah gave a roar of rage and raised a vengeful hand over his son.

It held a knife.

Gareth cried out a warning, far too late; Elijah bellowed as he struck; Luke screamed, the terrible noise of a trapped animal. Only Joss didn't make a sound. He simply moved, hurling himself at Elijah in an explosive lunge that knocked him flying.

Luke reeled away. The left side of his face was already a mask of blood.

"Oh Jesus." Gareth ran to him, gathering the boy into his arms. "Don't panic, don't panic. It's all right. I have a handkerchief." He fumbled the linen from a pocket and carefully put it to Luke's face, trying to control the violent shaking of his hand. The boy had twisted away as the knife descended. If he hadn't, Gareth was fairly sure he'd be dead. As it was—"Is your eye hurt?" he managed. Please God, let the knife have missed the eye. He couldn't see for the blood; he didn't want to look. "Luke?"

The watchers had run up now. Gareth vaguely recognised a couple of them from the Revelation. There was a babble of voices, all of them asking much the same thing, which boiled down to, "Joss?"

Gareth looked round in time to see Joss slam two short-range jabs into Elijah's face with his left hand. He was gripping the man by his throat with the right; Gareth thought he might be holding him up. "We need a doctor!"

"Get him to the Rev." Joss hit Elijah so hard that Gareth heard the crunch of his nose splintering. "I'll catch you up."

Eighteen

JOSS WENT SPRINTING AFTER GARETH AND GOLDIE, AS BEST he could on the sand. His knuckles were throbbing; two had split.

He'd left Elijah unconscious where he fell. Tom and the men who'd come to gawp with him, doubtless on the promise of seeing Elijah humble Joss Doomsday, could drag him out of the way of the incoming tide, or they could not. Joss didn't care. The look on Goldie's face, the fear—all Joss's fault, because he could surely have headed that hellish scene off somehow, and he hadn't. He hadn't done his work properly because of Gareth, and he hadn't done right by Gareth because of his work.

Gareth was stooping awkwardly. He had an arm under Goldie's shoulders, supporting him, and the other hand held a red cloth to the boy's face. No, a bloody handkerchief. Head wounds bled a lot. It would look worse than it was. Please God, it looked worse than it was.

Joss caught up. "It's me. Here, Goldie, need a shoulder?"

"Don't turn your head," Gareth said. "Joss, tell him he isn't in trouble. Tell him that *now*."

His voice had the edge Joss had heard before, but harder and sharper. It was something Joss would have liked to see pointed at someone else. "You're not in trouble," he said. "I swear, Goldie."

"His name is Luke." Gareth glared at him over the boy's head. "Maybe if more people bothered to so much as use his *name*, he might not have felt the need to curry favour with a monster!"

Joss wasn't sure how that followed, but he was pretty sure Gareth was only holding himself together for Goldie right now. "Luke," he said. "And yes. I should have dealt with Elijah a long time back. I'm sorry I didn't. I'm not angry with you."

"We need a doctor," Gareth said. "Is there one at the Revelation, and if not, perhaps you could summon one?"

The quack they usually used, Jabez Whalebone, was a decent bonesetter but his stitching left everything to be desired. "Ma will sew him up," Joss said. "I'll run ahead and let her know."

The next little while was chaotic. Joss and Ma had been in the middle of a blazing row about Elijah when Granda had sent him off, with regrettable things already said on both sides. The news that Elijah had stabbed Goldie was more than anyone needed. There was still shouting going on when Gareth came in with the boy, by now more or less holding him up.

Ma had overproof gin out for the wound, and a glass of best brandy for the patient to knock back, and hot water in which thyme and lavender steeped for her needle and thread. She said it made for neater scars that didn't go bad. Joss took her word, since she was the best hand at sewing up injuries on Romney Marsh.

Gareth got Goldie to a chair and took one by him, gripping his hand. Ma took a seat opposite. "Let me look at this now. You can go, Sir Gareth, thank you kindly."

"I'll stay with Luke."

"I said, you can go now. This is Doomsday business."

"This boy is under my protection," Gareth replied quite pleasantly. "So I will stay, madam."

Nobody told Ma no in the Revelation except Joss, and that rarely. Lucky for Gareth her mind was mostly occupied as she dabbed at the bloody mess on Luke's face with a cloth soaked in gin. The boy sucked in a shrill breath, and his knuckles whitened on Gareth's hand. "My nephew doesn't need your protection in his home."

"Really," Gareth said, and the word was a condemnation.

"You want him, Luke?" Joss asked, and got a tiny nod. "Right, he's staying, no more talk. We've enough to argue about."

"What happened, Joss?" Asa asked.

Tom came in then, with the other hangers-on, bringing a babble of noise. Joss said, "Shut your bleating mouths," in tones that didn't invite argument. "Nobody raises a voice till Ma's done sewing."

Sophy was watching him with wide, alarmed eyes. Joss just shook his head.

Ma cleaned and stitched, with a few brief comments—"Don't screw up your face, child," and "The eye's not harmed." Gareth sat by Luke, gripping his hand, whispering over and over that it was all right, it would be over soon, while Luke bit his lip against crying out. The room slowly filled around them: clearly word was spreading like wildfire.

At last she sat back. "That's done. Good boy."

"Well done," Gareth echoed. "It will be all right."

It wouldn't. The boy had a long, jagged wound that curved around his eye and over his cheekbone. Ma had made as neat a job of it as you could hope, but Joss reckoned he'd be wearing that reminder of betrayal and hate all his life.

"Right, young 'un, you sit for a moment," he said. "Don't try and stand or you'll probably puke. I know I did when I first got sewed up. Makes you feel like a quilt."

"I want to know what happened," Ma said. "How did this come to my nephew?"

"It was Elijah," Tom said. "He was arguing with Joss and then he turned on Goldie. I saw him do it, he just stabbed—"

"Elijah." Ma's face was stark. "Where is he?"

"I gave him not half the drubbing he deserved and left him on the sands."

"You raised your hand to your uncle?"

Joss locked eyes with her. "Next time I'll break his neck and throw the body in a dyke. I'm done with him."

They stared at each other. Ma's shoulders rose and fell, heaving in the struggle for control.

"Elijah cut Goldie, Joss?" Sophy sounded very young. "Cut his face? *Why?*"

"They were arguing," Tom said. "All of them. Sir Gareth too."

Every head turned. Joss had to lock his knees not to take a protective step over to Gareth. Asa said, "I asked Sir Gareth to talk to Luke about school."

He'd always called Goldie by his name, now Joss thought about it. He gave his grandfather a nod. "Elijah didn't like it. He came out with a lot of threats and nonsense."

"Yes," Tom said, his expression challenging. "He made some threats, all right."

Luke was huddled in his chair, looking terrified. Well he might, sat right in the middle of this much trouble. Gareth was looking pretty wary himself. "I reckon this part's family business," Joss said. "Excuse us, Sir Gareth. Luke, you need to go lie down. You've had a bad enough time of it. We'll sort it out without you."

"And what happens if Elijah returns?" Gareth enquired.

"There's enough of us to deal with him."

"Yes, there are." Anger crackled through Gareth's voice. "And yet it seems nobody has before now."

Several people breathed in sharply, and someone whistled. Ma's face was not a pretty sight.

"Want go with Sir Gareth." Luke's voice sounded odd, what with him trying to speak without moving his face, but it was clear enough.

Joss nodded. "Graveyard, give Go—Luke and Sir Gareth a lift to Tench House in the cart. Then stay there, you're on watch again. Sir Gareth will explain." He lifted his hand as his mother spoke. "No. I want the boy out of here. Come on, quiddy."

"Wait." Asa was trying to lever himself out of a chair. Joss went to lend an arm, and took his grandfather over to Luke and Gareth, where Asa gave the boy a careful hug, whispered something into his ear, then straightened and eyed Gareth. "Thank you, sir. I'm grateful."

"I'll take good care of him, Mr. Doomsday," Gareth said. "You have my word. Let's go, Luke."

He left without looking at Joss. That was fair, and also good because Joss wasn't quite ready to face him, certainly not in public. He waited for the two to leave, then turned to face the room. "Right. Let's have this out."

"Aye, let's," Tom said. "You've been spoiling for a fight with Elijah for a while. You laid into him today. Then you're arguing again, and you beat the bloody daylights out of him!"

"That's right," Joss said. "You saw Goldie. What did you want me to do, chat about it?"

"Why did he attack the boy, Josiah?" Asa asked, voice deep.

"He was thinking to use him against me. Goldie—*Luke*—wasn't having it. And now he's got a hole in his face, and he's scared as a cat of his own family. We can't go on like this. Elijah's been tearing us apart."

"Elijah, or you?" Tom said. "You took his place—"

"*Balls,*" Sophy said.

He ignored her. "You've pitted yourself against him every way. And he'd some things to say about you, Joss Doomsday; says there's things you're hiding from us. He told us to come with him acause he reckoned you'd murder him else. What's going on?"

"I want to know," Ma said. "My son sets himself against my brother, and my brother stabs his own son. I want to know what's happened to this family!"

Her voice echoed off the walls. Everyone was looking at Joss.

"You want to know?" he said. "Right. Reason I've been hard on Elijah is he's an idle braggart who's done nothing but sow trouble, drink, and bully anyone he's not scared of. You all know it. Maybe some of you think he has reason to be resentful; there's even some of you think he should be gaffer. He's left Ma and me to do his work for fifteen years, but we should all bow the knee when he wants acause he's the man of the family? Well, think as you like, but hear this." He looked around the room. "If that's what you want, have it. Anyone in this room thinks a drunkard who carved up his son will do better as gaffer, you can go pick him off the sand and let him give you orders. You put him in my place, and I'll leave you all to it. I've worked my arse off for this family since I was twelve years old. I'd be glad of the rest."

The room was entirely silent. Ma looked like a graven statue.

"As for hiding things, I've a life of my own, the little of it I can find time for, and I'll live it as I please. Anyone sticking his nose in my business will find it bloodied. That's all I have to say, and if you don't like it?" Joss stared round. "Fine with me. I can work anywhere I care to. But either I'm gaffer here and my affairs are my business, or that won't do for you, and I'll be off. No other choices. This is an—" He couldn't think of Gareth's cramp-word for a second. "An ultimatum. That means take it or leave it," he added, and saw Asa's eyebrow twitch.

His mother's face was rigid. "You'll walk away from this family, Josiah Doomsday?"

Would he? He was a Marshman to the bone, born and bred and breathing. He felt a deep duty to the place and its people; he loved his family, even when they maddened him. Ma, who was all hard edges because she'd been ground by life until the steel was sharp enough to cut; Granda and Sophy; his young cousins. He *liked* being Joss Doomsday.

But he needed space in his life to be just Joss. He wanted to look at the Marsh and see beetles and plants, as well as smuggling routes. He wanted a soft hand in his as he walked, flyaway hair in his face, long legs around him. Someone for himself, and on his side.

He wanted Gareth. He'd made a merciful mess of that, but it didn't stop him wanting. And if he'd made such a mess that Gareth would have no more of him, he still needed a life in which he could breathe.

"I don't want to, Ma," he said. "But I stay on my terms or I pack my things, and that's the long and short of it."

Sophy stood and walked to his side, folding her arms. "If Joss goes, I go with him."

"Sophia!"

"No, Ma. I'm not working for Elijah at any price. I've come close enough to hanging already."

Finty's voice came from the back of the room. "I'd be sorry to leave, Ma, very. But I'm with Joss, and so will Graveyard be."

"Are you Doomsday men, or Joss's?" Ma demanded.

"Some of us aren't anyone's men," Finty said calmly.

"Well, I'm a Doomsday man," Matt Molash said. "I'd follow Ma into hell, and trust Joss to get me out. I wouldn't let Elijah lead me to the next alehouse, and I don't give a farthing what Joss does on his evenings off. I'm begging you, Ma. Don't let bl-blasted Elijah do any more damage. He's done enough."

"He's not the only one," Joss said. "I've got plenty wrong. There's a lot of things I should have done better, and I'm not promising you I'll always get it right from now on either. If anyone objects to me staying in charge, they're welcome to say so, and no hard feelings. But you spit it out now or swallow it for good." He looked round the room. "Anyone? Tom?"

"Elijah said he knew things." Tom's jaw was rigid. "About you."

"Elijah said a lot before he cut Goldie's face open," Joss said. "I don't know what he told you. Maybe it was true, maybe it wasn't; I don't care. I'll walk the Marsh as I please, act as I see fit, and keep what company I like. And so will you, Tom Doomsday, and so will every Jack, Jill, and Will-Jill in this room, acause we're Doomsdays and Marshfolk and free traders, and we don't bow the knee to any man. Am I right?"

There was a full-throated roar at that, mostly out of relief at finding something to agree with. Joss shouted encouragement, got feet drumming on the floor, fists on tables. "Doomsday and Dymchurch!" he cried.

"Doomsday and Dymchurch!"

Joss gave it a minute, then raised his hands for silence. His split knuckles were oozing; they stung. "Let's be clear. Tom's the best boatman we've got, right? Good as Uncle Sam was. Give him time, maybe he'll be that good on land."

"Not likely, he's half fish," Matt said, and got a laugh.

"Every one of you knows Ma held this family and Dymchurch trade together when we lost Sam and my pa. She's led us to where we are now. When we stand together, me and Tom and Ma and Sophy and all of us—Doomsdays and Doomsday men—we can run rings round the Preventives. If we fall out—well, what's that they say? We hang together, or we hang separately. Right?"

"Right!"

"So," Joss said. "Ma. Young Luke will carry a scar all his life. If he wasn't fast, he'd be dead. What's your judgement on the man who did that?"

The room silenced. Ma looked levelly at him for a long moment. Her face wasn't showing much, but Joss knew his ma, and he could see the flickers of feeling: anger, pain, and, increasingly, shame.

"I've not been fair," she said at last. "Not for a long time, maybe. This—a child, his own son—No. You're right, Josiah. I wasn't fair and I can't be. You make the judgement."

Joss nodded, making it grave and respectful because Ma Doomsday admitting fault was not a thing you heard every day, or decade. "I say, Elijah needs to beg forgiveness of Luke, and of you, Ma. He's never to be alone with Luke again. He can do the odd jobs, carrying and sweeping or whatever needs doing, till he's earned our trust back. And the next time he raises a hand to anyone, Doomsday or not, without your or my say-so, he's out for good."

"And if he doesn't agree to that?" Ma asked.

"Then he's no man of ours, and let the whole Marsh know it." Which meant no free drinks, no consequence-free bullying, and likely a few unpleasant evenings for Elijah as the many people he'd offended took their chance for vengeance.

Ma considered a moment, then nodded. "Very well."

A babble erupted. Ma gestured to Aunt Mary to go behind the bar: ale would be in order.

"Got away with that, en," Sophy said from the corner of her mouth.

Granda, in the corner, nodded him over. Joss approached and knelt by his chair. "Granda?"

"Handled that as well as you might have," Asa said softly. "Tell me one thing, Joss. You risked a lot just now. Is he worth the risk?"

Joss looked up, breath stuttering. Asa put a hand to his face, gently brushing back stray hair. "I'm an old man: I've seen plenty of the world. You're a grandson to be proud of, and I love you. Now answer me."

"I, uh. I did that acause Elijah forced my hand."

"You could have lied. I've known you lie—otherwhiles."

Granda had often used Kentish words to make his young grand-children laugh at how they sounded in his Georgia drawl. Joss, a grown man, found his lips curving responsively even now, which made it almost easy to say, "I didn't want to, Granda."

Asa nodded slowly, as though Joss had said a lot more. "Well, he's a good-hearted man, and nicely mannered too. We could do with more of that. Bring him round to visit me."

Joss was not often lost for words, but he'd have needed a much longer run-up to this conversation. A full day to prepare would have been good, or maybe a week. "Don't know if he'll be wanting to come back after this," he managed.

"Not sure of yourself?" Asa said. "There's something I don't see every day." He gave Joss's head an affectionate push. "Get on, Josiah. I'll be waiting."

A few hours and far too much talk later, Joss went to Tench House. He did so openly, with Matt Molash and Sophy, who had insisted on getting the lay of the land, not to mention a nose-around. She was probably as good a watchman as any; she might not be as strong as the men, but he'd never known a more unrepentantly dirty fighter.

Graveyard was sitting out the front of the house, rather than in the lane. Someone had given him a chair to sit on. "Joss."

"Anyone come?"

Graveyard shook his head. Joss took a deep breath and knocked. Catherine Inglis answered. "Well. Joss Doomsday."

"May we come in, mistress? Think you've got my cousin."

"We do."

Joss wiped his feet carefully. Sophy followed suit. She was wearing breeches, he realised belatedly; that was probably not right for a Quality home. Mrs. Inglis didn't comment, but she was a Marshwoman.

Gareth and Luke were seated at the tea table with several empty plates and the remains of what had been a substantial cake, plus a couple of books between them. They both turned as Joss came in, Luke warily, Gareth with his face tense. Luke had on a clean shirt that looked too large for him in place of his own blood-soaked one. In Gareth's parlour, wearing his shirt, and Joss hated himself for the stupid stab of envy he felt.

"Mr. Doomsday."

"Sir Gareth," Joss said. "Can I have a word with you, and Mrs. Inglis too?"

"Certainly," Mrs. Inglis said. "Please go to the kitchen. Miss Sophy, help yourself to cake."

"Thank you kindly, mistress," Sophy said, already heading to the table. Marvellous. Luke and Sophy both got to sit in the parlour; Joss was firmly relegated to the kitchen.

They went through and shut the door. Joss said, "Look, first thing, how's Luke?"

"If you haven't beaten Elijah Doomsday to death, you ought to," Mrs. Inglis said, so calmly that it brought the hairs on Joss's arms up. "That child has bruises all over his arm and chest and back. There's a boot mark."

"The devil." Joss shut his eyes. "I didn't know it was that bad."

"I thought you knew everything," Gareth said. "He's in a great deal of pain, and ravaged by guilt. I've told him none of this is his fault—probably inaccurately, but there we are—and I expect you'll have to let him unburden himself too. He seems very concerned with your good opinion. I've been trying to take his mind off things with a Latin primer. Your grandfather wasn't joking about his intelligence, by the way. He's giving it half his attention with eight stitches in his face and he's on chapter three already."

Joss gathered that was good. "He should be at school, then?"

"He's wasted on the Marsh."

That stung, and Gareth would know it. Joss tried to meet his eyes, but Gareth wasn't looking at him. "Right. I'm grateful for you taking him off. It got a bit nasty."

"I promised him my protection."

Joss had no idea what protection Gareth thought he could provide if Elijah turned up angry. "I'm grateful," he said again.

"He can stay as long as he needs," Catherine Inglis said. "We have space. He needs feeding up."

We feed him! Joss wanted to protest, but his role in this conversation was clearly to be given a severe call-over while Luke and Sophy ate cake, and maybe he deserved it. "When your larder's bare, send him back. Should be about a day and a half."

That got a smile, at least from Mrs. Inglis. "We will."

"Right. And—can we talk about Mr. Henry Inglis?"

Gareth's face tightened. "I haven't had a chance to tell Catherine about that yet. I will later—actually, no, I'll tell you now. I wouldn't want you not to know something important that was going on, Catherine, since it involves you." He left a nasty little pause there to make sure Joss got the point. "I'm very much afraid my father was involved in guinea-smuggling with my uncle."

Her lips parted. "Oh, no. Gareth, *no*."

He went over it with impressive brevity. Lawyer training, probably. "So we can't trust my uncle, and Lionel's probably in on it. I don't want either of them in the house again, or near Cecy."

"No." Catherine Inglis was winding her fingers together. "But why? Hugo had plenty of money for his own wants. Why would he do this?"

"He'd made some losses on investments," Gareth said. "I suppose he started doing it for Uncle Henry as an easy way to replenish his coffers, and then realised if he stole the lot, he wouldn't have to make any more effort at all."

"Oh," she said. "When you put it that way...yes. Oh dear. So what now?"

"I'll have people watching," Joss said. "Best if you and Miss Cecy don't walk alone for a while, mistress, between this business and Elijah."

"That would be very kind." Mrs. Inglis's lips were pale. "Are we in danger?"

"From Sweetwater and Elijah, perhaps," Gareth said. "My family may be involved in smuggling, but at least they don't try to murder one another."

"There's ten thousand guineas in play," Joss said. "People have killed for a lot less."

"Perhaps, but there's no point in killing us for it, since we don't have it!"

"Tell your Uncle Henry that. You'll have Graveyard and Matt here tonight. I need a private word with Sir Gareth, mistress."

"Certainly," Mrs. Inglis said. "I'll be in the parlour."

She left, shutting the door, and they were alone. Gareth's expression didn't suggest he was pleased about this.

"Well," he said. "That was a delightful surprise you sprung on me. What the devil, Joss?"

"I'm sorry."

"Sorry? You let me chat away about my family troubles without telling me that your appalling *thing* of an uncle knew about us and was blackmailing you? We must have walked a mile and you didn't get round to *mentioning* it? My God, how much contempt do you hold me in?"

"I don't! Gareth—"

"You must. Indulging my worries about my uncle's foolery—"

"He's a guinea-runner!"

"Yours is an extortioner!" Gareth snarled back in the strangulated tone of a man trying to shout and whisper at the same time. "Your uncle *knew*, your cousin knew, and you didn't tell me because, what, I'd have panicked? You didn't think I needed to know? You're Joss Doomsday and you handle everything, and I'm merely the fancy man you pamper?"

"I do handle things, yes," Joss said. "I've done the best I can—"

"You said we were *safe*. You said we were safe in the Warren and the looker's hut, and I believed you!"

"I tried!"

Gareth wasn't listening. "And that poor little swine, crying all the way here and trying not to sniff in case I noticed. Do you have any idea what he's been through?"

"Look, I'm sorry for him too, but you realise he sneaked round after us and went running to Elijah with what he saw?" Joss snapped. "He can be grateful I'm not wringing his neck."

"*You* might have been a fully fledged man of action at thirteen. Most of us are stupid, spotty, and scared. He told me he wanted his father to think he was useful, do you realise that? His father, who threatened that revolting thing—My God. What good is all the talk of being Joss Doomsday and looking after your people when there's a boy being treated that way under your nose?"

"I didn't know!" Joss shouted. "You think I'd have let that go on if I'd realised it was that bad?"

"You should have realised!"

"How? I'm not a magician! I've been trying to manage the trade and the family and Elijah and Sweetwater—and us, too, acause you might say you don't want me doing anything, but someone's got to—"

"You said you'd handle things! You can't take charge of every-thing and then complain that other people let you!"

"You can't let people take charge and then complain when they do!"

Both their voices had risen. Gareth made a furious shushing noise. Joss scrubbed at his face, striving for calm. "Hell and the devil. I know I made a mess, Gareth. I was trying to sort it out."

"I'm sure you would have. And what then?" Gareth asked. "If we hadn't encountered your uncle, would you have ever told me what was happening, or would you have gone off and fixed it in some nefarious way and made sure I never knew?"

Joss opened his mouth, and shut it again. Gareth took a very long breath. When he spoke, it was in a clipped, controlled voice that sounded like he was keeping a grip on himself. "I didn't think so. I'm sure you're trying to do your best, Joss. And it's my fault too. My fault for believing we were safe in the Warren, just as much as yours for saying so. My fault for letting you run things, run us, because it's very easy to let you take charge. You're right. I shouldn't have done that."

"That's not what I meant."

Gareth ignored that. "I relied on you too much—unfairly, because as you say, you have too much on your plate—but you didn't rely on me at all. You couldn't say *I let you down* or even *Something's gone wrong* and trust me to listen or understand, let alone to help." His expressive face radiated hurt. "How can you be on my side when you don't give me a chance to be on yours? What does that mean when you don't trust me?"

"I do!"

"You don't, or you would have told me."

Joss couldn't find a reply. Gareth raised his hands hopelessly. "I needed to know, and that you didn't tell me makes me feel as though you consider me a-a responsibility. A problem to be solved, not someone you talk to on equal terms. And I dare say I deserve that—"

"No. Gareth—"

"I'm tired of being a problem," Gareth said. "My father considered me an inconvenience, you consider me an incapable, and my family considers me a-a sluice gate to the source of funding. I'm *tired* of it."

"I don't think you're an incapable, that's not true. But what were you going to do about Elijah if I'd told you?"

"I don't know. We might have found out if you had."

They looked at each other, then Gareth shook his head, looking very weary. "You should go. I expect you need to deal with your uncle, considering he's still in a position to destroy us."

"Nobody's going to listen to him now."

"I'm sure you can handle it. Go and be Joss Doomsday. It's what you do best."

He walked out on that. Joss stared after him.

Gareth had been quite reasonable, really. Fair, even, in the circumstances. Not losing his temper, not throwing blame around where it wasn't merited, talking about what he felt instead of flying off at a tangent. He'd said before he'd try to handle arguments better, and he had.

And he'd been right, and Joss had been entirely, shamefully wrong, and now he didn't know what to do.

Nineteen

Four days later, Gareth went into Dymchurch for divine service. It passed the time.

He hadn't seen Joss since the argument in the kitchen, which was probably for the best. It didn't *feel* like the best. It felt like Romney Marsh was a howling desolation of rank grass and foul water, an expense of spirit in a waste of shame. He didn't go near the looker's hut, or the Warren, or even the dyke where they'd sat, because if he did, he had a terrible feeling he'd end up riding to the Revelation post-haste and begging Joss to forgive him.

He wasn't going to do that. He'd leaned too much on Joss, and he'd known at the time it wasn't fair to his lover, but he hadn't realised quite how bad it was for himself. He'd been dependent far too much of his life and now that he could stand up for himself, he needed to get in the habit of doing so.

He'd made a good stab at taking charge with his cousin, which was a mild satisfaction amid the misery. Lionel had brought Cecilia back to the house a little while after Joss had left. He'd been all charm, she flattered and fluttering. Gareth had put something of a damper on the atmosphere by informing Lionel he wouldn't set foot on the property or escort Cecy again. Oddly, he'd been all the more effective for his heartsickness: he hadn't been remotely interested in arguing with Lionel, and his indifferent dismissal had worked better than strong words ever had. Doubtless Graveyard's sizeable presence in the garden had also helped persuade Lionel to leave, but still. Gareth felt it was another step in asserting himself. Maybe one day he'd feel like a baronet, or a man who could stand equal with Joss.

He had tried hard to think about other things, of which there was no shortage. Luke had stayed three nights in the end, having developed a slight fever on his first evening with them. Catherine had fed him enough to keep Napoleon's forces on the march; Gareth had dug out the rest of his old textbooks. They had talked, too, for hours, about being unwanted by one's father, and the absence of mothers, and families in which one didn't seem to belong. Luke had cried; so had Gareth, once or twice. He wasn't sure if he'd got things right—he hadn't talked to a thirteen-year-old boy since he'd been one—but Catherine seemed to approve.

Cecy didn't. There had been a scene of no common order after Lionel's dismissal, until at last Catherine sat her down and told her what they suspected. Gareth wasn't sure he'd have done that, but he wasn't in a position to recommend withholding information in order to protect people.

Not that she'd been grateful to be told. "But what about William?" she'd wept. "If he finds out—my own father a guinea-smuggler—If people know—I'll never be invited to the Topgoods again!"

"It's none of our faults," Catherine had repeated, but Cecilia was currently staying inside and refusing to show her face, except on occasional forays for cake. She had declined to accompany him to church. Catherine, curate's daughter turned mistress, never went. Gareth didn't ask about that.

Joss's absence also meant Gareth had no access to the vast Doomsday information network. He didn't have any idea if Uncle Henry was still in Dymchurch, or Lionel still staying with the Topgoods. He sincerely hoped they'd gone home and, once a few days had passed without incident, persuaded himself they must have done. They'd have cut their losses, accepted that Gareth didn't have the money, and returned to London, never to darken the Marsh again.

He'd hoped that very much, and it was therefore an unpleasant dose of reality to see Lionel walking down the aisle of St. Peter and St. Paul, following the Squire and Lady Topgood to their pew, Miss Topgood on his arm.

Gareth would have left if he could, but he was in the middle of a pew and didn't want to attract attention. He sat, therefore, and attempted to keep his mind on the service with only limited success. It didn't help that the vicar was not a talented sermoniser. Nobody could have paid close attention to whatever he had to say on whatever parable it was; Gareth couldn't afterwards have guessed.

The gentry left the church first, of course. Lionel processed down the aisle with the Topgoods, wearing a charming smile which stiffened and then broadened unpleasantly when he set eyes on Gareth.

Gareth dawdled. Perhaps it was cowardly; he preferred to think of it as tactics. He exchanged pleasantries with the few people he knew and left the church at a leisurely pace. It wasn't enough, because the Topgoods and Lionel were still outside as he came out onto the High Street.

He'd have liked to walk past but the Dymchurch Squire

couldn't be ignored, still less Lady Topgood. He greeted them both and received a response he couldn't persuade himself was warm. Lady Topgood gave him two fingers; the Squire frowned. He was horribly aware of Lionel lurking beside them, smiling.

"Now, Sir Gareth," Sir Anthony said in his bluff, frank, crass way. "What's this I hear about a falling-out between you and your cousin, and uncle too? It's a sorry business indeed when families can't be civil."

"Quite right," Lady Topgood said, with a chilly look at Gareth. "One may have disagreements, but magnanimity is the mark of a gentleman."

"I've a temper myself but I can accept when I'm in the wrong. You young men need to learn that much." The Squire gave Gareth a forceful nudge. "You haven't come to visit in an age. Come to dinner. You and young Lionel here can thrash things out. I tell you what, shake hands on it now and make up, hey?"

"I should be delighted," Lionel said, smile curling on his face, and extended his hand.

Gareth ignored it. "Thank you for your concern, Sir Anthony, but I shouldn't dream of troubling you with private family affairs."

"Nonsense. We're all friends, I hope. You'll accompany us home."

"Oh, don't pester Sir Gareth, Papa," Miss Topgood said sharply. "I'm sure Mr. Inglis will keep us very well entertained by himself. If Sir Gareth doesn't choose to apologise to his cousin, that is his affair."

Lionel had obviously done good work there, blackening his name. Gareth wasn't surprised; any surprise he felt was more around how little he cared. He opened his mouth to agree and bid them farewell, but Lionel got in first.

"I do hope you will at least one day let poor little Cecilia visit on the Marsh again. Really, she is *very* young, and I don't blame her in the slightest for her, ah, misapprehension or her very flattering enthusiasm." He spoke with patronising amusement. Miss Topgood, to whom Cecilia looked up as the most sophisticated young lady on the Marsh, gave a conspiratorial giggle.

Cecy. He'd claimed Gareth had thrown them out because of Cecy, and Gareth could all too easily imagine the picture he'd painted, with his charm and good looks, of embarrassing, unrequited girlish affections. He'd flung her to the wolves to make himself look better, and the wave of fury rushed through Gareth as if the Wall itself had burst.

"Cecilia may visit as she pleases, as long as I can be sure she will not meet unworthy company, because *her* behaviour has never merited criticism. And I thought you were here pursuing business, Lionel, not pleasure. Have you told Sir Anthony about your father's dealings in Romney Marsh yet? I'm sure he'd be fascinated by what you have been doing."

If he'd ever doubted Lionel's involvement, he couldn't now. The mask of the charmer dropped away for a second, Lionel's eyes widening and nostrils flaring before he got himself under control. "We needn't bore anyone with our tedious family transactions, need we?"

"Yours. Not mine," Gareth said. "I'm not involved, so talking about them to anyone wouldn't trouble me in the slightest. I will be very happy to, in fact. I expect you'll be leaving the Marsh soon."

"I'll stay here as long as I please," Lionel said savagely.

"I should think you had work to do in London. Isn't there something of a hole in Uncle Henry's accounts to repair?"

Lionel lunged. Gareth didn't expect it at all, and he stumbled backwards, even as Lionel caught himself and lowered his half-raised fist.

"Good God. Gentlemen!" Sir Anthony protested.

Lionel's mouth twisted, a snarl that was trying for a smile. "I do beg your pardon, Sir Anthony, Lady Topgood, but I cannot stand by to hear sneers against my father." He swung back to Gareth. "I don't know why you have set yourself up in enmity to the man who looked after you as a son, who gave you a home—"

"Oh, yes you do," Gareth snapped.

Lionel jabbed a finger at him, prodding his shoulder painfully hard. Gareth slapped his hand away; Lionel knocked his back. "I won't tolerate this malice." Prod. "You have never been grateful." Prod. "Ignoring my father's kindnesses—"

His jabbing finger came in again and bounced off a hand. A brown hand with scabbed knuckles, outstretched between Gareth and Lionel.

"That'll do, sir," Joss said.

"Who the devil are you? Get out of my way!"

"Can't do that, sir." Joss sounded very reasonable, but his hand had closed on Lionel's outstretched finger and Lionel's arm was bending steadily. "Outmarsh laying hand on Marshman? Can't have that in Dymchurch. Can we, Squire?"

"Now, Joss," Sir Anthony said.

"What are you blethering about, you insolent clodhopper?" Lionel demanded. "Let go!"

Joss shoved his hand away and stepped forward. Lionel recoiled, and bumped into Graveyard, who was behind him. "What—"

Joss was right up in his face, but his voice was level as the Marsh itself. "What I mean is, outmarsh—that's you, sir—doesn't lay hand on Marshman—that's Sir Gareth, sir. Hear me, *sir*?"

"There's no need for trouble, Joss," the Squire said, not quite assertively enough. "Mr. Inglis is my guest. He doesn't know the Marsh's ways."

Joss looked at Lionel for an unnervingly long and silent moment, then inclined his head respectfully to Sir Anthony. "Beg your pardon, Squire, very sorry to interfere. Didn't realise you were keeping order. If you'll excuse the interruption, I've a word for your ear."

"I dare say I can spare the time." The Squire's tone suggested he was conferring a boon. It was almost impressive. "Excuse me. And we shall have no more disputation, gentleman," he added firmly to Lionel and Gareth.

He and Joss stepped aside. Behind them, Sophy Doomsday had drawn Lady and Miss Topgood into an intent discussion. She was plainly dressed in drab brown skirts, while the gentlewomen were resplendent in the lace trim and satin gloves of their Sunday finery, but they were both listening to her in silence.

Lionel had taken a second to recover from the interruption. He turned back to Gareth now, red with anger.

As if Gareth cared. *Marshman—that's Sir Gareth.* Joss had said it in front of everyone, and nobody had laughed, or argued, or denied it. Joss Doomsday had said it, so it was true, and his cousin's bluster seemed suddenly absurd.

"Romney Marsh, Lionel," he said. "It's mostly like this. Go home. If you stay, I will not hesitate to give everything I know to the appropriate authorities, here and in London."

Lionel's face spasmed. "You would not dare."

"Try me. Get away, and stay away. And if you dare speak one more word about my sister, you wretched self-satisfied bully, I will give you the thrashing you deserve."

"You?" Lionel said, disbelieving. "You think *you* could lay a finger on me?"

He'd bullied Gareth all his life, always with Uncle Henry or a mob of friends at his back, and it was with no shame whatsoever and a gleeful sense of tables finally turning that Gareth replied, "Well, maybe I couldn't. But I know people who can."

Graveyard slapped a beefsteak-sized palm onto Lionel's shoulder, making him stagger. "Outmarsh," he said, in a voice like grinding boulders.

"What does that *mean*?"

"Excuse the interruption, Sir Gareth." It was Luke, manifesting out of thin air in true Doomsday style. Lionel recoiled. In fairness, the boy was not a lovely sight, with the inflamed wound curved round his eye and the black stitches across it.

"Luke, good morning. How are you feeling?"

"Excuse me," Lionel said furiously. "I am talking to you!"

"Well enough, thank you, sir." Luke slid between Gareth and his cousin as he spoke. Finty had drifted up too, with the result that Lionel was surrounded. Not that either Luke or Finty was physically impressive, but Graveyard skewed the average more than somewhat. "I've a message from my great-uncle, sir. He'd appreciate the favour of a visit, *if* you'd care for pleasanter company—"

Lionel was red with anger. Luke could have that effect. "Move, you revolting wretch! Get your damned repulsive face out of my sight!"

Luke's head jerked back, as if from a blow, and Gareth's fingers clenched to white-knuckled fists. "How dare you," he said, loud enough that heads snapped his way. "How *dare* you speak to him like that? If you have no compassion, have you not even manners? And you call yourself a gentleman? You contemptible scrub."

Lionel gave an incredulous laugh. "Cousin, you've been addled by country living."

"On the contrary," Gareth said. "I see many things more clearly these days, and one is that you are as cowardly as you are vicious." He didn't care if Lionel struck out. Let him, and Gareth would not hide behind Joss if he did. Luke was watching, hand raised to hide his disfigurement, and Gareth wanted to kick Lionel and his casual cruelty all the way to the Wall and off it. "Apologise to him. Apologise, damn you!"

Lionel gaped at him. "To an impertinent hick?"

Sophy came in there, with a plaintive quaver in her very carrying voice. "My own cousin, miss. A poor, hurt motherless boy, with no one to care for him."

"Shocking," Miss Topgood said with surprising indignation. "What a rude and heartless man."

Lionel's face changed. He turned to her, doubtless wanting to repair his position, and saw everyone was watching.

Lady Topgood had drawn herself to her full height with stiff offence, which Gareth could not believe was on Luke's behalf. Miss Topgood raised her chin and very markedly gave Lionel her shoulder. Sir Anthony, who still had Joss at his side, was looking daggers at his house guest.

Joss was watching Gareth. His gaze felt like a touch.

"Uh," Lionel said. "Of course, if I have misspoken—"

Joss bowed respectfully and stepped away from Sir Anthony. "Thank you, Squire, and I'm sorry for the trouble I've brought you. Your servant, my lady, Miss Topgood. That's a very charming shawl, if I may say, miss."

"Thank you, Joss." Miss Topgood gave him a coquettish smile. "I fear it's sadly worn."

"Ah, that's a shame. Dare say you'll need new. A brocaded silk would suit you well, maybe?"

She batted a hand at him. "Joss Doomsday, you're a dreadful rogue."

"Come, Laura, Sir Anthony," Lady Topgood said. "Good day, Sir Gareth, and we shall hope to see you soon. Mr. Inglis, we are returning." That last came out in a very different and exceedingly icy tone.

"Oh, dear," Gareth said. Lionel returned a look of baffled resentment and hurried to catch up with his hosts as they walked off.

Finty and Graveyard were both contemplating him. Gareth said, "Er, thank you."

"Thank *you*, sir," Finty said. "Nasty bit of work, that one, begging your pardon. Come on, young 'un, time for scran."

Luke hesitated. "You'll come and see Great-Uncle, Sir Gareth?"

"As soon as I can. And you must come to us again, very soon. Catherine won't know what else to do with her cake."

Luke opened his mouth, then flung his arms round Gareth's waist in a quick, hard, entirely unexpected hug, and darted off without a word.

Gareth looked after him, then back. Sophy had vanished. Joss was watching him with something raw and painful on his face, and his throat moved in a slight swallow.

"Um," Gareth said.

Joss's lips parted silently, then he blinked, and the usual self-possession was back in place. "Might I have a word at your convenience, Sir Gareth?"

"Now?"

"Bit fraped now, sir. I'll come to you later, if that'll do?"

He had to put the *sir* in: they were in the middle of the street as well as the middle of an argument. Gareth still hated it. "Very well."

Twenty

GARETH HAD LUNCHEON AT HOME. HE WEEDED THE GARDEN, alert to every rustle in case it might be Joss scaling the wall. He attempted to write up his observations from yesterday's walk, and then, failing that, tried to read a book. He didn't go out in case he missed Joss.

He was doubtless an idiot, and a weakling, and he ought to be marshalling arguments about how Joss's concealment had been utterly unforgivable, but he couldn't quite remember why.

Joss arrived after nightfall. He came to the front door, where Matt Molash was on duty.

"Evening, Sir Gareth. All right, you get off, Matt. I'm watching tonight."

"You, Joss?"

"Don't ask a man to do a job you wouldn't do yourself. A'night."

Molash headed off. Joss shot Gareth a look. "Can I come in?"

"Yes. Uh. Study, perhaps."

Cecy was in the parlour, and Catherine the kitchen. The study was clearly the appropriate room to conduct business. It was also on the side of the house where the window was screened by a wall, and he'd already drawn the curtains, not that those things were at all relevant.

They went in and Gareth secured the door and lit the lamp. Joss glanced around. "That's a lot of books."

"My father's, mostly."

Joss frowned at the annotated map of the Marsh. "What's this?"

"My father's key to where he found different creatures. He says there are stag beetles in Blackmanstone. I went yesterday but I didn't see any."

"Is that the big black ones with horns like antlers? Shorn-bugs, we say. Sorry you didn't see 'em."

"I'll look again. It might be a little early in the year." Gareth had no idea what to say, how to make a start. "About this morning—"

"I stuck my oar in," Joss said. "You didn't ask me to, and you could have handled him yourself. You *were*. Only, outmarsh doesn't raise a hand to Marshman, and I can't let that stand. No," he added, as if correcting himself before Gareth could. "I can't let it stand, but I couldn't watch that anyway, on the Marsh or off it, so I interfered. I know."

Gareth's skin was tingling all over again. *Marshman*. And not said for an audience, either: that was for him.

"I didn't ask you to," he said. "But I understand why you did it. And the truth is, he bullied me throughout my childhood, usually with his own gang of friends, and it was marvellous to see him get a taste of his own medicine."

"If I'd known you'd say that, I'd have proper leathered him." Joss shoved his hands into his hair. "I'm truly sorry for before, Gareth. I should have told you, and I knew it, and why I didn't... I was ashamed. Ashamed of Elijah, as who wouldn't be, and more ashamed of myself. I let you down. I promised we were safe when we weren't. I said I could handle everything, while all the time my own blood was turning on me. I boasted, is the truth. I liked you thinking I could do anything, but I can't. I made a mess for us both by trying, and a far worse one by trying to hide it. It's not I didn't trust you, I swear. It's that I didn't want to admit I'd failed you."

Gareth grabbed his hand. "You didn't fail me, Joss, for God's sake. It was bad luck and a foul man, and that hobbledehoy cousin of yours."

"No such thing as luck. And I failed Luke too, badly. You were right, about all of it. I need to do a lot of things better, and if I can't get things right because I've too much to do, well, it's up to me to see that and say it. There's other people ready and willing to take responsibility. Just, I've been fighting to be in charge for so long, it's hard to let go. Stupid." His hair was hanging loose round his shoulders; he pushed it back with a frustrated gesture. "And I'm sorry. For failing you, for being a coward about it, and for getting you wrong. It's truly not that I thought you were weak, but I had no idea how strong you were."

"Me?" Gareth said faintly.

"You. The way you stood for Luke, against Elijah, and Ma—you could have lost an arm there—and your cousin Lionel, too. Luke told me what he said."

"I'm so sorry about that. Is he all right?"

Joss exhaled. "Dare say a dunnamany arseholes will come out with things like that in his life. But that Lionel was the first, and you called him over proper-like, and Luke will remember that. You did my job for me there, London, and not for the first time. Because you're stronger than you think, or I knew, and that's on me for not seeing it. Not looking. There's a lot of things I never saw before you. And I've made a mess of us, and let Luke down, and got so many things wrong, and..." His golden-brown eyes were fixed on

Gareth, their intensity draining the air from the room. "And I need you on my side. Any chance I can lean on you a while?"

"You idiot," Gareth said, and somehow Joss was in his arms and they were kissing frantically, mouth to hungry mouth, locked in desperate need to be closer, hands clamped on heads and hips, pulling one another in. Gareth stumbled back and got his arse on the edge of the desk, which put his head at a more convenient height and Joss firmly between his thighs. They kissed their way past the hurt and the loneliness, kissed themselves back together, until at last Joss dropped his head onto Gareth's shoulder.

"Hearts alive. Gareth."

"I missed you."

"Me too."

Gareth kissed his ear. "Did you mean what you said?"

"All of it."

"Even calling me a Marshman?"

"Specially that." Joss nuzzled into his neck, lips buzzing against Gareth's skin as he spoke. "The way you look at things? Standing up for a Marsh lad? You belong here. I know it's not London or fancy and there's no grand society or baronet things to be had, but—you look *right* when you're out there. It's where you should be."

Gareth squeezed his eyes shut. He was *not* going to cry. That was a ridiculous thing to cry over. He pushed his face into Joss's hair. "I feel right here. I feel right with you."

"Better had. Acause there's nobody else I want, on the Marsh or off it. I told my ma I'd leave over this."

"What?"

"Over all of it. I said I'd go about my business without interference, or I'd be off and someone else could be gaffer in my stead. I didn't mention you." His hands tightened. "But I was thinking of you."

"Joss—"

Joss leaned back to look at him. "You told me once I smiled in London more than I smiled on the Marsh. Remember?"

Gareth had mentioned that one night in the looker's hut. Joss had given a vague sort of grunt in reply. "I said it. I didn't think you agreed."

"I maybe didn't, but it stuck. I've thought about it a fair few times since. And if I can't live free on my own ground, well, the world's bigger than Romney Marsh. Not better," he added quickly, "but bigger."

That was still a remarkable concession. "Would you really leave?"

"I'll do what I have to. But I said what I wanted, and looks like they don't have anyone else to do the dirty work. Well. And." He took a breath. "There's people who don't know what Elijah's been saying, and people who don't care, and seems there's people who didn't need him to tell them and they don't care either."

"Oh." Gareth pulled him tighter. "Oh, Joss."

"My granda." Joss burrowed into him. "He wants to meet you proper. Friendly-like."

"Your—oh, good God. Luke gave me a message from him earlier, asking me to call."

"If he had his legs we'd be in so much trouble," Joss muttered. "You don't have to."

"I will if you want me to. You do realise he made me promise to help Luke, before everything happened? How much of all that did he know was coming?"

"My granda sees a lot for a man who hardly leaves his chair."

"I'd love to meet him properly," Gareth said. "If you honestly think it's all right."

"He doesn't play games. And for the rest, well, that's how things are, and Sophy reckons I've got away with it, so we'll see."

That wasn't a ringing endorsement, but Gareth had a strong suspicion Joss was trying to avoid tempting fate. He tightened his arms. "And you threatened to leave the Marsh. I'm still struggling with that. What's happened to you?"

"You," Joss said simply, and kissed him.

Gareth broke free after some moments. "Let me breathe. You are absurdly demanding. A dreadful rogue," he added, mimicking Miss Topgood.

"Little madam. 'Oh, my sadly worn shawl, dear Joss,' every time. Still, it keeps the Squire sweet."

"What was Sophy saying to her and Lady Topgood?"

"Right. That." Joss sat back, which more or less put him sitting on Gareth's lap, arms round Gareth's neck for balance. Gareth briefly considered throwing out all his chairs. "So, there's been a few things happened since we spoke."

"Start with Elijah. Matt Molash said you'd disowned him."

"Well. Once he woke up—I gave him a fair drubbing—Ma told him what he'd have to do to make up. Learn a bit of humility and control his temper, is what it came to, and he didn't like it one bit. He whined and cajoled, but she wasn't having it, not after stitching Luke up. So that put him in middling order."

"Is that more or less angry than being two men?"

Joss grinned. Gareth had missed his smile so painfully; it bathed him in sunlight now. "Maybe a bit less, but he wasn't happy. He told her to go to hell, called her a jack whore and a rammish bitch and more. She heard him out patient-like, didn't say a word. Then she knocked him across the room with a frying pan, dragged him out of the Revelation by the scruff of his neck, and kicked him into the road."

"*Yes,*" Gareth said, with intense relish. "Good Lord, I wish I'd been there."

"It was a sight. And she apologised to me, after. My ma's not the easiest. She hasn't had it easy herself. But we had a proper talk, her and me. I got some things off my chest, she said some things I needed to hear. It was good."

"I'm so glad." Gareth leaned in for a swift kiss. "That's marvellous. So, Elijah..."

"Lurking around, whining. But everyone on the Marsh knows he's been thrown out of the family for trying to kill his own son, so I doubt anyone's listening to his spite. And there's a fair few folk owe him a kicking who'll be taking their chances. I reckon he's spiked his own guns."

"Good."

"So that's my uncle," Joss said. "Then there's yours. You know he's staying in Rye, at the Mermaid?"

"I didn't. What's he doing there?"

"That's what I wanted to know so I had young Emily go work there a night or two and see what she could learn."

"Of course you did," Gareth said.

Joss looked as close as he got to guilty. "Well, I thought you might need to know, and the chance wouldn't come twice. But it's only between me and Em so if you don't want to hear it—"

"No, I do want to hear. And I understand that you work for—for people you care about, and I'd be very sorry if I wasn't one of them. Only, I want to be part of it. Consulted."

"I did think of asking you," Joss said. "But you were angry, so I thought you'd say no—ah, drat, that's worse, isn't it? Sorry, London. I'm not good at this."

They'd been mid-argument, Gareth had dressed Joss down as badly as ever he had anyone, and he'd still gone out of his way to work on Gareth's behalf. Gareth wondered how it was possible to be at once annoyed and hopelessly charmed. "Practice more," he suggested.

"I truly will. I'm not closing you out, I promise. There's a fair few things I've got to tell you now, to that end."

He sounded serious. Gareth said, "Go on."

"Em's a good girl, with sharp ears. She says Uncle Henry and your boy Lionel had a bit of a set-to. She couldn't follow all of it, but what your uncle said was, *I can't hide those losses,* and *If I don't replace the funds we're ruined.* So—"

"Wait. 'Replace'? Is that the word he used?"

"Em wrote it down. She's quick with her letters. That mean something to you?"

"What it—let's say implies," Gareth said slowly, "is that if Uncle Henry borrowed the money, it was the sort of borrowing that doesn't involve asking the lender first. He's a trustee for several estates, which means he has control of large sums that he's meant to look after for other people. My God, Joss. What if he's been speculating in guineas with clients' money?"

"So he'd need to put the money back before anyone found it had gone?"

"If a trusteeship was coming to an end, say, or he had been asked to supply accounts unexpectedly. No wonder Lionel was so angry this morning. I threatened to report them to the authorities, which felt rather hollow as I've no way to prove they were involved in the guinea trade. But it would be child's play to discover that he'd misused funds, and that's a serious offence. Oh God. If they think I've threatened that—"

Joss's arms tightened. "They weren't keen on you anyway. And won't be any fonder of me now. I told Squire he'd do well to look into Mr. Inglis's finances before he let Lionel dance attendance on his daughter."

"The Squire takes that advice from you?" Gareth asked. "Good Lord. I suppose he expects you to know everything."

"Well, I'm gaffer, and he's bone idle. And Sophy told Miss Topgood and her ladyship how Lionel was with the barmaids at the Mermaid. They didn't like that."

"*Is* he offensive or was that a convenient fiction?"

"Em said he was free with his hands. Might have played that up a bit."

"And of course they'll believe you. Good Lord, Joss."

"I reckon he's outstayed his welcome at Squire's. Nothing to stop him going to stay with his old man in Rye, of course. Except that I reckon everyone there's heard by now that your Uncle Henry works for the Revenue in London—"

"What? He does not. Where did that come from?"

"I told Emily to set it about."

"You—"

"I had to," Joss said hastily. "Been talking my way out of a lot of trouble the last couple of days, explaining why I'm mixed up in your affairs. Had to look after myself."

Gareth very much doubted that was the sole reason, but he didn't want to argue, and also the thought of Uncle Henry and Lionel facing concerted Marsh hostility was deeply pleasing. He gave a pointed sigh in lieu of argument. "You are actually evil sometimes, do you know that?"

"Eh, outmarsh," Joss said, summarising Uncle Henry's ultimate offence and his own justification in a single word. "That's mostly where we are, but there's something else I should say. Something— ugh. I don't know. I might be wrong about this."

His tone made Gareth's skin prickle, and not pleasantly. "You're worrying me."

"I've worried myself. It might be nothing, but I thought it, so I'm telling you." He put his hands on Gareth's shoulders, eyes very serious for a man sitting on his lap. "See, I was thinking about how you'd handle the guineas. Your uncle would need to get the gold in London and have a trustworthy man bring it down here. Can't put coin on a mail coach."

"The regular deliveries from London," Gareth said. He'd worked that out himself. "My father said it was books and scientific instruments. Nobody asked. Cecy wasn't interested, and Catherine—well, it was rather her role to not be interested, if you know what I mean."

"Ask no questions and you'll hear no lies. The goods were delivered here. Then I reckon Sir Hugo would send a message to Sweetwater, who'd send a man to pick up the chests. That's how Sir Hugo could tell brother Henry that the guineas had been collected and then sunk, and tell Sweetwater that there weren't any coming, and have them both believe him. Follow me?"

"It makes sense."

"All right. But Sir Hugo didn't keep the chests here. So where did he put them?"

"I've been thinking about that. What about a dyke? The gold wouldn't come to any harm in the water."

"Thinking like a free trader," Joss said approvingly. "We do stash cargo in the dykes otherwhiles. Problem is, first, the Preventives might go fishing. Second, a dry summer and the water levels drop fast. Third, you need to be sure of the chest, that the wood won't split or rot. And mostly, it's a merciful nuisance to get the goods out again. Nothing funny about manhandling heavy chests out of a dyke at night on your own."

"I suppose not."

"Ten thousand guineas is a fair weight, Sir Hugo wasn't young, and the Marsh isn't friendly to hand carts. So if the guineas aren't here, how would he move 'em around by himself?"

"You think someone helped him hide the money?" Gareth

frowned. "But might they not have mentioned it by now? Or, more likely, gone back and stolen it? If I knew where someone had concealed ten thousand guineas—"

"Coming to that," Joss said. "So, this Adam Drake that Bill Sweetwater asked about, I put Finty on it. He's an allworks lives in East Guildford. Odd jobs, fetching and carrying, kegman for Sweetwater. Big man, strong as a bull but not as sweet-natured. And one evening in early February, he told his wife he was off Dymchurch way for night-work, and never came home."

"What?"

"He's not been seen since. Mrs. Drake went to ask Nate Sweetwater after two days and he said it was nothing to do with him, and Drake had probably gone off with another woman. Didn't give a curse, she said. Only, I asked Nate when I spoke to him the other day, and he said he had set Bill looking for Drake because he couldn't just have his men go missing."

"He's looking now, but he didn't care at the time this man vanished?"

"Right. So that's one odd thing. And the next is, Drake vanished in early February. Your uncle dismissed you twentieth of February, right? Probably when he heard from your father the money had been lost. But the guineas must have been delivered some time before that, what with moving the shipment around and setting up the run, and posting the letter and what not."

"In other words, in early February." Gareth didn't know where this was heading but he didn't like it. "Joss, what are you saying?"

"I rode out to East Guildford to see Mrs. Drake today. She said Drake had done night work in Dymchurch maybe every four months for the last year and a half, regular, and some odd jobs round this way too, lately. And I thought...suppose Drake was the man who carried the guineas from here to Sweetwater. Suppose Sir

Hugo said he had another job for him. Suppose he hired Drake to carry the chests otherwhere-else and hide them."

"And then?"

"That's the question. Maybe Adam Drake stole the gold and ran away. Mrs. Drake didn't sound like she missed him any. If there's no love lost at home, and money to hand, why not get away and start again?"

"Oh! So my father stole from Uncle Henry, and Drake stole from him, and perhaps that's what caused his heart to give out, even?"

"And that's where the money's gone. Could be. Could well have happened. It's what I hope."

There was that note in his voice again. "What do you fear?" Gareth whispered.

Joss looked steadily at him. "There's merciful few people I'd trust to know where I'd hidden ten thousand guineas. And dead men don't tell tales."

Gareth made a convulsive movement. Joss slipped off his lap to let him stand, and Gareth took a few jerky, pointless steps. "Jesus Christ. *Jesus.*"

"It's just something I thought. I wasn't sure I should say at all, except—"

Except Gareth had said he wanted to be informed, and now he rather missed the comfort of ignorance. "Do you have the dates Drake worked in Dymchurch?"

Joss fished out a grimy bit of paper. "Best as Mrs. Drake remembered."

Gareth found his own memorandum of those unaccounted sums paid to his father. "Two months later," he said, looking between the papers. "Adam Drake works here and two months later my father gets paid. Every time."

"He was the guinea-carrier."

"The man who knew about it, the strong one who my father gave odd jobs to, so of course he'd have taken an extra task, wouldn't he? Hell's teeth." Gareth scrubbed at his face with the heels of his hands. "Oh God, Cecy. What if anyone finds out? He was her *father*."

"I might be wrong about this," Joss said again. "Maybe Drake ran."

"But Sweetwater asked me about him, and they must have had a reason for that. Do you think they know something?"

"They've got all the information we do and doubtless more." Joss grimaced. "Which is what frapes me."

"How do you mean?"

"Bill Sweetwater wouldn't ask you about this if he could help it. I reckon he came to you because he's looked everywhere for Drake, and hasn't found hide nor hair. And that's a challenge on the Marsh. If Drake loaded up a cart with guinea chests and went offmarsh, odds are someone would have seen him go. You might disappear easier on foot with full pockets, but even so, there's usually someone who'll notice you till you get to busy places, and people would remember a working man spending guineas. I don't reckon Bill would have asked you where Drake was unless nobody else had seen him at all."

"Which raises the question of whether he's anywhere to be seen," Gareth said thinly. "So where are the damned guineas? And if there's a-a body, where's that?"

"No idea," Joss said. "There's plenty of places to hide things round here. Most of the churches are used regular-like, but there's the lost villages, there's the dykes, there's all the woodland on the higher ground. And Sir Hugo knew the Marsh well. Roamed it daily for twenty years. The body could be anywhere."

He wasn't saying 'your father', for which Gareth was profoundly grateful. "I need to think this through. Oh Lord. What do we do about this, Joss?" He caught himself. "I mean, I need to think about what to do. I'm not sure how this changes things."

"No. Might need to sleep on it."

"I doubt I'll be sleeping much tonight." He caught Joss's fingers in his own. "I dare say it's absurd, and I know you're here on watch but—I wish you could come upstairs with me."

"I'd like that too."

"I want a whole night with you. I want you in my bed, and for you not to have to leave." The words ached. "Even just holding you. That would be so much."

Joss tipped his head, considering. "Which is your room?"

"At the front of the house."

"More or less above this? Hmm. Know what I reckon? I reckon your uncle might have been looking for a clue to where the guineas are hidden so, if he came back, he'd want to break into the study. I reckon if I slept in your room—on your floor, course—I'd be in a good position to be woken by any noise from the road *or* the study. Practical, that would be."

Gareth's heart thudded. "Do you think so?"

Joss grinned. "Works for me."

They tidied each other back to respectability, then Joss went to have a look around and ensure the house was secure. Gareth checked that Cecilia had gone to bed; Catherine was still in the kitchen.

"Just to let you know," he said, as casually as possible. "Joss will be moving around the house tonight, so if you hear any noise, it will probably be him. I said he should sleep inside. Given my room's convenient position for the road and the study, he might take my floor."

"Oh, we can't have that, with the favour he's doing us," Catherine said. "Shall I make up a truckle bed so he'll be comfortable?"

"Yes, I suppose that would—"

"Or shall I not bother?"

Gareth stopped dead. Catherine walked up, went on tiptoes, and kissed his cheek. "You're a good man, Gareth Inglis, and I'm so glad you came to us. You deserve to be happy. And I'll make up a bed if you'd like me to, but I'd rather say I did and spare myself the work."

"I—uh—I—"

"I won't trouble, then. Good night." She gave him a quick flashing smile and took her candle up to bed.

Twenty-one

Joss was in Gareth's bedroom. *Sir* Gareth. Sir Gareth Inglis, baronet. It was enough to give a man ideas above his station.

He wasn't entirely surprised that Catherine Inglis had said that to Gareth. She was a practical woman. If she wanted to keep this comfortable home, she'd do well to make it as comfortable for its new owner, just as she wouldn't do herself any harm by being a secret-keeper for Joss Doomsday.

Practical, then, and sharp, but also kind. What she'd said hadn't taken Gareth's mind off the earlier conversation entirely, but it had decidedly lightened his heart. Which was good, because here they were, in his bedroom, and it felt so impossible that Joss was almost nervous.

Gareth had closed the shutters, lit the lamps, locked the door. They stood a moment, close but not touching, just watching one another, and Joss knew exactly what he wanted now.

"Strip for me, London," he said. "I want you naked. I want to look."

"Help me."

Joss came round behind him to ease the coat off his shoulders, and then got distracted, running his hands round Gareth's waist to the faint trail of hair at the front. Gareth pulled his shirt over his head. "You're not helping."

"Sorry about that." He slid his hands up to Gareth's chest, found his nipples hard. "Cold?"

"A bit. Feel free to warm me up."

Joss tweaked. Gareth yelped, and added, "Ssh!"

"Wasn't me," Joss protested. "Help, you say?" He caught Gareth's hips, pulling him close so he'd feel Joss's arousal against his arse, and held him there with one hand, running the other over the front of his breeches. "Mmm."

"How is that helping? Oh God."

"I want you bare and hard," Joss whispered. "I want to see you panting for me."

Gareth went for buttons, his fingers tangling with Joss's, getting in the way in a mock-tussle that had them both laughing. Gareth won, getting the buttons undone, sliding the breeches down and his drawers with them.

"I need to get these off."

Joss settled his hands firmly on Gareth's hips again. "Not stopping you."

Gareth twisted to cast a look over his shoulder, then very deliberately bent at the waist, pushing that beautiful pale arse of his back to rub against Joss, who took the opportunity to get a hold with both hands. Gareth made a strangled noise. Joss held on while he got his breeches and stockings off, enjoying the way Gareth's arse shifted and tightened with his movements.

And then Gareth stood and stepped back, naked to his gaze and fiercely erect, and Joss could have wept.

"You're beautiful," he said. "I thought you were beautiful in London, but I didn't know the half of it. I could look at you forever."

Gareth's cheeks were pink. "One day you'll have to explain why."

"Why I like looking at a merciful lovely man I'm going to fuck?"

"Why you like this so much. Me naked, you clothed."

"That. Right. It's a bit stupid."

"I don't think it's stupid," Gareth said. "There doesn't have to be any more reason than that it gets you excited, which I entirely support."

"It does that," Joss said. "But also—all right. Our first time. I asked you to come upstairs, and you said yes. And we had that room, and I said, I don't know. Just 'I want to see you naked.' Which, I did want to, but I didn't mean anything particular by it. And you looked at me with this little smile, like a bit of a laugh and a bit of a question, and you said, 'Now?' And I said yes, and you took your blessed clothes off and just stood there, waiting for me, and—" He couldn't describe the heart-stopping magic of it. The man he'd just met, the one he hadn't known he'd been looking for, right there in front of him.

Joss swallowed. "Only, the thing was, I didn't expect you to strip off then and there. I'd meant, you know, when we got to it. Not right away."

Gareth froze. "Oh. Oh God. I thought—"

"Yes, but you did it, and you looked at me nervous-like, as if you were wondering if it was all right, and I thought, well, I'd better show I appreciate it. So I took my time, and I looked at you, really looked. And the way you looked at me back, like half embarrassed and waiting and not sure of yourself, but you'd still done it, just acause I asked—"

"I thought people always did what you asked." Gareth sounded breathless.

"Not like that. Never like that. I looked at you proper then, and I don't think I've stopped seeing you since."

Gareth made a noise that might have been a sob, and Joss was in his arms, mouths crushing together, Gareth's skin under his hands. Perfect.

And a bed to lie on, not a straw pallet on a bench but a real bed with a mattress, of a generous size for two. Hands and hot breath, squirming around and over each other, tongues and fingers in constant tender, urgent touch until they were both panting.

Gareth rolled over so he was on top, braced on hands and knees, Joss looking up at him. "You keep saying I'm beautiful, but we never seem to discuss that you're the most ridiculously desirable man in England."

Joss narrowed his eyes threateningly. "In England? Who do you know in France?"

"Excuse me? I'm not the one being regularly ravished by French pirates."

"*One*. And he was a privateer."

"Details." Gareth leaned in to kiss his nose. "Talking of such things, I have oil."

His light hair, a messy length that needed to grow or be cut, was hanging down round his face. His pale eyes were smiling into Joss's, his lips red and swollen with fierce kissing, and the way he looked could break a man's heart and mend it all at once.

Joss cupped his head. "Going to fuck me, London?"

"I'd love to."

It took a bit of getting used to, since Joss hadn't taken this part for a while, and Gareth never. He was a little nervous, but tentative was better than over-eager in the circumstances, at least to Joss's mind. He could watch the intent look on Gareth's face forever as he explored, whispering as he went. "Like this? Here? Oh, you like that. God, Joss, you're lovely."

Two fingers gently fucking him while Gareth sucked him. Then rolling over onto hands and knees to make it easier, murmuring encouragement, feeling Gareth push in, liberally oiled. He'd forgotten the feel of it, the sensation of being filled, or filled in. Completed by Gareth.

And they had to be quiet with others in the house, but God, he didn't want to be. He wanted to howl at the moon and he let his body show it, bucking under Gareth, flexing shoulders and back because he well knew Gareth loved his muscles. Fingers digging into his upper arms, Gareth at once fucking him and hanging on for the ride, making whispery sobbing noises that turned to a cry muffled by clamped lips. Joss threw his head back as Gareth's fingers clenched painfully tight, and stifled his own gasps as Gareth drove into him with urgent, jerky movements, and finally collapsed on his back.

"Oh God." Gareth was panting. "Oh God, Joss. I couldn't stop. *God*, that was good. Why haven't I done that before?"

His first time, and he'd always remember it. Joss hugged that to himself, something to put in his box of treasures.

Gareth had got a cloth when he got the oil. He pulled out carefully and rolled Joss over so they both lay on their sides, then pressed against his back, stroking Joss's stand. "Sorry. I wanted you to come before I did but I'm only human."

"Wasn't far off."

"Well, then..." Gareth's fingers snaked between his legs. Joss widened his thighs to give access. Gareth was using both hands, working prick and balls at once with tantalising touches that were just firm enough, kissing his neck and his ear, all over him. "You were perfect," he whispered. "My smuggling prince. I want to fuck you again when I can see your face. I want to feel you come when I'm inside you and know I made you."

"Reckon you will. Ah, Jesus, Gareth—"

He was so close and he knew Gareth could tell, because his fingers tightened on Joss's balls and relaxed on his prick, exactly how he liked it. Joss bucked hard, biting back the cry as he shot and spent all over the quilt, helpless in Gareth's hands.

Gareth purred like a cat and shifted so he was wrapped around Joss, long arms and legs embracing him, lips against his neck. Joss stared at the ceiling and wondered how he'd deserved heaven.

Joss woke early. It was still dark out and Gareth was sprawled across the bed, snoring faintly. Joss slithered out from under him and moved silently round the room, finding his things by touch and piling Gareth's on a chair. He doubted Catherine Inglis brought him tea in bed, but even so.

Dressed, he made his silent way downstairs, hoping nobody had broken in and ransacked the study in his absence. They could well have done; he wouldn't have noticed Napoleon's forces invading while he'd been fucking—fucked by—Gareth, and he'd slept like the dead after.

The house appeared intact. He checked the study and the front, then padded into the kitchen, where he encountered Mrs. Inglis.

"Beg pardon, mistress," he said, retreating a step.

"No, come in. Tea?"

"I'd be grateful."

"We don't seem to have been attacked. I dare say that's because you were here protecting us."

Not a twitch on her lips. Joss took a sideways look at her. She returned a glinting smile.

"Mrs. Inglis—"

"Catherine," she said. "In the circumstances. Tell me how Luke is."

That took up the next little while as she made tea. Joss took the mug she gave him. "What sort of man was Sir Hugo, mistress? I didn't know him myself and I've a reason for asking."

"What sort? A selfish one," she said, with a remote sound to her voice.

"That's no uncommon thing."

"But he was uncommonly selfish. Not cruel, as such, but he didn't see that anyone else needed consideration. His slightest comfort was more important than Gareth's home, or Cecy's future, or my honour. He was a man and a baronet, so he mattered. We, women and children, didn't."

"And servants?" Joss asked. "A man who did odd jobs, say, would he matter?"

Her eyes snapped to his. "A man like Adam Drake?"

"Very like."

"Not at all. Not in the slightest. Why?"

He shook his head. "Best not to ask, mistress. And I don't say that lightly."

"He was Cecy's father. For all his faults, he was her father, and she has his name. If there's more trouble coming around all this business, I want to know."

"It's not for me to say."

She gave him a long look. "I don't like this. I love my girl, and I care for Gareth. He is a kind man and a good one, and you had better not be adding to his problems, Joss Doomsday."

Joss hoped not. "I'll head off what trouble I can for you. That's all I can say, but you've my word I'll do my best."

She considered him for a long, unnerving moment and gave a nod. "I dare say that will do."

Gareth came down then, looking as though he'd dressed in a hurry, not to say in the dark. He stopped when he saw Joss, with a smile of relief that would have been a hopeless giveaway in company, only Joss didn't have a leg to stand on because he was smiling back. "A'right."

"Watcher, Joss," Gareth returned in a creditable Kentish brogue. "We seem to have had an uneventful night." Said with a straight face too. "Is there tea in the pot, Catherine?"

There was. She made ham and eggs, too, and they ate together. In the kitchen because of course free traders didn't get the fancy china and Miss Cecy might appear at any time, but together, and a meal with Gareth. It felt like a privilege.

What he'd have liked to do was take Gareth off for a rambling walk over the Marsh. Unfortunately he had a lot to do today, starting with getting rid of the other Inglises, then a frank and comprehensive discussion with Nate Sweetwater. All of that meant Gareth confirming what he wanted done.

"I'd best be off," he said. "Thank you kindly for breakfast, Catherine. Quick word, Sir Gareth?"

"I'll show you out," Gareth said politely. They walked through to the hallway, where Gareth grabbed his arm and dragged him into the study for an urgent kiss that almost had him off his feet.

Joss staggered back a step to find his balance. "Steady, you."

"I don't feel steady," Gareth assured him. "I'm bouncing between thinking about you and wanting to dance, and thinking about my family and wanting to cry."

"I know that feeling."

"I wish you could stay. Last night was *glorious*. And—I got distracted yesterday but I meant to thank you for everything you said. You listened to what I said, and that matters so much. And I know there's lots of people you have to be Mr. Joss Doomsday for, but I'd love to be the person you don't." His eyes were so intent. "Because you need to be afraid or weak or wrong or vulnerable now and then, if only to balance out how marvellous you usually are. And if you want to be those things with me, if you can just be *you* with me—I'd love that."

"Oh, London." Joss rested his head on Gareth's chest a moment. "You're the best thing in my life, you know that?"

"Same. God, Joss. I thought last night would be a wonderful treat but all it means is I want you here tonight too. Can you come?"

"I'll have to see how things are, but I'll try. I'd be here every night if I could. If you'd have me."

"I'd have you."

"Ah, Gareth," Joss said, leaning back a little to see his face. "I love you. It's stupid how I love you. *Baronet*, for mercy's sake. I've got no business loving you, and I can't seem to do a blessed thing else."

"It's not my fault my great-grandmother was a trollop by royal appointment. And I love you so much, it's hard to breathe."

Gareth's eyes were wide with much the same look of wondering joy Joss felt. He was so lovely that Joss couldn't breathe either, and then they both moved at once and the problem only got worse because kissing that hard didn't allow for much air. He grabbed Gareth's hair and arse, pulling him close. Pulling them together because you had to pull that much harder when the world wanted you apart.

They released each other only when feet thundered in the hall outside the closed study door.

"Cecilia's fairy footsteps," Gareth said in an undertone. "She's perfectly ladylike in person and sounds like a herd of bulls on the stairs. Will I see you soon?"

"Soon as I can. I'll send to you. Look, I want to get this whole business of the guineas done with. Reckon I'm going to go talk to Nate Sweetwater in plain language, if you're all right with that. I thought we might say he's welcome to go treasure-hunting, as long as he doesn't involve you or your old man in any of it. Not the trading, not the finding, not anything he might find along of the gold. What do you think?"

"But if he finds Drake—?"

Joss shrugged. "He can take the guineas, then send for the crowner. After three months nobody's going to look too close at a body if there isn't a knife sticking out of it."

Gareth winced. "Is that right? Should there not be, well, justice?"

"There's none to be had. Sir Hugo's dead and gone and there's nobody else to blame. Or do you mean your uncle ought to get the money back?"

"The rightful owners should have it back, but if Uncle Henry has to ruin himself replacing what he took, that's his problem," Gareth said. "I would prefer Sweetwater not to have it either, but I don't suppose there's much to be done about that."

"Not without a lot more trouble."

"No. Talking of my uncle, I really do think he and Lionel ought to go away, and if everyone here thinks they're Revenue, I expect they'll want to. Only, if I tell them to clear off, will that make them dig their heels in? They really don't like me."

"Mph. You had your cousin on the back foot before, but he was on his own. And bullying sorts don't listen when it's two against one."

"That's exactly it," Gareth said. "Lionel won't back down with his father there, and Uncle Henry won't with his son there. Would you mind making it two against two, at all?"

Joss had to take a moment there. Gareth *wanted* his help, he just wanted to ask for it, not have it foisted on him without asking, and that was so obvious now Joss looked at it that he could have kicked himself raw. "Course. I'll have a word with Sweetwater first, then we'll go. You talk to 'em, and if they're fool enough not to listen, I'll be there."

"Thank you," Gareth said, and his smile was all the reward Joss needed.

He walked back to Globsden Gut, thinking things through. Easy enough to talk to Sweetwater; the question was if he'd be believed. After all, if he was looking for ten thousand guineas and a missing man, he wouldn't accept claims of ignorance from the son of the culprit at face value. He certainly wouldn't credit a word if Nate Sweetwater announced *There's ten thousand guineas for the taking but I'm not interested*, so he very much doubted Nate would credit it of him, and there was no way he could explain that he was only concerned to keep Gareth out of it. He'd need to present the whole business in a way a covetous man would understand.

He was still chewing that over as he approached the Revelation, until he saw what was going on.

The place was an overset beehive. The doors stood open and there were people standing in the road, running in and out, talking in little huddles. No sign of Granda on the porch either. Had they been raided by the Preventives? They'd find nothing but it would be a merciful inconvenience, and he paid the local Excisemen lavishly to avoid that very thing.

He lengthened his stride a little, walking briskly without being seen to hurry, because confidence was all. Only, as he approached, he saw the moment someone saw him and said something. One by one the various hangers-on stopped talking and turned to stare. They were all silent and gaping as Joss came up to the Revelation's steps.

"Watcher," he said in a general sort of way. There were a couple of faint mumbles in reply.

What the blazes was this? He went in rather than get his information second-hand or betray ignorance.

The room was full of Doomsdays. Ma was seated, holding Luke by the shoulders. The boy was white as chalk, the ugly wound standing out vividly on his pallid skin. Sophy and Emily and Aunt Mary were clustered round Ma, and her face was anguished in a way Joss hadn't seen in a long time. Not since Pa and the others had died. Tables had been shoved haphazardly to the sides of the room, and several men were clustered around something in the centre.

"What's going on?"

Everyone turned, some of them sharply. Sophy sprang up. "Joss! Where have you been?"

"Tench House. You know that. What's happened?"

People stepped aside, moving to left and right, clearing the way for Joss to see two tables pulled together, and the body lying on them. Joss had one horrible second thinking *Adam Drake* before his brain caught up, because this wasn't a three-month corpse. He took a step forward.

It wasn't Drake, or anyone else. It was Elijah. His head lolled unpleasantly; his face was livid and bruised from Joss's fists and Ma's frying pan; his clothes were wet through but not dripping, and smelled musty. He was dead.

"The devil," Joss said. "He drowned?"

"Broken neck," Jabez Whalebone, their sawbones, said.

"Broken *neck*?"

Whalebone shrugged. He was generally reliable when sober, and since it was not yet ten in the morning, there was a moderate chance of that. "What happened?" Joss demanded. "Where was he found?"

Tom darted a look. "Why'd you say that?"

"What?"

"That he was found. How d'you know he was found?"

"He didn't walk in here soaking wet and then break his own neck on that table," Joss snapped. "Or if he did, I'd be interested."

"Josiah," Asa said warningly.

"The Royal Military Canal where it passes by High Knock Channel," Sophy said. "This morning, at dawn, by a looker."

"Reckon he'd been in a while," Whalebone said. "Since last night. You can see, something's started nibbling on his lips—ouch!"

Joss gave Isaac a nod of gratitude for the timely kick. "Any witnesses? What was he doing round that way?" It was in Walland Marsh, close to the Isle of Oxney, maybe three miles north of Rye. "And why the blazes is everyone looking at me?"

"You said you'd kill him, Joss." Isaac's voice was thin. "That you'd break his neck and throw him into a dyke. I mean...you *said*."

"I said that right after he carved Luke's face up," Joss said as levelly as possible. "I spent last night at Tench House in case of trouble there. I didn't borrow Sir Gareth's horse and cross the breadth of the Marsh at night in the hope of finding Elijah skulking round Sweetwater territory as if we didn't have plenty of dykes on our doorstep. Don't be a fool."

"You wanted him dead," Tom said. "We all knew that."

"No, I wanted him gone. If I'd wanted him dead, I'd have killed him when he cut Luke and not one of you would have raised a voice against me. He's been a thorn in my side for fifteen years and I didn't kill him all that time. Why would I do it when I was finally rid of him?"

"Josiah," Ma said. Her voice was flat, but the pain hummed through it.

Her little brother, he reminded himself. "I'm sorry, Ma. That was disrespectful. But I had nothing to do with this."

"I know that. My son wouldn't hurt me so."

He came over and gripped her hand. She pulled him close, clutching him. "The last words I said to him—the last he said to me—"

"It shouldn't have ended this way, Ma." He kissed her rough cheek, then straightened. "Jabez. His neck. Could he have fallen badly or what-have-you, or was it done deliberate?"

Whalebone gave him an incredulous look. "How'm I supposed to tell that?"

"I don't know, do I? Look at the blessed body and see what you find out."

"Why don't you?"

"Oh, for goodness' sake," Aunt Mary said, pulling her sleeves back. "I've laid out plenty of dead. Out of my way, you lot. Jabez, make yourself useful or make yourself scarce."

Everyone else retreated as bristling quack and determined aunt went to work. Joss said, "Right. Who knows anything I need to know? What he's been doing the last days. Where he's been. Who he's talked to."

"He was talking to them Inglises."

That came from Emily, a nervous voice. Joss turned fast. "What?"

"He was in Rye yesterday. I went to the Mermaid again, to listen in on that Mr. Henry Inglis and the son, the one Squire kicked out."

"I didn't tell you to do that yesterday."

"You didn't tell me to stop doing it."

"Why do we care about the damn Inglises?" Tom demanded. "Watching outside Tench House and spying on them in Rye? What's this all about?"

Joss raised a hand. "Tell you later. Go on, Emily."

"Just that. Elijah was in a private room with both of them Inglises. Didn't hear anything, I couldn't get to a keyhole."

"Why didn't you tell me before?"

"You'd gone off when I got back!" She looked alarmed. "I thought it would wait."

"Any other night, you'd have been right. Good work, Em. So Elijah was talking to Henry and Lionel Inglis in Rye last evening. And died that night and his body was in the canal up Oxney way. Hell's bells. What was he telling 'em?"

Everyone looked blank. "Why would they care what he had to say?" Tom asked. "What could he tell 'em?"

How to blackmail Gareth, Joss thought savagely. And now what? Gareth wouldn't want his father's dealings made public, but this was feeling increasingly like a case of picking the least worst option. He went for a fraction of the truth, given the roomful of listening ears. "This Henry Inglis fellow has been up to something. Any of you know that old Sir Hugo had dealings with Sweetwater? No? Well, seems he did, and seems like brother Henry was mixed up in it. It was Sweetwater men who attacked Miss Cecy Inglis and then Sir Gareth. We saw them off, and then Henry came down here with his son to stick his nose in. I don't know what they're up to exactly; I've been trying to find out. But this Henry's an attorney."

"And works for the Revenue!" Emily put in.

There were sharp intakes of breath. Lawyers were only marginally less unpopular than tax officials: the combination was noxious. Ma frowned. "And what does all that mean?"

"I don't know yet," Joss said. "But I don't like that Elijah had something to say to him in private."

That set off a predictable uproar. Joss folded his arms and waited it out. He had the sense of heightened nerves he got on a run, when you were dancing along the line between excitement and panic, knowing that if you once stumbled you'd never recover.

Ma slammed a hand on the arm of her chair for silence. "Are you saying my brother betrayed us, Josiah?"

"Why would they kill him for that, Ma?" Sophy said. "They'd want an informer alive."

"Who says he was informing?" Joss said. "Elijah had a grudge against Sir Gareth over Luke. I dare say you've heard the spite he's been coming out with." He looked around. Nobody met his eye, which suggested they all knew exactly what Elijah had been saying. "Well, Sir Gareth's fallen out with his family pretty loudly. Elijah might have wanted to cause him trouble. What if he went to keg-meg to Henry Inglis and got mixed up in whatever him and Sweetwater have been up to?"

"And what's that?"

"I don't know yet, but I'll get some answers," Joss said. "From Henry Inglis and Nate Sweetwater too."

"You can start with that his neck's clean broke," Aunt Mary said from the corpse. "Twisted right round, I reckon. That was no accident."

Ma inhaled sharply. "Find who did this, Joss. Find them for me."

"I will, Ma." Joss gripped her hand. "I promise. Sophy, Graveyard, Tom, you're with me. We're going to ask some questions round High Knock way, talk to anyone who saw anything. Everyone else, I want silence on this, hear me? The word until I'm ready is that it was an accident, nobody's to blame so far as we know, we're just finding out his last movements. Anyone at all who flaps their lips on this will answer to me."

"And to me," Ma said grimly.

"Elijah did wrong. He did badly wrong by his own son, and his sister too. But he was a Doomsday and he's dead and by God we'll find what happened to him. Let's go."

Twenty-two

JOSS RODE OFF WITH HIS SQUAD. IT WAS A SLOW BUSINESS JOG-
ging through the Marsh; the few tracks ran from village to village,
making for maundering journeys. Outmarsh sometimes attempted
to ride straight across what looked like flat, empty land, only to
discover themselves blocked by dykes eight feet wide.

Joss wasn't in a hurry. He needed to think.

He had absolutely no desire to admit, *There's ten thousand
stolen guineas maybe hidden on the Marsh, probably with a corpse.*
Nothing good would come of that. Sweetwater and the Inglises
would know, though, and he'd need to speak frankly to have a
conversation. In an ideal world he'd have Gareth with him for
this, or at least tell him what was happening, but right now he was
running to keep up.

They spent two long, frustrating hours around the place where
Elijah had been found, in the shadow of the Isle of Oxney. It
wasn't a heavily populated area to start with, and nobody on the
Marsh made a habit of curiosity when people moved around in
the night, which Joss would normally applaud. They caught up

with the looker who'd found the body, who Joss rewarded with five guineas. They rode up to Appledore, the closest village, and down again. They even stopped at a Preventive station on the Canal, which didn't get them the friendliest reception. One of the Revenue men seemed to find it highly amusing that a Doomsday was dead, and Graveyard had to take Tom outside while Joss asked questions.

Joss was beginning to despair when they returned to High Knock Channel at the point where it ran by the Canal and the Isle of Oxney's wooded slopes rose on the other side. This was where Elijah had been found, and what the blazes he'd been doing up here, Joss couldn't imagine.

"There's someone," Sophy said.

It was Pagan d'Aumesty, the Earl's brother. He was another one always maundering around the Marsh to no purpose. Joss was beginning to harbour views on rich old men who took pointless walks.

"Good afternoon, sir," he said in his best voice. "Have you heard about a body found round here?"

"A body? Ah, you mean Sir Hugo. Yes, a great shame."

"Sir Hugo? No, sir. Found this morning."

"No, no, he's been dead some time, I'm told."

"Yes, sir, but I don't mean Sir Hugo."

"Oh, his son? I'm sure he's not dead. I spoke to him quite recently. He had some interesting observations on my Mithraic cult theory."

Joss set his teeth. "Not Sir Gareth either, sir."

"Who's that?"

"Sir Hugo's son. I'm asking about a dead man."

"Is he dead? Good heavens, how unfortunate, so soon after his father. What was his name? Lancelot? No, Gawain."

Sophy, who hadn't met Pagan before, was gaping. Joss nailed

a smile into place. "Gareth. The son is Sir Gareth Inglis, and he's alive and well. The dead man I mean is Elijah Doomsday."

"Doomsday? Ah, the cognate branch of the family."

"The what did you call us?" Tom demanded.

"Cognate. The name is a corruption. A bastardisation if you will: d'Aumesty, dome-sty, Doomsday. A noble patronym slurred into a familiar, if absurd, form by unlettered rustics," Pagan explained, oblivious to Tom's darkening expression.

"Hold on," Sophy said. "Branch? You saying the Doomsdays and the d'Aumestys are related?"

"On the bar sinister, of course."

"What?"

"That's very interesting," Joss said, wresting back control of the conversation, "only Elijah Doomsday is dead. He was found in the Canal this morning and looks like he went in there last night. Did you hear anything, sir?"

"I could hardly have heard a dead man. What absurdity."

"*Before* he was dead." There was going to be another corpse in about thirty seconds. "Any disturbance last night. Anything?"

"Disturbance? Not at all. I slept extremely well, thank you."

Joss hung onto his patience with both hands. "Good to hear. Marvellous. Sorry to have troubled you."

"Oh, was it you?"

"What?"

"The argument," Pagan said. "I shouldn't say it troubled me, but it was excessively loud and most inconsiderate. I walk in order to consider my theories and I prefer not to have my thoughts interrupted. Don't do it again."

Joss's skin was prickling. "Beg your pardon, sir. Who was it arguing?"

"You, of course. You told me so yourself. Who are you?"

"The other people arguing," Joss said. "Apart from me."

"Some pack of fellows yesterday evening, very near here. Four of them, in fact."

"Is that right, sir?" Joss smiled at him. "Tell me more."

The Inglis father and son were staying at the Mermaid in Rye. It was an old building, all blackened wood beams, on a steep cobbled street. The landlord was a friend to free traders and took no sides except against the Preventives; he was happy to direct Joss to the little parlour where the Inglises were sitting.

They were speaking urgently in lowered voices as Joss walked in without knocking.

"Hey, fellow. This is a private room," the older man snapped.

"Good," Joss said. "I want a private talk."

Lionel Inglis jumped to his feet. "What the devil—Get out!"

Joss strolled over. "Mr. Henry Inglis? I'm Joss Doomsday. Shut up." That was to Lionel's address, as he'd kept blustering. Lionel raised a fist; Graveyard moved up into his face, walking Lionel backwards until he bumped into a chair, then helping him sit with a firm hand. "I expect you know my name."

"Why would I know any such thing?" Henry Inglis didn't look too good. Pallid skin and dark-ringed eyes, like he hadn't slept.

"Acause you met my uncle Elijah Doomsday just yesterday in this very inn, maybe this room. Any reason you wouldn't say so?"

"I do not choose to engage in conversation with Captain Hackums. Leave this room at once or I shall summon assistance."

Joss sighed. "I know what you've been up to. I know what you were doing with your brother, and what you came here to search for. Think on that, and then answer me properly."

"You are insolent. I shall summon a watchman."

"Look, I'm busy, so I'll get to the point," Joss said. "Tell me everything I want to know, or I'll ruin your life."

"I beg your pardon? In what possible manner could you do that?"

"Drop a word in the right ear to look through your books." Joss wished he'd got the proper legal language off Gareth. "They can see where the money is that you ought to be looking after for people. How long do you think it'll take a good clerk to find a ten-thousand-guinea-sized hole in your accounts?"

Henry kept his face impressively still, but he couldn't do anything about the blood that drained from his cheeks, leaving his skin a clammy grey. Lionel attempted to surge up from his chair. Graveyard prodded him back with a sausage-sized finger.

"That is a calumny." Henry's voice was thin. "I deny and repudiate all your allegations. I don't object to answering civil questions, but I warn you to draw no inference from that. What do you want?"

"What were you up to with my uncle last night?" Joss saw that hit, in the way Henry Inglis's face clamped tight, and took a stab. "Yesterday evening, couple of miles north of here. What were you doing together? What were you talking about with him?"

"Why don't you ask your uncle?" Lionel struck in. "I dare say he'll explain if he wants to."

Joss looked round at him. "Two things I don't like, outmarsh. One, people who think they're clever when they're not, and two, you. If you say one more thing that isn't the truth, the whole truth, and nothing but the truth, I'm going to tell the Preventives you used the money you stole to run guineas to France."

Henry Inglis physically wobbled. "How do you know?"

"Shut up!" Lionel hissed at his father, too late.

"No more tithering," Joss told Henry. "Sit down. Talk."

Henry sat. Lionel, sounding pardonably exasperated, said, "We don't have the money. Gareth has it, my cousin. It was his father had it, stole it—"

Sophy and Graveyard gaped in unison. Joss cursed mentally. "He doesn't have it."

"Of course he does! Or he knows where to find it. He's been sneaking around the Marsh looking for it."

"That's right." Henry sounded a bit short of breath. "Secretive. Hiding his dealings from me. A wildly extravagant portion for his half-sister. He unquestionably knows where the money is."

"You're talking to the wrong men," Lionel added. "Gareth knows. You go to him."

"I'm not here about the money," Joss said. "I'm here about my uncle Elijah, who you two were with yesterday. Why? And if you don't tell me the truth you're going to wish you had, acause your chance of getting away with this is getting smaller with every tick of the clock. What were you doing with Elijah Doomsday?"

The Inglises exchanged looks. Lionel said, "He claimed to know where the money was hidden."

"What?" Tom said.

If Elijah had known where to find ten thousand guineas, Joss had no doubt he'd have shown the Marsh a clean pair of heels. "Go on."

"He said he knew where Gareth had been looking, that he'd seen him. He said he knew secrets. That he'd tell us anything we wanted to know, for the right price."

Tom bristled. Joss put out a hand to halt him. "How'd you and him meet?"

"He came to us. He said he had information to sell that we'd find interesting."

"Is that right," Joss said. "Did he say, 'I can tell you where all that money is,' before you asked him if he knew about it? Or did he say he could tell you what Sir Gareth's been doing, and you said, oh, you mean you know where he's hidden the guineas?"

"Uh—"

"Idiots," Sophy muttered. "And, what, he led you out on a wild-goose chase and you didn't find anything."

"Hours of stumbling around in the mud of this godforsaken hole." Lionel looked sour.

"I bet," Joss said. "You got wet and tired, and you found nothing. Probably you worked out he'd been lying to you. And that's when you got angry with him."

"No," Henry said. "No, we did not. You cannot say we did."

"I can't say you got angry with a man who lied to you? Funny. Most people get angry when they're lied to. Me, for example." Joss leaned over the man in the chair. "Or were you denying something else?"

"Of course I deny it! I didn't touch him!"

"Who did?"

"None of us," Lionel said over him. "None of us touched him. I told him he was a drunken liar and we returned to this place for a warm bath. He was alive and well when we left him. I swear it!"

"You're merciful bad at this," Sophy said. "You ever heard anyone so bad at this, Joss?"

"Not much," Joss said. "I thought you tosspots were lawyers."

"I don't get it," Tom said.

Sophy patted him on the arm. "They just told us they didn't touch Elijah and he was alive and well. Only, we never said anything about him *not* being alive and well." She paused, waiting for enlightenment to dawn. "So how would they know to say that if they didn't know he got killed?"

"Oh, right!" Tom looked pleased for a moment, then his face changed. "Bastards."

"You missed something, Soph," Joss said. "Smart-arse here said, 'None of us touched him'. Does that sound like two men?"

Sophy clicked her fingers. "You'd say 'neither', wouldn't you? 'Neither of us two, none of us three.' That's grammar, that is. Granda always said we'd need it one day."

"Tell him, he'll be pleased." The byplay had put the Inglises nicely on edge. Joss grinned at them. "Who else was there?"

Lionel was a bad shade of puce. "I will not be interrogated. You are not officers of the law."

"You want to bring the law into it?" Joss asked. "We can do that."

"There is no information we can give you," Henry said. "We don't know anything about your uncle. He dragged us around the countryside for several hours under false pretences, then we returned here. If any harm has come to him, it was not our doing."

"Who were you with?"

"I refuse to discuss this."

"Someone you're more scared of than you are me," Joss said. "Someone with more on you than I've got, and I've got plenty. Someone you made sure not to mention when you said you were with Elijah. Who are you covering for?"

Henry's throat worked. "I have no idea what you mean."

"That would sound better if you didn't look like you were about to shit through your teeth," Sophy remarked.

"Let's not mess about," Joss said. "We've got a witness who saw you two up by the Isle, with Elijah and another man, and I know exactly who the other fellow is. Did he wring Elijah's neck or what?"

"My son and I had nothing to do with any harm to Mr. Doomsday. I know nothing of this."

Joss took a deep breath. "Listen. There's two ways out of this for you. One of them is that you clear off the Marsh and never come back, and if I was you, that's the one I'd take. All I need to know is what happened last night. Tell me that and you can go." He looked from face to face. "I don't care about who stole whose money, or your family squabbles. I care about who killed my uncle and I need to hear your account of what happened, acause I've got my mother at home crying her eyes out for her little brother and begging me pitiful-like to find the man who killed him. And I'm sorry I came in here angry, but if it was your poor widowed old mother weeping and grieving like her heart might break, you'd know how I feel."

Sophy and Tom both had their mouths clamped shut and their gazes fixed on the ceiling. Graveyard was going a slightly odd colour.

"I won't lie," Joss went on inaccurately. "We'll have our vengeance on the man who killed my poor old Uncle Eli, and on the whole merciful lot of them as stand behind him. The Marsh won't be a pretty place when we've done. But beyond that, it's not my business what anyone was up to last night. I've bigger fish to fry."

Henry and Lionel exchanged looks. Henry frowned; Lionel gave him a meaningful gaze; Henry shook his head in warning.

"Oh, be damned to you, you old fool," Lionel said, apparently tired of the pantomime. "What? I'm not protecting him at our expense. Listen, fellow." That was to Joss's address. "Bill Sweetwater killed your uncle. We were out—yes, searching for the guineas. *Our* guineas. The Doomsday fellow claimed he knew where they were, that he had seen Gareth looking around there. It became apparent he had lied. He was drunk, and belligerent. He and Sweetwater exchanged words, then blows. They struggled. Doomsday shouted, and Sweetwater—" His expression of horror looked altogether real. "His head twisted in the most appalling manner. He was dead. Sweetwater told us to keep silent—"

Henry had gone a lurid shade of puce. Now he made a sound like a boiling kettle. Lionel glowered at him. "What? If he finds the money without us, he'll take it all. You should never have spoken to him. He murdered this poor fellow's uncle, and he's the one who should face the consequences. It would be wrong of us not to say so," he finished nobly.

"That'll be why you went to the magistrates first thing," Joss said.

"No, no, I didn't," Lionel assured him.

"Jesus wept," Sophy muttered. "What now, Joss?"

"Word with Sweetwater," Joss said. "And while I'm at that, you two will be leaving the Marsh whipsticks, and that means right away, you guinea-trading, backstabbing, treacherous outmarsh scum. Get out, don't come back. If I so much as hear your names spoken again, I'll come to London after you."

"You said—" Lionel began.

"Our money—!" Henry protested.

"Shove your guineas up your arse," Joss told them both. "There's a Doomsday lying dead, you were part of it, and if you're still on Romney Marsh tonight, you won't live to see dawn."

He led the way out of the Mermaid. Sophy kept quiet until they were mounted and riding towards Camber, then said, "That wasn't like you."

"I'm not in the mood," Joss said. "This is going to be a nightmare. Oi, all of you." He reined Fleurie in and waited for the group to gather round. "Listen well. Bill Sweetwater's going to pay for this in full, but I'm not persuaded Nate was involved. I've a suspicion Bill went off maggoty, so we'll give Nate a chance. If that's wrong we'll go in high and hard on him and the whole lot of them, but I'm not starting a war till I know it's warranted. So we all keep our heads, hear? Tom?"

"Yes, Joss. But what is this money?" Tom demanded.

"That Henry was shipping guineas to France, with old Sir Hugo as middleman and Sweetwater running the cargo. A shipment got lost along the way and they're all saying Sir Hugo took it. Which is easy, what with he's dead."

"So are we looking for it?"

"No," Joss said. "Reason being, it's long gone. Sir Gareth doesn't know a thing about it, and believe me, I've tried to find out."

Tom's jaw dropped. "Is *that* what you've been up to there?"

Joss shrugged. "Seemed worth asking. He doesn't have it. I reckon the fellow who fetched and carried for Sir Hugo took it off-marsh, whether for Sir Hugo or of his own accord." Joss hoped that was true, and apologised mentally to Drake's shade if it wasn't. "All I know is, it's nowhere to be found and I've had too much trouble from this. I want those two Inglises off the Marsh tonight, and Bill Sweetwater to answer for Elijah, and after that I'm calling the whole business a middling waste of breath."

There was no sign of Nate Sweetwater in Camber, nor could they learn where he'd gone. Joss had an inkling that Nate would be working along similar lines of thought to himself. He wouldn't want to go to war with Ma Doomsday, so Bill Sweetwater was probably being unceremoniously removed from the Marsh even now to prevent further bloodshed. Joss didn't care. Elijah's death wasn't something he regretted, and his only interest was in getting Gareth out of this mess intact.

It was a long ride home across Walland Marsh and through New Romney. At the Revelation, Ma was in a state, which didn't improve when the family sat down to discuss what measures they might be obliged by honour to take.

"Fact is, we told Elijah to fend for himself," Sophy said. "He was outside the family by his own choice."

Ma clenched her fists. "He was still a Doomsday!"

"Give Nate time to clean his own house," Joss said. "Elijah was your brother but Bill is his, and better if Nate acts on him of his own will. If he doesn't, we'll do it, but we'll take this steady, all right?"

That was easier said than done. Talking and arguing took up too long, not to mention the preparations for Elijah's burying. Joss was uncomfortably aware, too, that Gareth might consider his visit to the Inglises overstepping. It had been on his own business, and hardly avoidable, but even so, he didn't want to lose time letting him know.

He took Luke aside close to seven o'clock. "Go see Sir Gareth. Tell him there's been developments, a lot of them, and I'll be over later. After dark, probably. If he wants to meet me outside, he's to tell you where."

"Yes, Joss." Luke swallowed. "Thanks, Joss."

That might be either *Thank you for trusting me,* or *Thank you for giving me something to do.* Joss clapped him on the shoulder. "You all right?"

Luke made a face, and winced as the scabbing wound pulled. Gareth or Catherine might get more out of him. "Go on, then. If you're invited for supper or to stay, do as you please, long as I get any message in good time."

Luke darted away. Joss fully expected him to be detained by Catherine Inglis's lavish table, so he was startled to see him back in little more than twenty minutes. The boy was red-faced and gasping, and he grabbed Joss's sleeve and dragged him outside with determination, ignoring Asa in his rocking chair.

"What the blazes is it?"

"Sir Gareth," Luke managed, between sucking breaths. He looked to have run the mile back at full speed. "Mrs. Inglis—you sent a note."

"I what?"

"Man came, with a note, before. From *you,* Joss. He said he was from you." Luke shook his arm. "Sir Gareth went with him."

"Who—"

"She didn't know. Doesn't know where they went." He stared up at Joss with wild eyes. "A man came, and he's *gone.*"

Twenty-three

GARETH HAD A DELIGHTFUL MORNING. MUCH OF IT, ADMIT-
tedly, was taken up by daydreams of last night, and Joss, and *It's
stupid how I love you.* He could think about that for hours. There
was Catherine too, serenely moving around the house as though
she hadn't given him that gift of love and trust and support. He
wondered what he could best do for her, and attempted to do it by
having a sensible conversation with Cecilia.

"I know things have been difficult," he said. "And I am very
sorry for my part in causing problems for you and Bovey. You know
there's no hurry at all to marry. That's not a reflection on Bovey,
naturally, he seems a fine man—"

"Are you going to tell me I'll grow out of it in a few years?" Cecy
asked a little shrilly.

"I've no idea what you'll do. I've known you for two months: I
shouldn't presume to predict what you'll think in years. There are
things I felt at seventeen that I still feel just as much, and things I
don't. All I meant was, whether you choose to wait for one year, or
five, or ten, I shall support you. I want you to have a free choice."

"You didn't give me the choice to go out for a trip with Cousin Lionel."

"No, I didn't," Gareth said. "And I can't apologise for that. I've only hit two people in my whole life, but I would strike him if he tried to make up to you again. He's not a good man."

"Aunty Cathy said you were being protective," she remarked, watching him curiously. "Would you really strike him?"

"Well, I'd try. I have a duty to look after you. And Lionel isn't kind."

"I heard he was making up dreadfully to Laura Topgood *and* bothering the girls at the Mermaid. And I didn't like how Mr. Inglis was to Aunty Cathy."

"I don't like either of them in the slightest. Lionel is very plausible and charming, of course."

"Much more charming than William. He has very polished manners, and—and poise, and pays pretty compliments, which is terribly exhilarating. But it's not *real*, is it?"

"Some men are real and honest, and pay pretty compliments too," Gareth said, thinking of one who had told him he was beautiful. "But if I had to choose between the two, I'd want a man I could trust to be on my side. If I were a young lady, I mean."

"Yes, I think so too. I dare say one could easily be fooled by superficial charm, if one didn't know any better," she added wisely.

Gareth forbore to smile. "That is a danger. But I'm sure you will make a sensible choice in due course, whether you settle on Bovey or not."

"He says I have to be at least twenty-one before we marry," she said, a little mutinously. "He says that's only fair, to give me time to change my mind. Really, it would serve him right if I eloped with someone terribly dashing."

"I think that's extremely honourable of him." Gareth wondered if he could impose conditions on her portion without causing mayhem. "It gives you time to consider. And, if I can be selfish, it gives me a little longer to know you, which I would like. Actually, I was wondering if we might take a holiday."

"A holiday?"

"I was thinking of a trip to Tunbridge Wells. I need to visit a tailor"—and had no desire to go strolling round Rye—"and I imagine you and Catherine might both want to replenish your wardrobes. I thought we could go for a week? Take the waters and see the sights and so on, and spend a great deal of money?"

Cecy put her hands to her mouth. "Really?"

"We all deserve a treat after everything that's happened. And I've never had a sister to treat before, so I have some catching up to do. May I?"

She opened her mouth, gestured wildly, shrieked, then flew to give him a hug. Gareth hugged her back.

That, when communicated to Catherine, put the whole household into a better spirit. It was certainly a pleasanter topic of conversation than most recent ones, and the holiday mood lasted until John Groom arrived with the news that Elijah Doomsday was dead.

"All over the Marsh, it is. Some say Joss Doomsday quarrelled with him."

"Well, that can't be true, if he was found in the morning," Catherine said. "Joss was here all night."

"Ah, but he's a clever man, is Joss Doomsday."

"Don't slander," Gareth said sharply. "Why would Joss do such a thing to his own uncle?"

John Groom tapped the side of his nose. "Elijah Doomsday was talking to that there Revenue lawyer-man, Sir Hugo's brother, that's why. Doomsdays won't have liked that."

Gareth removed himself from the conversation at that point to worry. He doubted the authorities would be troubled by, or trouble themselves with, Elijah's death, but he didn't like the idea of people gossiping about Joss or spreading spite. Gareth would swear Joss had slept in the house all night, even on the bedroom floor, unless that would make things worse overall. He hoped that if Joss needed him to say anything, he'd be told what it was in advance.

They'd spoken this morning about telling Uncle Henry to clear off together. Joss was probably busy, Gareth thought, and decided it could wait, with a little guilty hope the man would just go away. Surely he must realise that Gareth had nothing to do with any of it.

He wanted to speak to Joss. He resented that he couldn't simply walk down to the Revelation, give his condolences for what they were worth, and offer to help. But he couldn't, so he got on with his own business until, around six in the evening, a youth came to the door.

Gareth didn't recognise him, but that meant nothing: Joss had a lot of people. He took the rather battered note he was proffered and broke the plain wax seal.

To Sir Gareth Inglis (London)
From Josiah Doomsday (Kent)

Sir—Will you please accompany the bearer. A talk is needful between us, due to our earlier aquaintence and the current situation. Please go with the bearer.

Yrs
Jos. Doomsday

That was bafflingly formal: presumably Joss had suspected it might be read by others. It was unquestionably his writing, not to mention the names. "Very well," Gareth said. "I'll get my coat."

The youth walked with him up the path behind Tench House, towards the dyke where they'd sat, beyond which was the looker's hut. Gareth wanted to say, *I know where I'm going*, but decided against it. He might be wrong.

He wasn't. The youth took him to the looker's hut and them made an 'after you' gesture.

The hut was pitch dark inside, thanks to the shutters. Gareth took two steps in and the door shut behind him, leaving him in complete blackness. "What—Joss?"

A bolt scraped. It sounded like it was on the outside of the door. "Joss?" Gareth repeated.

Nothing. The room didn't *feel* occupied; he couldn't hear breath. He stepped back to the door in the blackness and pulled, tugged, then he was struggling, jerking at the handle, to no effect. It was bolted or locked from outside. He was inside, and he was trapped.

Calm down, he told himself. *Think.*

Joss wouldn't have left orders to lock him in the darkness. Unless Gareth had ever expressed a desire to be kidnapped by a handsome smuggler, which he was sure he hadn't but the rising panic was making him a little uncertain of his memory. *Why yes, there was a conversation, you said you wanted to be locked up...*

No. But maybe the youth had misunderstood Joss's orders? Maybe he'd said, 'Get him to the looker's hut and keep him there till I arrive.' That was perfectly possible, except that the words *Wait for me* would have done the same job.

The note had been Joss's handwriting, round and determined. He was sure of it. And the reference to London and Kent proved it anyway—

The answer crashed into his mind. He stood a second, feeling dizzy and sick, then groped his way round the side of the hut to find the bench, patted the mattress to be absolutely sure Joss wasn't lying there in some perverse practical joke (*please, please*), and sat heavily.

Joss hadn't needed to say London and Kent to prove anything in a note sent today. But before their reunion... Gareth could all but see the memory in the blackness. Luke holding a letter. Joss offering it to him in the garden.

Someone else had taken the note; someone who knew about the looker's hut, and that Gareth would go there willingly and unquestioningly. And by 'someone' Gareth meant Elijah bloody Doomsday, who was dead. Which meant, unavoidably, dreadfully, that he had talked first.

Gareth faced that head-on for a long moment in the dark. Then he got up, made his way carefully across the little hut, shuffling and hands out, found the window, and started trying to get through the shutters.

He shook. He rattled. He found a stool after a frustrating ten minutes of groping in the darkness and slammed it against the shutters till it broke. He stood by the window and shouted until his throat hurt, hoping against hope that someone might be passing by the middle of an empty field.

None of it did any good, because he was on Romney Marsh, and so isolated he might as well be on the moon.

He had no idea how long it took before the door opened, but when it did, the man in the doorway was silhouetted against late twilight.

Gareth leapt up. He stopped as the man raised his arm, and he made out a pistol. "Don't move."

"Mr. Sweetwater." Gareth's voice rasped. "What's going on?"

Bill Sweetwater came in, followed by another man, with a lantern, and a third hulking shape. That was Bowring, the huge man who had attacked him in the lane. The man with the lantern was Lionel.

Gareth stared. "What the—"

"Shut up," Sweetwater said. "Bolt the door, Bowring. Now, Sir Gareth, I've done asking nicely. Where's the money?"

"I don't know."

Sweetwater shook his head in a mockery of sadness. "There's no point lying, Sir Gareth. You're a long way from help here, and we're all tired of your games."

"It's not a game. I don't *know*. I didn't speak to my father for twenty years before he died. I wasn't involved in his dealings."

"But you know about them."

"I do now, because you and my uncle Henry started demanding money from me! For heaven's sake, I only came to the Marsh in February."

"And you've been all over it, just like your old man, fossicking in dykes and nosing round crannies," Sweetwater said. "You've been looking for it. Elijah saw you searching at the Isle. I saw your map."

"I'm a naturalist, like my father. That's what the map shows. I was looking for great crested newts! For God's sake, Lionel, you can tell them—"

"You do know," Lionel said. "You're hand in glove with smugglers."

"I? What about you? I wasn't running guineas!"

"Your man tried to drive us off today," Lionel snarled. "Well, I won't be driven. We'll have the money out of you, and you'd better give it over now or you won't like what's coming."

"You know very well I don't have it. Your father was searching my house for days—"

"And you kept your study well locked to stop him finding anything."

"My private business!" Gareth shouted. "Why should I let him make himself master of my affairs?"

"I'm the master here," Sweetwater said flatly, cutting across Lionel's reply. "There's ten thousand guineas missing. I want it."

"I don't have it!"

"You have money in funds," Lionel said. "You can give us the guineas or a draft on your bank, I don't care which."

"You don't believe I have it at all," Gareth said, numb. "You're just making this an excuse for robbery. You're stealing my inheritance and pretending you have a right—"

"Your father stole mine! Ten thousand guineas! We're ruined if we can't repay it!"

"You stole it first! Why on earth would you *do* that? You're rich!"

Lionel sent him a look of pure hate. "Not since that damned old fool acquired a taste for speculation."

"That and your taste for gambling," Sweetwater remarked. "Mr. Inglis had plenty to say on that. Lot of family trouble and none of it mine to care about. I want half, tonight."

"This is absurd," Gareth said. "You can't just demand I pay you a fortune for nothing."

Sweetwater turned to look directly at him. His eyes were bland, even a little amused. "It's not for nothing, Sir Gareth. It's for you lying to me, and your father stealing from us and our hard work. For you walking out of this hut on your own feet instead of crawling on broken legs. Even for me not asking questions about you meeting Joss Doomsday in this here hut." He smiled without mirth. "You're in no position to argue."

"I don't have it!" Gareth's voice cracked. "How many times—"

Sweetwater hit him. It was an open-handed slap that sent Gareth's head snapping to the side, so he staggered and half fell. "As many times as you like until you tell us where the money is."

"Or a draft—" Lionel began.

"No." Sweetwater's voice was still level. "The guineas. You swore he knew where the money is, and I don't like being lied to. Did you lie to me?"

"No. No, he knows. He's been searching since he got here. The Doomsday man said that everyone's seen him."

"Newts and beetles," Gareth said. His cheek stung painfully. "I was looking for newts and beetles!"

"Liar." Sweetwater hit him again, this time a backhander that had him reeling. "Where's the guineas? Tell me or I'll take you apart."

"He's got the money in funds," Lionel said urgently as Gareth clutched his face. His eye was throbbing. "He can sign a promissory note—"

"What use is that to me? Or will he sign it all to you and you'll pay me my share?" Sweetwater appeared genuinely amused by this. "And I'm to trust you as an honest broker? No, Sir Gareth here will tell me where the coin is, and you'll help make him. And if we can't persuade him to talk between us, maybe I'll have to decide he was telling the truth and you were lying."

"I'm not lying," Lionel said urgently. "He is. Do it to him."

Gareth stared at him. "You're going to let him assault me when you know damned well I don't have the money? Lionel!"

Sweetwater moved. Gareth flailed desperately at him, trying to fend him off, and found himself caught by both arms with Sweetwater behind him, pinioning him. He struggled to nightmarishly little effect against the strong grip.

"Have a go," Sweetwater said.

Lionel looked blank. "At—?"

"You want him to talk? Make him."

"Me?"

"You think I should do all the work? You said he knows where it is, so make him tell us."

Lionel looked around as though assuring himself this wasn't a jest. Gareth said, "For God's sake!"

"Do it," Sweetwater said. "Or I might think you don't mean it."

Lionel's mouth worked, as if he were assuring himself of something, then he stepped forward and threw a punch to Gareth's stomach. It was a puny blow, almost flinching, nothing compared to the force Sweetwater had used. It still hurt immensely.

"Lionel!" he gasped.

Lionel was avoiding his eyes. "I never liked you." It sounded as though he was reminding himself. "Your father stole our money."

"Again," Sweetwater said. "He pays or you will. In the face, and harder."

Lionel's hands were shaking. He'd hit Gareth often enough in their boyhood, but they both knew this was different. Gentlemen let other people get their hands dirty.

Lionel made a fist, then lowered it, and licked his lips. "I've a better idea. He has a sister. Seventeen. If you threatened her, he'd talk."

The words buzzed in Gareth's ears for a second, then he was thrashing, fighting harder than he'd known he could. He slammed his heel on Sweetwater's foot, tore an arm free with nothing in mind except getting to Lionel, and managed to smash one furious, vengeful punch into his cousin's face before Sweetwater hauled him back. "I'll kill you! If you touch her, I will kill you!"

"There," Sweetwater said. "Well done, Lionel. I should have thought of that myself. Now, Sir Gareth. Guineas, or we get your sister in here and take our time with her. What's the name again?"

Lionel dabbed at his split lip with a handkerchief and sent Gareth a savage look. "Cecilia. She's got nice tits."

Gareth was still struggling fruitlessly. "You bastard. Joss will kill you! When he finds out, he'll leave you in pieces from here to Hythe!"

Sweetwater laughed softly, the noise vibrating near Gareth's ear. "Guineas or Miss Cecilia, Sir Gareth. Choose."

"I don't have the bloody money!" Gareth shouted. "You could have it if I knew where it was, but I cannot simply produce ten thousand guineas now!" Or pounds either, but he'd worry about that later; he could not have these bastards go to Tench House, where Cecy and Catherine would be unprotected. "I'll pay you five thousand, Mr. Sweetwater. Whatever I can withdraw tomorrow and a draft on the rest."

"Mmm," Sweetwater said. "That's a good offer, but if you're sitting on ten thousand guineas, well, you might give five thousand away and still feel pleased with yourself for keeping the rest. So how do I know you're not holding it back?"

"You said you wanted half!" Gareth almost screamed. "I am *offering* you—"

"Drafts can be stopped. I want coin, and you've got it. I saw your map, Sir Gareth. I've seen you searching the Marsh with my own eyes, and don't tell me that's for beetles. No I don't think I'm taking your offer. I've got a better idea."

They walked through the Marsh, Gareth with a gag in his mouth, his hands pinioned behind his back, flanked by Bowring and Sweetwater. They'd made clear what he could expect if he attempted to make a noise or a run for it. He'd have tried anyway, if only he'd seen another human soul who might have helped. He didn't.

There was a half moon, enough light that Gareth found himself able to put his feet where they should go. Lionel, with no practice nightwalking or traversing the Marsh, stumbled, slipped, and swore. The wet sucking sound of him stepping into unexpected liquid was a tiny consolation in a hellish situation. Gareth had no idea where they were going, or what Sweetwater expected, and the curdling fear for himself was only equalled by his terror for Catherine and Cecy.

Would they worry about him? Probably not. He often roamed the Marsh at night without much explanation or saying when he'd be back, and Catherine believed he'd gone to meet Joss. They had no reason to be concerned. And Lionel had said Joss had told the Inglises to leave the Marsh; would he imagine the threat to Gareth had passed? Would he be too busy, with Elijah killed and himself suspected?

Gareth tried to tell himself not to panic, to focus on what he could do instead of things he couldn't. Unfortunately, he couldn't think of anything to do at all.

After trudging a mile or so, they struck off to the right, in the direction of the coast, approaching the Wall. They were some-where north of Dymchurch, up past Marshland Gut, in the long empty stretch between Dymchurch and Hythe. He couldn't imag-ine why they were here, instead of on Walland Marsh. This wasn't Sweetwater territory.

Here the coast road ran along the top of the Wall, twenty feet above ground level. They ascended to join it, Sweetwater and Bowring pushing Gareth between them, Lionel squelching furi-ously behind. Gareth looked around, breath short in his despera-tion to see someone, anyone. Surely from this height—?

He had a view across the Marsh from here, over the dark plain studded with thorn trees and the occasional building. A handful of faint lights, pinpricks from Burmarsh. Not a human soul.

"Down," Sweetwater said, and gave him a shove.

Down meant to the strand, on the far side of the Wall. Bowring went first, then Gareth, his hands loosed for the purpose, clambered down. Cold water slopped over his shoes. The tide was coming in.

"Right," Sweetwater said. "Tie him to the Wall."

Gareth couldn't understand that for a second, and then he fought. He lashed out viciously, smacking Bowring in the eye, and turned to flee, except that Sweetwater was in his way. He kicked and struggled, and found himself slammed against the Wall, a blow to the stomach stealing his breath.

"Lash him," Sweetwater growled. He and Lionel, face grey in the moonlight, held Gareth pinned while Bowring pinioned his wrists, knotting a strong cord around his hands and looping it around a couple of jutting spars. By the time Bowring was done, the tide was over their ankles. When it was full in, it would reach almost to the top of the Wall.

Sweetwater tested the knots. "Right. Last chance. Where's the money? Only, don't lie to me. Acause here's what: you tell me where the guineas are, and once I've found 'em I'll come back for you. You don't tell me, or they aren't there, and I'll fetch your sister instead and make her scream while you drown. So this is your last chance. Where are the guineas?"

He jerked the gag up. Gareth said desperately, "I'll give you anything. I don't *have* the guineas. But you can—"

Sweetwater shoved the gag back into place. "Obstinate, ain't he? We'll leave you here, Sir Gareth, and fetch your pretty sister. Maybe by the time we're back you'll be ready to talk."

Gareth shouted into the cloth, desperately trying to make himself heard. Sweetwater ignored him. "Bowring, you keep watch. Lionel, you come with me. I dare say you can persuade the lady nicely."

Gareth screamed into his gag. He tried to pour everything he felt into his expression, as though he could strike Lionel dead with the force of his gaze, but his cousin didn't even meet his eyes.

They clambered back up onto the Wall. Gareth jerked violently at his bonds, till Bowring batted him across the side of the head. "Stop that. I'm going up. You make me come down and get wet, you'll be sorry." He clambered up the wall, a laborious process from the grunting.

Now what? The tide would rise inexorably, faster and faster as it moved towards its peak. The water was already painfully cold on his feet and calves. In an hour it might be up to his chest. He didn't want to imagine the slow rise. What if they didn't return? What would it be like when it reached his chin, when he was expecting it to reach his nose and mouth? He wondered how long he might stand on tiptoes, and if one might plunge one's face into the water simply to end the torture of waiting.

Surely they wouldn't just leave him tied here to drown, he told himself. Except Lionel wasn't going to go against Bill Sweetwater, that much was clear. Nobody knew where he was. And even if anyone happened to pass along the road at this hour they wouldn't see him here, on the wrong side of the Wall.

He attempted to convey via urgent noises that he wanted to talk to Bowring. He was ready to offer everything he had for his freedom, but the big man didn't respond. Maybe he'd gone. Maybe Gareth was entirely alone.

The moon shone on the shifting sea. The water rose and rose.

Eternity passed. Gareth had no idea how long it was; he could see nothing but dark water, hear nothing but the splash of the waves and the occasional hoot of owls. The water had reached his thighs and he could barely feel his toes; his wrists hurt from the rope and his shoulders were afire from the stretching, but that was the least of his concerns. He wanted Joss, so painfully and miserably that he found tears running down his face into the gag, but Joss had no way of knowing where he was. He'd be found eventually, but tucked against this side of the Wall, it might be days. Unless they cut his body loose and let it drift away on the tide.

They won't kill you like this, he told himself, except Bill Sweetwater had killed Elijah just last night. And if Gareth died, Uncle Henry would become baronet, with Lionel to succeed him. That alone might sway his cousin to let this happen, but the fact was, Gareth knew too much and had threatened to tell it.

They were going to kill him. They had to: it had all gone too far, and he would never see Joss again. The only question was what they might do to Cecy first.

The icy water swelled, over his thighs and groin and waist, rising at horrible speed. He stared out at the sea, utterly alone.

Twenty-four

THE SUN WAS SETTING. WITH JOSS RIDING WESTWARD, IT WAS catching him in the eyes. He just hoped the horse wouldn't stumble.

He was riding Elijah's foul-tempered bay at the fastest canter he could risk. He could have pushed his own Fleurie a fraction faster and had a smoother ride of it, but she'd already carried him across the Marsh and back today. Beside him, Sophy was urging on Isaac's ratty grey mare, the last of the Doomsday horseflesh. Everyone out looking for Gareth would be doing so on foot.

He was thinking about horses because he didn't want to think about Gareth.

Taken off by a man with a letter, and he bet he knew which letter that was. If he'd only told Gareth it had been stolen. He hadn't meant to keep it from him, it just hadn't come up in the course of the argument, and had honestly slipped his mind after, with everything else going on, and now look. All Joss's fault, and Gareth would pay the price.

No. He would not. Joss would get him back unharmed, and Bill bloody Sweetwater would pay for every minute's fear on both their parts. That was why Joss was heading to Camber in an all but straight line, cantering over the marshland rather than keeping to the maundering paths, setting the bay at dykes with gritted teeth.

Nobody could ride this way who didn't know the Marsh intimately: every point where a dyke could be leapt to avoid a dog-legged path, every unexpected thorn hedge or treacherous bit of boggy ground. Outmarsh would be confounded; most Marshfolk wouldn't risk it. But Joss had lived and breathed the Marsh all his life, and taken Fleurie on many a frantic night-time gallop with the Revenue at his heels. This was his heartland, and he rode accordingly.

He had to restrain himself from kicking the bay to a gallop now. It was ten miles from Globsden Gut to Camber Sands: he needed to pace the horse, though the urge for *faster, faster* thrummed through his veins.

At least Elijah hadn't stinted when spending Doomsday money on himself. The bay was a powerful beast and a good jumper: Joss set him at a dyke and soared across, grunting as he landed. He'd done close to thirty miles in the saddle already today, not to mention having Gareth ride him last night, and everything from hips to knees was aching.

That was fine. He'd take it all out on Bill Sweetwater.

The path ran their way a little while past Great Cheyne Court. Joss took the bay onto it, heard the double sound of hooves as Sophy came up behind him on the grey.

Joss hadn't been able to think after Luke's news, his mind a frantic cloud of rage and fear, but Sophy had taken charge like...well, like Ma Doomsday's daughter. She'd dragged him over to Tench House, talked to Catherine, forced him to sit down and think about what was going on, made what plans they could, and told him she was riding with him. He wasn't sure what he'd have done without her, but it would probably have been something stupid.

What was going on: well, that seemed clear enough. Bill Sweetwater had to flee the Marsh, and he wanted to do that rich. He thought that he could get money out of Gareth. And Joss's protection, his threats and promises and authority, were worth nothing in this situation, because Bill had killed Elijah Doomsday, and he might as well hang for a sheep as a lamb.

Joss hated that saying. *Been bad? Do worse.*

Bill was out there on the Marsh somewhere, with Gareth. Maybe with the Inglises too, since Joss had made enemies of them as well, but he couldn't think now about how badly he'd handled this. He'd learn his lessons once he got Gareth back unharmed. And if he couldn't do that—

He would do it. He was Joss Doomsday and he *would* find Gareth before anything happened to him, because no other outcome was bearable.

He'd got his people out, combing the Marsh: Matt and Finty and Isaac and Emily. Graveyard was at Tench House in case of trouble; anyone with news would bring it back to Asa at the Revelation. He'd left Luke with his grandfather to serve as messenger boy. And he was riding to Camber to confront Nate Sweetwater now, with only his little sister at his side.

Some people might call that foolhardy.

The sun had disappeared as they approached the Kent Ditch, far too wide to jump, though that didn't stop Joss thinking about it for a reckless moment. He took the wiser course, and directed the horse south toward Broomhill and the crossing there.

Sophy caught up, riding alongside him. "A'right, Joss?"

"No."

"We'll get him back."

"Will we?"

He could feel her glare on his skin. "I *said*, we'll get him back."

They cantered past the sand hills into Camber, as the distant church bells of Rye chimed the hour. Nine. Gareth had been taken some time after six o'clock.

The dusk was thickening to night. There was a light burning in Nate Sweetwater's house. Joss stalked to the door and banged on it with a fist, and Mrs. Sweetwater answered.

"Mistress," Joss snapped. "Where's your man?"

She moved out of the way, calling, "Nate!" Joss walked in past her, trying not to show how much his thighs ached, a hand resting on each hip, where he had his knives. Sophy was close behind, at his shoulder.

Nate Sweetwater's front room was full. Eight or nine men, all or most of his closest crew, none of them looking pleased to see the Doomsdays. No Bill.

"Joss," Nate said, rising. He looked wary. Well he might.

"Where's Bill?"

"You've not come here for Bill."

"I have that," Joss said. The knife-hilts were smooth and inviting under his hands. "Where is he?"

There was a general murmur from the Sweetwater men. One at the back rose, and Joss recognised the ratty man he'd thrashed for attacking Gareth. Nadgett. "You telling Nate what to do, Joss Doomsday?"

"Quiet," Nate said. "Now, listen. I don't know what happened to your man Elijah—"

"Yeah, you do," Sophy said. "Bill broke his neck and threw him in the Canal."

"Three witnesses," Joss added. "Don't tither."

"Don't pretend you liked the arsehole," said Nadgett. "If Bill rid you of him, maybe you should be thanking us."

"I'd like to hear you say that to Ma's face," Sophy remarked. "You'd piss your breeches first, big mouth." She wiggled her little finger to indicate what wasn't big about the speaker. Several men laughed; he gave a snarl of anger. Joss and Nate said, in chorus, "Shut up!"

"I said quiet," Nate added, glaring at his men. "We're talking. All right, Joss, we've wronged the Doomsdays. I won't argue that. I don't know where Bill is right now—"

"He's kidnapped Sir Gareth Inglis."

Nate's jaw dropped. It looked entirely unfeigned. "He what?"

"You told him to clear off the Marsh before anyone came to blows over him, right?" It was what Joss would do with a murderous relative. Exile the troublemaker, prevent further trouble. "Well, he didn't. He went after Sir Gareth. A Dymchurch man. *Mine*."

"Shit," Nate said.

"I warned you, Nate Sweetwater." Joss held his gaze, letting his pulsing rage sound in his voice. "I told you to lay off Dymchurch folk. We shook hands on it."

"For Christ's sake, the chuckleheaded, contrary dolt. I told him to leave Sir Gareth be. *And* I told him to get his arse off the Marsh by nightfall, so—You." He swung to one of his men whose grumbling had become audible. "Got something to say?"

"Aye, I do," the man said, coming to his feet. He was a thickset fellow with an aggressive look. "I say be damned to Elijah Doomsday and all the Doomsdays with him. I say Bill's been right all along. You're losing your nerve, Nate, and if you can't lead proper-like, we won't follow. I say Bill made a good start to the job, and now we put this pair of Doomsdays in the water along with their uncle."

Joss's hands closed on the hilts of his knives, but Nate was already moving, and there was a very solid crack as his huge fist connected with the speaker's face. He went down cold, head wobbling as he fell in a way that didn't look good for getting up again.

"Anyone agree with him?" Nate asked.

Apparently nobody did. Nate looked around until the silence became painful, then nodded. "Good." He turned back to the Doomsdays, and narrowed his eyes as he saw the pistol Sophy held. "No need for that."

"I'm sure there's not," she agreed, unmoving.

"Put it away, Soph." Joss took his own hands from his knives, though not too far. "We understand each other, Nate and me. I understand this is Bill's doing. Nate understands that Bill's run up a hefty reckoning, and there'll be devil to pay." He met Nate's eyes with a hard look. "I want Sir Gareth back, safe, tonight. You said he'd be unharmed, you shook hands on that, and I'm trusting you to make it happen. Acause you don't bring harm to two Dymchurch men and not expect a war."

There was a growl from the assembled men. Sophy stepped forward, pistol raised. "We can start it here if you like."

"Every bastard get back!" Nate snarled.

"Meaning you too, Sophy Doomsday," Joss said. "Enough of this. Nate, if you want to deal with Bill, that's your right. If you don't, I will."

Nate scowled in thought. He was in a tricky spot here: Sweetwater in the wrong; his brother disobeying him and, it seemed, undermining him too; needing to keep his authority, but newly reluctant to take risks. "You're sure about this, are you? Kidnapping the new baronet?"

"Your Bill was working with Henry Inglis when he killed Elijah. Sir Gareth's been taken, and we both know what that's about. Yes, I'm sure." Joss glanced around the room. "And where's Bowring? Your big lunk who attacked him before?"

Nate frowned. "Anyone? Nadgett?"

"Bill said he had a job for him," Nadgett allowed reluctantly. "Early afternoon."

"What? Where?"

Nadgett's eyes dropped. "Might have been up Dymchurch way."

"Fucking hell," Nate said. "All right, you bastards, on your use-less feet, we've work to do. Joss—"

"Sir Gareth back tonight, unharmed, and you and I have no quarrel," Joss said. "And I need two horses, right now. The best you've got."

The ride back felt like a nightmare, one of those that never seemed to end. The half moon didn't cast nearly enough light for safety and they were mounted on unknown horses, a pair of rawboned crea-tures Joss didn't trust to keep their footing. It would have been sensible to walk them, or at least keep to the paths, and Joss would have recommended Sophy to do so if he hadn't thought she might shoot him.

He couldn't be sensible. Gareth had been taken hours ago, and Bill Sweetwater was an outlaw now, a doomed man with nothing to lose. So Joss urged his borrowed mount to the fastest speed he dared, flying over the dykes and plunging across the Marsh, through the clutching wisps of mist and treacherous tufty ground, hooves splashing, stum-bling now and then, never slowing. A steady stream of foul language told him Sophy was at his side, and he took some comfort in that.

For all his effort, the clocks struck ten as they passed Old Romney, and it was the best part of a half hour from there to the Revelation. Home ground though, and Joss urged the horse to greater speed, apologising mentally to the beast as they covered the last, endless bit of distance.

His legs almost gave way as he dismounted outside the inn; he clutched at the saddle to stay upright. "Granda?"

"Joss." Asa sounded tense. "Any news?"

It wasn't that Joss had thought Gareth would have got safely home in his absence. He hadn't thought that at all, so he didn't know why the words felt like a blow.

"No news," Sophy said for him. "Went and stirred Nate Sweetwater up. Nothing here?"

"Nobody's come back," Asa said. "Joss, Luke has gone."

"What?"

"Luke. Said he had an idea and ran off. More than an hour ago, didn't say where he was going, and not come back."

The last, the *very last* thing in the sodding world Joss needed was that plaguesome brat causing more trouble. Luke had been told to stay here: if he'd gone off and broken his ankle in a dyke, he could drown in it for all Joss cared.

Because nobody had come back to say they knew where Gareth was. Nobody was here to help. There was the whole Marsh to search, and only him and Sophy to do it, and the impossibility of the task stretched over him like the night sky. He was briefly grateful for the darkness hiding his face.

"Joss?" Asa said. "I know you're fearful for Sir Gareth. But the boy is lost."

Joss's fists clenched so tight, the nails dug into his palms. He took a deep breath, not knowing what he'd reply, and Sophy said, "What's that?"

"What?"

"Listen. Something... Come here, you evil bitch." She swung herself up onto the borrowed horse again with a startling oath— Joss wasn't the only one with painful legs, sounded like—and trotted off down the road towards Dymchurch.

"What was that?" Asa demanded.

"I don't know." Joss hadn't heard anything, and couldn't now but the scrape of distant hoofbeats, but Sophy had hearing like a bat.

Endless moments later she was back, the borrowed horse trudging resentfully out of the night, and she had a smaller shape in front of her. Luke slipped off the horse almost before it halted, stumbling forward. "Joss!"

"Where've you—"

"I found him!" Luke blurted. His shoulders were heaving as he struggled to regain his breath.

Joss grabbed his arm and dragged him over towards the Revelation and the pool of light from its lantern. The boy was scarlet and filthy, his brown eyes wide and frantic under the thick brows, the wound an ugly red bracket to his face, and Joss had never welcomed a sight more. "I found him, but you've got to come quick. *Quick*, Joss. It's the tide."

They took Fleurie, who'd been dozing in her stall. She seemed to be reasonably rested, but Joss whispered an apology anyway, promised her oats, reassured them both it was only a mile. Luke, sitting behind him, gave his story as they rode.

"I went to the looker's hut. The one where you and Sir Gareth— you know."

Joss hadn't realised Luke had known about the hut, as well as the Warren. Doubtless he had told Elijah, who had told Bill Sweetwater. If Luke had mentioned that bit of prying, Joss would have had the looker's hut searched hours ago. He choked down the urge to point that out. "Go on."

"I thought of it when it was getting dark. Only, I didn't want to explain why he might have gone there, so I didn't say to anyone.

I just thought I'd check, to be sure. And when I got there I saw Bill Sweetwater, and that Lionel Inglis, and Sweetwater's big man, Bowring."

"Hell's teeth."

"You'd gone to Camber and everyone was all over. I didn't know where to go for help. So I stopped and listened. Bill was asking Sir Gareth for money. They, uh, they hit him a few times. And then Bill said he was going to take him somewhere and they set off crossmarsh. And I thought, if I don't follow I'll lose him, so I went by-bush." Sneaking along dykes and hedges, that meant, and Joss could only be grateful for this most sneaking of boys. "Went a good mile, down to the Wall. And they took him over the Wall, to the sand, and—and Joss, they *tied* him to it, and the tide's coming in."

Joss's lips moved soundlessly. Luke said, "Joss?"

"I heard you. I heard. How far in is it?"

"Rising fast. We've time, I'm sure we do, but—" He shuddered, the movement vibrating through Joss too.

"All right," Joss said with a calm he didn't feel, urging Fleurie to a faster trot. "What then?"

"Bill and that Lionel left him there while they went to get Miss Cecy." He'd already told them that part back at the Revelation. Sophy had headed straight to Tench House to aid Graveyard, who was on guard there. "They left Bowring with Sir Gareth, so I came to find you. And that's all, but—but you'll get him safe, Joss, won't you?"

"I'll get him," Joss said. "Where is he?"

"Next rise. What about Bowring?"

"Don't worry about him. Mind the horse. I'll be back soon."

Bowring had heard them coming. He stood at the top of the path that led up to the Wall, a huge form dimly silhouetted against the dark sky. Joss called, "Evening."

"You," Bowring growled.

"Me." Joss pushed back his long leather coat, took a knife in each hand, tossed and caught one with a casual gesture. Foolery with blades was a trick he'd learned off the French privateer: it concentrated people's minds. "Here's how it is, Bowring. The Doomsdays are coming. Nate Sweetwater's on his way, and he's in middling order with Bill and everyone who helped him. And you've got Sir Gareth down there, so I'm going to get him, and the only question is if I walk past you or over you to do it. My advice is, point your face to Hythe and start running."

Bowring started to say something, but a call drifted past them, very like an owl hoot, except it wasn't an owl. That was the Doomsday night-call, so often heard echoing over the Marsh, and Bowring knew it as well as Joss.

He didn't know it was being made by a thirteen-year-old. He hesitated, but then another call echoed back from further away, the direction of Dymchurch. A Doomsday had heard, and would be on their way.

Joss turned his wrists so his blades glittered as they caught the moonlight. Bowring weighed up the odds, said, "Ah, sod Bill," turned, and lumbered off without farewell.

That was a relief, because Joss had not fancied his chances in a fight. He hurried up the path, peered over the top of the Wall, looked down to where the dark waves splashed against it, and made out a dim shape.

Gareth.

He only just had the sense to pull off his coat and drop it on the path. Then he was scrambling down the Wall like a squirrel, painful thighs forgotten. "Gareth! *Gareth!*"

No response. He leapt down into the water with a splash and a curse—it was up to mid-chest on him and merciful cold—and there was Gareth, strung up and gagged, his eyes wide, alive.

"Oh Jesus." Joss couldn't seem to catch his breath. He grabbed Gareth's face, wet and icy cold. "Fuckers, fuckers, merciful anointed *fuckers*. I'm here, London. I'm here." He carefully edged a knife under the gag, then sliced through the cloth.

Gareth gasped as Joss pulled the sodden material away. "Oh God, oh God." He was shuddering convulsively and his teeth were chattering. "Joss!"

Joss kissed him, a hard press of lips, and then swung to his right wrist to cut the cord. "Hold on. I'll get you out."

"Cecy," Gareth gasped.

"She's all right."

"No! Sweetwater, gone after Cecy!"

Joss paused in his work to press a hand to Gareth's face. "I *know*, sweetheart. Hear me? Graveyard's at Tench House with Sophy, and they know Bill's coming. Dare say him and Lionel are getting leathered to pulp right now. Miss Cecy's safe as houses."

"Are you sure?"

"Promise."

He should maybe not have said that, because the relief seemed to cut whatever last strings had been keeping Gareth vertical, and he sagged against the Wall.

"Hold up." Joss sawed through the last strands and Gareth's wrist came free. He grabbed at Joss, who pulled him as close as he could. "I've got you. I've got you. Hearts alive, London. Let go now, I need to do your other hand. And they'd better not have killed Bill over there, because I need to kick his head in."

"Lionel," Gareth managed. "His idea to go after Cecy."

"Both their heads." Joss had no objection. It was something to look forward to, just as soon as he'd got himself and Gareth out of the sea, ideally before anyone's balls froze off. He sawed at the wet rope. "Let me get your hand free, and—"

An urgent owl-hoot caught his ear. He knew the sound well: it meant *trouble*. "Drat. We need to hurry." The sodden cord finally gave way. He helped Gareth pull his wrist free. "Got to climb now."

"Climb?" Gareth whispered.

Joss wasn't looking forward to this himself, with tired thighs, drenched breeches, and boots full of water. Gareth was soaked to above the waist; his arms must be screaming from being stretched out so long; he was shaking with cold, and his feet and fingers would be numb. He stared up at the twenty-foot ascent as though it was a mountain.

Joss squeezed his arm. "I know you're tired. But you've got to. *We've* got to."

Gareth swallowed. "I can't. So cold."

"You can," Joss told him, willing it to be true. "I'm telling you you can, and I'll be with you every step. I'll keep you safe, London. I won't leave you."

"Promise?" Gareth whispered.

Another hoot: Luke, calling his warning. Joss grabbed both his hands. "Promise. I love you. But the tide's not waiting and we're not getting any drier down here, so up we go, and quiddy with it."

The climb was one more nightmare in an evening full of them. Gareth clearly didn't have the strength but he did it anyway, with agonising slowness but never giving up, seawater streaming off his sodden trousers as he emerged from the waves. He moved from one foothold to the next, breath coming in desperate sobs, with Joss straddling him all the way, pushing and pulling, using all his muscle to force and drag Gareth up the impossible, endless Wall, until at last he rolled and sprawled onto the path at the top.

Joss clambered over him as he lay, soaked and gasping and shudderingly cold. He grabbed Gareth's arm. "Up. Come on."

Gareth made it to his knees, but that was it: they were out of time now, because Joss could hear footsteps approaching. He draped his coat over Gareth's shoulders, carefully, lovingly. "There you go, sweetheart. Hold on for me, now. I'll just be a minute."

"Joss?"

No more time, none at all. He stepped forward, guarding Gareth, as two figures plodded up the path that led to the top of the Wall.

Bill Sweetwater had a pistol in one hand, a knife in the other. Behind him, Lionel Inglis was soaked from head to foot, and streaked with mud.

"Fall into a dyke, lawyer?" Joss enquired.

Lionel swore at him. Sweetwater's expression hardened as he looked around. "Bowring?"

"Cleared off," Joss said. "Just you and me, Bill."

Sweetwater snarled. Joss pulled his knives from their sheaths, settling them in his hands. He and Bill were both slightly crouched, watching each other like dogs ready to spring. Except Joss's breeches were soaked and heavy, and his waterlogged boots sloshed when he moved, and his legs felt like lead.

Didn't matter. Bill had tied Gareth to the Wall. Joss would kill him with one hand behind his back if he had to.

"Looks like two against one to me," Bill said. "You sure you want to do this, Joss? I put a bullet in your head, what's to stop me carving your boyfriend up till he tells me where the guineas are?"

"I've men all over the Marsh looking for you. Fire that pistol, you'll have minutes to live."

"And you'll be dead."

Joss grinned at him. "Unless you miss. Talking of misses, what happened to your plans for Miss Cecilia? Didn't go so well?"

Bill swore at him, from which Joss gathered that he'd seen the welcome awaiting him at Tench House and decided not to try his luck. Lionel said, "For God's sake, do something!" He sounded like he was cracking. The Marsh at night could do that.

"Run," Joss suggested. "Both of you. Nate's on his way, and he's an angry man. You've lost, Bill. Get offmarsh now and you might save your skin."

Bill shook his head and raised the pistol, levelling it directly at Joss. "Not without the money. Tell me where it is. Last warning, Joss."

Moonlight flared off Joss's blade as he turned it. "That a promise? I've heard enough talk."

"No!" A croak of a sound, from Gareth, behind him. "Don't shoot, Mr. Sweetwater, please. I'll tell you where the money is, if you don't shoot. Hurt him and you'll never see it."

"I *told* you," Lionel said. "I told you he knew! Kill the other one and make him say!"

"I didn't tell you when you tied me up to drown," Gareth said. "If you hurt a hair of Joss's head, I won't say another word."

"Want to bet?" Bill asked.

"I would," Joss said. He didn't know what Gareth was up to; he'd back him to the hilt anyway. "Right obstinate fellow, the new squire."

"I know where the money is." Gareth sounded raw and desperate. Joss might have believed him himself if he hadn't known better. "It's not far. I'll tell you as long as you don't hurt Joss. And if you promise not to give any of it to Lionel."

"What?" Lionel said.

"Not a penny, you shit," Gareth said, with feeling. "You and your father started this over money you stole in the first place. I hate you both, and I hope you hang. Promise me, Mr. Sweetwater. Take it all every penny. Leave him with nothing."

Lionel gaped in horror. "Good idea," Joss said. "Cut him out."

"No skin off my nose," Bill said.

"No." Lionel's mouth was working. "No. It's my money. You *promised—*"

Bill grinned like a dog. "Piss off, lawyer."

"We said halves!"

"Shut your face. Where is it, Sir Gareth?"

"You'll make sure Lionel gets nothing?" Gareth demanded.

Bill shrugged. "Kill him for you if you want. I can put the ball in his head as easy as Joss's. Up to you."

Lionel's face convulsed. "What? No! *Gareth!*"

"Yes," Gareth said. "Do that. Kill him."

Lionel screamed as he lunged, grabbing for the pistol. Bill wrenched his arm away. The two men struggled for a second, and the gun went off with a deafening report.

"*Joss!*"

Gareth shrieked the name, and then he was somehow on his feet, legs wobbling like a newborn colt as he lunged, apparently unaware Joss had a sodding razor-sharp knife in each hand. Joss dropped one like a hot coal and caught his lover with the hand that freed, pulling him in and holding the other blade well away. "It's all right. I'm all right."

He was; Lionel wasn't. Lionel had slid down to his knees, face incredulous, a dark stain spreading on his chest. His lips worked soundlessly and he fell forward.

Bill Sweetwater flung the empty pistol away. "Right! Where the—"

"Bill." It was Nate Sweetwater's voice, from the path.

Joss had heard the hoofbeats approaching. Bill apparently hadn't: perhaps he'd been concentrating too hard on Gareth's lies. Certainly, his big frame stiffened at his brother's voice.

Joss very gently pushed Gareth away and back, impressed that he stayed on his feet, and scooped the knife off the path. "Here. Take this."

Gareth took the knife like a man who'd never held one before. His eyes were wide and appalled, and his hand shook, but he managed a tiny nod.

Nate had tramped up to the top of the Wall. He was alone, or he'd left his men on the road, whichever. "Bill," he said.

"Nate," Bill said. "Sir Gareth was just saying he knows where the money is."

"Don't be a fool all your life," Nate said wearily. "Who's that dead?"

"Lionel Inglis. Lawyer's son," Joss said.

"My cousin," Gareth added. He was at Joss's shoulder, clutching the knife in a too-tight grip. A child could probably push him over, the state he was in, but he wasn't backing down. "Your brother murdered him."

Nate sighed. "You arsehole, Bill. Look what you did."

"Who cares? Sea'll take him. Sea'll take all of 'em. It's good, Nate, don't you see? Lionel can't blab about the guineas. We'll scare his old man off, or silence him. We get rid of Doomsday now—two of us, we'll take him no trouble—and make the baronet hand the money over. Easy as pie. See?"

"Ah, Bill," Nate said. "You should have gone when I told you."

"I know what's happening," Bill said, low and vicious. "Your bitch is breeding, and you've turned milk-hearted. Well, I haven't and there's a dunnamany Sweetwater men ready and waiting for my word. Pull yourself together and we'll see the sodding Doomsdays off, between us. We'll start it here."

"Bill," Nate said heavily.

"We can have the money, move in on the Doomsdays, take over the Marsh. You and me, Nate! We'll finish Joss now, and do as we please! Why the devil not? Or have you lost your guts?"

Nate let out a breath that rattled. "You rammed stupid chuckleheaded bastard. How many fucking Doomsdays d'you think are listening to you right now?"

The chorus of hoots at that would have sent any real owl into panicked flight. Joss recognised Luke and Sophy—he'd bet she'd followed Bill from Tench House—Matt and Finty, all summoned by Luke's call. His own blessed wonderful crew, God love them. And—

"That you, Tom?" he called.

"A'right, Joss," Tom shouted from ground level.

"What you doing here?"

"Ma sent me. She's in a pretty dobbin over this, I can tell you."

"That's you fucked," Joss told Bill.

"You stupid bastard," Nate said again. "Trying to take over behind my back, like I wouldn't notice. Words about my wife. Killing a Doomsday and kidnapping a baronet and shooting a sodding *lawyer*, you worthless fool!"

Joss could almost have thought he was growing in his wrath, from his outline in the dark. "Nate," he said. "What do you want to do?"

Nate's big shoulders heaved. "I'll deal with him. *Family*."

"I'm sorry for your trouble," Joss said with perfect truth, then raised his voice. "I'll take Sir Gareth back now. Doomsdays, Nate's going safe home to his wife at the end of this business, you all make sure of that. Everyone hear me?"

"Yes, Joss," came the chorus, and Joss heard a certain amount of anticipation in their voices.

"No," Bill said. "No! Nate! You fucking coward!"

Joss didn't wait for what would happen next. Nate could deal with it, and if he didn't, there were a lot of angry Doomsdays, the cover of night, the ever-hungry sea.

He took the knife off Gareth, got a shoulder under his shaking arm, and took him away.

Twenty-five

JOSS WOKE WITH HAIR IN HIS FACE. NOT HIS OWN EITHER. Pale flyaway hair, and a pale shoulder under his arm. Gareth, snoring softly by him.

He could snore and welcome, as long as he was breathing. As long as he was here and alive, and those brutal hours of cold, sick fear were past and gone.

Joss lay back and let himself remember it all—the fear, the rage, the cold, the dreadful not knowing—and then breathed the memories out, making the pictures in his head blur and fade, like rain washing away chalk. It wouldn't make the bad parts disappear right away, but it helped take the sting out. He'd probably need to teach Gareth how to do the same.

He lay there dealing with the memories for what seemed a very long time, until Gareth stirred gently in his arms, mumbled, "Joss," and jerked awake with a cry.

"Here. Here. Got you."

"Joss." Gareth was wide-eyed with fear. "I—Am I at home?"

"Home and safe. Everyone's safe."

"Cecy? Catherine?"

"As houses. I promise. It's all right."

Gareth gave a long, shaky breath out. "How are you here?"

"Brought you back last night. Stayed." Wild horses wouldn't have removed him. They hadn't needed to try, because Catherine Inglis had taken one look at him and announced that he absolutely had to keep guard in Gareth's room, in case of more trouble. Joss made a mental note to send the fine brocaded silk shawl he'd ordered her way; Miss Topgood could make do with calico print. "I wanted to be sure you were warm."

Gareth clutched his arm. He was breathing fast, but it slowed after a moment. "Right. Yes. Uh, Bill Sweetwater—"

"I don't know yet."

"Oh God, what a ghastly mess." Gareth slumped back on the bolster. His face was badly bruised. Joss would have liked a word with Bill Sweetwater or Lionel Inglis, except nobody would be having any more of those. "How did you find me? What *happened*?"

"Luke, mostly. Not such a brat after all." He gave Gareth the story, including the letter, and how that had been all his fault. Gareth didn't say anything to that. He just listened in trembling silence, and at last let out a long breath.

"God, Joss. I was terrified. I thought I was going to die out there, alone, that Cecy would be hurt and I was helpless to do anything. And all the time you were looking for me. The entire Doomsday clan was out looking for me?"

"I said I wouldn't leave you," Joss said. "I won't. Not till you make me, and you'll have to try middling hard on that."

Gareth made a sound like a laugh, but it didn't come out quite right. His mouth worked, and then he buried his face in Joss's shoulder, and Joss held on as he sobbed. That worked pretty well too, to draw memories' teeth.

They got dressed eventually, and reluctantly, and came downstairs, where calm, remote Catherine Inglis grappled Gareth to her in the sort of embrace that had fear and relief boiling off it. There was a deal of hugging and a bit of crying with all three Inglises, and then Miss Cecy turned and held her hand out to Joss.

"Thank you so much, Mr. Doomsday. For saving my brother, and for taking care of us all this time. I'm very grateful." She swallowed. "Is it true that my cousin tried to kill Gareth and came here for—for me?"

Joss hoped nobody had told her what exactly Lionel and Bill Sweetwater had had in mind. "I'm sorry to say it, Miss Cecy. Don't frape, though. You've no more call to worry about either of them."

"Good," she said. "Good."

Probably Joss should have gone back to the Revelation. He didn't, because he needed to be with Gareth, and Gareth and Catherine and Miss Cecy needed each other. Anyway, he had a fair inkling that people would be turning up here.

Sophy and Luke arrived around noon, to nobody's surprise and a heroes' welcome. Catherine, who had spent much of the morning cooking her fears away, insisted they stay to eat, which meant that Joss found himself lunching with not just Gareth but his family too, this time in the dining room of Tench House.

Catherine got Luke to recount his heroic efforts stalking the villains across the Marsh. He did that with particular attention to Lionel falling into a dyke, which got everyone laughing, the kind of can't-breathe unstoppable laugh you needed after too much tension.

Someone had to ask eventually. Joss wasn't surprised it was Catherine. "So what will all this mean for us?"

"Might not be much," Joss said. "Nate doesn't want trouble.

Soph, remind me to get Ma to knit a cap for his baby that's coming. Henry Inglis—"

"Nate'll be talking to him today," Sophy said. "Telling him to keep his trap shut about guineas and get offmarsh if he knows what's good for him. Nate wants all this to go away."

"Don't we all," Gareth said. "I suppose that's best. Or, no, it would be *best* to inform the Revenue about all of this, but—"

"Our father's name," Cecilia said softly. "Our name."

"Let sleeping dogs lie," Joss said. "Your father's dead, and Henry's been punished enough."

"Oh God," Gareth said. "I almost forgot. Lionel."

"Terrible accident, lost to the sea along with Bill, shame," Sophy said cheerfully. "Talking of lost, what about those guineas?" She raised her hands at Joss's glower. "What? We all want to know."

"No," Joss said. "No treasure-seeking."

"There's ten thousand guineas out there!"

"I said, leave it. There's enough people dead over that gold already. You won't be adding to their number, Sophia Doomsday, hear me?"

She glared, then subsided. "Yes, Joss."

"My pa," Luke said. That brought a sudden silence to the table as everyone remembered his father was not even in the ground yet. "He was killed for it."

He'd got himself killed for spite and stupidity in Joss's view, but Luke doubtless needed to make his own tale. "It's blood money," Joss said, in lieu of agreement. "Ill-starred. As to where it is, maybe Sir Hugo or someone else hid it on the Marsh, but far more like it's long gone with Adam Drake. I don't intend to look."

"Nor do I," Gareth said with a shudder. "I don't ever want to hear of guineas again. I'll be very happy to deal in banknotes for the rest of my life."

Miss Cecy and Catherine agreed in strong terms. Joss couldn't help noticing that Luke did not.

They went walking on the Marsh afterwards, across the fields to Blackmanstone rather than to the sea. Joss reckoned Gareth had seen enough of the sea for the next while.

They talked a little. Joss told him about the trick for making memories fade faster, and Gareth listened and nodded, but what really brought the colour back to his cheeks was coming across a great black shorn-bug in the ruined chapel.

"Stag beetle," Gareth said, crouching to look.

"I can see why you call it that. Fine pair of antlers on him."

"Those are mandibles, actually. Jaws."

"They never are." Joss flexed his own jaw with mild horror. "Imagine carrying that around."

"Mmm. My father promised I'd find them here."

Joss didn't comment on that. He squatted down and watched, eyes flicking between the beetle and Gareth's face, and he was ready when Gareth's mouth turned down in a sudden, painful spasm.

"Hey. London." He went onto a knee to keep his balance and put an arm around Gareth's shoulders. They were in the lee of the chapel; they'd see anyone a mile off. "It's all right."

"It truly isn't." Gareth dashed a hand over his eyes. "He was such a selfish, awful man. All this misery because of him. Lionel and Elijah were both dreadful, but now there's Luke and your mother and Uncle Henry mourning them. Not that I care for Uncle Henry, but Lionel was his only child and he loved him. All the pain that's been caused. I spent so much time longing for my father, longing and wishing. And this misery is his legacy. *This* is what he left me."

"He left you the Marsh," Joss said. "He left you bugs and beetles and birds. He left you Catherine, and Miss Cecy. And if you hadn't come here, I'd probably never have seen you again, so you might say he left you us too."

Gareth took a deep breath, calming himself. "Perhaps. I suppose that's true. It might mean more if I thought he'd intended a single part of it."

"Which he didn't, what with being a selfish, shuckish, arbitry arsehole."

Gareth gave a breathy laugh. "No, please. Say what you truly think."

"We'd be here a while if I did that. But all the same, you're here where you belong acause of him, and that's something."

Gareth leaned into him. "It's everything."

"No need to thank him for it, mind."

"God, no. To think that the first time we spoke about this, I was concerned for my family name. A name titled by adultery and distinguished by treason, embezzlement, and murder. That's something to be proud of."

"Oi. Leave your great-grandma out of it." Joss tugged Gareth's hand up and kissed the knuckles. "What's a bar sinister?"

"A heraldic symbol that denotes illegitimacy. Why on earth do you ask?"

"Names," Joss said. "You can run around being proud of them, or ashamed too, but it's all a lot of rubbish, isn't it? A name's no better or worse than the man who bears it."

"Your grandfather changed his," Gareth pointed out.

"He had the chance to be a Doomsday. Wouldn't you?"

"Yes. Yes, I really would." His fingers tightened. "I wish I had the chance."

"So do I," Joss said. "I wish I could offer it. I'd be on one knee right now to ask you, if I could."

Gareth's lips parted. He tried out a few words that didn't come, and then said, "But you are on one knee."

He was, at that. Joss gripped his hand harder. "Well, I can't give you my name, but I love you, London. I do better with you by me, I can't say how much. I like the way the world looks with you. I'm on your side, and I want to stay there for good and all."

"I want you there too," Gareth said. "You make me stronger. You make me *think*. And I want to be there whenever you need me because you're always there for me. I want you on my side. I want to be on yours."

"Just one side," Joss said. "Ours. And us both on it, always."

Gareth leaned forward and Joss met his mouth. Kissing gently, for the first time today because it had all been too raw, kissing away too many hurts that had lasted too long. Kissing to seal a promise, and then just kissing because it was Gareth, and there was nowhere else Joss wanted to be and nothing else he wanted to do.

He pulled away at last. Gareth was looking at him with the wondering expression that never failed to make Joss's breath catch.

"You realise we're in a chapel," he said.

"Middling ruined, though," Joss had to point out.

"I grant you, it lacks walls, pews, and a roof," Gareth allowed. "But it has grass, sky, and a thriving population of invertebrates— bugs—so in my view, that's an improvement. *And* nobody's preaching a sermon."

"True. In that case..." Joss groped for long grass and plucked a tough blade. He twisted it into a ring without looking away from Gareth's face—he'd used to do this a lot for Sophy when she wanted to be a princess, along with daisy chains—then took his right hand and slipped it on the fourth finger. The twisted grass would stain his finger green. Joss liked that thought, of marking him in even a tiny, temporary way. "There. Marsh ring for a Marshman."

Gareth's expression was a glory. "Do another?"

Joss twisted another blade into a ring. Gareth took his hand in turn. "If I were king, I'd dub you the Prince of Romney Marsh, and not for your performance in bed either. Or, not only for that," he added with a flickering look. "I can't give you any of the titles you so richly deserve. But I'm all yours, and I want to be with you for as long as you'll have me, so…"

He eased the grass circlet on. Joss had an emerald ring and a gold fob watch in his treasure box. Both expensive, valuable things, both good memories. Neither worth a snap against a single strand of twisted grass on his finger, and what it meant.

He smiled into Gareth's Marsh-mist eyes. Everything in the world he needed, right here, all and only his. "I'll have you, London. I promise."

**KEEP READING FOR A SNEAK PEEK AT
A NOBLEMAN'S GUIDE TO SEDUCING A SCOUNDREL,
COMING SEPTEMBER 2023.**

One

April 1823
THE ISLE OF OXNEY, ROMNEY MARSH

RUFUS D'AUMESTY, NINETEENTH EARL OF OXNEY, TWENTY-second Baron Stone, and inheritor of the ancient and unbroken d'Aumesty lineage, glared at his uncle Conrad and said, "Balls."

"Your vulgarity is regrettable." Conrad wore a little smirk on his smug face. Rufus regretted the near-thirty-year age difference that prevented him knocking it off.

"We've been through this," he said in lieu of violence. "The Committee for Privileges took seven months to assess my right. You dredged up every calumny and speculation you could think of against my mother and invented God alone knows what nonsense about me in your effort to claim the title, and you still lost. They said so, it's done with, and you cannot start it all again!"

Conrad's smirk stayed in place. "Of course I have accepted the decision of the Committee. I can scarcely be blamed for taking pains to ensure the title continues down the true line in lawful fashion—"

"You speculated my mother bore a girl and switched me at birth with an orphan boy, as though she were a Bourbon queen, not a draper's daughter," Rufus said with all the patience he could muster, which was scant. "Then you said I was an impostor who'd stolen a dying man's identity on the battlefield."

"I merely raised the question."

"You called my mother a liar and me a fraud, and I've had enough of it. The title has been awarded. The matter is closed."

"Then it must be reopened. Some very serious information has only recently come to light, as a matter of chance. It requires investigation."

Rufus's back teeth were grinding together. "It does not, because the title has been awarded. I'm the legitimate son of Raymond d'Aumesty, there's nobody in front of me in the line of inheritance, I am the sodding earl, and there is no more to be said!"

"Certainly you are Raymond's son. The question is your legitimacy."

Rufus clenched his fist hard in lieu of saying something his uncle would regret. He was going to stop trying to hold on to his temper very shortly. "The Committee examined the proof thoroughly. My mother was married to my father. That is incontestable."

"Oh, the marriage is unquestionable," said the man who'd spent months questioning it. "I do not argue that Raymond went through a ceremony with your mother. The question is whether he was legally able to do so."

"Legally able to—what, marry?"

"Indeed."

"He was twenty-five years old and of sound mind, insofar as any d'Aumestys are of sound mind, which—"

"He was already married."

"What?"

Conrad plastered on a sympathy-shaped smile. "Or such is the allegation. Raymond was my brother, but he was a rash, irresponsible, foolish man, easily led, with uncontrollable enthusiasms—"

"What do you mean, already married?" Rufus demanded. "Get to the facts!"

"Before Raymond became...entangled with your mother, he had a dalliance with a local girl. The junior nursemaid to my own children, who abandoned her duties to sport with a son of the house."

"You mean he pestered one of the staff. So what? If my father had married all the girls he bothered—"

"He married this one!" His uncle spat the words out, then went on, more in his usual condescending tone, "Or so it is suggested."

"By whom? And why wasn't it 'suggested' while you were scrabbling round for a way to make yourself earl?"

"I could not say." Conrad looked sour about this. "But I have now received this information, and it must be investigated. Whatever the Committee for Privileges has ruled, this would change everything. If your father was already married at the time he wed your mother, that marriage was invalid, and you are not legitimate."

"If," Rufus said. "Where's the proof? Who is this woman, and if she was married to my father, why hasn't anyone heard of it till now?"

"Her name is Louisa Brightling. She is or was a local woman from Fairfield. She no longer lives in the area and her whereabouts are not known."

"Then who's making this claim?"

Conrad gave him an exceedingly unpleasant smile. "Her son."

They sent the claimant orders to present himself at Stone Manor the next day. Rufus would have preferred to ride down and confront the fellow at once, but he lived in Dymchurch, halfway across Romney Marsh. It would probably be bad tactics anyway: he didn't

want to treat this latest freak of Conrad's as having any more substance than all his other accusations.

The conversation had been unsettling and infuriating, and he
decided to get out of Stone Manor. It was raining, as it always did in
this blasted place and this blasted country, but he ordered his horse
anyway, and rode out for Buds Farm. He'd been meaning to go,
given the numbers of complaints that had come from that source,
and hopefully an unheralded visit on such a dismal day would
make him look like a good landlord who took his duty seriously.

Little chance of that, he reflected sourly as he rode along the
wooded, dripping lane to Wittersham, what with the pile of unread
or half-read letters accumulating on his desk, and the nightmar-
ish labyrinth of accounts to which he had no clue, and the state of
his lands, which showed itself to be worse and worse the closer he
looked.

This was, or should be, a prosperous area, since the Weald
supported an amazing number of sheep per acre. The d'Aumestys
ought to be a prosperous family with prosperous tenants. He might
easily have inherited the earldom as a well-run concern, with a
smooth transition of authority from his grandfather to himself. No
such luck.

Rufus had spent seven miserable months in the legal mire as the
Committee for Privileges examined his claim to the title. Months
hearing Conrad attack his mother for her hasty and deeply regretted marriage to Raymond d'Aumesty, calling her character and
honour into question. Months where Rufus's honesty, legitimacy,
and even identity had been subjected to his uncle's insinuations
and dissected by a pack of superior old men. It had been a scarify-
ing experience, of which the only good thing he could say was that
it was over.

Well, and also that he'd won. Rufus was the Earl of Oxney,

immovably in place unless he committed treason, which he didn't intend, or was proven illegitimate, which he was determined not to worry about. This was doubtless just another desperate throw of Conrad's, and Rufus was tired of putting up with nonsense because his uncle couldn't let go of his disappointment.

In fairness, Conrad had good reason to be disappointed, and angry too. Rufus couldn't blame him for that. He just didn't want to be the target of his wrath.

The previous Lord Oxney had had three sons, of whom Conrad was the youngest. The eldest, Baldwin, Lord Stone, had never married; Raymond, the second son, had eloped with a draper's daughter. The old earl had promptly disowned him, and disavowed any responsibility to Rufus, his grandson.

The old man had never softened his stance. He didn't respond to pleas for help when Raymond abandoned his young wife and child, and when Rufus was reported killed in action, and his grieving mother wrote to let the Earl know, he had replied that he was glad to hear it. She never forgave that cruelty, and Rufus didn't blame her. But it meant that she didn't trouble to write to Stone Manor when Rufus turned up thin, ill, scarred, but alive after five months as a prisoner of war. She hadn't wanted the Earl's poison tainting her joy.

And then Baldwin died. Rufus's mother saw the notice in a newspaper, and took intense, vengeful pleasure in advising the Earl that his despised commoner grandson was alive, and now his heir. The Earl replied with a single line of crabbed acknowledgment. He did not suggest meeting, which was a pity because Rufus would have enjoyed refusing: he had nothing civil to say to the man.

Rufus had gone on with his life as a soldier. He hadn't thought of himself as an earl in waiting because that seemed ghoulish. Still, he'd known the position would be his one day, and when the old man shuffled off at last, he'd expected to assume it without too much trouble.

He'd expected wrongly. Because, over the three and a half years since Baldwin's death, the old earl had not broken the news to his family that Rufus was alive.

For all that time, his third son Conrad had been under the impression that Baldwin, Raymond, and Rufus's deaths made him heir. For all that time, Conrad had awaited his decrepit, bedbound father's death in the belief that the coronet was a breath away from his own brows, and the old earl hadn't troubled to disabuse him.

That absurd, cruel silence had given Conrad years of hope and anticipation and expectation, and then snatched everything from his grasp. Rufus could not imagine what had been in the old fool's mind, unless he'd had a particular dislike of Conrad. Which was not unreasonable: Rufus couldn't abide the man.

Conrad hadn't taken the news with good grace. Half-crazed by disappointment and shock, he had wasted a vast amount of money and time in increasingly far-fetched efforts to oust Rufus, making accusations that verged on the slanderous, inventing more and more far-fetched speculations. The Committee had heard him out with decreasing patience and awarded Rufus the title. That should have been the end of it. Apparently, it was not.

Conrad had been treated with gross injustice and had a real grievance. Rufus often reminded himself of that. So he'd meet this individual who claimed Rufus's father had married his mother first, and he'd hear him out and examine the evidence fairly. And if it proved to be a pack of lies, he'd kick the swine all the way down the Isle, and into the Marsh he came from.

On that invigorating thought, he arrived at Buds Farm.

Rufus wasn't a countryman. He'd been brought up in the house-hold of his stepfather, a successful draper; he'd followed the drum from the age of sixteen. He didn't know anything about farms, or farming. But he knew what makeshift repairs looked like, when you had to keep shoring-up and patching-up because there was no time or money to do a proper job, and he saw it here.

The tenant farmer, Hughes, didn't seem overjoyed by a visit from his new landlord. He spoke respectfully, but there was a lot of resentment under the polite words.

"Been asking for repairs a long time now, my lord. I wrote to Mr. Smallbone time and again. Didn't happen when the old master was alive, and as for after he died, with you and Lord Oxney—Mr. Conrad, I should say—fighting over the title for seven months..." He let that hang meaningfully.

"Surely the work of the estate was carried on in that period," Rufus said.

"No. It weren't. And I've an agreement says what costs I bear, and what the Earl, and that ain't been done. I've got *rights*—"

"Now, Hughes," his wife said, warning in her voice, and something more than that. Alarm, perhaps.

Rufus had a temper. He was well aware his face showed his feelings, and he was undeniably angry at this moment, so he made an extra effort to look and sound calm. "Have you given Mr. Smallbone the full list of repairs due?"

"Three time."

"I'll talk to him," Rufus promised, trying not to make it sound like *I'll wring his neck.*

Hughes snorted. His wife dug a finger into his side with an urgent expression, and he shot her a glower. "Stop that, woman. I've talked to Mr. Smallbone plenty, and written too, and he's made plenty of promises of this and that. Well, it ain't happened yet and I don't see it happening now, and I'm weary of asking for the same thing over and over. I got my rights!"

The battle cry of an Englishman digging in to be an awkward son of a bitch. Rufus knew it well. "Yes, you have rights, Mr. Hughes, and the estate has duties to you. I'm going to get this under control. Can you tell me, this situation, with repairs due—"

"All over," Hughes said, with a sort of gloomy glee. "There's nothing been done to speak of anywhere on the estates, not since Lord Stone died, and that's the truth. Everyone'll tell you the same. The loss took the heart out of old master, your lordship, and nobody could blame him for that, but it's been more'n four year now—No, I will not mind my tongue!" he snapped at his wife. "His lordship asked, and we've had nothing done in all this time, and if he wants to turn me off my land for saying so—"

"I shall do no such thing," Rufus said. "I asked you a question because I wanted you to answer it. I'm grateful for your frankness."

Hughes gave him a short nod. Mrs. Hughes didn't look convinced.

Rufus was still turning over that unsatisfactory encounter in his mind the next morning as he sat in the study, swamped by paper.

He was supposed to have the assistance of his cousin Odo, Conrad's younger son, who had acted as his grandfather's clerk. Unfortunately, Odo was a vague sort of man, nervous to the point of imbecility, who only seemed happy talking about ancient history and the family heritage, subjects in which Rufus had no interest at all. He reacted as though he might be struck whenever Rufus expressed the slightest sign of annoyance, and since Rufus did that a lot, matters were not going well. Rufus didn't want to upset the fellow—Odo was the only one of his family to show any sort of civility, and he was clearly trying—but he was also useless, and

Rufus had been obliged to send him away earlier, in case he swore at him.

There was a lot to swear about. Odo's hand was appalling, a chaotic close-written chicken-scratch that slanted erratically up the page, with endless crossings-out and insertions, so a wooden rule under the lines was no help. It danced in front of Rufus's eyes, the words tangling themselves into incomprehensible knots, and the most ferocious concentration wasn't giving him anything more than a headache. There were entire books of this that he needed to make sense of, but he could barely get through a page in an hour, leaving him in a state of shame, rage and frustration.

And there were sheaves of unanswered letters from the seven-month interregnum, when it seemed nobody had taken any responsibility at all, and new ones coming in every day, and Rufus was beginning to panic. The steward Smallbone was entirely useless, affairs were all too visibly deteriorating, and everyone he spoke to was hostile. The family hated him, and the staff were stiff and unwelcoming, siding firmly against the interloper who had stolen Mr. Conrad's birthright. They eyed Rufus with distrust and took his orders to Mrs. Conrad for confirmation.

It was enraging, and miserable, and exceedingly lonely. Rufus would not have compared his situation as earl of Oxney with his time as a prisoner of war, or at least not out loud, but in the last weeks he had sat through too many meals where the company was even colder than the food, and spent too much time mired in the study, struggling with books he didn't understand and an inheritance he didn't know how to manage, and he was beginning to feel something rather like despair.

He didn't intend to give in to that. Still, he sat in the study alone, achieving nothing, cursing Conrad and the books and this damned pretender fellow, until he was informed that the visitor had arrived.

Odo was in the hall, looking even more like a surprised owl than usual. He gave Rufus one of his twitchy smiles. "Oh—ah—Oxney."

"Busy," Rufus said, to head off whatever gibbering he was likely to be subjected to.

"Is it the, uh, the—"

"Fellow who claims he's the earl. Some ridiculous name."

"Perkin Warbeck."

"What? No, nothing like that."

"No—I mean the claimant—Perkin Warbeck was a pretender to the throne," Odo explained earnestly, falling into step by him. "He declared himself to be one of the Princes in the Tower, you know, and attempted to take the throne from Henry the Seventh."

"Good for him. Did it work?"

"Well—er—no? He was captured, and Henry hanged him."

"Even better," Rufus said, and kept walking.

Conrad was waiting for him in Stone Manor's drawing room, along with the pretender, who Rufus was now inevitably going to call Perkin at some point. Conrad was in a flow of oratory; the other man was listening in silence.

He stood when Rufus arrived. "Lord Oxney. Good day. I'm Luke Doomsday."

It was a ridiculous name. Even Perkin Warbeck would be better, and come to that would suit him better. Someone named Doomsday should be villainous-looking: shabby and sinister and scarred.

This fellow was not shabby. He was respectably dressed, even rather smartly, with a well-fitted coat that showed off a pair of decent shoulders for his height. He had a bright head of guinea-gold hair that gleamed in the little sunlight allowed by Stone Manor's miserable windows, and a clean, clear look to him, with nothing sinister or piratical about it.

But by God, he was scarred.

It was a hell of a scar, a raised welt easily four inches long that slashed down his temple, made a jagged curve around his left eye, and ended over his cheekbone. It was clearly old, which invited questions because he looked to be in his mid-twenties, and it must have made a bloody mess of his face at the time. It was the kind of scar someone called Doomsday ought to have. People of a sensitive nature would recoil from a scar like that.

Rufus wasn't sensitive, and had seen a lot worse, and the face it bracketed was otherwise rather pleasing. Dark brown eyes that made a nice contrast to the shining hair, finger-thick near-black brows over them—as though a couple of caterpillars had found a resting place, Rufus thought unkindly—and a generous mouth.

Doomsday, Rufus reminded himself. *Pretender.*

"Sit down," he said. "So. You think you should have my earldom."

Acknowledgements

I would like to thank David Allen Green, who, unbelievably, took time out of his extremely important work to look at legal history stuff for me. I'm staggered at his kindness and extremely grateful. Any errors are, obviously, mine.

I'm very grateful to Mary Altman for a fantastic edit that sharpened the book up immeasurably, and to the entire Sourcebooks team. My agent, Courtney Miller-Callihan, is an ever-present support without whom none of this would be happening.

There's been a lot going on in the world while I've been writing this book, and I've participated in some fundraisers that have left me astonished at people's generosity and kindness. Candy Tan, Michael Cumpsty, and Claire Trottier: my profound thanks and love to you all.

I couldn't do this without Charlie, who's never failed to support me. And a big shout-out to the kids, who came on two research trips to Romney Marsh without a single word of complaint. (It was *paragraphs*. They're still moaning about Dungeness. ALL RIGHT I'M SORRY IT RAINED.)

About the Author

KJ Charles spent twenty years as an editor in British publishing before fleeing the scene to become a full-time historical romance novelist. She has written over twenty-five novels since then and her books have been translated into eight languages. She lives in London.